lowering his chi a depth Andy had never seen before. Knowledge and understanding and something else in those pupils.

"Your black belt won't always save you, you know."

Andy turned away. He continued to follow her.

For some reason, his persistence irked her. She thrust a hand to his chest. Rock solid. "Don't. I could take you down if I had to."

"I'm sure you could." A cocky grin started at one side of his mouth, before spreading to the other. "Goodnight, then." With a salute to her, he marched backward. When he rounded the corner out of sight, Andy found her phone and dialed Carla.

"What did the guy want?" Carla asked.

"Karate lessons."

"Are you sure? I think he was into you."

Andy changed the subject. "What did your mom want?"

Before Carla answered, two men in rubber masks rushed Andy, sliding up beside her, grabbing her phone and purse. She immediately let go of the burner phone, but her tote! Everything she needed was in there.

She was not giving up her bag without a fight.

Joyce—

Baker's Dozen

by

Amey Zeigler

"Verify first, then trust."

Amey Zeigler

Baker's Dozen

Cover Art by *Debbie Taylor*

The Wild Rose Press, Inc.
PO Box 708
Adams Basin, NY 14410-0708
Visit us at www.thewildrosepress.com

Publishing History
First Crimson Edition, 2017
Print ISBN 978-1-5092-1837-0
Digital ISBN 978-1-5092-1838-7

Published in the United States of America

Dedication

To my husband for his unfailing loving support

Chapter One

Men lie. They lie about how many women they've been with, their alcohol tolerance, and the size of their, uh, paycheck. Which was exactly what Jack, sitting across from Andy Miller, was lying about.

He tapped his coffee mug with the tip of his finger, stretching his lean body against the booth at Ronney Dell's. "Ninety grand this year alone," he claimed.

Closer to fifty grand, according to his secretary. Though maybe he was taking into account all the vehicles he had sabotaged before fixing which weren't on the books.

But Andy didn't contradict him. Instead, she demurely batted her lashes and smiled into her shoulder. "Ninety grand," she cooed, snapping her gum. "I don't believe it!" she said.

And that *was* the truth.

Andy brushed back the bleached wig of her "Mary Lou" persona covering her natural brown hair. *Brown as the Mississippi mud*, her dad always said. She fingered a necklace just above the plunging neckline of a tank top and Daisy Dukes combo. Oh, the depths she sank to for a story. But to avenge poor, old Mrs. Wheyland, it was worth it.

"It's been all this overtime, you know." He gave her a crusty smile. It had been too long since he'd seen the inside of the toothpaste cap.

1

"Are you going in to work tonight?"

She wanted one more peek at Jack's books. Something was amiss, something more than the sabotage. After doing some research on how much small repair shops made, she wanted to recalculate the figures.

"I'm just about to finish up your BMW. Want to come?"

She nodded. "Watching you work gives me such a thrill."

Andy smiled in anticipation of sharing all seventeen of Jack's dishonest dealings with her ten thousand Twitter followers @BakersDozen. And if there was a bigger story in the books, it would be the cream on top of all the corruption and scandal. Lies à la mode.

"Let's go." He tossed his head.

He gulped one last swig of coffee. Andy slid from the booth, arms jangling with bracelets, her stiletto boots nearly entangling in the table legs. At the register, Jack patted his back pockets, then his shirt pockets, and swore.

"Forgot my wallet in my other pants. Mary Lou, will you?"

Andy flashed a tight smile as she did some mental math. She had paid for dinner five of the six times they'd been out. If this had been a real date with a real boyfriend, Andy would have left him to wash dishes for their meal. At least Jack was a tax deduction. She slid her wallet from her red weekender tote. "Sure, hon."

"Last time, I promise," he whispered in her ear. This was the only truth he'd uttered their entire relationship. He didn't even know how true it was.

Andy paid and headed for the doors while Jack lingered near the waitress, smiling coyly as he attempted small talk.

Blinking in the setting sun, Andy shoved open the first set of glass doors and reached for the sunglasses nestled in her wig just as a broad-shouldered guy entered from the opposite set of glass doors.

At first, she didn't pay much attention to him. To be sure, his glance swept up her body. But Andy was used to men ogling her, especially in her current attire. Shorts barely to there and legs up to here. Andy's legs were sexy, her torso tight, her body desirable, and she didn't mind using it to get what she wanted—information.

And normally, when Andy worked on a story, she didn't get distracted. It was a cardinal rule. It could mean life or death to even let an eyeball roll in the wrong direction. But this man's physique begged her to look. She couldn't help it.

Tall. Strong jaw, with a hint of stubble. Discriminating blue eyes. Sandy blond hair falling in just the right places. Lithe, toned, perfectly built.

Perfectly distracting.

Three seconds was too long to stare. She ripped her gaze away to refocus on her cover. But as she did, the man did the most unexpected thing—he raised his eyebrows and smiled at her.

Recognition?

Andy jerked in surprise. Her jerk disrupted the delicate balance of her weight hovering over heels the size of sharpened pencils. Mid-stride, Andy's ankle faltered. She tried to recover by setting down her other foot. But it never made it safely under her as the heel caught on the area rug, pitching her forward.

Her hand flew out to grasp something, anything to keep her from toppling. She caught nothing but air.

Until she caught hold of...*him.*

With swift reflexes and amazing agility, Andy noted, the man caught her about the waist, saving her from a most assuredly embarrassing tumble to the floor with more leg and perhaps a little inseam exposed.

"You all right?" he asked, holding her aloft with warm hands, his face hovering inches from hers. They paused there, suspended in an almost tango-like bend over the checkered tile.

She absorbed him, memorizing every detail, the curl of his lip, the arch of his eyebrows, the smooth planes of his nose. A small scar split his left eyebrow in two. It was a nice face. But his arresting gaze held her, perceptive, sparkling with amusement—and familiar. Definitely memorable.

Andy searched deeper into his eyes. He was taking in detail, too. Some static or lightning or maybe indigestion from Ronney's jalapeno spaghetti and meatballs flashed in her stomach.

"Andy, isn't it?" he whispered.

A pleasing smell of leather from his flight jacket radiated from his body. And something else. Sandalwood incense? The stranger quickly righted her, his gaze never leaving hers.

"Do I know you?" she asked, struggling to remain in character, patting her wig, hoping it was not jostled. It was fine, secured with no fewer than a hundred bobby pins. But still her gaze locked on his.

"You don't remember," he said.

"Do you know this guy?" Jack demanded behind

her. He placed a possessive hand on her back, attempting to ease her away from the man.

Strong. Handsome. Andy was still dazed. She had been dating dross too long.

"No," Andy, as Mary Lou, said.

Jack scowled at the stranger. But Andy barely noticed. Jack and the whole world disappeared. Only she and the stranger existed, encased between sets of glass doors and Andy balancing like a flamingo.

She set her foot down. A streak of lightning shot up her leg. Her yelp broke the trance. She glanced down at her foot, wincing in pain. The stranger jumped into action, crouching to examine Andy's ankle.

"You're hurt."

"She's fine," Jack said, shoving her toward the next set of doors, Andy limping. Jack glared at the man as he wrapped a protective arm around her waist.

"Want ice?" the man asked, opening the door and moving toward the dining area.

"No, thank you," Andy said. Jack continued to lead her toward the parking lot doors. Every step caused her body to shake with pain. She was losing her cool and her cover. The guy needed to go away.

The stranger glanced from Andy to Jack, then back to Andy. He abruptly strode ahead of them to the doors, propping one open for the couple.

Andy hobbled past the man, feeling, rather than seeing, his gaze. She peeked from the corner of her eyes. A split second was all Mary Lou could give him, although Andy wanted to see more, feel more.

"Name's Hugh, if you ever need anything," he whispered to her as she passed, giving Jack a nervy stare.

"Thank you." Her voice, pinched with pain, almost lost the dumb laziness of Mary Lou, but she quickly recovered. Her mind searched through her cerebral database, grasping for recognition, dismayed at her near-photographic memory for forgetting a guy like him. Little glimpses flashed in her eyes. She remembered him outside, but she couldn't recall where.

"We can get ice at the Shaft," Jack said, pulling her farther from the restaurant. "I've got an ice maker there." Her leg radiated with pain. Those hooker shoes! Had to wear the six-inch heels tonight, didn't she.

In the parking lot, Jack paused by his pick-up. "Why don't we go in my truck?"

"But we always walk." Second rule. As a twenty-three-year-old woman, she never rode in the same car as one of her marks. She had left a dynamic ten-speed chained to a nearby tree.

"But traffic's terrible tonight. And your ankle looks swollen."

Truth be told, her ankle was a *lot* swollen. And painful, too. But rules were rules. Andy couldn't let anyone give her rides. Never. Not when she was working, anyway. Too easy to lose control of the situation.

Jack persisted. "And the crosswalk is so far from here."

The shop was just across the street. And the spring weather in St. Louis, though warm during the day, was still chilly at night, and she hadn't remembered a coat. And the traffic was bad this evening. And if her ankle was sprained, hobbling to the shop might aggravate it.

Andy weighed the options in her mind. Just a jaunt. It was still early. Plus, Jack was not a threat. They'd been "together" for four weeks, and he'd never tried anything. His smell was worse than his bite. Which was saying something, because with those teeth, his bite was probably infectious.

"Sure thing, hon," she said at last.

With her red weekender tote on her shoulder, she hopped into his truck and set aside wrenches, invoices, napkins, and bills still in their envelopes. A rancid smell from either the oil stains or the rock-hard french fries hidden in the seats rose to meet her.

This story had better break big.

If she could just dig a little deeper into the books. The income Shaft Auto reported to the IRS was high for the number of repairs Andy had observed. Even with the tampered vehicles.

"Where we goin'?" Her voice almost cracked. She'd been so involved in her thoughts to realize he'd passed Shaft Auto Shop.

"Oh," he said chuckling. "Some place I've wanted to take you for a while."

"I thought we were finishin' up my car." After picking up the car tonight, she was supposed to wrap up the investigation and dump Jack.

"Don't worry. We can finish tomorrow morning." He gave her a little wink. "Or afternoon."

Andy suppressed a shudder. "But I need ice for my ankle."

"There'll be ice where we're going."

A pit formed in her stomach. And she would never get another chance to study Jack's books. Or get back Carla's car. She'd relinquished control.

She glanced at her watch. Six p.m.. Two hours until absolute deadline. She still had to write up her lead and send her story to Mr. Hershal, her editor at *Gateway Times*. Her tight deadline left no time for dallying.

When they arrived at his apartment, Andy pasted on a fake smile. "Is this your place? Why, it's so nice." On this neglected facade hung a once white, now bleeding rust, Latin Quarter-style lattice. "I love the pretty iron-work."

But Jack only had eyes for Mary Lou. He jingled his keys in anticipation before exiting the car. Andy dreaded this part. It happened too often.

Andy opened her own door slowly. There comes a point in every relationship, even fake ones, when someone, usually the guy, wants to take it to the next step—bed. In the last three years as a freelance investigative journalist, Andy had developed three cures for the grabbies. Two of them she learned from Sensei Tanaka.

They climbed the stairs together to his door arm-in-arm. At least the drive in the car rested her ankle. With jingling keys, he opened the door, then faced her.

"Let's take a selfie, shall we? I want to remember tonight." He stuck out his phone in front of them.

Andy's hand flew to her face. "No, Jackie, you know I don't like my picture taken." Andy couldn't afford to leave any photographic evidence of her with Jack.

"But," he still persisted.

Desperate times called for desperate actions.

"There is something I want more." Holding her breath, she snuggled into him, nuzzling his chest, turning her face away from the camera. Andy paused before pressing her lips against his.

"Honey, you—" But her lips were on his. His

initial shock only lasted half a breath before he gnawed at her lips, forcibly parting her teeth for greater depth, their teeth clanking in his unrestrained desire.

One of the reasons she didn't date much in her personal life was because she still hadn't found anyone who could satisfy her in the kissing area. And if the kissing wasn't good, nothing was good.

While he was distracted, she held down the arm holding his phone. He slipped it in his pocket then grabbed her with both hands on her shoulders, clutching her into him.

Andy broke away, almost suffocated by his embrace. Then, keeping her facial expression seductive, Andy grabbed him around his bristling neck. His eyes lit up in delight. Drawing closer and massaging his neck, her fingers found the pressure point.

Three seconds later, Jack collapsed inside the door in a heap.

"Sorry, Jack," she said to his almost corpse, moving his legs inside before writing a breakup note to leave in his hand. "But I just couldn't kiss you one more time. Not even for poor, old Mrs. Wheyland." She paused, observing his crumpled body with a sigh. "Be glad I put you to sleep the nice way."

Law-breakers always looked so peaceful in their sleep. Made you wonder how they sleep at night, though, robbing little old ladies of their Social Security and all. Not to mention the other customers who had also had cars tampered with.

"I hope you sleep well after this hits the news," she said out loud while closing the door. She wished she could be in the room of the mysterious corporate owner of Shaft Auto when the story broke. Still, she regretted not being able to follow up on the irregularities in the books. There might have been an even bigger story. She would have to leave any bigger story to the police investigation.

Slipping off her shoes, she descended the stairs, her ankle finally feeling better. This little detour cost her too much time. Deadline was an hour and half. She had to act fast.

****

Hugh parked his car outside the Kwik-E-Mart just after sunset. He checked his watch. He had a few minutes before his meet up with Antonio Guterelli.

He opened his car door. The hot dogs and corn dogs plastered on the windows of the gas station matched the smells wafting from the place and encouraged his hunger. It's not what he would've called food, but neither was anything at Ronney Dell's.

Ronney Dell's was a disaster. He clearly interrupted something. An op, or whatever you call it when you're not a professional. Hugh might've blown her cover. Though it was most amusing to catch her in action. Most amusing indeed. He wouldn't soon forget those shorts.

Once inside, he nabbed two dogs from under the heating element and slid them into the sleeves. The door pinged behind him as a large man entered the store. Not Antonio. This guy had on a tattered unbuttoned shirt open over an even more tattered t-shirt exposing a diamond playing card tattoo on his neck. He picked up a bag of chips as he moved to the cashier's desk. Hugh stood in line behind him, his hot dogs warming his hands. The girl at the cashier rang up the bag of chips and gave the total.

10

The tattooed man slapped his hand on the counter and leaned toward her, pointing to a sticker on the bag of chips. "The price tag says two forty-nine, not three forty-nine. Are you stupid or something?" he said.

The young clerk's face flushed red as she realized her mistake. "I'm sorry. I'm not sure how the mix-up happened. Let me void the transaction."

She fumbled through the keys at the computer. The man sighed and set his foot down heavily.

"I'm sorry," the cashier said again. She squinted at the screen, fully absorbed, her fingers unsure, as she typed on the keyboard.

While the clerk was distracted, the man lifted a pack of gum from below the counter and slid it into his pocket. "This is taking too long. Just forget it," he said. "I don't need the chips."

"I got it," she said at last, tossing a strand of hair behind her ear and ringing up the chips again. "It worked."

"About time," the man said, plopping down some cash.

The clerk handed him his change.

"Idiot," he said, not quite under his breath, as he left.

When Hugh stepped up to the counter, he laid down his two hot dogs. "Want him to pay for that?" he asked.

She glanced up from ringing up the hot dogs, her face still red. "For what?"

"He just stole a pack of gum. You want him to come back and pay for it?"

The clerk smiled and nodded her head. "Yeah!"

"I'll be right back."

"Who are you the police or something?"

But Hugh was already out the door. He approached the man as he opened his car. "Hey, you going to pay for the pack of gum?"

The man opened the door and arched an eyebrow at Hugh. "Excuse me?"

"You lifted a pack of gum inside. And I think you owe the clerk an apology. You were rather rude."

"Not going to happen." The man ducked into his red Camaro. Hugh caught his door before he could close it. The man yanked at the door.

Hugh held firm. "You will go in, pay for the gum, and apologize to the store clerk."

The man jumped to his feet and puffed out his chest as he faced Hugh. "You gonna make me?" He whipped out a gun from his waistband. He pointed it four inches from Hugh's nose.

Hugh smiled slightly, amused. "A gun? You think you're going to shoot me? I only asked you to do the right thing." In a flash, Hugh knocked the gun from the man's hand and joint locked his arm, forcing him down, immobilizing him. Still controlling the man's arm, Hugh trapped his face against the black tar of the parking lot with his foot. "Are you going to apologize?"

Before he could answer, sirens blared and blue and red lights of two police cars splashed over Hugh and his captive. The store clerk approached him. "I didn't know what to do so I called the police," she said.

"Brilliant," Hugh said under his breath, lifting the thug from off the ground.

"What's going on here?" the first cop asked, approaching with caution unsure who was the good guy and who was the bad guy. Hugh released the thug to two officers but a third grabbed Hugh. The clerk hurried over, talking fast.

"The other guy pulled a gun on this guy," she said, pointing first to the man and then to Hugh.

"Yeah?" the officer said. He opened a pad of paper and wrote down what the clerk said. "Why'd he threaten you with a gun?" he asked Hugh.

Hugh sort of shrugged, still held by the officer.

"He was a real hero," the clerk continued with shining eyes. "First, he spotted the man shoplifting a pack of gum, but then when he confronted him, the other guy pulled out a gun. This guy disarmed him completely."

The officer turned to Hugh, eyebrows raised. "He lifted a pack of gum, and you were going to stop him?"

Hugh gave him a short nod.

One of the other cops interrupted the questioning after they cuffed the man and escorted him to the back of the police car. "Looks like we picked up a winner. Driving a stolen vehicle, has four warrants for his arrest here in Missouri. Two in Illinois."

The interrogating officer returned to Hugh. "I guess we owe you some gratitude for stopping him. But you shouldn't have confronted him. You never know if you're going to come across a hardened criminal like this guy. Still, I am glad no one was hurt. Next time leave it to the trained professionals."

"I'll remember your good advice, sir." Hugh glanced over to a man in a suit watching outside his car. He had a huge grin on his face.

The clerk slipped Hugh his hot dogs. "They're on the house," she whispered to him. Hugh remembered his hunger and grabbed the now cold dogs.

"Thank you," he said to the girl with admiration shining in her eyes. He bowed to the officer. "Am I free to go, sir?" he asked.

The cop arched an eyebrow at Hugh. "I want your number in case we need to ask you further questions."

Hugh nodded and gave him a number, then joined the man in the suit who had his elbows resting on the roof of his Mercedes and an open car door. Antonio laughed at Hugh as the cop cars departed, lights flashing, sirens *whupping*.

"You sow chaos wherever you go," Antonio said, with a slight Italian accent, shaking his head, his lips drawn up in a smile.

"The man stole a pack of gum." Hugh stuffed a hot dog in his mouth and chewed.

"You can't let anything slip by you, can you?"

"And he was rude to the clerk."

"Double jeopardy."

"You would've done the same."

"No, I would've let him have the pack of gum and done nothing. It's like you want to be discovered or something. You're lucky they didn't ask for identification."

Hugh didn't say anything until the police and the clerk finally dispersed. "You have my laptop?"

Antonio smiled and ducked inside the car to retrieve the computer. He held it to his chest. "Don't break this one so fast. It's got to last a long time."

"Or not so long." Hugh held out his hand for the laptop, but Antonio smirked and shook his head.

"Why are you so eager to leave? Are you planning on retiring at twenty-eight?"

"I have some unfinished business to attend to. I'm

just here to hone my skills. *'Bǎoshí méiyǒu mó guāng, méiyǒu mósǔn, yě méiyǒu rén wánchéng méiyǒu shìyàn.'* "

"Say what?"

"Chinese proverb: A stone isn't polished without hits, or something." He was grateful they hired him on with his special circumstances. "Can I have my laptop now?"

"You have, how do you say in English, a grinding ax?"

"I think you mean an ax to grind."

"Ah," Antonio said, nodding. "Why volunteer for this case?"

Hugh shook his head.

"You are such an enigma. Secretive about your past, yet you jump to bring justice to a man most people thought arrogant and pompous."

Hugh didn't reply for a few seconds. "You're not going to give me the laptop until I tell you, are you?"

Antonio smiled again, this time showing white teeth. "I just want to know why a man like you volunteered to take this mission."

Though they'd worked together for the last year, sometimes Hugh wanted to wipe Antonio's charming smile off his face. Hugh could totally take him. But punching a superior was out of the question. And he liked Antonio. Most of the time. "The victim knew my parents."

Antonio didn't speak, but arched an eyebrow.

In a flash, Hugh snatched the laptop from the Italian. "He also offered me help when I was at a real low point in my life. He may have been arrogant, but he was a good man. He didn't deserve to die." Hugh popped open the laptop on the car's rooftop and clicked a few strokes to login.

"And have you found justice for him?"

"I'm getting close."

"You made contact with the girl?"

"Contact, yes. But no questions." Hugh remembered her arms grasping around him when she fell.

Antonio shrugged. "Maybe she's not important."

"Maybe. Something keeps me coming back to her. She's more than what she appears to be. I've been keeping tabs on her on and off for the last year. I have a theory about her. Her POI report is really intriguing."

Antonio leaned in, his eyes shining in mockery. "Sounds like you are interested."

Hugh glanced up from his screen. "It's not like that. You know it's not." Her Person of Interest report filled the screen. "I'm going to catch her at work. It should be in here." He scrolled to find it. "White Fang Dojo. Says she's a master. Impressive. My interrogation will be all the more fun." Hugh smiled as he clicked the lid down on his laptop. "I've always wanted to learn Japanese karate."

Chapter Two

Andy's heels and wig disappeared into her bag before the long, but fast-paced, hike to retrieve her ten-speed at Ronney Dell's. Wearing sensible shoes and a baseball cap unearthed from her bag, she biked in haste to her place, dodging obstacles, jumping curbs like a BMXer. Deadlines were deadlines.

Once inside the door, her phone rang. She knew who it was. Mr. Hershal. Her editor. Andy chewed her finger before answering.

"Amanda," he said, unusually calm.

Andy's heart plummeted. "I know, I know! I'm almost done. I'm typing it up as we speak." As Mr. Hershal droned on about deadlines, Andy peeled off the remaining essence of Mary Lou, threw on some yoga pants and a t-shirt. "I'll have it in before the deadline."

"It's due in ten minutes."

"I know. I had something ugly come up in my schedule." In the kitchen, she poured herself some water and knocked it back, swallowing hard. "Really ugly."

"I want it now. You have a contract."

"It's all written, I just have to—"

"If it's not here in ten, I'm putting in Hansen's column instead."

"The foodie? He waxes on about the texture of bisque and the lusty thump of French bread." What a waste of cyberspace.

"Send me the piece." He clicked off.

Andy opened the lid of her laptop, fingers flying over the keyboard. Before hitting send, she paused, reading it one last time to ensure proper vindication for Mrs. Wheyland's sabotaged car. Satisfied, she hit send. She shifted the desktop to the Internet, then headed to the kitchen for a snack.

From the freezer, she grabbed a quart of ice cream. She needed a calorie boost after her crazy ride from Ronney Dell's. She threw three auto mechanic books from the couch before falling into it, spooning chocolatey goodness into her mouth. Every girl deserved chocolate after a breakup.

When the phone rang again, Mr. Hershal sounded more cheerful. "Cutting it close, Amanda. But it was brilliant."

The compliment gave her a burst of energy. "I always come through."

"Yeah. Just like your old man. Finding the stories other journalists were too afraid to investigate. It takes guts to go undercover like this, Amanda."

"I only use it for self-preservation. Andrew Baker makes a lot of enemies. Thanks again for letting me use my father's pseudonym. I owe you a lot."

"Just as long as I don't get sued for libel."

"My father always taught me, 'Seek truth to uphold justice.'"

His voice turned somber. "He was a great man. Never had ambitions to be some well-known Pulitzer Prize winner. He just wanted the simple truth." He coughed. "Did you get the bigger story? The one you begged me for an extension for?"

Andy's stomach tightened. Mostly she was angry at herself. Caving for the ride when she just should've sucked it up. "No. It didn't work out."

"Disappointing. But at least all the auto shops in the metro area will think twice about tampering with cars. You've empowered consumers. We'll run it through copyedit tonight for your blog posting tomorrow."

"Thank you."

"Ok, then. Until next month. Don't cut it so close next time."

With a half-smile and a shake of her head, Andy hung up the phone.

Now to scrub Mary Lou.

She positioned four pay-per-use burner phones in front of her and placed a pile of SIM cards on the coffee table. Prying up a scoop of Rocky Road, she stuck the spoon in her mouth and held it there while she removed the SIM from the cell phone she used to call Jack, labeling it "Mary Lou" and adding the date. In a few months, when he'd given up, she might try using it again.

She needed a new project. She glanced at her list on the laptop. On the screen was the website for CIA application. She'd forgotten it was still up. Sighing, she changed desktops to her list of problems to be solved.

Mr. Hershal suspected his mother's nursing home was skimming money off their food budget and pocketing it. Or she could track down the group of masked purse-snatchers who stole one of Carla's designer bags.

Andy flipped back to the CIA tab. She studied it for the zillionth time. Then closed it.

Removing the spoon for another bite, she picked another SIM card from her pile, the name Cindy was scrawled in black sharpie. Her heart squeezed a little when she remembered Cindy. The time right after the breakup with Conner. One year ago.

With a fresh bite, she slipped the SIM card into her phone. She set it down and waited for her phone to initialize. She scooped up another bite while the phone dinged.

Andy peeked to count how many. Thirteen messages.

There'd never been so many before. Curious, she played back the messages.

A deeper voice said, "Hey, Cindy, this is Ian."

Oh, Ian. A portly clerk who was "helping" the Honorable Nechler receive gifts for turning a blind eye when the defendant was young and nubile. Persistent guy, Ian was. He was the reason she had to leave the card out longer than the normal few months.

Most of the messages were from him.

"Cindy, this is Ian, call me, please, we need to talk." Skip.

"I'm having kind of a bad day. The Judge has been arraigned. I hope it doesn't go to trial." Skip. Andy's heart shuddered. What mess of lies, sex, and bribery.

"Cindy, I've testified in exchange for a plea bargain." Skip.

The DA was interested in bigger fish than the clerk.

Andy continued to listen to the other messages.

"Check your credit—" Skip.

"Get out of debt—." Skip.

"This is Juan Martinez—" Andy didn't remember him. Perhaps a telemarketer or stalker. One advantage to having multiple phone numbers. Skip.

"Andy—" She recognized Bradbury's voice. "I, uh, just wanna talk. This was the last number you called me on. Sorry it's been so long. Anyway, call me."

Andy checked the time stamp. Yesterday at eleven forty-five p.m.

She raised an eyebrow at the cryptic message. No guy, not even a stepbrother, just called late at night to talk. "I wonder what's up," she whispered, dialing his number. "Hey, Brad-berry!" she said when he answered. "How's it going?"

He laughed at her use of her pet name for him. "You'll never stop calling me Brad-berry, will you?" he asked.

"No way. Too much fun!" Andy sat into her couch, curling her legs under her. "Sorry, when my dad and your mom were dating, I honestly thought Sandra said your name was Brad-berry. Give me a break, I was only three."

"I'm pretty sure my mom named me after Ray Bradbury."

"She does have a whole stack of his books on her coffee table."

"I know. She's such a hoarder."

"Don't be mean. She practically raised me." Andy paused, waiting for him to speak. When the silence lengthened, she continued. "So, I can't even remember the last time you called. What's up?"

Brad's end fell silent for a few heartbeats. "I'm having a little trouble at work," he managed to get out.

"You? Mr. Perfect SAT scores? Class Valedictorian? The man with the perfect job? Your mom isn't worried about your future. She's worried about mine." As far as Sandra knew, Andy only had a dead-end job teaching karate at White Fang Dojo. And Andy planned on keeping it that way. "So, what's going on?"

"I'd rather tell you in person. Wanna meet for dinner tomorrow?"

"Sure. Class ends at six." She began searching through her clothes.

"Meet me at seven?"

"Sure." Andy laughed, fingering a fuzzy shrug lying on her couch.

"What are you planning?"

"You'll have to find me."

****

Early in the morning, Michael J. Tyrone's board meeting for Imperial Energy was interrupted with a rap on the glass doors of the Executive Suite in the high-rise T-Building. Several men and two women all dressed in dark suits sitting in leather chairs faced Bobby Sharp. From the head of the table, Tyrone waved him in.

"Excuse us, gentlemen of the board, and ladies," he said, dismissing them.

The board filed out, leaving Tyrone and Bobby alone. Leather squeaked as Tyrone leaned back, scrutinizing Bobby. Someone must have told him brown was his color. Hazel probably, because he always wore brown.

Tyrone stared hard at Bobby keeping his face calm. Bobby was the only man Tyrone allowed to interrupt his board meetings. "It must be very important."

Something was wrong. Bobby's gaze was low. His eyes didn't meet Tyrone's. Bobby nervously lifted one lanky arm to rub his morning five o'clock shadow. Bobby drew out his phone from his suit pocket.

"Baker's been to Jack's shop. Story's in the news." He tossed the phone on the sleek surface of the table.

Sitting up, moisture fell from Tyrone's squinted eyes. He hated these sneak attacks. One day, business as usual. Next day, *bang*, social media flared, and another of his fronts bit the dust. Andrew Baker disgusted him. "Another one?"

"Exposed."

"Did they mention any money laundering?"

"No. But Jack ain't wise."

Tyrone leaned across the desk, taking the phone. On the display was *Baker's Dozen,* a once-a-month squealing blog. "Why does he pick on me? This is the sixth shop he's closed in the last few years. And he ratted out our judge."

Tyrone scrolled down the screen, scanning the words but not reading them. He swore under his breath. From his inside suit pocket, he slipped out a pin-tucked handkerchief, a navy monogrammed MJT on the corner.

Bobby averted his gaze. Tyrone wiped his eyes, smearing white puss-filled tears across the white cotton. He folded it back and tucked it into his pocket. Pollution irritated his eyes.

Bobby continued. "Jack did some tinkering of his own. Triggered the investigation by Baker."

Heat flashed at Tyrone's neck. Wasn't anyone an honest crook anymore?

Tyrone threw the phone. It fell to the floor, shattering the screen. Bobby bent to retrieve it, but Tyrone grabbed him by his collar, drawing him nose to nose. "I want Andrew Baker," he said, feeling his hair displaced by the rough action.

"Nobody knows who he is." Bobby fidgeted. He had a weak bladder. Tyrone had made him piss his pants a few times. "Uses different aliases. Maybe has a whole army of people working for him."

"What about the *Times*?"

"Checked before. Works freelance. Has a registered agent and an LLC with automatic deposit to some bank in Texas. This guy's smart. No one knows who he is."

Tyrone grit his teeth. "Pressure the editor. Somebody has to know." Tyrone dropped the stringy man. "And I need a conference with Jack."

Bobby nodded. He knew what conference meant.

Tyrone wiped his hair back into place. He sat in his seat, sighing. Then he glanced at the phone on the floor. "Go buy a new one." He sat for a moment. "Please don't tell Hazel."

"Never." Bobby shrugged. "Business don't concern her."

"How are the wedding plans?"

"Outrageous. What'd you expect? Talked her out of filling the pool with champagne."

Tyrone twisted the ring on his right pinky, the one from his wife. "Hazel is costing me a lot of money with her plans."

Bobby laughed. "Not as much as she'll cost me after the wedding."

"But someday you'll inherit all of this." His arms swept wide. Bobby scowled. Eyeing him from the corner of his lid, Tyrone gave him a fleeting smile. "Good thing I like you so much."

"Good thing I *know* so much."

Tyrone huffed a bit deep in his diaphragm, a sound like the beginnings of a chuckle. But he didn't want to give Bobby the satisfaction of making him laugh. Tyrone waved his hands.

Bobby nodded at his cue to exit. On the way out, he bent to pick up the phone. "Don't worry. We'll find Baker."

****

Sweat dripped down Andy's brow as she tucked into a corner of the dojo to undress from her Master's *gi* at the end of class.

"Thanks for a great session," Carla said over the din of kids preparing to line up on the mats. "Going for dinner?"

"I have something to tell you," Andy said when she had finished tucking her pants into her bag.

"You finally applied for the CIA?" Carla's deep brown eyes lit up. Her dark skin contrasted with her white uniform. Only Carla could still be feminine in a *gi* built for a block.

"No."

"How far did you get last time?" Carla asked, admiring her luminous black hair in the wall of mirrors behind a row of chairs surrounding the perimeter of the dojo.

"I decided on careers I was qualified for and placed them in the Job Cart. But that's not what I was going to tell you."

"Next time, hit the Apply button." She smoothed her soft curls with the palm of her hand, her perfectly placed lipstick unsmudged by her physical exertion. "Hey, when do I get my BMW back? Was it in the sting op for that car repair shop? I read your blog this morning. Amazing."

"Thanks," Andy said. "Yeah. Sadly, it's no longer in perfection condition. Jack jimmied with the powertrain; the drive shaft is broken. It'll probably get confiscated as evidence, now." Andy wrinkled her nose. "It was my fault. I got a ride instead of insisting we go to the shop. Sorry."

Carla shrugged. "Daddy will buy me another. Scott wrecked the McLaren 650S he got for graduation, and he didn't even get into trouble. But of course, he is the golden child so he gets away with everything," Carla said, still focusing on herself in the mirror. "Now, what did you want to tell me?"

Andy leaned closer as Carla faced her. "Somebody detected my disguise," she whispered.

Carla's glossy lips parted in surprise. "Nobody recognizes you, ever. You even fooled Sandra."

Andy smiled remembering her first test run. Dressed as a FedEx man, she delivered a package to Sandra at work. Disguised in a short red-headed wig and prosthetics, Andy had a fifteen-minute conversation with her about begonias. Sandra never suspected. Andy was that skilled.

"Who was it?" Carla asked, her perfectly shaped brows gathered in a furrow.

"Some guy," she said, tugging her yoga pants over her spandex.

Carla leaned close. "Was he cute?"

Andy didn't reply. She wrapped up her belt and stuck it in the bag, slipping on her shoes.

Carla continued through Andy's silence, giving her a sly smile. "What scares you more? A guy *noticing* you or him seeing through your disguise?"

"Carla, this isn't about guys. This is about my safety. My disguises are my Maginot line. If it's penetrated, I'm done for."

"Did you just say penetrated?" Carla cast her a wicked smile. Andy frowned. "And you shouldn't compare yourself to failed foreign policy."

Andy nodded, throwing her bag over her shoulder. "Let's go."

"When are you going to start dating again?" Carla asked, her gaze roamed to the black belts shouting their reps of push-ups.

"I've dated."

"You mean José? Your Latin lover? Scott was jealous you were seeing his bodyguard."

Andy rolled her eyes trying to hide her blush. "We weren't seeing each other. We just trained together."

"Some of those punches steamed up the room. What happened with him?"

Andy shrugged. "Nothing." Andy wasn't sure if it was because of her or him. "He returned to Mexico. But he did say to look him up if I'm ever down there. So that's something. And Scott was not jealous."

"Oh, I almost forgot. My mom wants you to call," Carla said, following Andy to the door.

"Right now?"

"It's an emergency, she claimed."

"Everything is an emergency with your mom."

Carla laughed. "True."

Distracted, Andy opened the door, digging in her bag for her phone. Instead of finding it, Andy glanced up, startled to find *him* standing outside.

"Hello," Hugh said. Andy immediately straightened, wishing her face was not so red.

Carla thrust out a manicured hand, never missing a beat to meet a hunky guy. "I'm Carla Vehemia of Vehemia Manufacturing."

Hugh shook her hand, introduced himself, then turned to Andy. "Actually, I was hoping *you* could help me."

Carla glanced at each of them, then she perked up, as if hearing a cue. "I think I forgot my black belt inside," she said, opening the door to return inside. "Call me." Andy got a text from her a heartbeat later.

—*Cute guy. Don't forget to call my mom.*—

"I was pretty impressed with your work in there." Hugh's eyes glowed, burning into hers. He edged toward her. The dimness of the street lamps accentuated his chiseled features and his scar was bright white in his eyebrow. Even the shadows could not hide his penetrating blue eyes.

The phone call was completely forgotten.

"You shouldn't be so easily impressed," Andy said, but she hid a smile, basking in the glowy light of the compliment. She reminded herself to never completely let her guard down. Hitching her red weekender bag over her shoulder, she sized him up. She could take him. "You said you needed something?" she asked.

"Two weeks of your time. Private lessons. To master karate."

"Two weeks?" Andy scoffed. "I studied for years to master karate." She pointed to herself. "Black belt. Sixth degree."

"Is that what all those stripes mean?" he asked.

"You don't know much about karate, do you?"

He smiled. He licked his lips as if savoring a funny joke or *crème brûlée*. "I'd better not mess with you

28

then?" His eyes shone with amusement, his lips curved at the corners of his mouth.

"Not unless you want to get hurt," she said with a toss of her chin. She was tough, and she knew it. He was supposed to be intimidated. This was not going the way she wanted. Or was it? She couldn't decide.

He held out his hands in protest. "I don't want to get hurt." He glanced sideways at her, with a sly smile. "Maybe I do. Just a little."

Andy caught him winking at her. She focused straight ahead again. "I accept you as a pupil just because I pity you. Meet me here tomorrow at six."

He bent low in a sweeping bow. "I will be eternally grateful. For two weeks. I can tell we're going to get along great."

"So, do I know you? I mean, what were you doing at Ronney Dell's?"

"Funny. I was going to ask you the same thing." His eyes twinkled when he asked her.

"None of your business."

"You had quite an outfit."

Andy returned to the original subject. "Have we met before?"

"We have." He smiled. His lips, the perfect contrast to white teeth, were enough to make her forget anything else. She struggled to remain in control, to keep from softening. Even if he had a nice smile. And twenty-inch biceps. "Hugh Donaldson. You really don't remember."

He was right. And Andy was bugged. She never forgot a face. As a journalist, remembering people was essential. How could she forget him? He was certainly memorable.

"It will come to me." Already her mind raced with

scenarios, cocktail parties, yacht clubs, bars, conferences. In one month alone, Andy attended at least ten functions each as a different person, snooping, gleaning snatches of conversations while hobnobbing with mayors, governors, lobbyists, state workers, union men, and oil execs.

In her line of work, exposing law-breakers made few friends. In fact, she probably made more than a few enemies. Anonymity was not just a protection against lawsuits, it was protection for her life. If this one man could detect her, track her down, she was not safe.

"Shall I give you a hint?" He caught up to her, keeping stride beside her. "Last May…" He gazed at her with anxious anticipation. "Forest Park."

Andy stopped. Her mind shot with as much speed and heat as lightning to Forest Park, last year. What an amazing coincidence.

The night of her breakup with Conner. She had expected a ring. She got dumped instead.

"The Foreign Film Festival," she murmured. Andy didn't want to relive that day, but visualized it in her mind. "After a really crappy day—a huge misunderstanding—my stepbrother invited me to watch my favorite movie with Bruce Lee and Chuck Norris."

"*The Way of the Dragon*. It's my favorite as well."

Andy noted his response with interest.

Pausing under the dimmed street lamps now, Andy scrutinized Hugh. She noticed how much more attractive he was now than a year ago. "You sat next to us," she said. "You laughed at a part no one else did." She had always wondered why. Brad acted uncomfortable when Hugh spoke with them.

"You do remember," he said, his lips parting in a

smile. "As I said, we're not complete strangers. We even like the same movies. I was thinking about catching up over a taco tonight, if you wanted to get reacquainted."

At the mention of dinner, she remembered Brad. "Oh, no!" She checked her phone. "Sorry. I've got a previous engagement. Right now." She quickened her pace.

"Later?"

"I'm going to be late."

"Can I at least escort you home?" He kept up with her.

"I'm fine."

"In this neighborhood?" His skeptical glance swept the tall, run-down buildings. This neighborhood wasn't the safest part of town, but the rent was cheap.

Andy stopped. "Did you miss the part of me being a black belt?"

He stepped closer, lowering his chin, giving her a deep stare. His eyes had a depth Andy had never seen before. Knowledge and understanding and something else in those pupils.

"Your black belt won't always save you, you know."

Andy turned away. He continued to follow her.

For some reason, his persistence irked her. She thrust a hand to his chest. Rock solid. "Don't. I could take you down if I had to."

"I'm sure you could." A cocky grin started at one side of his mouth, before spreading to the other. "Goodnight, then." With a salute to her, he marched backward. When he rounded the corner out of sight, Andy found her phone and dialed Carla.

"What did the guy want?" Carla asked.

"Karate lessons."

"Are you sure? I think he was into you."

Andy changed the subject. "What did your mom want?"

Before Carla answered, two men in rubber masks rushed Andy, sliding up beside her, grabbing her phone and purse. She immediately let go of the burner phone, but her tote! Everything she needed was in there.

She was not giving up her bag without a fight.

Spinning, Andy halted, the cold barrel of a gun pressed against her forehead.

The shorter, wider thug with a distorted Daffy Duck mask tucked her bag under his arm. "Thank you," he said.

The taller of the two, with a sagging exaggerated Bill Clinton head, continued to press her with the gun. Andy almost laughed at his bulbous nose flopping around.

"Let's go," the shorter said, his voice muffled through the grinning duck.

Bill Clinton tilted slightly. A distraction was all she needed.

In a flash, she hit Bill, knocking the gun from his grip. As it clattered to the ground, it fired. Shocked, but not thrown, she lifted her leg in a sidekick, knocking Daffy down. Pain shot through her foot and leg. She re-injured her ankle. Not bad, but it needed some rest. She hopped on her uninjured foot to retrieve her bag from the fallen Daffy, kicking him once more for good measure.

Breathing deep, she swallowed her pain as Bill Clinton snatched at her bag again, knocking her off balance. Holding his shoulders, Andy balanced on her good foot, kicked him in the crouch with the pained one, then kneed him in the chest, finally finishing by stomping on his insole.

Just when Daffy had roused, ready to help Bill Clinton, the sound of footfalls echoed behind her. Hugh appeared, sizing up the situation. Though he must have run half a block, he wasn't even winded.

After elbowing the former president, she smashed her fists into the neck of his bent form, still hopping on one foot. "Grab the gun!"

"You're doing great without it," Hugh said.

Andy assumed he would nab it, but instead, he kicked it into a pile of trash in an alleyway just as Daffy threw Andy to the street. Andy held on, taking him down with her fighting over the tote.

Hugh shouted, "Let it go. It's just a bag! It's not worth it."

"You don't understand," Andy said. The man held tight but still she persisted. "It's my life, my everything."

"Girls and their purses… I was talking to the duck."

Daffy managed to stand, still holding the purse. Andy was too slow to return to her feet, but Hugh jumped into action. Andy had never seen anyone so agile. He grappled the Daffy around his neck, then crashed him into his knee. Andy recognized the Russian Sambo technique. Even with the rubber mask, the wallop hurt. Daffy probably had a broken nose.

Andy stood still. This was the same man who asked for karate lessons a few minutes before?

Holding his nose, Daffy ran with Bill from the

alleyway leaving the tote. Andy retrieved it from the sidewalk.

"What were you doing?" she asked.

He shrugged. A bit of blood trickled from his lip where the attacker got in a lucky punch. He cocked an eyebrow. "Don't you have a date tonight?"

Hugh wrapped his arm around her, helping to stabilize her. Andy stiffened. He dodged her question.

He continued, "I'll call the police and report the attempted theft. Not much they can do anyway. I can't give them facial descriptions."

Shaking, she couldn't figure it out. A man who wanted karate lessons twenty minutes ago just executed a Russian Sambo tactic. Flawlessly. There was more to Hugh Donaldson than he was letting on. She stared at him.

"You're still a little ruffled." He found a scrap of paper and a pen. "Here's my address and phone number if you need it."

"I'll be fine," she said, pocketing the information without even reading it. "I have to go."

Andy headed toward her apartment, a nagging feeling in her gut.

****

The man in the tailored brown suit was out of place in the filthy bar full of people like Jack, men who didn't wear suits, even to funerals.

Jack noticed the lanky man, who was a little too tall for his suit, when he lifted his head above his bottle. Jack hadn't showered the last three days and smelled as greasy as Mel's bar kitchen. He glanced up to his reflection in the mirror across from his seat. The dim lights of the bar accentuated the deep lines in his face, the circles under his eyes. He hadn't slept well. He needed refuge. To drown his sorrows in booze and loud music.

The man stood next to Jack and waited. Jack just stared at him. Finally, the man spoke.

"Boss isn't happy," he said.

Jack had worked with the man before. Somewhere out of his foggy brain he managed to pluck out his name. Bobby. Bobby Sharp.

"Screw Tyrone."

Bobby tsked. "Not nice to talk to someone who takes care of you. Who could've made you rich, if you wouldn't have gotten greedy. Very rich."

Jack snorted. He was lucky he wasn't in prison. In just one day, social media and police investigations cost him everything. And he didn't need Tyrone now, he needed beer, a girl, and some peace.

"Now Tyrone needs something from you."

"You think I'm afraid of Tyrone?" Actually, he was. But it wouldn't matter. If Jack was convicted, his life would be over anyway.

"You should be." Bobby leaned close, close enough to whisper in his ear over the loud music. "Tyrone has a new set of chef's knives he'd like to try out."

Jack knocked over his beer bottle. He snatched up some cocktail napkins and mopped up the mess.

Bobby waited until the napkins were soaked through before continuing. "Need the identity of Andrew Baker. Help us find him, then Tyrone might forgive this little indiscretion."

"How would I know who he is?"

"He's been to your shop. Found evidence. Maybe

he showed up on your cameras."

His mind was clouded with alcohol. "I don't know. I don't know. The police confiscated everything."

Bobby stood, grabbing Jack's shoulder. "Think about it, Jack. Something's got to be suspicious. Get your revenge on Andrew Baker." Bobby dropped a card with a deadline. "We need information before then."

Chapter Three

After a shower, she had ten minutes to choose an *ensemble* then dress and get out the door. There was no way she could assemble everything in time. She called Brad.

"I'm running late," she said, not telling him why. "But I'm almost ready."

While still on the phone, she threw on a tiered peasant skirt. Pressing speaker, she dropped the phone on a bench to tuck her hair up in a spiky Tina Turner wig. She shook her head to allow the spiny ends to flutter around her, like having a slinky on your head.

Brad responded, laughing a little. "Someday it will be a matter of life and death."

Hopping on one foot to the mirror, because she stepped on an errant earring left on the floor, she pried open bobby pins with her teeth, securing the wig to her head. "Yeah, but hopefully not today."

Now, makeup.

"You're not coming dressed in one of your funny costumes again, are you?" he asked.

She smiled. Man, he knew her so well. She shook her head as she applied rouge to the apples of her cheeks like she was painting a barn. "Meet you in a few…if you can recognize me."

"You're well-disguised, Andy, but I always spot you."

"Not the last two times."

"Yeah, okay, so you cheated with the kabuki mask."

Andy smiled. "Whatever. This one won't be too tough."

Tiered peasant skirt, equestrian thigh-highs transformable to ankle boots, a purple fuzzy shrug over a baby tee, and she was ready to go. She smiled. She would blend right in. Total disappearance in an outfit like this. "Be there in a bit."

Hurrying, she picked up her clothes. Usually she just left them on the floor, but these she'd worn for three days in a row, and they were starting to stand on their own. As she gathered them, a little piece of paper floated out.

Hugh's digits.

After hesitating, she pocketed the scrap and tossed the clothes toward the basket, missing it completely. She'd come back and clean it all up.

Then she grabbed her bag.

****

As soon as she crossed the gangplank to the entrance of the refurbished riverboat of the Riverfront Casino, Andy blended in. After passing security in the lobby, she slid into a chair at the slots, scanning the dimly lit room for Brad. When she didn't spot him after a few minutes, she stood, surveying the crowd. People from every class tried their luck, from the guys with the impoverished hope of betting their last hundred bucks to the wealthy recreational gamblers. But she still didn't spy Brad.

Someone approached her. A man with sunken, purple wells beneath his eyes. She didn't recognize him.

"Gotcha, Andy!"

"Brad!" Andy stepped back in surprise at Brad's lined and pale face. She stopped herself from blurting out, "You've aged."

Stress robbed his boyish youth, replacing it with this old man. Andy's heart clenched at the change in such a short time.

"You look great, Andy," he said, smiling, but it did little to improve the tension in his face.

Andy wished she could say the same about him. But managed to say, "You look well, too." A lie, but it was a compliment, so it didn't count.

He arched an eyebrow with a disbelieving half-smile. "Our table is ready. Shall we?" He held out his arm for Andy.

He escorted her through the Riverfront Casino which was docked forever on the Mississippi River. Andy doubted it even had a motor. They probably gutted the engine room to make way for more lucrative activities.

A glass spiral staircase climbed to the seventh story to the outdoor dining room where the wealthier class of patrons overlooked the water sparkling with reflected light. At the top of the stairs, they waited to be seated. The wind picked up, blowing the strands of her wig around.

When the seating host, a man with dark receding hair in short waistcoat and tails, showed them their secluded table for two, Andy plunked down her bag beside the chair leg as he seated her. Menus appeared out of nowhere. With a foreign accent, the waiter told them about the house specials for the evening and served their drinks. She waited impatiently for him to be gone.

After he disappeared, Andy ignored her hunger and the desire to open the menu to discover what smelled so delicious at the table next to them. Brad fidgeted with his flatware.

"What's up?" Andy said, thumbing her menu. "Your face tells the whole story. Is work at Imperial Energy more stressful than what you expected?"

Grimacing, he peeked around to make sure no one was within ear shot of the table. He whispered, "Have you received any texts from Conner recently?"

"Not since he dumped me last year after his big promotion."

"I haven't seen him for two weeks. I think he's... I think he's been killed."

Andy's throat tightened. "You think he's been killed?"

"He discovered something. Something big. And he uncovered some stuff at work."

Andy was silent. Staring at the lines in the tablecloth.

"I hoped you might be able to, you know, investigate."

"What do you mean?" Andy's face warmed.

"I think you know what I mean."

"No."

"Your dad's column?"

Andy exhaled. So he did know. Or he guessed. "How did you find out?"

"Andy, I know you. I know you use those disguises for things. When Mike disappeared, but his column didn't, it wasn't hard to guess who picked up the torch."

"What do you want me to do?" she asked.

"Conner gave me something. I've stashed it in my office." He slid a small envelope across the table. "Here is a map to it, as well as the entry code to the room it's in. I hid it behind the aquarium. I left you two things."

"You didn't bring them tonight?"

"I can't take anything out of the office without getting frisked. It's too dangerous."

"You can't email it?"

"Andy, they frisk us at the door, what makes you think our email is secure?" He sighed, annoyed. "Sorry, I'm a little stressed. You could get in using your disguises. You could dress up as a cleaning lady or something."

"What am I supposed to find?"

"Conner said all the leads are on a jump drive under the folder labeled 'Pictures of Amanda.' There's an encryption code to get into the jump drive." He passed Andy a piece of paper with an authentication code of seventeen numbers.

Andy picked up the paper. "What's on the jump drive?"

"As far as I know it's the only copy of emails, reports incriminating Tyrone. Conner gave me the jump drive a few weeks before he disappeared. With it is a sticky note with the name of Conner's contact. He'll be able to tell you more about who is involved because he was one of the ones who discovered the cover-up. You must convince him to testify. Without this, it will be hard to get a conviction. I think everybody else connected with the case is dead or missing." He glanced around. A chill rose up Andy's spine.

"We don't have much time." He bent forward,

whispering. "Also, Dr. Victor Armstrong. You'll need to find him. He's missing, too. I tried to call him but they said he was no longer at Boston University. Find a home number or address. Try to find out his connection to another professor at BU. I can't remember his name. Something foreign."

"I'm confused." Andy leaned forward, "What's the story?"

He glanced around again, as if he were a young boy, so small, his sunken eyes, large, in his white face. "When I started working for Imperial Energy, I made some connections."

"Connections?"

He hesitated. "Like an association of powerful men. Men who make things happen in this city. We had to commit to an oath of loyalty."

Andy's throat constricted. The mob. She didn't want to get involved in organized crime. Those guys operated way beyond her skills.

Brad confirmed her fear. "This will be more serious than chasing down federal agents caught with their pants down." Last fall. Literally, she caught Ross Underlee with another federal agent in a, well, *compromising* position. They were trading sexual favors for top secret cover-ups. She was pleased he had kept up on her articles. "They make blood oaths." He emphasized this by pointing his finger on the table. "What I am about to give you violates my blood oath."

"Blood oaths?"

"We make compacts to never tell the secrets discussed in our meetings, to protect one another, to help each brother in Imperium."

"So, why are you telling me?"

"Because there are other people out there searching for this information, too."

Andy's heart quickened.

Brad continued, leaning over and whispering to Andy. "Conner said a man approached him saying he was from Concordant."

"What is Concordant?"

"Another syndicate across town. He *persuaded* him to help him find some dope on Tyrone."

"He blackmailed Conner?"

Brad nodded.

"What did Conner do to incriminate himself?"

His lips crumpled into a frown. "I don't know everything about Conner. But the guy from Concordant said Tyrone had some guy killed, and he wanted to convict him but needed evidence."

Andy nodded, encouraging him to go on.

"Under duress, he snooped around Tyrone's affairs. What he found was way worse than what the Concordant guy told him. Conner tried to tell him, but the Concordant guy just shrugged and said he only wanted a conviction for Tyrone." His gaze grew tense. "Andy, I don't know what's going on, but Conner hasn't responded to any texts in the last two weeks. He always responds to my texts. We were close."

A memory of her dad flashed for a second in her mind. He didn't respond to her texts either. It had been three years. Then immediately refocused.

"So, why not go to the police?"

"Because I don't know if the police are in on it."

"Surely you could go to Fred."

"You mean Frederick Alexander Hillsdale III? Carla's old boyfriend? I doubt I can trust him.

Hillsdales are in Imperium."

"He's rejected his family's money. And doing his own thing should mean something."

"He's also a weirdo."

"Just because he wears basketball shorts with combat boots doesn't make him weird. He's someone I trust on the St. Louis Police Department. He's been a reliable asset for me."

"Oh, yeah, how did you get to know him?"

"It just so happens Fred likes old movies in the park and so does Bethany."

"Who's Bethany?"

Andy whipped her head. Her voice switched to an exaggerated Californian accent. "She's, like, an alter ego, okay!" Andy dropped back to her normal voice. "It's my way of milking him for information without compromising my identity."

Brad just shook his head. "Anyway."

Andy leaned close. "How about the FBI, then? Go there for a witness protection program."

"Probably on Tyrone's payroll, too. I can't trust anyone else because I'm not sure how far the corruption goes. You don't know Imperium. They are everywhere." He paused, glancing around again before leaning in. "Everybody lies. Don't believe me? Here's the real kicker: I found out the guy claiming to be from Concordant doesn't work there." Brad paused. "One of my contacts in the association has never heard of him. Conner says he's been following him for about a year."

She bit her lip, her fingers twirling the stem of her empty wine glass, thinking. It was all coming too fast. Andy didn't know anything about organized crime. "What's in it for you?" she asked.

"Freedom. I didn't realize what I was getting into, and I want out. There are only two ways out. Death or the downfall of Imperium." Now she understood his haggard appearance. "I'd prefer the latter."

A silence passed between them. Her gaze darted to the other couples seated with hurricane lamps between them, the flames wavering in the open breeze. It was all so ironic. All those years growing up, Brad convinced Sandra and her dad he was the obedient one, and Andy was the rebellious one. And now she was having this conversation.

Brad broke the silence. "Listen, I'm sure they're watching me, so we don't have time. Are you in or out?"

Seeing Brad so scared, so small, so internally sick with fear, made her all the more afraid.

She understood when she replaced her father as Andrew Baker there might be some retaliation from those she exposed. But a lone wolf breaking the law was different than taking on organized crime. This was the mob he was talking about.

"Give me a minute to think about it," she said. She wasn't even sure she had the skills to do this. Picking up the codes and stuff, she stuffed them in her bag, hefting it over her shoulder. "I'm going to the bathroom to freshen up my face."

Before she left the table, he stopped her by touching her forearm. "Conner told me he was going to propose to you last year."

Andy faced him, snorting. "Why didn't he?"

"I think he was afraid. Maybe he feared his boss would find out who you are. Or maybe he was afraid you'd discover who he really was, deep inside." He paused. "He had a ring, Andy."

Andy nodded and left the table. She'd had too much disappointment for the night. Her beloved stepbrother was in a mob. Her ex-boyfriend was killed, and he hadn't proposed last year out of fear.

Just as she was about to enter the restroom, she noticed a sign on the door.

Closed for cleaning

Even better. No one would be coming in to disturb her. She glanced across the foyer at a stooped, old man in a janitor jumpsuit, gray wisps of hair falling over his balding head with each back and forth of his mopping motion in the men's bathroom.

While he faced away, she slipped past the cleaning cart and large gray garbage bin into the bathroom, and slipped into a stall. Digging through her bag to find her phone without success, she placed her mirror and lipstick on the toilet paper dispenser to freshen her makeup later.

She sat on top of the black box at the back of the toilet, her skirt covering the automatic flushing device. She hooked the heels of her boots on the inside of the toilet bowl. A little uncomfortable, but not bad. So much better than those manual flushers with a two-inch hexagon riding up your rear when you sat on them. She'd been in more awkward places, for sure; between mattresses, in a dessert cart, and up a fireplace flue just to name a few.

She just wanted a quiet moment alone. To think.

The door slammed open, stuttering her heart, shaking the stalls, and making her lipstick roll to the edge of the dispenser. Her ears pricked alert to voices.

"In here," a gruff voice said. Her breath halted at

the shuffling of feet. The sound of *men* in the ladies' room was more than disorienting.

"I'm cleaning in here," the janitor said. "You can't—"

"No one comes in," the same voice interrupted. "You got it?"

The door closed with a bang, and the men continued to shuffle around and struggle. Her heart thundered in her chest. Andy trembled. She couldn't swallow. Couldn't breathe.

"Toss him over here."

Andy didn't dare budge as something large smashed up against the mirror. Her gut sank.

"So, Mr. Potts, squealing, are you?" a man said.

Brad! She counted the voices of three men.

A familiar accent spoke next. "There was a girl with him."

The seating host ratted her out.

Four men. Too many for her. If she were armed, it would be different.

She couldn't get to her phone or recorder because the noise to wade through her purse would alert them. She just sat and listened.

"What were you telling the girl, Mr. Potts?" one of the men said.

"Nothing." His voice sounded pinched, wheezing, like they were strangling him. "We were just meeting for some drinks, dinner. A friendly date."

"She was no date. You know you aren't supposed to share secrets. Why did you break your promise, Mr. Potts? You know the Grand Master doesn't like broken promises. She must be some girl for you to risk your life for her."

Brad whimpered. An unmanly, *inhumanly* whimper.

"You must have had something very important to tell her. What was it? What did you risk *her* life to tell her?"

Only a pause. Andy held her breath.

The man continued. "Now you are forcing my hand to do some very unpleasant things."

A groan of pain grated at her heart. But the man still continued.

Another groan from Brad. Andy was frozen. She wanted to throw her hands over her ears to block out the sound, but she was paralyzed.

"I didn't do anything," Brad said through breaths, exerting great effort to speak. "Leave the girl alone."

"Depends on what you've told her."

"Nothing." The reply was too quick. "She doesn't know anything. It's just an old friend."

"An old friend?" He sounded intrigued. "I'm surprised such a beauty could," he paused, "only be a friend. I'd like to get to know your friend. Where is she?"

"I don't know. She left."

"I doubt she went very far." The timbre of his voice, the proximity to her made Andy's veins freeze. "Sergio, please inform security to detain our little beauty." He paused. "But I'm afraid she will not be so beautiful when we get done with her."

"No," Brad started, but it was cut short by thumping. Each hit like hamburger being tenderized.

"Don't worry, we'll find her. If you tell us her name, maybe we won't kill her as slowly. You, my friend, will not be so lucky."

They were killing him. Tears pricked Andy's eyes, exerting self-control not to go shooting out of the stall, whipping them all. But she realized the futility of it all. She couldn't save him. Andy bit her lip almost to bloodshed. She could only endure.

"Her name." More beatings, groans. "Her name!"

Andy just couldn't stand it. She closed her eyes trying to stop the sound, but only squeezing out more tears. *Stop, stop, stop, stop*, she repeated in her mind after each beating. *Stop*!

Then it stopped. When she opened her eyes, a stream of blood, as thin as a marker line, flowed to the drain in the next stall. It was eerily quiet.

"Toss him in the river. Make sure they don't find the body." A large thump sounded, like they stuffed Brad in the large gray garbage can. Wheels started to roll.

"Clean this up," a voice said. "Send all pictures of him and any girl to the boss. Alert security to search for a girl with a red bag."

"Yes, Rodgers."

Someone bumped into the stalls again. The lipstick rolled to the edge of the dispenser. Through the thin crack in the stall doors, she spied the back of the man leaning over the sink, preening in the mirror. He said before leaving, "Red bag. Weird hair. Boots up to here. Shouldn't be hard to find. Talk to security. Find her. Question her. If he squealed anything, kill her."

Her legs ached from crouching on the toilet seat. Her thighs burned. Sweat beaded on her forehead, waiting. She held her breath, expecting the door to spring open any second.

The silence burned in her ears, tears streaming

down her face before the mop passed over the blood. Brad's blood. His essence of life, drying brown, trickling down the patterned drain. She sat there immovable, staring at the coat hook unaware of anything but tasting her own fear, her own brush with death.

The janitor left. Silence reined for a few minutes. Maybe a few hours. Andy couldn't be sure. Then at last, two women entered.

"I can't believe she bought her vest at the Demi Prix," one said.

"Well, you know Katalina, she hasn't always had the best taste," the other replied.

The conversation snapped Andy out of her shock. There was still a world going on outside the bathroom. Someone concerned about a vest. A flood of women entered in after them.

Hands washing. Paper towels dispensed, trash. Hair fluffing, lipstick on. Still talking about shoes or sunglasses or something. More women entered, clicking in high heels across the white tile where there was once a stream of blood. Brad's blood.

Brad's blood.
Brad's blood.
Brad's blood.
Stop!

She needed to snap out of it. She had to get out of here. Sergio was probably searching every inch of the restaurant and casino.

Her bag, where she had always thought it was a help, it was now a tell. Stupid, stupid, Andy.

Finally, she shifted, unhooking one foot then the other off the rim. She stretched out her legs, letting the blood prickle into her limbs. She had to get out of there. Standing in the middle of the stall, she realized the sound of flushing toilets all around hurt her head.

She needed a new disguise. She stared at her bag

Chapter Four

The wig was off first. With her head much lighter, cooler, a weight lifted off her shoulders. She stuffed it in the bag, her hands shaking. Adrenaline ran through her, giving her clarity and focus.

Next, she removed the shrug. An easy fix. They'd be searching for someone with a purple fuzzy shrug. And her boots. Trembling, she removed the convertible equestrian boot shafts from around her calves, sporting ankle-high boots, hoping the transformation would be enough.

Digging into it with her elbows, she reversed her printed t-shirt. The inside was nondescript gray. To further transform it, she dug a pocket knife from her bag and cut out the mid-drift of her shirt, tossing the scraps into the sani-bin. She worked mechanically, trying not to think of what just happened, or to think of what could happen if they discovered her. She shuddered. She just had to focus on getting out.

She plucked her mid-calf tiered skirt, biting her lip, searching through her bag once more. After finding her sewing kit, she tucked under two layers of the tiered skirt up to her waistline, turning it into a shorter balloon-type skirt, securing it with large basting stitches across the waist. It was too short for the ankle-high boots. But right now, she was not going for a fashion statement, she needed a transformation. Wrapping up the sewing kit, she tucked it and everything else in her bag.

Her bag. It was an obvious tell. Brad's killers knew it. They mentioned it. They'd be hunting for it.

Andy gulped. She had gathered stuff for over three years for her bag: lock picks, compass, socket wrenches, and medical tape. Some of it her father had given her. The rest was a collection of survival gear and emergency supplies gathered for preparation for any situation. She couldn't part with it. It held too much.

But if it risked her life, it wouldn't be worth holding on to. She'd have to find a place to hide it. She stuffed Brad's code into it, knowing she'd have to come back for both tomorrow when she could be in disguise.

She leaned against the door, her hand on the latch, heart pounding. Sliding the latch back, she creaked open the door, peeking out.

The toilet flushed behind her. She jumped at the sudden whooshing, her heart beating furiously.

"Stupid automatic flushers," she said with a nervous laugh, feeling a rush of energy. "They get you every time."

She checked her reflection. Her makeup streaked down her face. She wiped away the stain on her cheeks and lips with moist towelettes from her bag. Usually, she wore a disguise to make sure she wasn't seen. But this was even scarier, going out as herself. This was her. All her. No disguises. Plain ol' Andy.

Andy waited while the last lady washed her hands. By the sinks, a stainless-steel trash bin fit into the wall. Once the bathroom cleared, she slipped her bag into it, marking the outside of the plastic with some tape from her tote. She stuffed tons of paper towels over the top to make sure it was out of sight. She didn't want it stolen either.

She'd have to come back tomorrow. Early. Staring into the trash filled with white fluff, her heart ached. Everything she loved was in there. The second loss of the day.

When the door opened, she straightened up. A woman held the door open for Andy as she exited behind her.

Returning to the first floor, she searched for the casino exit through the maze of slot machines and card tables, dodging servers and patrons, in a haze of cigarette smoke. She hurried, but not so much she attracted attention. At last, the glass doors promised freedom. But a man in a suit with an earpiece patrolled the large front doors.

Security.

She shied away from the door, waiting, heart pounding. Pure adrenaline surged through her veins. She couldn't sit still. Security just waited there until an elderly woman asked him something, and he led her away by the arm.

Half-running, half-walking, she skipped through the doors, down the bridge. Outside, a group of suited men scanned cars as they drove by, checking passengers. She held her breath, sliding along the building. Cameras hung from every light post in the parking lot. With her face down, she dodged through the cars, strategically avoiding the men in golf carts patrolling the lot with lights.

The trek was unbearably long. She didn't glance behind until she neared the end of the lot. Finally, she arrived at Market Street. The brilliant casino flashed as the skyline swallowed the sun behind her.

Crowds gathered at the entrance, advertisements flashed for decadent buffets, money changed hands, neon signs showed coins falling from machines. Promises made. Promises broken.

Her stomach soured realizing how much they entice people to come in, like Brad who got sucked up in it all. She couldn't think of where he was now. Probably at the bottom of the Mississippi.

She shook the image from her head. *Goodbye, Brad.*

Andy ran. And ran.

Feeling too nervous to go home, Andy wandered the street grateful for the painkillers she swallowed earlier. Her ankle mostly healed.

With every car speeding by, she jumped. Too nervous to think right, she left her keys and her phones in her bag. Sandra would fall apart if Andy brought the mafia after her. She couldn't face her and tell her about Brad. Not tonight.

And on foot, hiking to the county would take forever. Thanks to cell phones, there weren't any pay phones either. And she didn't have any numbers memorized.

After an hour of wandering the city, she was sure no one followed her. But still, she hesitated going home.

A car horn blasted behind her. Car lights illuminated the street before her. Andy shuddered, naked without her bag. Out of resources. She had nothing. Nothing.

Glancing behind, she slid her hand into her pocket and slipped out the rolled-up sliver of paper and read it.

Hugh's phone number and address. She'd forgotten she'd slipped it in there earlier.

But she still didn't trust him completely.

The address was only two blocks from where she was. Definite bonus. Andy paced the sidewalk. She had nowhere else to go. He, at least, wouldn't ask her questions. All she needed was a place to rest and think of what she was going to do next.

She found the address, a loft in the restored warehouses common in the downtown area of South City. Trembling, she mounted the staircase, jumping at every noise echoing off the brick walls and concrete stairs in the industrial loft. Once on the second floor, she knocked at one of two high metal doors and waited.

"This was a dumb idea," she said aloud, ready to leave. When the door squeaked open, Andy squealed.

Hugh's head peeked from the thick metal door, startled at seeing Andy there. His hair hung in wet strings on his forehead. Andy didn't know what time it was, but she guessed late.

"Can I come in?" Andy mustered all her strength.

"You all right?" Hugh asked.

Andy ran her fingers through her hair. Her neck and shoulders ached with tension.

"Rough night." All the emotion of the last few hours finally strangled her. Andy collapsed against the brick wall, her legs losing strength.

Hugh, alarmed, caught her. He glanced her over and asked, "Are you okay?"

After closing the door behind him, Hugh stepped out into the hallway, ushering her to the stairs. Sitting side by side on the top stair, Andy held her face in her hands, quietly sobbing. Hugh held her. She craved being with him, his gaze aroused her, enlivened her. Like taking a deep breath of fresh air, like sated thirst. But could she trust him?

"Is everything all right?" he asked.

"Can I sleep here tonight?"

An eyebrow raised. "Girls don't usually ask until after the first date."

Andy attempted a smile. "I can't go home."

His brow furrowed a bit, and her heart lunged with shame or regret.

"Upset about the purse snatchers?" he asked.

Andy nodded. A lie. But it wasn't spoken. So it didn't count. She was grateful to have an excuse to appear so weak. Hugh bit his lip. "Let me rearrange a few things, and then you can come in. You all right out here by yourself?"

She nodded.

"It will just be a few seconds."

He stood and entered the thick, industrial door, leaving Andy to contemplate the brick wall and exposed ceiling, trying to think of anything other than her horrific evening. Everything jarred her senses. Where dark rust stains splotched the banister and the floor, Andy imagined blood. She closed her eyes, aching.

In a flash, Hugh opened the door, inviting her inside.

Andy, usually attentive to detail, didn't catch anything as she entered and sat on his contemporary couch. Her eyes were glazed, seeing *through* objects rather than seeing them. But she noticed the darkened room was lit by only a single bulb hanging from the exposed ceiling far above. The musky smell of incense clung to the fabric of the futon.

"Can I get you something to eat?" he asked.

Andy's stomach growled. Although she'd met Brad for dinner hours ago, they never ordered. After all the wandering and the emotional distress, she was hungry, but Andy shrugged. Eating was a burden. She needed to decompress, to think about how to get her bag, how to carry on. It was late. Her mind wandered. Hugh was asking her something, but she just blinked it away, not hearing anything.

"I'll just run and go shopping," he said.

"Don't go," she said. Suddenly, all energy drained from her. Frequent late nights and the emotional stress from Brad's death weighed on her. "I just need a place to rest. Then I'll be out of your hair."

He pointed to one of two doors on the only sheet-rocked wall. "You can sleep in there. Sheets are clean."

"I'll be comfortable on the couch."

"I'm not letting my first guest sleep on the futon, I don't even have sheets for it yet. Just take the bed."

Andy ambled zombie-like to the bedroom. It was small, as big as a walk-in closet with a bed, a nightstand, and an overstuffed chair with pants draped over the back. The small room was filled with clothes and boxes and two identical trunks on the floor. No windows.

"Bathroom's in there." He pointed to a small door inside the room. She nodded.

"If you need anything else, I'll be out there."

"Will you stay?"

"I'm not going anywhere."

"No. In here. Until I'm asleep. I'm afraid."

He didn't say anything, but strolled to the chair and sat. Andy was grateful for his patience and for the fact he didn't ask any questions.

Andy couldn't sleep. She lay on the bed with her clothes on. The cracks in the ceiling were trails of blood. When she closed her eyes she again, the thin line of blood on white tile haunted her.

She must have slept briefly. She woke to darkness. Hugh had switched off the lamp and left. Andy's heart pounded as she slid her covers off, dropping her feet to the concrete floor.

She tiptoed to the door. Voices echoed in the spacious living area. Andy cracked the door. An eerie blue glow of the computer lit Hugh's face in the darkened space.

"I'll ask her," he said, his voice low. "Nothing I could do, though, without compromise."

A voice replied from the computer, "You did right. Anything else would've been risking too much."

"What about the girl?"

"I trust you."

Intrigued, Andy craned her ear. The door creaked. Andy swore in her mind. Hugh glanced up, silencing his computer. "You okay?" he asked.

"I woke up. Did I disturb you?"

Hugh didn't blink an eye. "Just watching a movie." He lied.

Andy's heart thundered in her ears. With all senses on alert, Andy, very much awake, halted at the door.

Hugh rose from the couch and followed her into the bedroom. But this time, it was not comforting to have him close. Her body was still rigid as he resumed his place in his chair.

Andy clutched the covers.

"You're still nervous." He rose from the chair and

sat at the foot of her bed. "You okay?"

Andy swallowed, retracting her legs. "Nightmares."

"How about I tell you a story?"

He arose slowly, waiting for Andy to open the covers for him. Finally, Andy scooted toward the wall. He sat next to her without saying a word.

"A story?" She swallowed. "What kind of story?"

"What kind of story would you like?"

"Something happy."

A long pause. Andy wished she could catch a glimpse of his face in the dark.

His tone changed to thoughtful. "All right. I've got a story. My favorite memories from the summers living in Manhattan."

Andy perked up a little. "New York?"

"Kansas."

Andy couldn't help be a little disappointed.

"I lived with my grandparents on a farm in the middle of Kansas. It was hot and filled with sunshine and wheat. I used to run through the fields with my black lab, Rhiner, and lay on my back and stare into the sky to ask those white clouds about life. Anyway, my happiest days were spent running around the farm with Rhiner on my heels, his ears flapping, his tongue out. I can still smell the crisp burnt leaves of the harvest in fall, the smell of Pappie's aftershave, and Meemaw's cooking."

Listening to the steady intonation of his voice eased her, releasing her fear, her body relaxing. Her eyes grew weary, imagining Hugh as a little boy on a Kansas farm. A little Hugh running through the wheat, the sun shining.

"What did you say you did for a living?" Andy wasn't sure she asked it, or if she just thought it, but she didn't remember him answering.

****

When Andy woke it was dark. The clock said eight a.m.. Alarmed, Andy sat up. Only a sliver of light shone under the door.

Hugh was gone from her side. She huddled back under the covers. Then, the memories of Brad crashed upon her like a cold shower on a hot day.

Slipping from the bed, she paced around the bedroom, trying to control her fear. She couldn't remember what Brad needed her to do. The trauma of the night had made her forget.

Rubbing her hands across her face, she searched her painful memories. Then she remembered. Get the jump drive from behind the aquarium in his office, use the code to access information, and call the name of the person on the sticky note. First step, she needed her bag and the code, then she could think about the next step. Calmness settled over her, resolute calmness. She needed to get back to the casino and dig through the trash to get her bag.

At last, she had something to focus on, something she needed to do. What she needed the most was a purpose, a drive, something to propel her forward. She needed a plan to get it.

Andy had just the idea.

She opened the door to the rest of the apartment. What she didn't notice last night was how neat and tidy his spacious loft apartment was. The high ceilings of exposed pipes and vent ducting worked with what he was achieving with the sparse decor. The industrial-style kitchen with stainless-steel countertops, brick backsplash, and wrought iron lights, was empty. Hugh must've left for the morning. He couldn't have been gone too long, the incense was still burning. But his laptop was gone.

She should be on her way.

But a top investigative journalist couldn't just stay at a mysterious guy's house without at least snooping a little bit. Especially after the conversation she overheard last night.

She touched her fingertips together, thinking.

The bathroom.

His life was surprisingly sparse. No years' worth of junk gathering dust like at Andy's apartment. It was as if he'd just moved in last night.

Disappointed at only finding toiletries in the bathroom, she opened the door to the bedroom glancing around. Two trunks sat against the far wall. She knelt down beside one of the giant, black sea chests. A military grade lock hung from the latch. She held it in her hand. She pulled. Worth a try. The other chest was also locked. Not necessarily suspicious. Maybe he had a snoopy roommate before and had to be cautious. She stood, glancing around his clothes. Normal. There wasn't much to his room. She glanced around. This guy was really boring.

Or he was hiding something.

Andy checked the bedside table. Nothing on top. As she opened the drawer, something rolled around inside.

A tie tack.

An odd thing to keep in the side of the drawer. It was just all alone. Andy picked it up, then seeing the red triangle and the initials BDP, she nearly dropped it.

It was Brad's tie tack. One she gave him for graduation a few years back. Her eyes widened.

The front door opened.

Trembling, Andy stuffed the tie tack in her pocket and closed the drawer. Keeping her breath even, she opened the bedroom door just as Hugh set down a bag of groceries and his laptop.

He eyed her keenly. "You look guilty," he said upon examination.

"Who are you?" she asked, eying him, her heart beating.

He broke into a smile. "Directness. I like that." He dug into his bag and pulled out a carton of eggs and a bag of spinach. "Want an omelet?"

Andy retrieved the tie tack from her pocket. Probably not the wisest approach, but she wanted answers. And she figured she could take him if things went south.

"Where did you get this?" she asked.

Hugh stopped with an onion in his hand. He chewed the inside of his mouth. But remained quiet.

"Mine," he finally said.

Andy slammed it down on the stainless-steel counter. "Initials BDP? I don't think so. It's my brother Brad's. I gave it to him."

Hugh's eyebrows raised.

Andy's eyes narrowed. She hated being played. "Who are you? Not some guy who wants karate lessons, I bet."

Hugh set down the onion, watching her carefully. "No," he said. "I'm not."

"Where did you get this?" Brad had warned her of

a man lying about his membership in Concordant. She let her emotions cloud her judgment and fell right into a trap. She snatched a knife from the block on the counter and held it out, threateningly.

Hugh scoffed at her, amused at her brashness. "Do you really think you could best me?"

Andy half wondered if she could. He may be bigger. And he had some skills, but Andy could hold her own.

"It is Brad's." Hugh spoke quietly, patiently, trying to disarm her with his words. "Listen, drop the knife. You're right. I'm not who I said I was."

Andy didn't lower the knife. "Surprise me."

Backing from where he stood, he opened a drawer behind him, removing a flatware tray. Andy tensed.

"I didn't want to have to tell you. My name is Hugh Donaldson. *Detective* Donaldson. I'm working undercover for the St. Louis Police Department."

Underneath the tray, he removed a panel. From there he retrieved a wallet-sized object. He flipped over to show Andy a police badge. Andy's jaw dropped. If it hadn't been attached so securely to the rest of her skull, it literally would have fallen on the floor.

He flipped it closed and dropped it in the drawer. "I didn't know it was your brother's. I found it when Brad was meeting with another contact I had, Conner Flannery. We've been tracking Conner for a year in deep cover, investigating his involvement in a secret society called Imperium. Conner may have given Brad some leads. We think a man named Tyrone, the leader of Imperium, may have killed someone important."

Andy nodded her head, but the information like a leaf floating on a pond—not sinking in. She pocketed the tie tack.

Hugh continued. "I know you'll keep my little secret. It may mean the difference of life or death, to me or to you. Only you and the STLPD know my cover."

"He's gone," she whispered.

"What do you mean?"

"Brad," she said, then caught herself. "Both Conner and Brad. They killed them both."

"They got to them last night, didn't they?"

Andy shook her head. "Not Conner. He's been gone for a while. Brad." Andy almost couldn't say it. Her throat was so tight.

"That's why you were so traumatized last night."

"I wanted to stop them. But there were four men. I should've tried. It was the first time my life was in real danger. But instead of using my skills to protect someone I love, I was so scared. I hid and let them kill Brad."

"You couldn't have stopped them. Even with a sixth-degree black belt. While impressive, you do the math. I'm sure they were armed. And trained. You would've been in over your head."

"I can handle my own." But was she sure? In all her stories, in all her investigating, never once was her life in danger. Sure, there were guys who had the grabbies, but she could've kicked their butts at any moment. But these guys, these mobsters, they could kill without even wondering what to do with the body.

"Did Brad give you any information?"

Andy's mind flashed to her bag. She needed to get it. But she wasn't sure she bought Hugh's story. "He wanted me to do something for him."

"What was it?"

"Help him. He was hoping to be free, but now he'll never be free."

Hugh faced her with seriousness in his face. "You can help me. I have been trying to track down Tyrone. If you help, we can end Imperium."

But to track down Tyrone, she needed her bag. "Mind if I borrow your computer?" She sat down at his laptop.

"Sure. Go ahead." Hugh continued with a cocky grin. "What you are supposed to say now is, 'What a pleasant surprise, you are in on it, too. Now we can work together.' You've got some skills. You're brave. I'm a professional. I think we'd make a good team." But Andy still had nagging thoughts as she searched for the information on garbage pick-up. She finally glanced up at him. "I'd like to work together on this thing, if you'd let me," he said. His eyes were so soft, so sincere. He was so confident, so *trustworthy.* He couldn't be working for the bad guys. "Two people are better than one. And I've got resources."

"Interesting suggestion," she said, sitting back in her chair. "I've always worked solo. Having a *sidekick* might slow me down, or," she said, giving him a nasty glare—"encumber my work. But it could also be an advantage." She didn't have time to mull the pros and cons. Her lifelong mantra popped into her mind: Verify *first* then trust.

She'd need all the help she could get going up against the mob. Before she told him anything, she needed to make one phone call.

And she needed her bag.

"Okay," she said at last, with a hint of bravado. "You can work with me. But I call the shots. We have to do something first. Get my bag." She pointed at the screen. "Today is garbage day at the casino. We have to hurry."

"You say such interesting things. What's in your bag anyway?"

Andy was already at the door. "Flashlights, lock picks, emergency rain ponchos, credit card-sized cameras, wall-climbing robotic devices. Other things, too, water-purifying tablets, military issue magnesium fire starter, nail polish, sewing kit, duct tape, toilet seat covers. Plus hair bands, bobby pins, an extra wig, mint floss, and an inflatable PFD. A girl needs her stuff."

Hugh flashed her an exaggerated eye-roll. "Girls and their purses."

Chapter Five

As Tyrone gathered ingredients for dinner in his penthouse kitchen, Bobby's number flashed on his phone. He picked it up.

"Tyrone here."

"Jack called. Says he has something for you. Thinks he might have a picture of an accomplice working with Baker."

"He thinks, huh? Doesn't mean much. I want to meet with Jack." He hung up the phone after setting a time and date. He sat at the table stroking his face.

Tyrone didn't like squealers, and Andrew Baker was his least favorite. The man was a fly on his seared filet mignon. Tyrone shuddered.

"What's the matter, Daddy?" Hazel asked. Tyrone couldn't believe this blonde beauty was his daughter. She sat across from him at the dark ebony table searching for decorations for her wedding on a tablet. Next to her sat champagne lists, a caterer's menu, and one bakery pamphlet. Plus, she had fabric samples, names of musicians, florists' quotes, and pastry chef recommendations. She carried all of this in a designer tote to show him.

Tyrone sneered at the clutter. "You're nearly thirty. Do you have to talk to me like you're four?"

"What shall I call you? *Master*?" She arched an eyebrow at him.

Tyrone sniffed a little and stared out of the view of the city. It was a gray day. Yesterday was sunny, not a cloud in the sky. Today was rainy. Weather in St. Louis was inconsistent. He loved it. Not too much of one thing.

"You didn't answer me," she said, glancing at him over her brochure she consulted. "You've obviously got something on your mind."

"Business. Doesn't concern you."

"Daddy this isn't the Dark Ages. Women run businesses all the time."

"Not my business." He said this over his shoulder.

"You are so archaic."

He leaned toward her in his chair. "You want to know what plagues me? People keep squealing. Accountants, workers. I've got leaks all over the place. Am I an incompetent plumber? I had to terminate someone at the casino this week. I hate it when they make me do that. I didn't even get to do it myself."

He stood and crossed to the fridge and pulled out the raw chicken carcass. "But worst of all. Worst of all is Andrew Baker."

"Who Daddy?"

"A journalist." He set the chicken on the counter.

"If he were my enemy, I'd call out a hit on him."

Tyrone faced her. "You're not supposed to know about those things."

"You can't keep shielding me forever. You think I don't know what goes on here?"

"Plan your wedding," he said, pointing at her stuff with his chin. "The only planning you'll get to do."

For dinner, he was making *poulet aux quarante grosses d'ail*, a French dish of stewing forty cloves of garlic with a whole chicken, a favorite from his days at the École de Cuisine in Paris. If only his father had allowed him to become a chef instead of taking over the family business.

He slid a meat cleaver from the knife rack. Holding it near his head, he dropped the knife. The cleaver sliced through the breast, the sound of bone cracking. A prickling sensation enhanced his senses, energizing him.

This time it was personal. He wanted Baker to get the message loud and clear. St. Louis was Tyrone's city. He would order the hit himself.

Baker would get the message.

****

Hugh led Andy to the parking garage where his Porsche was parked. Andy crossed her arms, studying it suspiciously.

"They gave this to me to do undercover work." He grimaced as he clicked the doors open. No beat cop could afford one of these unless he had a rich grandmother who recently passed away. He should've chosen a different car. It might give him away. But he loved his Porsche, the hum of the GT3 Cup R engine and the sheer power of V8.

Andy rolled her eyes. "Not very inconspicuous."

Hugh grunted, wanting to change the subject. "Now, you're probably safe to go up to your flat and get whatever you need. I doubt Imperium has identified you yet. But if you're worried, I'll go with you to check it out."

Once at the apartment, Andy trembled a bit as she punched in numbers in the security pad as they stood on the cement stoop. "I have to get the spare keys from the concierge."

"This is your place?" Hugh asked, gazing at the brick multi-level rising on a wooded street, in a safe but older part of South City. He pointed to the keypad. "Security."

"Yes," Andy said as she opened the door. "But Mrs. Wheyland lets people in. She's just being nice and holding the door. A coded entry might keep out small time punks." But not the Imperium and trained killers. They got the spare key. She hesitated as they climbed the stairs to her apartment.

She slid her key in the lock and waited.

"Want me to go in first?" he asked.

She nodded.

After he opened the door, Hugh glanced around then shouted, "Somebody's broken in and ransacked the place!"

Clothes spilled from everywhere, dinner plates on the couch. Shoes of varying styles lay overturned in the front foyer, papers scattered on every flat surface. Andy, behind him peeked in, panicked, then blushed deeply. She was rather cute.

"Har, har!" Letting out a nervous laugh, she hit him on his bicep. "This is how my apartment always is."

"You should probably be cleaner. You could attract pests."

"Well, I was *planning* on coming home right after dinner last night and cleaning up."

She rushed about tossing stale breadsticks in the overflowing trash can, stacking the reusable plastic containers to wash.

"So many take-away boxes," he said, tsking his tongue. She glared at him.

Still, he continued poking his head around every nook and cranny of her place, while Andy thought she was being sneaky by picking up clothes and tossing them on the couch behind Hugh's back as he investigated her apartment.

"So, we're here to get your bag?" he asked as he stepped over a few shirts and plates with bits of pizza crusts hardening on them. He wrinkled his eyebrows at a Chinese carton dripping sweet and sour sauce all over a shoe.

"No," she said. "We're here to get dressed up so I can get my bag."

"You know," he said glancing around. "Your *Baker's Dozen* stories were actually quite well written."

Andy stopped cold, holding the pantry open, her hand on the door.

"How did you know I was Andrew Baker?"

"Your campus rape culture one was perfection."

"DNA all the way. If you can get DNA, you can get a conviction." She eyed him. "How exactly did you figure out I'm Andrew Baker?"

He shot her a smile, opening the fridge. "Oh, my. Do you ever go grocery shopping? This thing is so empty someone could've been hiding in here." He picked up a half-gallon of milk, inspecting it. "And it smells rotten. What's the expiry date on this carton?"

"You're evading my question."

He replaced the carton, feeling weary. So many secrets. "Well, you made one big mistake." Andy paled. He continued. "You wrote about your college campus."

"So?" She shrugged. He hated crushing her spirit.

"When I created an analytical map of where Andrew Baker worked, I noticed a pattern."

"Oh?"

"He sniffed out political corruption in the city, helping senior citizens and teenagers, all within one square mile."

Andy breathed out audibly, her eyes widening.

He reveled in her shock. "I cross-referenced college records from those years with everybody who lived in this square mile. And guess whose name showed up."

Andy trembled as she closed her eyes.

Hugh could tell she was really upset. "Don't worry," he said. "You'd have to be some really great hacker to be able to discover your information."

"You did."

"We're on the same side."

"But the bad guys could find it, too."

"Not likely." He had to reassure her without exposing all his secrets.

"And why not?"

"Because they are not as smart as I am."

Andy wasn't at all reassured, but he couldn't tell her how he actually got the information without revealing his sources.

Andy paused beside the second bedroom. "Just wait right here, will you?" Andy said as she unlocked and slipped in the door of a second bedroom. So secretive. His curiosity was piqued. But when she was gone longer than a few minutes, Hugh began to worry.

"Hey, where'd you go?" Hugh opened the door. Andy stuck her head out to stop him.

"No." She clutched the knob, closing the door farther, speaking through the frame and the door. "This closet-room is kind of my biggest secret. You have to pinkie-swear to be best friends for the rest of our lives. Seeing this part of my life is like seeing me naked."

A wide smile played across his lips. She scowled.

"What? You were the one who said it." Hugh couldn't help smirking.

She held out her pinkie. "Do you swear?"

"I swear to someday see you naked."

"Hugh! It's a part of me no one has ever seen, not even Conner. And I'm sharing it with you. Because we're"—the words were hard to say—"working together."

"Okay, I swear I'll be your best friend or whatever you want."

He stuck his hand between the door and the frame. They locked pinkies.

She opened it a bit and paused. "And no wise-cracks." The door fully opened to let him peek in.

"No, nothing but pure admiration." He stepped over the threshold in awe, gazing at the double rungs encircling the room.

Where rest of the apartment was in disordered chaos, her closet room was precise organization. All around the perimeter were closet rails full of different types of clothes, hipster, youthful, old ladyish. In the center, stood more free-standing garment racks, each laden with costumes, doctor's scrubs, uniforms, graduation gowns, unitards, overalls. And one wall had rows of wigs, labeled make-up jars, and jewelry hanging from stands, scarves, fake nails, and prosthetics. "You collected all of this on your own?"

"Yup."

"No help from anybody?"

She shook her head. "I mean the lady at the thrift

shop helped me find some things. And Carla paid for maybe half of it in exchange for the nitty-gritty details."

He raised his eye brows in admiration and nodded his head approvingly. "Andy Baker you are amazing. You don't mind if I call you that, do you?"

Andy was in her element, searching through things for just the right stuff, gathering it. He didn't expect her serious concentration. "No, but as you are now part of my secret you must help me."

She handed him a cup.

"What's this for?" he asked.

"When was the last time you peed? I just went."

"Wait—you want me to…" He couldn't finish the thought let alone the sentence.

Pointing into the mouth of the cup, she finished for him. "Pee in the cup."

He tilted the cup in his hand, examining the outside label. "Is this for a drug test?"

"Should I test you?" She raised an eyebrow. "I have one."

He held his hands out, puffing out his chest. "I'm clean."

"Urine. I need it. Hopefully you're dehydrated." She rummaged around underneath hanging clothes. "The smellier the better."

"You are one odd girl, Andy Baker."

"It's all in the details."

He smiled slyly. "At least you're not asking for any other types of body fluids."

She glanced over her shoulder and blinked at him innocently. "Oh, like your blood?"

He stepped back. "You are so scary."

"I hope so."

When he returned from the bathroom, she'd found a double-bagged sack. She unwound one of the red twisted ties, allowing the smell to escape.

"Woah, your bag stinks," Hugh said, handing her the cup of yellow pee.

"Vinegar, vodka, soured milk, garlic, cumin—which I find always smells like body odor—stale smoke"—she paused for effect—"and a shot of urine." She tossed the warm plastic cup of yellow liquid after dashing it into the bag, wincing as she tied.

"Sounds like a terrible recipe."

"The recipe for overnight hobo smell. It's hard to fake months of no showering, but this is the best I can do." She mashed the bag together. "Gotta take it to the laundromat, stick it in the dryer to set the smell. There's one next door."

His eyes grew big. "Remind me never to use public laundromats again."

"Yeah, I wouldn't." She hefted the sack, hoping to throw it over her shoulder, but Hugh caught it.

"If you're going to have to wear it, the least I can do is take it to the dryer for you."

"Thanks." She handed him a fistful of change she dug from a box on a vanity. "Quarters. While you're doing laundry, I'll get my hair and makeup done and teeth in."

"Teeth?"

Several sets of dentures sat on her table, one with gaping holes, others with large gaps, or big horsey tombstone teeth or small pointy teeth. "I won't ask for your secrets. Just do your thing."

When Hugh returned, he almost didn't recognize Andy. Tangled hair covered her face. And her face, covered in who knows what, was filthy, leathery instead of smooth. In place of her beautiful teeth, a rack of yellowed broken choppers launched from diseased gums.

"Repulsive," he said.

"Thank you." Even her voice eked its way out of her hideous mouth. "Rancid olive oil sprayed in my hair. Do you have my clothes?"

"Yes." He handed her the bag.

"Ah, the sweet smell of stench."

"Do you want me to leave so you can change?"

"No need." As she opened the bag, she suppressed the gag reflex. "You are an angel to take this to the dryer." He shrugged.

As she lifted the jacket over her head, she gagged. "Well, at least I'll have a little bit of you to go with me. Man, this reeks."

She slipped the skirt over the top of her ratty leggings and filled pockets within the skirt with lock picks and other oddities. When she tucked a canister in her jacket pocket, Hugh raised his eyebrows.

"What are you pocketing?" he asked.

"Hexachloroethane and zinc for smoke screen. Just in case. I've never faced the mob before."

Her fingers trembled as she slid on a jacket, hat, and several sweaters. Padding in the shirt. Gloves with fingers missing. A ratty scarf.

"What do you think?" Andy asked him, smugly satisfied with her appearance.

She was so unprepared to face the mob. He wanted to stop her and tell her he'd take care of it. But some part of him wondered if she could do it.

"You're really going to go through with this?" he

asked.

"I have to."

He leaned closer. "What is on your face?"

"Glue."

"Glue?"

"Yes, just dried school glue with bronzer and charcoal." A briquette laid on the counter.

Amazing. He examined her makeup job. The smell kept him from getting too close. Age spots, freckles, even white over the lips from wind burn or dehydration. He absorbed every detail, her hands, the hair. Only the eyes were Andy's. They were still bright and attractive. And focused on him, laughing, enjoying her success in such an utter transformation. He leaned nearer, holding his nose in blatant mockery. Maybe she could pull it off. He'd be watching close by just in case.

"It's amazing up close. Although I don't know anybody who would stay close." She had transformed into a hideous hag, but he couldn't help admire her for having the guts to do this, the knowledge. But she hesitated.

"I'm still scared," she said, her expression serious. "They killed Brad, and they will have no problem killing me, if they catch me. Before I was always in control. I could out-man any of those guys. They may have done bad things. But they weren't bad people. These guys are bad. They kill and they don't care."

"If you want, I can go instead."

She cocked an eyebrow at him. "You are much too big to be a homeless man. No, I am the one who has to go. I am the only one who can go."

"You can leave it. You can buy all your stuff again."

She paused. "You're right. I could but it's not just the stuff. Brad gave me some information about Tyrone. It's in the bag. I have to get it if we want to continue. And I have to prove to myself I can do this."

Hugh nodded. He understood. He just hoped it worked.

****

Jack waited by the side of the abandoned warehouse. The river gurgled to his left, the sounds of the city murmured to his right. Cold blew through him, and he stomped his boots a bit, waiting. He hadn't eaten much the last few days, and the cold bit his body like a beast.

Maybe after tonight, he could eat like a king, drink imported beer, and get him a girl. Best way to get the last girl out of the mind—a new girl.

How was he going to bargain? He had what they wanted, didn't he? He glanced at the picture. They should be the one to pay him. Like all those spy shows. Those who had the information had the power.

He checked the time. A little past seven. He said seven, didn't he? Maybe he got the dates mixed up or the wrong warehouse. This was the old Hodgekins coal supplier building. Boarded up. Used to be quite booming, loading and stashing coal for years into the brick seven-story building until the trains out-pulled the steamboats.

The sound of crushed gravel alerted Jack. The limo made his heart flutter. He'd only seen them around town and at his high school prom. He'd never hoped to ride in one. The door of the sleek limo opened, and though all was dark inside, he climbed in, feeling the warmth and smelling something foul.

"I'm glad you didn't leave," Tyrone said as Jack crawled into the seat.

Jack situated himself into the leather seats, sizing up the man across from him. He'd never met Tyrone before. His coal-black eyes leaked liquid, as if crying. Jack couldn't for the life of him figure out why he was crying. No. Not crying. Tyrone had no other tells of emotion.

The smell overpowered his empty stomach, and the overwhelming heat made his stomach lurch as the limo returned to the road.

"So, you know something of this Andrew Baker?" Tyrone asked.

Okay, so Jack lied on the phone when he'd called. He only knew what he had. A picture of his girlfriend.

"Yeah, well, you know." Jack couldn't remember the story he'd rehearsed. He flipped the phone in his hand. He hadn't expected Tyrone to be so stern and confident. It made Jack lose all courage, as though the man read his thoughts. Tyrone unfolded a white handkerchief and wiped his watering eyes.

Jack trembled like a shirt on a clothes line.

"So, what do you have for me?" His voice grated Jack's ears, like tires across gravel.

"Well." Jack ran his finger along the leather stitching of his seat.

"Please tell me you did not waste my time."

Jack couldn't speak. Tyrone's voice sent serious tremors under his skin. He was a man who did not waste time.

Jack winced a bit. "There was this girl." He fidgeted in his seat when the man with the weeping eyes, stared more distinctly into his own. "She really was a sweetheart." He smiled like a schoolboy admitting to his first crush. "I don't think it was her. But she was being awfully friendly with a guy the night before the story broke. The beginning of my bad luck."

Jack hadn't a chance to tell anyone about his broken heart, first the girl left him on his doorstep, although he didn't remember how or why. He hadn't had too much beer. Then the story. Then social media lit up like a bonfire. The phone calls. The police interrogation. The lawyers. It was too much. This man before him was the least likely person to listen to his heartbreak. Maybe he was getting revenge because he didn't like the way Mary Lou flirted with the man at Ronney Dell's.

Tyrone wiped his eyes again but remained as stoic as ever, perhaps even a little bored, like Jack was wasting his time. But Jack continued on. He didn't care if he had an attentive audience, it just all tumbled out.

"I called her, but her phone number was disconnected." Tears stung his eyes. "I swung by her place where I always met her before, and they said they'd never seen or heard of her. She disappeared."

"Interesting."

Eager to have a listening ear, Jack began to blather forth about all his troubles.

Tyrone stopped him. "Yes, so this girl. How did you meet her?"

"Who?" Tyrone's expression made Jack focus. "Oh, Mary Lou? It's kind of a funny story. She dropped off her car. A nice one. BMW 7 series." When he thought about it, why was a girl like Mary Lou driving such a nice car?

"At the shop?"

Jack nodded, pleased he was interested. "She flirted with me pretty hard core. Even asked me out." His chest puffed a little, remembering how flirtatious Mary Lou had been when they first met. Boy, she came on hot and heavy, and it pleased him.

"Do you have a picture of Mary Lou?" Tyrone asked.

"Yes, it's not a great one. But you should be able to recognize her."

Seeing Tyrone was interested, Jack grew bolder. "But I want money for this. Lots of it." Jack couldn't remember the exact figure he'd planned.

"Oh?" Tyrone's gaze shifted from the phone to Jack.

"I know how this works. The man with the information gets paid. He gets what he's worked hard for."

Tyrone leaned forward and plucked up Jack's phone. "Oh, don't worry, you'll get what you deserve."

Jack leaned back, satisfied with his bargaining. He'd managed to score big. This guy must have millions. Jack relaxed even when they parked at an abandoned warehouse. This must be where they keep their money. Perhaps he could score himself a woman tonight.

Chapter Six

Andy stood outside his parked car. Hugh spoke behind her. "Wait, you want me to give you a ride in my Porsche?" he asked with an arched eyebrow.

"Of course." Andy had already broken her rule riding with him over here. She hoped he was indeed the police detective he said he was. Besides, he wasn't a mark. He was a partner. Maybe. Andy couldn't shake the unsettled feeling.

"You can't have a bag lady coming out of a Porsche," he said.

"Drop me off a block from the casino."

He pinched his lips together in a frown. "You are not sitting on my leather interior in your costume."

"You're such a baby." Andy furrowed her brow, her face hurt as it puckered under the glue. Facial movements would have to be kept to a minimum. "How am I supposed to get downtown?"

"Bus?"

"It would take four times as long. We are a little pressed for time. I have no idea when the city picks up the trash."

Hugh grabbed some plastic bags from his trunk. "Place these over the seats, and we ride with the windows open."

"It's still chilly and wet outside."

"I am not staying in a car with your stench. No

close proximity, no enclosures."

Andy rolled her eyes. "You are such a wimp. You could not handle doing my job."

Hugh snorted. Andy spread the plastic bags out on the seat, then opened one and slid it over the back, starting with the headrest. "You should've been there when I was a sewer worker, wading through waste water trying to find…"

"Enough, girl. Get in."

Hugh murmured about having to get the seats professionally cleaned and settled into the car. The car ride was silent. Silent because you can't really talk when the windows are open and you're driving down the highway. Andy had to hold on her knit cap to keep it from flying away. At least the wind messed her hair up more. When they exited for downtown, Andy elbowed him. He recoiled, checking if she'd rubbed off on him.

"Just a bit farther," she said.

"If I could, I'd drop you off sooner."

"Enough cracks about the costume."

"This had better be worth it."

"It will be." Two blocks from the casino, Andy directed him to an alleyway where no one would witness a homeless woman descending from a steel-gray Porsche. Andy struggled to get out of the car, carrying several carrier bags and an opaque plastic bag to slip her weekender tote in to. With her many scarves, multiple jackets, she was a coat closet come to life. Maneuvering was a problem.

"Why are these cars so low to the ground?" she asked through the cracked teeth, tumbling toward the door.

"It makes them go faster." The engine *vroomed* as

he raised his eyebrows.

"Enough. Are you going to help me?"

"What would people think if I helped a bag lady out of my car?"

"Never mind." She placed a grimy hand on his window sill with a purposeful stare in his direction and was on her feet. "Meet you back here in say, an hour?"

"Sure." And he zoomed off.

Andy waited until the sound of his engine faded. She wanted so much to trust him, to be able to let go her apprehension.

Andy rummaged through her bags, feeling quite like a bag lady, until she found her cell phone she picked up at home with "Bethany's" SIM. Badges were hard to fake, easier to steal, but she wasn't taking anyone's word. She was calling Fred.

"Oh, Fred," she sighed aloud as she dialed his number, thinking of the red-headed freckled guy with a smile.

Andy actually found it quite respectable he wanted to make it on his own steam, to not use his father's money as a crutch. To Carla it was unforgivable. Being a black sheep who dated bottom-dwellers was one thing; leaving the fold another. Standing in the alley dressed as a bag lady, Andy needed confirmation of one name. But his voicemail answered.

"Is your refrigerator running? You'd better go catch it! Leave a message. Or not. I don't care."

Immediately, she switched into character. "You'll never guess who I ran into," cooed ditzy "Bethany" into the phone after the beep. It was weird being Bethany while reeking of trash. "Detective Donaldson. He says he knows you from the STLPD. He just wanted me to say hello. Give me a holler when you get this message."

She hung up, stashing the phone in her pocket. Why was she so suspicious of Hugh? It was possible the police department had a special forces she knew nothing about. Operatives trained in vice or narcs. Matters they didn't want to get the feds involved with. Andy chewed her lip. Without further information, she had to trust him. She wanted to trust him. She just couldn't trust him completely.

Andy headed for the casino. She judged her success on their reactions. Good, good. She must be convincing. People on the street avoided her gaze and her person. Their reactions caused tears to sting her eyes.

Meeting with Brad, she realized she missed family, close relationships. Even Carla was more of a fangirl.

Slumping slightly, she shuffled in her worn, mismatched shoes, one of which pinched her small toe. The meandering cost her some time, but it had to be real. She had to be completely in character. They might still be searching for her.

Just outside the backdoor of the docked boat casino, she found an array of dumpsters. She paused.

She could leave it all. Let the garbage man throw Brad's codes in a landfill. Wash her hands of the whole deal and just be Andrew Baker. Did she really want to risk her life for this?

A uniform truck idled by the loading dock. A man in a gray suit patrolled the dock with a walkie-talkie on his hip, surveying the area. And there were cameras. Lots of them. One near the back door, focused on the point of entry. One scanning the courtyard and at least one more focused on the alley. It rotated to span the length of the back lot, including the green oozing garbage containers. Her heartbeat quickened realizing this was all recorded.

The trash might have already come. It might already be gone. Then fate made her decision for her.

A little lump in the pocket of her pants pressed against her thigh. Brad's tie-tack.

Her eyes stung with tears. She had to do it. For him. He wanted to be free. He wanted justice to be served. She had to make it happen. This had to be her best performance yet.

It pained her to shuffle slowly across the bottle and litter strewn asphalt when she wanted to run. But shuffle she must.

She had to suppress her gag reflex when the stark odor of the trash reached her nose. It was worse than expected, sweeter. It smelled like alcohol and rotten fruit mixed with week-old diapers. All she had to do was jump in and rummage through the flotsam for a bag with purple tape on it.

Jumping in the dumpster required fifteen minutes just to scale the side of the first looming green beast. She searched for a foothold. The truck tine hole sat waste high. She slid her feet inside the holes. A giant first step. The bulk around her midsection made it difficult to grab the top of the container at first attempt. Falling, her ankle knocked against the metal making a resounding clang. She was glad Hugh wasn't around to witness this. Not her most flattering of moments.

Usually she had the agility of a cat, the grace of a swan. Right now, she resembled a renegade, greenish marshmallow scaling a metallic mountain. Her second attempt proved successful, launching her bag over the top to lock her into place like a grappling hook.

The trash had not come yet. In the first container, she rummaged neck high in plastic bags. The sides of the stained garbage bags had bits of discolored, matted paper towels stuck to them. Dozens of bags filled the container. The bathroom plastic bags would be easy to identify. They were clear with bunches of white paper in them. She searched top to bottom, tossing each inspected bag to the other side of the canister, grateful she had the protection of layers of clothing and gloves. She was sure there was some needle usage going on inside the casino, and she didn't want to accidentally get stuck with something toxic.

After throwing several sticky bags around, her bag was nowhere to be found. Her arms ached, her neck hurt.

Not in the first dumpster. Rubbing her neck, she wasn't discouraged. Four more awaited. She scaled the bags to slip into the neighboring dumpster. A startled cry scared her when she landed.

"What are you trying to do, kill me?" A toothless mouth flapped open in accusation. A tallish man—or perhaps he only seemed tall because he was so lean—dressed in a ratty sweater and with a tangled mess of hair and scraggly beard, holding a chipped glass ashtray. Andy had to pinch back a laugh. She wasn't expecting anyone else to be rummaging around in the dumpsters.

"Oh, sorry," Andy murmured, her quick eye noticed at once this one was filled with black bags from the gaming floor. It was awkward with the two of them; she couldn't be quite as systematic and quite as vigorous. She gave up and headed for the next one.

With a thump, she landed on a not so soft bed of trash. What if her tote was stolen? Throwing bags around, she continued scouring until she spied it. Tucked in a dimmed corner sat the marked bag. The tape hadn't been necessary, although it was there, hanging off. A smear of red through the diaphanous plastic gave it away. She tore at the plastic, grateful to be there before the guy next door found it. What a relief! Peeling her tote out of the bag, she plucked used paper towels from off it. After hugging it, she slipped it inside her carrier bag.

A noise above her sounded familiar. It wasn't helicopters. One time, when she was doing a story on homelessness, the first time she used this costume, she had a run-in with the ghetto birds. Not pleasant.

No, this wasn't a helicopter. Andy blinked in sober recognition. It was a truck.

A garbage truck.

Andy's heart seized. She had to get out and now. There weren't as many bags in this one as in the other two. Anxiously, she piled them to help her scale the wall. Easy to get into, hard to get out of. The bags rolled and refused to stay stacked. The first dumpster landed to the ground with a horrid clunk—emptied. Metal scraped against the asphalt as the truck returned it.

Beep! Beep! The truck backed up. Her dumpster was next.

Then the close sound of the motor and the sound of metal scraping metal was louder than the boom of the heartbeat in her ears. As she climbed the hill of rolling bags, the dumpster rose off the ground. She climbed to the top, just in time to see the whites of the eyes of the driver as she floated above the windshield in her chariot of trash.

The mechanism stopped with a jolt and a whine. Andy breathed in silent relief. The dumpster lowered. Andy fell back again, the ground becoming suddenly steady under her. Maybe he would come and help her out.

"Hey, you," the driver yelled. "Get outta there! I'll call the cops."

Or not. Andy did her best to scale the garbage and leaped an eight-foot jump to black asphalt. But she lost the trash bag around her red weekender tote as she hitched it to her shoulder.

"Crazy lady! You could've gotten killed." The real homeless man was yelling at her now, too.

The scene garnered the attention of security. The man on the loading dock faced her way. Andy, clutching her bag to her chest, glanced up in time to notice him. He recognized the bag. The security man raised the walkie-talkie to his mouth, following after her with his gaze.

Andy's heart lunged, spurring her to a run. As she rounded the first corner, pattering feet followed her. The security detail was after her. Andy's adrenaline zoomed, powering her through the extra bulk of the costume as she ducked right through a darkened alley. With a great lead, she managed to withdraw the smokescreen from her pocket, igniting it as she ran. She tossed it into the debris collecting in a doorway. A small stream of smoke billowed from the canister until it began to fill the compact space between the two brick buildings, making her lungs hurt and obscuring her sight. Hidden from view, Andy dashed to the next street, crossed, and entered another alley.

When she was sure she no longer had a tail, she hugged the bag to her chest. She made it. The codes to the jump drive and the office were in her bag, safe. She sank down and breathed for a few breaths to rest. She rubbed off the glue and make up, pocketed her teeth, combed her hair into a pony. Then, transformation nearly reversed, she stuffed her coat into the trash and ran for the rendezvous point.

****

"Did you find your bag?" Hugh asked when he picked her up.

"Yup." She climbed in, her face grim, slightly out of breath.

"You got it?" He was impressed. She outsmarted the mob. Maybe she would be an asset in this case after all.

Biting her lip, Andy hugged the red bag on her lap. He smelled bathroom tissue. She shrugged and inspected the contents.

He glanced at her again. She should've been happy to have just rescued her bag. "What's wrong?"

"I think I was spotted."

"By security?"

"Yup." Her frown deepened as she faced away from him. Even with her disguise, facial recognition on the security cameras was terribly accurate. Casinos had top of the line stuff. "I always thought this bag was my greatest asset. But no more. It's an obvious tell."

"They'll go back and review the camera footage."

"Yup."

Though focused on the road, he frequently glanced over at his companion, at her sunken eyes. "Can you remove your makeup now?" He wrinkled up his nose. Traces of bronzer and charcoal clung to bits of glue, like a leper. "I'd really like you to be beautiful again."

"I'll have to wash it off," Andy said, glancing at herself though the window to the passenger-side mirror.

"At least you don't smell as bad," he said, checking his rearview mirror. "Want me to drop you off at your place?"

Andy swallowed hard.

Hugh detected her silence. "You're nervous about going back there."

Andy nodded.

"I'm also the only one with food." He glanced over to Andy seated next to him in his car. "You'll just have to shower at my flat."

****

At the loft, Andy showered in his micro bathroom, exited in his bathrobe over the top of her sports bra and a pair of his unused boxers. He glanced up from his omelets.

"You don't need makeup," he said.

"I do, so I won't get caught."

"No, I mean, the makeup you usually wear," he said. His expression was earnest. "I prefer you *au naturel*."

Andy couldn't decipher her feelings. She couldn't be super attractive with a shiny, red nose. Her eyes appeared smaller without mascara, too. But she was flattered by the compliment. She mumbled a thank you and loved feeling his eyes shining on her, taking her in. A glow germinated in her heart. She stepped closer to him in the kitchen, standing in front of the stainless-steel fridge. Nearly touching, his breath warmed her.

"How do you want it?" he asked, peaking his eyebrows, propping his elbow up on the corner of the fridge, and leaning into her. Andy blushed, feeling a physical rush. Her heartbeat quickened. They were close enough to kiss. She caught him staring at her lips. Her brain turned to mush. What was he talking about?

Oh, the omelet.

She should push him away. But she welcomed his lusty glances, returning with her own appreciative smile. It was like she'd been living in a foreign country and finally found someone who spoke her native language, passing some innate understanding between the two of them. If Fred would just call and tell her what an awesome guy Hugh was, the nagging in her gut could relax. As if on cue, her phone buzzed in her bag. Andy, let it go a few times, clinging to the moment with Hugh, then stepped away. He caught her arm, stopping her.

"You don't have to get it," Hugh said.

"It might be important."

She just needed confirmation before she can truly let herself be free. Hoping it was Fred, she fished through the bag for her phone. Carla's mom. Sighing, Andy held it in her hand. She'd procrastinated long enough. She should take it, no matter how much she wanted a hot…Omelet.

The call had already gone to voicemail.

Andy faced Hugh, who was opening cupboards. "Is there someplace private I can go to listen to this?"

He pointed the spatula to the second door.

Andy opened the door and stepped into the darkness, playing the voicemail. Mrs. Vehemia was brief. "Amanda, call me at your earliest convenience."

Andy forgot all about Mrs. Vehemia with the trauma of Brad. Andy hesitated, her finger over the redial button, but she was in a new, unexplored room in Hugh's flat. Curiosity burned within her.

Switching on the flashlight app on her phone, she inspected the room. Wooden hat rack-like structures lined the walls. The ceilings climbed about thirty feet above. It was bigger than she supposed. Bigger than the other two rooms combined. The floor gave under her feet, her light reflected off mirrors on the walls. He's either vain or…

She knew what this was.

Searching the walls, she found the switch behind the door. She flipped it on, her eyes blinking, adjusting to the light.

"This is a martial arts gym." A *serious* martial arts gym. The "hat rack" stands were places to practice forms. Mats for sparring.

Hugh opened the door.

"You're a master," she said with awe and wonder. She had to change her paradigm. Here she was thinking he was some two-bit cop with a little training.

He smiled broadly, arching his scarred eyebrow. "Depends on your definition of a master."

"How many?" she asked, gulping.

His eyebrows peaked. "Years? Seventeen."

And she thought she was going to teach him something. In the light, she discerned more equipment, shurikens, swords, and a ball and mace. "No. Disciplines."

"Depends on how you break it up. Do you count Muay Thai different from Tomoi? Is Taekwondo separate from Tang Soo Do? If you count them all

94

individually, nineteen."

Andy ran a hand over her face to hide her embarrassment from her first conversation with him. How she must've sounded like an idiot.

She faced him, poking his solid shoulder. "And you wanted to learn karate? You lied!"

"I didn't lie."

"You said you didn't know martial arts."

"No, I said I wanted karate lessons. It's true. I do."

"But you implied you don't know any." Andy's face burned.

"I've never taken karate." He shrugged. "Even I can learn something."

Andy's eyes narrowed. "Don't even try to sound humble."

He cocked his blondish head toward the mats, grinning wickedly. "Like to run a bout? I recall you bragging about your superiority."

Andy wanted to die. Her ears burned but she kept her chin high. She was not going down without a fight. It was on! She was a sixth-degree black belt with judo training and a little Taekwondo. "I can totally take you."

His eyes brightened. "Let's take it to the mats."

"Fine."

He removed his shirt with slow and deliberate effort, his challenging gaze never flinching from hers. Muscles rippled down his back as he tugged his shirt over his head and off his arms.

Andy caught her breath. Every inch of his body was perfectly toned, his abs flat, his latissimus dorsi the perfect shape. He was attractive with clothes on, but with clothes off, he was chiseled art.

In the small of his perfectly sculpted back, she caught sight of a tattoo of a black seraph with words written above each of the three paired wings as well as the head and tail.

"Rules?" she asked, stripping down to her fitness bra and shorts, hoping she affected him. His gaze absorbed her, passing up and down her body. She savored the moment.

The muscles in his shoulders rippled as he gave a little shrug, then crossing his arms, warming up his shoulders. "*Shinkyokushin* rules, then?"

Without admitting she didn't even know what he meant, Andy agreed.

"Anything goes," he said, smirking a little.

"Anything goes," she agreed.

She began limbering up, purposefully striking the most seductive poses, clasping her hands behind her back, thrusting out her chest. "How will we determine the winner?"

"Last man standing."

"Or woman."

He barely peaked an eyebrow to express, what? Doubt in her ability? No, confidence in his own. But there was something else. A sly smile. If she hadn't been paying astute attention, she would've missed it. He enjoyed this.

"Before I engage in any sport, I always provide the proper protection." He tossed her boxing gloves.

"So gentlemanly of you."

He nodded in the direction of some pegs on the wall. "Wrap up."

On the pegs were hand wraps. He grabbed a multi-colored, woven band, looping it over his thumb. "Given to me by a monk when I studied Muay Thai at a Buddhist temple in Southeast Asia for several months."

He was only bragging to try to intimidate her. It worked. A little tickle of anticipation sprung inside her.

She grabbed black straps encircling her wrists, threading them carefully around her knuckles. Quick movement caught her out of the corner of her eye. Wrapping exceedingly fast, Hugh eyed her in goading competition. She stepped it up a pace, binding her fists and starting on her right hand, where she had more practice.

Her practiced fingers could've threaded this blindfolded, and she was quick. Maybe it was her smaller hands, her nimble fingers, her ample repetition but whatever it was, she finished weaving the cotton through her fingers just as he'd finished. Hugh still smiled smugly, smacking his fist into his other hand, but there was a nod of admiration.

But she didn't want to get cocky. Boxing gloves on, the only protection needed, they faced each other on the tatami. Bowing to each other, they each formed a stance. She recognized the dragon stance from kung-fu.

"Want me to go easy on you?" he asked, just as she crescent-kicked at his head. He easily avoided it, lithely stepping to the side, but she smiled at his bemused expression. It was momentary, but it was there. He quickly recovered and blocked her right hook. "Woah, where's the respect?"

"No rules," she said, huffing as she blocked his attack then did a sweep of his leg. He grinned wide. Right before she socked him in the face with a right feint followed by a left uppercut. Now it was time to get on to business. Next, she used a judo hold and flip, grabbing him by shoulder but he escaped. He wasn't a novice after all. Music thrilled in her. Far from it. It was nice to have someone outman her.

She couldn't just use standard attacks. She'd have to plan a strategy. Catch him off guard. A man with this much training had almost pre-cognition. With a swift step around him, she attacked with a strike to his back. But he swiveled in time to block it, missing her with a kick, but knocking her off balance.

"Did you use Krav Maga?" she asked when he attacked in an unfair but vaguely familiar form. Krav Maga was the big guns of martial arts, with no formal katas. They trained recruits how to fight with the odds of ten to one, how to use the M-16 as a weapon, even after the bullets were spent. Kill or be killed. Certainly not standard repertoire for an undercover street cop in St. Louis. "Where did you learn that?"

"I trained with the Israel Defense League."

"Are you allowed to train with them?"

"If you know the right people. Which I do."

He circled her seeking an opening. Andy blocked his left hook, grabbing it, turning under his hand to a hold. He countered with a wheelhouse kick, which she blocked, sending them both downward with force.

They tumbled to the ground, him on top of her, pressing down. The moisture of his sweat wet her skin. The movement stopped. Their gaze locked in an intense stare. Both breathing heavily into each other. Then with all the intensity of the last few minutes of fighting, he bent over her and kissed her, hungrily eating her lips, her jaw line, anything he could touch. She reciprocated, pressing upward to meet him.

He tore at his gloves, releasing them. Tugging at

the wraps binding his hands, tearing at them in one long string as they unwound. His hands, now free, immediately released her hair, letting it loose in strands all around her. His thumbs followed the length of her throat, the base of her neck, her bare shoulders. Andy tugged at her gloves to touch his skin, his hair. But being overcome, overwhelmed, she succumbed. Her heart pounded as if they still fought. No more lies. She could just love and be loved. He broke her down. And she liked it.

Then Hugh stopped and released her, rolling to his side. "I can't let it go this far," he said, wiping his hand down his face, freeing the perspiration.

"Oh?" Andy said.

"I'm sorry. I just can't." Sighing, he sat back against a punching bag lying on the floor, allowing her to settle into him. He slid his arm around her, holding her tight, letting his lips brush her jaw line. "Not now."

He drew her in closer. Kissing her again.

When they finally broke for air, Andy's throat ached for more.

"I am sorry you had to suffer so much these last few days," he said, stroking her bangs back to where her hair fell in pools on the mat.

Tears pricked at her eyes. Her gaze met his, so full of concern, deeply searching hers.

"Brad." Her voice broke. "And then Conner."

Hugh waited patiently for her to speak. Calmly, he leaned forward and kissed the tip of her nose. The act of intimacy warmed her heart.

"It was so hard to lose him, even if I hadn't seen him in ages," she said.

"How long had it been?"

Andy's heart bled it all out. Things she'd never been ever allowed herself to give expression to before, let alone confess to anyone bubbled to the surface. "He broke up with me the night of the movie festival in the park."

Hugh nodded, continuing to stroke her hair, letting her talk. Up close, she could count the scars on his face, marking his jaw, marring his rugged five o'clock shadow, not just his eyebrow. Slits of white. What hid behind those eyes? Other pent secrets? Some pain, some suffering, an understanding of her ache and longing?

"I thought he was going to propose." Her heart heaved when she said it, as if for the first time she was admitting this to herself. A burning in her nose was a sure tell the tears would come. "He finally had the right job, making a lot of money and *bam!* It hurt. It hurt so bad I couldn't believe emotional pain could hurt so bad, real physical pain."

Tears leaked from the corners of her eyes, dribbling in her ears. "Brad told me he was planning on proposing. He broke up with me instead."

"Did he give a reason to breakup?" Hugh asked.

"He said we were going in different directions, but there was more. Last night Brad said Conner was afraid."

Hugh's face crumpled with disapproval. "He was a fool." Andy smiled wryly. Hugh's gaze focused on where his thumb and forefinger stroked a strand of hair above her head. Hugh continued, "So, what else did Brad tell you?"

Silence passed. His chest rose underneath her as he breathed, his nose breath blowing fly-a-ways on her neck. "He said he belonged to some secret organization called Imperium. They were doing something bad. Something huge. He wanted me to investigate and expose them."

"What was it?"

Andy shrugged.

"Why was he telling you?"

Andy shook her head. "He wanted to relieve his conscience, I guess."

"You don't think there was some other reason?"

She'd never considered anything else. "Could there be another reason?"

"I don't know, I'm just asking. Why didn't he go to the police? Or why didn't he go to the newspapers himself." His eyes narrowed, focusing on her. "Why you?"

Andy pondered on the simple two-word question. "I guess he trusted me."

"What specifically did he ask you to do?"

Andy gulped, feeling coerced to share this burden. "There's an encrypted jump drive with information he wanted me to recover behind an aquarium by his desk."

Hugh listened intently, but didn't speak.

"I had to get my bag because I had Brad's entry code for his office." She didn't reveal she had an authentication code for the jump drive or say anything about Dr. Armstrong. She wasn't even sure of Hugh's connection yet. She hadn't even had time to search the Internet. Besides, you shouldn't tell all your secrets.

Andy finished. "I've told you everything I know. It's only fair if you tell me everything you know."

He struggled internally.

"Aren't you going to tell me what you know?" she

asked.

"I don't have anything."

"You don't have anything?" Andy elbowed him away.

"All the information we know, I got from you. We need the jump drive. And we need to get into the T-Building."

Andy fumed. She'd been dealt her own medicine, and she didn't like it. He must be who he said he was because if he was part of Imperium, he would've killed her already.

Hugh bit his lip. "We just need a way in."

"Can the police help us?" Andy asked.

He shook his head. "No, they might be able to set us up with communications and back up, but access, no. Requires warrants."

Her phone buzzed in her purse on the other side of the room.

Supposing it was Mrs. Vehemia, Andy sighed. She'd put her off too long. "I'd better answer it."

Reluctantly, Hugh let her up, kissing anywhere there was exposed skin.

Frantically, she raked through her stuff to find the right phone in the midst of flashlights, toothpicks, matches, and ammo clips. With her purse tucked under her arm, she found the phone just as voicemail picked up. She recognized the number. Fred. Her heart leapt.

She flashed Hugh a nervous smile. He waited for her, propped up against a punching bag lying on the floor. "Someone important?"

She hoped he would leave a message. An icon blinked red.

Perfect.

"Nah," she said, her voice wavering. "It already went to voicemail."

He stood, heading to the door. "While you're listening, how 'bout I get cleaned up and make those long-awaited omelets?"

Shaking, she held the phone to her ear, eager for Fred's validation of Detective Donaldson as an upright member of the STLPD despite his scars and his exceedingly scary tattoo. And his IDF experience.

Her throat tightened at Fred's baritone voice.

"Hey, Brittany. I was a little confused by your message. As far as I know there is no Donaldson on the force. Maybe he's with the St. Charles PD or from some small town like Bella Villa or Georgetown. Or the guy's messing with you. Impersonating a cop isn't cool, Brittany. If you need me, call. I'm a little worried about this guy." Andy's phone slipped from her ear.

Andy swallowed, her breath jagged.

There was no Donaldson on the force. Andy's heart thundered. Lied. Again.

And she fell for it, let her heart go, let him in.

Trembling, Andy searched her bag again. Found it. She had retrieved it from her apartment. Her Sig Sauer. She laid it on top of her bag. Just in case.

Chapter Seven

Hugh returned to the gym with the omelets. Andy punched the hanging bag in a corner, metal chain clanking with each strike. Andy powered up for a roundhouse kick, sending the bag swinging, the chain like wind chimes in a violent storm.

"Nice hit," he called from the other side of the gym, his voice echoing across the wooden floors and high brick walls.

Andy didn't turn. When the bag swung back she gave the bag a powerful strike sending it sailing away.

Without facing him she asked, "What's your name?"

Hugh was taken aback. Her voice sounded defensive. Not this again. They've discussed this already.

"Hugh Donaldson."

When the bag swung back, she caught it quickly, steadied it before turning to stare him straight in the eyes, a beautiful, furious storm. "My connections say there are no special forces. No Detective Donaldson."

A wave of guilt swept through him. She had connections. The phone call. Damn. He worried about that.

She fired another question at him. "Who are you?"

Hugh's mind raced. He needed to stall her. "Truth?"

"Yeah, the truth. People want to hear the truth."

He studied her expression. She was ravishing, flushed and sweaty in her sports bra, even when angry. He wished he could wrap her in his arms and tell her everything was all right. But he couldn't. He wasn't sure it was going to be okay. "I have to make a call."

"Whatever." Andy faced away.

Hugh entered the living room, eyeing the door behind him just to be sure Andy couldn't eavesdrop. He picked up his phone and dialed his boss.

"Yes," a cold voice answered.

"Cover blown. She knows local police."

A simple swear passed through the phone. "Plan B."

"Are you sure?"

"Are you questioning my orders?"

"You know I never would. Andy's a smart girl, though." They'd worked through the protocol before he really knew her.

"Plan B." Hugh clicked off the phone, shaking his head.

Sighing, he returned to Andy. "They said I could tell you the truth."

"They?" Andy crossed her arms, her chin forward, her expression expectant. "Okay, what's your name? Let's start there."

"Tyler."

"First or last name?"

"Tyler Hansen." He closed in.

"Okay, 'Tyler,' if that is your name, what are you? CIA? HSA? FBI? Terrorist or spy?"

Tyler winced when she said his name in mock quotations. He was treading water in dangerous seas. As long as he didn't lose her, this could still work.

"Tyler Hansen. FBI." Thankfully, he controlled his bodily reactions. She was staring at his naked chest. He smiled slightly. "I should've known I couldn't outsmart you."

"So, all the garbage about your grandmother on the farm, your training in the Thai monks. It was all a lie."

Hugh, now Tyler shoved away hurt feelings. "Not entirely." He stepped closer. She backed away, keeping the same distance.

"What do you mean?" she asked.

"I never lied to you straight out. I related parts from my childhood and wove them into something you could understand. Yes, I lived with my grandparents on a farm. It wasn't in Kansas. I was in California. I ran away from my grandparents, and I wandered the streets in south-central L.A. where I learned how to street fight. I roamed Crenshaw Boulevard to the Santa Monica freeway, sleeping on the dirty Metro stations, dodging cops. I told the essence of truth, Andy. I couldn't tell you where I'm from, or why I'm here, but I could tell you about me, without blowing my cover."

"You never told me a lie?" she asked.

"Never. Not a complete falsehood."

"The best lies are always mixed with a bit of truth."

"They weren't lies. Not to me, Andy."

"How can I ever trust you?"

"You can't, I guess. But deep down in your heart, you know you can trust me." Tyler silently prayed she'd believe him. "I'm sorry I used you. My assignment was to get information," he said at last.

"You used me to get information?" she asked. "All the flirting, the kissing." She shook her head.

"Oh, and you never do the same thing?"

Andy flushed. He hit the nail on the head. For some reason, he wanted to drive it in.

"You lecture me about kissing to get information? What a little hypocrite. It's okay for you to use your body but if someone else does it, it's wrong? I've got news for you, girlie, turnabout is fair play."

Andy's eyes blazed with fiery light. Her voice transformed into a growl. "I work alone. I don't need back up. I don't need you. Brad"—the name choked in her throat as she said it—"asked me to help him. I am doing it for him. He didn't ask you and certainly not the FBI. If it is indeed the FBI you work for."

"Andy." Maybe he'd said too much.

"Lies, lies, lies. All men lie."

He didn't want to hurt her. Then again, maybe he did. Maybe he wanted to take her down a notch. "And so do women." A shiver shot through her. But he couldn't stop. "You should let us handle it. Leave, go someplace safe. Just give me the entry code so we retrieve the jump drive. If not, you might get hurt."

Her eyes flattened to little slits. "Are you threatening me?"

"What? No."

Tyler stepped forward. Andy slipped her hand into her bag, whipping out a Sig Sauer. Tyler scoffed.

Andy aimed the gun straight at him, picked up her bag and slung it over her shoulder. "Goodbye Hugh or Tyler. Nice knowing you."

He couldn't let her leave. Not now. And quite frankly using the gun pissed him off.

He stepped closer. "What if I don't let you go. You're going to shoot me? And then what?"

Andy held her steely gaze. Beautiful rage.

"Can't you understand?" he asked, growing impatient. "It's naïve to think you can waltz in there with a few disguises and a bag full of tricks and be invincible." As soon as he said it, he instantly regretted it. He might have gone too far. Whatever cool Andy had been harboring just blew away. Anger, shock, a full flush covered her face. She headed again toward the door. His arm flew out to stop her. Her gun raised again. They were close now. Close enough he could breathe her scent.

"You want to spar again?" she asked, anger flashing in her eyes, her face inches from his. He had to admit, it turned him on. A feisty, fiery girl—just how he liked them. "This time, it won't end the same as the last."

He didn't want to have to do this, but it might be the only way she'd listen to him. He seized her gun hand, twisted it around, wresting away the gun, dropping it to the mat. He kicked it away and pinned her in a joint lock against the door with his body.

She kicked, she elbow-jabbed, but he was relentless. Sheer muscle and weight gave him the advantage, all combined against her. "I'm not saying you can't do it, but I'm saying leave it to the professionals or join with us. Don't try to do this alone. Brad would want you to be safe." He had to invoke his name. He had to evoke whatever emotional sway Brad had over her. Her gaze scorched him with burning intensity, her chest heaving into his with such passion. Conner was a fool to have let such a creature go.

"Let go of me." She scrambled around powerless against his strength.

"Are you still resisting?" He bent his head to whisper in her ear, his face lost its kindness. "If you work alone, then I will use you as bait. You will go bumbling around in the dark and I will capitalize on your bumbling and stumbling. I will get what I want. With or without you."

Andy finally relaxed her body. Tyler hated taking the spirit out of her. But it was the only way to keep her from getting killed.

"Okay, I concede," she said. He smiled inwardly, the rush of victory, conquering a well-matched foe.

"I knew I could persuade you."

Her smile warmed him, he released his body from hers. In a flash, her leg flew up and hit him square in the nads, opened the door behind her, and slipped out by saying, "Brad asked me to do this. So I will do this."

Through the purple haze of pain, he called out, "Where will you go Andy Baker?" The front door opened. "They're hunting you," he called.

The door slammed shut again.

He smiled despite the throbbing.

He liked her.

****

Too afraid to go home, Andy rented a cheap hotel room to rest and to plan her next move. Tyler ruined her trust. Andy fumed, staring at the dingy framed art above the bed. She was working alone, now. Nothing would change her mind.

The hotel room carpet was so crusty, she was afraid of even sitting on the floor. She'd seen several cockroaches already in her room. Lying on top of the striped bed cloth, she searched online for Dr. Armstrong. She scrolled through the list of links.

Taught chemistry in Boston, but was no longer listed on a faculty list. Stumped. Since she couldn't make any more progress for the time being, Andy decided to call Mrs. Vehemia using the sticky phone in the motel.

Andy had rarely talked to Mrs. Vehemia, an intimidating lady with an impressive plastic surgeon on retainer. The greatest compliment she received was when someone asked if she was Carla's sister. The woman worried for a passion yet none of it lined her face.

Her personal assistant answered the phone then put Andy on hold. Finally, Mrs. Vehemia's silken voice oozed from the phone.

"I'm sorry about keeping you waiting, Andy. I had to find a private place to discuss this matter."

Keeping secrets from the help was vital for privacy. For one of her stories, she was a ladies' maid for St. Louis's old-money Mrs. Groggen and uncovered heaps of information about their profiteering. Mrs. Vehemia knew who to hire and how to keep them loyal. Her desire to keep this completely confidential worried Andy.

"I'd love to help you in any way." Andy sat up on the faded bedspread, hesitating to touch the carpet and chairs coated with stickiness.

This would be a challenging task but she owed the family since they paid her so generously for Carla's private lessons.

"What a relief, Amanda. And of course, I'd gladly pay your expenses and for your time."

"Thank you," Andy said, graciously. You don't turn away money for your time and expenses.

"You know my son, Scott."

Was this a trick question? He was one of the most eligible bachelors in the Harvard MBA program right now. Not only was he hot, but he had a brilliant mind for strategy, a knack for new technology, and was expected to inherit his father's manufacturing business when he graduated. Hardworking and driven, even without his money and connections, he would've earned his way into any Ivy League school.

They had met a few times. Although Andy had a rule never to crush on a best friend's brother, it was tempting to make an exception for Scott. But Scott was so out of her league, and they rarely crossed paths. Still, Carla sometimes told her little things about him. What interesting new ventures he wanted to invest in. How he asked about Andy all the time. Andy recalled their last conversation.

"You haven't told him I'm Andrew Baker have you? Because you promised to keep my secret."

"Of course not! But it would up your wow factor in his eyes. He asks about you all the time. I think he's into you."

"Uh, Carla, guys like your brother don't go for girls like me. I know you like guys in my class, but your brother dates debutants." In "America's 50 Most Eligible Bachelors" by *Gossip* magazine, he ranked third.

"He thinks you're smart."

"How would he know?"

"Because I told him."

Andy had shaken her head then, but now on the phone, the prospect of seeing him intrigued her.

Andy's heart beat a little quicker when she spoke to Mrs. Vehemia. "Yes, I believe I've had the pleasure of meeting him a few times, with Carla."

"Oh." Her voice was strained. "He was supposed to graduate and direct the business affairs of Vehemia Manufacturing. If only he hadn't gotten himself into this predicament."

Andy stopped. She wasn't a lawyer. "What kind of predicament?"

Mrs. Vehemia's voice cracked as she began. "He's so diligent in his studies. I know it's stressful. But I guess the stress got to him."

"Stress?" Andy asked.

"Well, one night before a particularly difficult exam, he just went crazy."

"What do you mean crazy?"

She said something in the phone Andy strained to hear.

"Uh, I didn't catch that."

Mrs. Vehemia whispered again, but Andy didn't want to pain her by asking her again. In agony, she racked her brain to figure the cadence of the sentence. She didn't make sense. It sounded like…

"He ate his own flesh?" Andy half whispered, half questioned, disbelieving her own ears. But the barrage of tears from Mrs. Vehemia confirmed it. Andy's stomach lurched. Self-cannibalism. No wonder she didn't want it splashed all over *People* magazine.

"There's more. He terrorized some students, taking bites out of them."

Andy recoiled in horror. Speechless, she just listened.

"You must promise never to tell anyone. We've already paid a lot of money to the victims not to tell the news about this incident."

"I promise."

"I didn't know where to turn. Carla said she trusts you."

"Thank you for your trust." Andy paused, unsure what to do next.

"Normally, I'd ask for references, but in this case, if Carla feels you are qualified, I'm satisfied. The less the professionals know, the better."

Andy wasn't offended Mrs. Vehemia didn't consider her professional. "What would you like me to do?"

"Find out what is wrong." Andy's heart sank. There were a few lines you should never cross when you do investigations. Investigating family secrets of your best friend had to be in at least the top three. Especially when they were rich and powerful.

If she could find the jump drive and expose Imperium, maybe she could invest the time, but she was still working on plans on how to get in the T-Building. "What kind of information were you hoping to find out?"

"I don't know. I just know something's not right. We don't have crazy in our family. A little anxiety, maybe. But don't we all? Maybe someone drugged him and…" It was too horrible for her to get out. "Are they competitive? Was he feeling too much pressure? It certainly didn't come from us. We never forced him. I just don't understand."

"Was it possible your son was doing drugs?"

"No. He is studious and hardworking."

Andy's heart ached. Any mother would be grateful to have her son exonerated. "I would love to help you. As soon as I can get to Boston, I will."

Mrs. Vehemia's voice cheered a bit. "I've set up a flight voucher for you to fly at any time. You just have to call for the first available flight. And I've sent some funds to your account for expenses. Just be as discreet as you can."

Andy already had too much on her plate right now. But she accepted. Relief flooded Mrs. Vehemia's voice "Thank you, Amanda."

After hanging up, Andy scrolled through searches for any news on Scott. Image after image of one of the most sought-after men flipped on her screen. One snapshot with a movie star, this next one with a model and a pimped-out car. This one he wore a blazer with a careless smile, his hair tossed and gelled. It would be a lie to say she didn't enjoy her homework.

****

Three days later, Andy readied to stake out the T-Building for possible entry points. She was tired of being in this dingy hotel infested with cockroaches. Try as she might, she could not kill them.

She flipped to the news as she dressed in black. Depressing really. Nothing ever positive in the news. But it was chatter. It wrapped her in safety somehow, hearing the voices. As Andy swooped up her hair, a name caught her attention on the news.

"…Jack Reynolds from Shaft Auto was found in his apartment from an apparent suicide."

Andy jerked her head to the TV. The screen showed the outside of Jack's apartment with yellow police tape wrapped around the New Orleans-style lattice. A roiling in her heart made her ill. The newscaster continued. "Mr. Reynolds's property manager found him this evening strung to the shower rod. The manager checked on the tenant as he was behind on his rent, finally opening the door to find his body.

"The only clue was a hastily scrawled suicide note saying, 'For Andrew Baker.' Police can only speculate he was upset about the article Mr. Baker ran in the local press last week accusing him of fraud and tax evasion. Shaft Auto planned to file for bankruptcy after the many threats of court action from customers. In other news…"

Andy shuddered. She couldn't speak. Andy's heart churned. She almost didn't register her cell phone ringing. In a daze, she answered it without checking the caller ID.

"Have you seen the news?" It was her editor, Mr. Hershal. She nodded. He continued without her verbal response. "I think the bad publicity isn't going to help the newspaper."

With the phone still to her ear, Andy changed the channel to another news station also reporting the story.

"And have you seen your Twitter feed? It's blown up." Andy grabbed her phone, scrolling through the blaming #bakerkills. People called for her to be fired. Her heart lunged, her face flamed red. Mr. Hershal continued. "I think we'd better lay off the Andrew Baker column for a while. Not permanently. We'll write our regrets, of course." Andy barely grasped what he said.

"I killed him," Andy said at last, her eyes hot with fresh tears. Her nose stung. "I ratted out his business, and it killed him."

"I wouldn't listen to all the social media babble."

Andy plopped down on the bed, her chest tight

with anguish.

"Consider it a leave of absence," her editor said. Andy snapped to attention.

"You mean, no more Andrew Baker."

"Not for a while. A few months maybe. Until this whole thing has died down."

Andy nodded into the phone, her voice swollen with tears.

"I'll call you when this has blown over," he said at last.

An awkward goodbye passed on both ends.

Andy stared at the TV, the images of police and hazard tape all over his apartment complex. Interviewing a neighbor.

A knock sounded at the door. She ignored it.

Tyler strode into the room.

"You pick locks, too?" she asked.

"I told them you were my girlfriend. They gave me a key."

"What are you doing here?" Andy stood ready for a fight.

"This." He nodded toward the news story, then flicked off the TV with the remote.

Andy's heart burned. "Go away. I don't need your help. I'm a professional."

Tyler didn't say anything. Andy didn't feel very professional. Her mark killed himself for what she exposed. It was haunting. Not just the news, but in her mind an image of Jack, swinging, hanging from the shower rail. Acid boiled up in her stomach. She couldn't pass the image out of her mind.

"Someone left you a calling card," Tyler said, so matter-of-fact, so unemotional.

"Huh?" Andy wished he'd go away and let her feel unprofessional and sick all by herself.

"He didn't commit suicide."

Andy may have been in shock but she understood. "How can you be sure?"

"Someone wants Andrew Baker."

Goosebumps pricked Andy's skin.

"When you investigated Jack's tax evasion and fraud, was he acting on his own?"

"I don't really know. There was money coming from an unknown corporate source only marked as 'Bearing Inc.' on the books." Andy didn't have time to track down all the weird things on Jack's books. She wanted the evidence of fraud, found the tax evasion which was enough.

"Money has to come from somewhere. These little stores are usually a front for bigger operations. What have you stumbled onto, Miss Andy Baker?"

Andy bit her lip. Even with all her precautions, she might have bitten off more than she could chew.

"And speaking of money, Ms. Baker. Where are you going to get yours? Your job has dried up for the time being, and I happen to know the dojo gig doesn't pay much. Where are you going to get resources now?"

He folded his arms across his chest, thrusting out his chin, his eyes gleaming. He won. He knew too much.

"How did you know this?" Probably bugged her phone. Andy hated him for needing him. Hated him for being so attractive and likable.

"You noticed a few cockroaches around?"

"I complained to the manager about them."

"They're bugs."

"Of course they're bugs." Then it dawned on her. "Bugs, right. What do you want from me?"

Tyler gave her a sideways glance.

She grunted. "You want the entry code."

"Yup."

"Then I want a place to stay. Full disclosure. And a new wardrobe. And some operating cash. And no more spying."

He smiled. "Welcome to our team."

****

Tyler dropped her off at a little condo they rented for her two blocks north of his place. "Here's the deal," she said, hand on the car door. "About the entry code."

He proffered his hand. "I'll take it now, if you want."

Andy shook her head. "No deal. I will give it only after we are safely inside the T-Building."

"And who is going to get us inside?"

"I am."

Tyler raised an eyebrow.

Before opening the door, she said, "Find out what you can about Imperium from your side, and we'll meet tomorrow."

Tyler smiled as Andy opened the door. She knew how to maintain control.

"Sure you don't want to leave it to us?" he asked. "The professionals."

"I'm a professional."

He smirked. She slammed the door. Tyler returned to his loft.

Their next meeting at the refurbished condo was more pleasant. When he entered, Andy was studying a map of the T-Building spread like a tablecloth over a granite-covered island. Carla sipped a latte on the cappuccino-colored barstools.

"What did you find out from the FBI about Imperium?" she asked.

Tyler consulted his phone. "Locals. Powerful men who run things, own things. They manipulate laws, businesses. The list of men is highly secretive. We don't know who the leaders are or what their goals are."

"You're thinking the leader is Tyrone?" she asked.

He nodded. "He's already got one strike against him."

"Our game plan is to retrieve the jump drive," Andy said.

Tyler eyed Carla, who sat in the corner, texting someone on the phone. "Why is she here?"

"She's on my team."

Tyler scowled. "Okay, how do we get in to Tyrone's building?"

Andy threw up her hands. "I don't know. It's impossible. I did a quick rundown of the building. Nobody can get past his security. These people pride themselves on being able to hire people who know how to keep enemies at bay. What about just breaking in? You have tech?"

Tyler tucked his hands under his armpits, which made his biceps bulge. "Even with government resources, we couldn't get through. His security system outranks anything the government has, so no breaking in. His detail, the men working for him, are ruthless gunmen. I was thinking you could go as a cleaning lady."

Andy shook her head. "It takes a year to get staffed there. Tyrone requires thorough background checks and usually they need to be related to someone to be hired, or even considered." This was how Brad got hired. His dad had worked at the office. "Hiring requirements are more strict than a government job," Andy said, smirking.

"Har, har. How about window washers? Those have to be contracted out."

"They do. In fact, I checked and they have a bi-monthly contract..." Tyler hoped for an in. "With his brother's company."

He sat back. "So, no getting hired on there."

She shook his head. "Unless you're related, no. I know hundreds of ways of getting in buildings. I've done FedEx, a client, new hire, carpet cleaners, IT consultants, EMT, electrical engineers, building inspectors, union bosses." He shook his head at each mention, but he was still impressed. Although she was still an amateur.

"Florist?" he asked.

"They drop the flowers off at the front desk. You're not going to get much farther."

He leaned back on the patterned sofa, showing off his extremely toned chest through his shirt. "Man, Andy. I don't know how we're going to get in his building."

"What building?" Carla asked, glued to her phone.

Tyler glanced at her. "Really, you've been here this whole time and you don't know what we're talking about?"

Carla blinked innocently over her iced latte.

"You're talking about the T-Building, right?" Carla asked, glancing up briefly through her eyelash implants.

He gave an impatient nod.

"And you want to get in?" Carla continued. "You want to go when no one is paying attention to security but everyone is there."

"Are you the Sphinx talking in riddles?" he asked with slight impatience.

Carla ignored him. "Easy. You only need an invitation."

"Okay, when she starts making sense, will someone please translate?" Tyler held his head high, using a patronizing tone.

She smiled slyly, relishing the moment. "You need to go to Hazel Tyrone's engagement party."

Andy's eyebrows shot to her hairline. "Engagement party?"

"Everybody who's anybody's going to be there."

"How do you know?" Tyler asked.

Carla held out her purse. Unclasping the latch, she dug around in her Vuitton bag, producing a lush embossed paper with a gold seal. She flipped it back and forth in front of Tyler's face. "Because I have an invitation."

Tyler snatched it from her. In one week, Hazel Tyrone was throwing a shin-dig. Carla's invite included a plus one. *At the Grand Ballroom in the T-Building.*

"Hazel knows how to plan and execute in epic proportions," Carla said. She waved at it like it was trash. "I have a prior engagement and have no interest in going to a stuffy party or breaking and entering. So you may use it."

"It's the perfect way in. Want to be my plus one?" Tyler asked.

Andy was already calculating the cost of a disguise so complete. "There's waxing and heels and panty hose and an appointment at a salon and a very expensive, custom-made dress."

"Whatever you need, my boss will pay for it."

Andy's expression relaxed but was still grumpy.

"And the best part, I'll be your date." He gauged her reaction. Andy's gaze slid sideways to him. He grinned and bowed. "I'll be the perfect gentleman."

"You'd better."

"Or not, if you prefer."

She side kicked him. Not hard. Just hard enough to let him know she was serious.

"Walk me home?" Tyler asked, nudging her with his elbow when they finished hashing out the details.

"You afraid to go home alone?" Andy teased.

"I think you're the scariest thing in this 'hood." He smiled back. "I want to talk."

Andy enjoyed the crisp night air.

"How come you didn't tell me Carla has so many connections?" he asked.

"I didn't know myself."

"Right. You've known her for how long and you didn't know her dad is connected to Tyrone? You don't think she could be connected with Imperium do you?"

Andy scowled. "I've known Carla and her parents for seven years. They are not killers."

Tyler conceded and changed the subject. "I'm excited to go with you all dressed up. It's nice to have a beautiful girl on the arm."

"Oh, yeah? Isn't that every guy's dream?"

"Not me." He paused. "I want *two* at my side, like a pair of cufflinks."

Andy raised her leg for a front kick.

"Kidding," he yelled, blocking the kick. "I'm

actually anticipating seeing you disguised as a debutant. I have a feeling it will be much more pleasant than, uh, the bag lady."

Andy sniffed in disbelief.

"Don't trust me?"

Andy faced him. "If you want my trust, Tyler, you're going to have to earn it."

His insides tightened. She was right. After all the lies, how could he possibly be worthy of her trust? He didn't want to have to lie to her. Hopefully this was the last alias he had to give her. After retrieving the jump drive, the mission would be over, and they'd never be together again.

"I'll prove it to you," he said. Turning toward her, his breath glowed in the lamplight when he exhaled, his flight jacket open, his hands stuffed in the pockets. She stopped, too, facing him. He stared at her, deep into her brown eyes. If only he didn't admire her so much. "Until next week, then. Text me if you have any questions."

Chapter Eight

Tyrone's men discovered other pictures of Jack's woman on his phone. Her hair bleached, her shorts too short to be decent.

Tyrone stared at the pictures projected on a wall of his penthouse, savoring his little glass cup of *avocat, crevettes, et pamplemousse*, a greenish frothy mixture of avocado and grapefruit with shrimp. His little weeping eyes stared hard at the images, disgusted.

"Could Andrew Baker be a woman?" he muttered to himself.

Tyrone shook his head. Unfortunately, Jack's shop could no longer play into his schemes. He had other shops to be sure. But it bugged him someone sniffed it out.

The woman faced the camera in the next shot.

"Pause it," he said to Bobby, who controlled the remote.

His dish forgotten, his gaze focused on her face. He'd seen it somewhere before.

"Get the images the casino sent over," he said, remembering some incident early last week.

Bobby clicked open a file.

Jack's pictures were haphazard and fuzzier.

"Do a side-by-side." He motioned to Bobby.

On one side, Jack's girlfriend. The other, a young woman dressed to meet an underling in Imperium.

Tyrone couldn't even remember his name. Some punk kid whose dad worked here, then squealed on them. Other images flipped through. Then he recognized it.

A bag. In both images.

"The bag."

Tyrone stared harder, concentrating on the face. Fear gripped his stomach, his appetite gone—the worst thing he could think of. He cursed.

"Where's the footage of the loading dock security camera Rodgers sent up. The bag lady running away a few days ago."

"Think he's still got the clip."

"I want to review it."

Bobby called Rogers who emailed him a clip. Bobby threw it up on the big screen in front of them. A bag lady had a red bag clutched under her arm.

"Bobby, I think we've found Andrew Baker." Tyrone wiped his mouth, then his puss from his face, sitting forward meeting Bobby's gaze. "Run a facial recog on her. I want her. Priority one. Alive. I want to have a little talk with her."

Bobby nodded, his cheeks dimpling into creases. "Right boss."

****

Tyrone's penthouse elevator opened and Hazel, her blond hair curled, red lipstick shining on her lips, marched in. Her long, trailing chocolate-sequined gown—Dior, maybe she said—brushed the gilded ebony columns flanking either side of the elevators. Where his executive suite was designed for business and efficiency, his personal apartments were all about aesthetics. French antiques from the Empire Age lined the walls, their straight and strong lines pleasing to their owner. A massive walnut secretary adorned with gilt Roman laurels, and heads of eagles of the Neoclassical age filled the hallway beyond the columns where Hazel Tyrone, radiating all the beauty wealth and influence could give her, stood with hands on her hips.

"You're not going to hang out in here the whole party, Daddy, are you?" she asked.

"I don't eat catered meals." He bent over his counter tops, arranging slices of bread. He couldn't stand the disappointment on her face.

"Catered? It's Chef Teamon. My own. Personal. Chef." She pounded her heart with each word.

Over three hundred people were invited. Champagne and chocolate was the theme. He'd spent a small fortune importing Delafée gold-plated chocolates. A waste of money in his opinion. But she'd begged for it with those large blue eyes like her mother, and he consented.

And this was just the engagement party. Wait until the wedding bills arrived.

With a large knife, Tyrone cut off the crusts of his bread. "You know I don't eat anything I do not make myself."

"Oh, Daddy!" Hazel checked her lipstick in the reflection of her pocket compact. "You're so paranoid."

"When I am done dining, I shall come down and greet your friends."

She wrapped her arms around him and kissed his neck. Then rubbed her lipstick mark away. "They're your friends too, Daddy."

He never once stopped preparing his meal. "I don't have friends. I have people I work with and people who work for me." He moved the crusts to the side.

Hazel just sort of laughed. "What are you making?"

"*Croque-mie*," he said, focused on his counter tops where he rolled thinly sliced meat with Gruyere.

"I think I shall be happy with Robert," she sighed, leaning against the counter picking up a piece of crust.

"If not, I'll bump him off." Tyrone honestly didn't know why she loved the man. Sure, he was loyal, a crack shot, and the best shake-down man he had, but those things weren't the foundation for a strong marriage. And not what he imagined for his Hazel, who was a miniature of her mother, God rest her soul. Sheer beauty and grace. Of course, Hazel had more spunk and passion. But what did he know about young girls and their hearts. Marianne had loved him, though Tyrone never understood why. If Hazel wanted Bobby, she could have Bobby.

"You're so funny, Daddy." She laughed, her brilliant red lips parting in a smile.

He grunted. "Your guests should be arriving. You should go and greet them."

"Oh, I have people doing it. I want to spend time with Bobby." With her hand on her chin, leaning over the counter, Hazel observed her father for a few minutes, absorbed in his cooking. Then, she stood. "I'll expect you later tonight."

****

The night of the party, Andy stepped from the door of her condo. Tyler leaned against his steel-gray Porsche, arms folded across his chest, his hulking biceps tugging at the rigid sleeve of his tuxedo. His blondish hair shone in the streetlight. He hadn't seen her yet. Some part of her heart wished they could start over. Or they hadn't met. Or had met under different circumstances.

How could she trust him? She wasn't even sure if he was FBI. At this point it didn't matter. She was just using him to help her get into the T-Building. Once she had the jump drive, *sayonara* to him. Andy wanted to eradicate all of Imperium, not just Tyrone.

When she teetered to the stairs, a little flutter of excitement made her glad she hadn't eaten. It would've all come up. This was her first big heist.

At the top of the stair, she paused, observing him. What did he think about when he didn't have anything he must think about. Lies to create, spin, weave, make believable? He didn't look sinister. His expression was thoughtful, almost playful. This was a whole new Tyler. He wasn't the same man she first met.

Andy laughed to herself. It was actually true. Tyler was FBI not Hugh, the Detective. If he was even FBI.

She wrapped a length of baby pink organza over her bare shoulders and continued down the stairs, careful not to trip on the overflowing dress. This was her best disguise ever. An alluring, sultry, and powerful Andy.

"Where were you all week?" she asked, doubted he'd been making the same harried preparations she'd been making over her dress and hair. Every detail had to be planned. "You never answered my text on Thursday."

He glanced at her, speechless, his eyes full of surprise and innocence. Maybe he was playing some role, and he really was trustworthy.

"Thursday?" he asked, recovering from his shock. His gaze shot upward, as if recalling details. "I was somewhere over the Yangtze River." Trustworthy, until he said some outrageous lie.

Andy let out an exasperated sigh. "Why do I even bother asking you questions? You just lie."

Frowning, she faced away from him. With a gentle touch to her shoulder, he stilled her, turning her toward him. Raising her chin, he made her face him, leaning close enough she could smell his manly scent of shaving cream or aftershave, and whispered to her. "Not everything I say to you is a lie, Andy."

"All right," she challenged, straight into his eyes. "Tell me something I know is absolutely true."

"You are indescribably beautiful."

Andy flushed. A gooey warmth flooded her body but she forced it away. She glanced at her reflection in his Porsche. A complete transformation from her norm. Her hair coiled around her head, slicked with plenty of pomade, bobby pins, and a cloud of hairspray the stylist promised would create a bulletproof protection around her head. Her custom-made dress hugging her toned body overflowed with pale pink ruffles, and sported beaded sequins down the boned bodice. Whoever Tyler's boss was, he was generous. She'd never paid so much for a costume piece. And her makeup, contoured and air-brushed, her eyebrows aristocratic and shaped all made her feel like an electric outlet that couldn't keep the electricity in.

She gave him a shove. "Har, har."

He caught her arm with considerable tenderness. "I'm serious, you are absolutely breathtaking."

Unable to believe him, she readied an uppercut meant for his jaw, but he blocked it squarely, catching her fist in his hand. He held her hand in the warmth of his palm, then drew her nearer.

"No fighting tonight," he said, close enough to warm her cheek with his breath, his gaze staring into hers with intensity, maybe a little bit of hurt. She caught her breath, stunned by his seriousness, the deep penetrating steadiness of his gaze. "Truce. For one night," he said, gently taking her arm, wrapping it around his firm bicep, pressing it there longer than necessary. "You can at least pretend to like me."

"You are a great liar," she said, stifling her breath, her whole body tingling from his touch. "It's a compliment."

"Thank you. It's my job."

"Are we going in this?" she asked nodding toward the Porsche.

"Not that piece of junk." Her heart sank just a tad, to at least to her belly button. "I ordered something unassuming." Andy frowned. She would've liked to have taken the Porsche when she wasn't dressed as a bag lady.

She cocked her head, scanning the street lined with Volkswagens and Toyotas. He didn't approach any car, but stood, staring at her.

From down the lightly damp street, clopping echoed off the high rise, glass and concrete buildings. She caught her breath.

"No," she sighed, her eyes widening, her lips parting in a smile. Then the white horse-drawn open-air carriage and driver pulled into view.

Andy couldn't believe this was happening. When it stopped in front of them, Tyler opened the carriage door. A smile crept on his usually stoic lips, his eyes dancing in her delight. He held out his hand to her, his smile broadening. "Shall we?"

The most romantic night of her life, her legs waxed smooth, nails, hair, makeup all for a bride rather than a party, and it was all to obtain information. It was surreal.

"You know how to soften a girl up. You're smooth."

Tyler held the door open, his face fallen. Once they entered the carriage, he reviewed their plans, face taut and stressed, serious again. She nodded as he spoke, but wasn't paying attention. She concentrated on his face, so near, wishing to see his carefree smile again. Sadly, his face hardened.

Before they descended from the carriage at the impressive, impregnable, and historical T-Building nestled at the bank of the Mississippi, Tyler handed her something smaller and flatter than a pencil eraser.

"What's this?" she asked, taking it.

"Comms unit. You put it here." He slipped the little bug in her ear. "In case we get separated."

"Can *they* hear us?"

"Of course. They are just ears tonight. No interfering. Only for emergency extraction, if things get bad. But they mostly want to stay out of it. Covert. You understand."

Andy frowned as she placed the bug in her ear. She didn't like this, this spying, not on other people, but on her. She was a solo gal, and this intrusion made her nervous.

The carriage stopped at the foot of an impressive limestone staircase, leading up to a well-lit building. She'd studied the plans for the spacious historical building. The first floor held reception and a ballroom.

The other twenty or so floors had office spaces. The very top, Tyrone's penthouse suite. But they only had to get to the seventeenth floor.

"Do you have the coded entry key?" Tyler asked, descending the carriage first.

"Yes. I hid it someplace you will never find it."

"Where would that be?"

"My bra."

Tyler frowned and held out a hand for Andy to descend to the carpet leading to the doors. Andy glanced up, counting the stories to Conner's floor.

Seventeen. Darkness.

A shiver of excitement tickled her stomach as she exited the carriage. Behind them, a line of BMWs and Audis dropped off guests. Andy absorbed it all.

"Is that a Bentley?" she asked.

Andy swallowed, holding the outlandish invite in her hand. The paper and the wax seal weighed heavy in her hand. A lady in a red sheath gown and white elbow length gloves checked her invitation. A sprig of diamonds nestled in her pompadour-style hair-do. She smiled through her matching red lipstick.

People stared at them. Andy touched her hair, trembling a bit.

"Can they tell we're not supposed to be here?" Andy whispered to Tyler. "Everyone's staring at us."

"They are staring because you are so beautiful."

Surely, he was joking, but his expression was true. Not a lie or a tease. Pure earnestness.

She patted her bobby pins, still in place. "Yeah, and I'm really intimidating in this outfit," she said tugging at the detachable frothy pink chiffon skirt of her dress. "I look more like sherbet punch than a fighting machine. And it weighs a ton. Sure, I'm irresistible."

"You are." He passed her sly sideways glance, a smile in the corner of his mouth. "Admit it. You want me to lust after you."

"I do not."

"Do too. I can feel it."

"Shhhhh."

A couple passed them on the plush carpet talking about their stock portfolios. Andy's bodice slipped, her underarms were too exposed. And too sweaty. She yanked uncomfortably at her bodice, tugging it up again. Or maybe being with Tyler made her uncomfortable. "I am out of my league here."

"I thought you could adapt to any situation."

"Usually I can. Usually, I'm dealing with the dross of society, petty people trying to get away with petty crime. Not used to rubbing elbows with mega-millionaires."

"Billionaires."

"I was using alliteration. Allow me some poetic license, will you?" They stopped as the people ahead of them stopped.

"Just wanted you to be accurate. How about brilliant billionaires? Or brainy billionaires."

Another woman in an emerald green dress, her red hair held in place with emeralds stopped them. "Step this way for the photo shoot."

They glanced at each other. They didn't realize they were standing in the photo line.

"The photos will be available on the couple's website," the woman with emeralds said.

Tyler kind of shook his head. "No pictures tonight."

The red-headed lady was taken aback. "But why not?"

He jabbed a thumb in Andy's direction. "My wife doesn't know I'm with her, and I don't want any photographic evidence," he said, scooting Andy out of line and into the main flow of the dance floor while the lady stared after them, opened mouthed.

"It often shocks me how easily you lie," Andy accused.

He faced her, his expression earnest. "Does it shock you how easily you lie?"

Andy's heart burned with shame.

In the slow music, he wrapped his arm around her and led her to the dance floor. His head bent toward her, his face near hers. "I don't care if you hate me lying, but don't be a hypocrite. Especially in the line of work we do."

"*We* do?" Andy didn't think he'd think the FBI and her investigative journalist gig should be mentioned in the same category.

"Lying protects us while we seek justice," he said.

"Yes, but I don't lie to people who trust me."

His eyes narrowed, his face too close to hers. "You don't lie to say, your stepmom?" He spun her around.

Andy burned again with guilt. "She couldn't handle the truth."

"And you've decided for her?"

"Those lies protect her."

"I knew you'd understand."

Before Andy refuted him, he moved again, taking a sharp spin.

"Avoid the photographers," he said.

"There are tons of them." Men in tuxes and women

in simpler dresses with cameras hanging around their necks were everywhere—taking pictures of the couples dancing, at the table sampling the hor d'oeuvres with caviar and fois gras.

Other photographers scanned the room, photographing the fresh flowers, lights, liquor, and couples.

Andy had no idea which couple was Hazel and her fiancé, and she didn't care.

Andy glanced around. "We need a distraction to get upstairs."

"Let me go scope out the elevators," Tyler said, leaving her in the middle of the dance floor. "I'll be on comms."

Andy scanned the room, wondering if it was inappropriate to snag some beautifully crafted chocolate while on the job when a voice stopped her.

"Hello, Amanda." She swiveled. Carla's dad stood with an older man and woman. His larger than life smile fit his larger than life body. "It's been a while. You know the Senator and his wife, don't you?"

"Please repeat their names, so we know who you are talking to," Tyler said in the earpiece. Andy exercised all her self-control to not roll her eyes or heave a sigh. Working alone was much easier.

"Hello, Mr. Vehemia," she said with some exaggeration as she shook his hand. She swiveled to greet the couple. Handsome, both of them, in their early sixties, maybe fifties. The Senator's quick movements, the energy of his eyes, and the agility of mind belied his age. Andy kept up in politics, local as well as national. One could never be too informed.

"Of course, Senator Granger," she said, her gaze

taking him in. "I'm always interested in national politics. I'm a huge fan of your Elimination of Greenhouse Gas bill in Congress requiring the new emissions converters. If you gain the presidential nominee, you can count on my vote this fall."

His eyes shone all the more. "Thank you, and thank you." He smiled at Mr. Vehemia. "These are the young votes we can count on." Then he turned to the woman with him. "This is my wife, Annette."

Senator Granger let go of his wife's hand as she raised it for the introduction. Her lipstick was a little too bright for her faded colored hair. Her eyes were glassy and her gaze distant. Then the Senator grasped Andy's hand in his. Andy's knees wobbled a bit. She was shaking hands with one of the most powerful men in the whole country.

The Senator was gorgeous, as you might expect from an actor-turned-politician. And an extremely skilled politician with oratory skills, charisma, and an ability to put everyone at ease. His completely gray hair betrayed his shockingly white, youthful smile. A genuine smile. He held her hand longer than necessary, and Andy realized his smile was flirtatious. Right here in front of his wife. Andy flushed.

The Senator's gaze, exploring and alert, never left Andy's as he asked Carla's dad for an introduction. "And who is this rapturously beautiful woman I have the pleasure of meeting?"

Andy couldn't meet his wife's eye out of guilt. No, not guilt. She wasn't flirting. But some weird feeling, some mixture of abhorrence and embarrassment made her ashamed to face the older woman. She wanted to retract her hand from his too-soft hand and run away.

But the Senator held tight, his grip firm.

Mr. Vehemia made the introductions. "Yes, Amanda Miller is as thick as thieves with my daughter Carla. You remember Carla?" The Senator nodded, dropping Andy's hand. Then Mr. Vehemia asked Andy, "Is she here tonight?"

Andy was amused. Mr. Vehemia could tell you the price of stock for his company, the rate of coal production, or the amount of wind energy produced by windmills, but he didn't know his daughter's schedule. Perhaps every father was like that. "I believe she had another engagement tonight, sir."

His phone must've buzzed because he removed it from his pocket and began texting. Carla's dad shrugged his shoulders. "Girls," he said, his gaze not leaving his device. "I can't keep up with them."

Andy faced to the politician. "Senator Granger, I had the pleasure of performing in your eponymous theatre. I was in the troupe at the University."

"Oh? A fellow thespian, are you?"

"Yes."

"You're coming to my presidential fundraiser party in the theatre in two weeks?"

Her earpiece talked over the question. "Okay, fangirl. Don't waste time talking to the Senator."

"Yes, of course," she said to the Senator. "You'll excuse me. I think my date is searching for me."

She waved a little goodbye to Mrs. Granger who was more interested in her drink than social graces, and hurried away. Awkward.

Conversation sparkled around the room from the best dressed in the city, arrayed in white elbow gloves. Yards of sequins, satins, gauze. And jewelry and tiaras.

Bling worth more than several fortunes. The heavy smell of designer perfumes activated by heat, and cloying fresh flowers. She rushed to the other side of the room hoping to avoid any more awkward conversations.

Too late.

She bumped into a man wearing a powder-blue, early-sixties tux with a frothy, pink shirt front. At least his date dressed for this century. They made eye contact. Andy couldn't avoid the conversation now. She switched modes, changing her body language to an insecure girl at a party.

"Bethany," Fred exclaimed. "I almost didn't recognize you."

"Fred. Imagine me, like, bumping into you. Like, literally," she said with her exaggerated ditzy "Bethany" voice.

Fred stepped back to fully examine Andy. "Wow! You look, you look"—he gave her a melodramatic up-down, one influenced by too much bubbly—"you look amazing."

"Thanks. OMG. Like, what are you doing here?" Andy asked, glancing all around searching for Tyler, hoping he wouldn't catch this interaction.

Tyler whispered into her ear. "Now who are you talking to?" She wished the earpiece would go away.

"Can I get you a drink, Bethany?" Fred asked. Andy caught the eye of his date who hadn't been introduced yet. His date's smile faded to a pasty frown as Fred effervesced.

"You're so sweet. I'm all good. But, like, thanks," Andy said.

"Bethany? Who is Bethany?" Tyler hissed in her

ear. Andy exhaled, wishing to silence the questions. She just babbled on to Fred.

"So, imagine us talking two times in one week," Fred mused.

"I don't remember talking to you this week." Andy didn't have to try hard to be ditzy this time.

Tyler spoke in her earpiece again. "Names, Andy, we need names."

Andy breathed deeply. There was no way she was divulging her contacts.

Fred continued. "Well, I guess it's been longer than a week now."

Andy's reaction was true. Her confusion was not an act.

Fred faced to his date. "Daryn, will you get me a drink?" Daryn frowned, giving Andy a poisoned stare before slipping away. Once she was gone, Fred moved closer, whispering. "You know," he said. "The phone call."

Andy's eyes widened. She caught her breath. The phone call. Andy's face burned. "Uh," she said.

"The jackass who claimed to be on the police special forces. Did you ever figure out who he was?"

Tyler cackled in her ear again, desperate and forceful. "What is he talking about, Andy?"

Andy slid her comms unit out of her ear, smothering it between her thumb and forefinger. "Yeah, totally cleared it up. He's, like, with the FBI." Saying it aloud, she wasn't so confident about her reply. "With, like, a totally different name."

"Interesting." Fred absorbed this, thoughtfulness contracting his features. His date returned with a drink.

"The music's got a great beat," Daryn said,

handing him the drink, moving her shoulders, forcing herself against him. "We should try it."

Fred nodded. He shrugged to Andy with a reluctant half-grin, saying goodbye over his shoulder as Daryn drew him away. "I'd be careful with a guy who can't even tell you his name. I'd want some proof."

Andy's stomach clenched. Fred had a point. She didn't have any proof. Just the word from an admitted liar.

She slipped her comms unit into her drink and gave it to a waiter to discard. Her stomach clenched and roiled.

****

Tyler slid up behind Andy. "Where have you been?"

"My comms unit. I think it fell out," she managed to say from a tight-lipped smile.

Tyler didn't challenge her on it, though he knew it was a lie. He bowed a bit, speaking to his mike. "Andy's ears are gone." Brushing his tuxedo, he returned to Andy. "At least I have mine. We'll just have to make sure we don't get separated. You can't leave my side the rest of the night. Here's the low-down. There's security at every exit. At the elevators and at every door."

Andy stiffened. "What's our next move?"

"Dance." He held out his gloved hand.

"Excuse me?" Andy leaned forward to catch what he said.

The music filled the air, couples moved toward the dance floor in droves, gracefully turning in circles to the music.

Tyler persisted. "Will you dance with me?"

"You don't think this is very serious."

"I'm improvising. We have to dance or it will be obvious we don't know anyone here."

Andy stood rigid even as he slid his hands around her. She kept her distance from Tyler, but allowed him to guide her in a circle around the floor.

"Relax," Tyler said. "While I was gone, I put in place a diversion to evade security. It will be an easy in-and-out job. We go upstairs, find the aquarium, pluck up our jump drive, and come back to rejoin the party. We won't need communications unless something goes wrong. And," he quickly added before Andy could contradict him, "nothing will go wrong. Enjoy the music, the dancing."

Andy's shoulders relaxed a little. He moved closer, mentally blocking everything else out. He only had eyes for the girl in shimmering pink in front of him.

Tyler leaned closer, tilting his head. "You are dancing with"—he scanned the room of gray-haired and simpering men in way overdone tuxes—"what appears to be the hottest guy in the room."

"With the smallest paycheck."

"But the greatest kick-ass skills."

Andy snorted. "Are you always on?"

"What do you mean?" he asked.

"Are you always, you know, playing some role, telling some lie, trying to get information out of a mark? How can I ever trust you?"

Tyler's hurt only passed briefly on his face as he searched her hard expression. He'd been taught to control his emotions. But in this case, he wanted her to see it. To make him appear more vulnerable. Sometimes he wondered if he was always acting. Some part of him hoped not. He didn't want to lose his humanity. Sometimes he didn't know if he was acting with her.

"And how can I trust you? You know using deception in journalism isn't always considered ethical."

Andy's eyebrows gathered. "You think I like lying? I only use it as a last resort, for particularly nasty cases where it would be impossible to obtain the truth otherwise. Most of the time it's just sheer hard work and elbow grease like every other journalist."

"I just think you could use those skills in a better way."

In the midst of the press of people, she stepped back from his embrace in the middle of the dance floor. "I need some air."

"Andy what I meant—" But she was gone.

Hiking up her skirt, she shouldered her way out of the well-heeled, well-jeweled dancing tangle around them. She slipped out an open French door near a glittering pink fountain, foaming with drink. The doors opened to a terrace, ensconced with greenery and bushes, overlooking a garden and farther away, a boat dock to the Mississippi. Once outside, the fresh air and moon glow softened her anger, but the muffled music soothed her nerves. Who was he to talk to her that way? Her throat was dry, she wished she'd grabbed a drink on her way out the door.

The wind picked up, blowing her hair, raising goosebumps on her skin. The weather had turned chilly. Andy moved to an unoccupied stone bench next to a couple deep in conversation and stared out across the black, swiftly moving Mississippi River.

Andy wondered if Tyler was even real. FBI. Police.

It didn't matter. She only wanted one thing to be real. But he told her he lies. And he picked at her. But their emotional connection meant something to her, even if it didn't mean anything to him. Something happened to her, something burned him into her heart, and she couldn't let it go. Ironically, when she finally found someone, someone she could love with all of her heart, someone who instinctively understood her, he ended up being a compulsive liar and dangerous.

A tear slipped down her check. Ah, a measure of weakness. She couldn't cry when her dad didn't return. She didn't cry when Conner broke her heart. She didn't even cry when Brad was brutally beaten to death. She wasn't about to cry over a stupid guy. She wiped it away with her gloved fingertip. She loved him, and she wished she hated him.

"There you are," said a voice behind her.

She swiveled. Tyler was back-lit by the large French doors, his broad shoulders and his unmistakable build filled the doorway. Andy quickly hid her tears, stuffed them down deep. "We should stay together," he said.

Andy couldn't tell if he was annoyed. There was an edge in his voice. He stalked toward her. "Never leave your partner on an assignment without comms. I didn't know where you were going."

"I told you I needed air."

"What is up with you anyway?"

Andy gulped, but she hoped it wasn't obvious. "What do you mean?"

"You can be honest. I removed my unit. I know the comms have been bothering you all night." He held out the little, silver device in his palm, then stuffed it in his pocket.

Andy averted her gaze from him to the glittering reflection across the river.

She couldn't tell him how she ached for him, how dancing in his arms was torture far worse than any needles or hacksaws could do. She craved intimacy with him, yet couldn't trust him. He used her. If she could force those negative experiences to crowd out her growing admiration and respect for him, then she could remain in control.

"I know what you need," he said, stepping nearer.

Suspicious, Andy readied herself for an attack. Even in her dress, she could still give a roundhouse kick to the head. "You do? What?"

Instead of answering, he slid his arms around her waist, drawing her close, crushing her bodice into his chest. At first, she struggled, fighting it physically and in her heart. But he calmed her with a fingertip on her chin. He tilted it upward, placing his warm lips on hers. Andy softened in the security of his strong arms.

Andy's heart raced, a warmth spreading through her. She fought desire as he tenderly parted her lips with his, slipped his hands onto her skin on her back, and secured her against him. Andy couldn't fight him any longer. He wasn't a mark with poor hygiene, bad manners and a prison record. This was a man. A real man.

She encircled his neck stroking his velvety hair, inhaling his intoxicating breath, surrendering to his enticing smell, the strength of his embrace.

Then the fire alarm sounded.

Chapter Nine

Tyler broke first from the embrace, lips swollen, breathing heavy, questioning the sound coming from the building. It was just too coincidental.

"Is this part of your plan?" Andy asked.

Tyler shifted, glancing back to her. "No, but we're going to take advantage of it." *And hopefully arrive first.*

Grabbing her hand, they slalomed through thick skirted guests and panicked musicians scurrying toward the exit.

Tyler tugged on Andy's hand. "Stay at the back of the crowd."

Without drawing too much attention, he scanned the security detail, waiting for their break. He needed a distraction.

Then he recognized an opening. Security stepped away to convince an inebriated elderly lady to leave behind her mink.

"Now's our chance," Tyler said.

Hand in hand, they sprinted away from security and the crowd down the hall to the elevator lobby.

He punched the button. Nothing lit up. No little bells dinged. He swore. "The elevators automatically stop when the fire alarm goes off."

"I've got a fireman's key." Andy hiked up her skirt.

"No time."

"Stairs?" Andy asked.

"Stairs." Tyler led the way and opened the door. The sirens continued to scream as they mounted the first flight of stairs. "Your dress is slowing us down," Tyler said, his voice echoing off the cement walls. "Does it come off?"

"It is detachable. But we need this stuff. You'll thank me later."

"Stuff? Is that why it's so floofy?"

"Floofy? Do you get to make up your own English?"

"Pshaw."

With her arms full of skirt, Andy bounded past him. "Stop talking," she said over her shoulder to him. "You're slowing us down."

He chuckled as he climbed the stairs two at a time to keep up with her.

When they arrived at the seventeenth floor, she was scarce out of breath.

"Through there," he said consulting the map which Andy had taken from her purse. They threaded through the halls to the coded door.

"Do you trust me with the entry code now?" he asked.

Andy's eyebrow arched. She faced away from him and dug into her bodice. Tyler rolled his eyes. Andy punched in the entry code.

Peeking in the windowed door, he noticed the office divided into four sections. Across from them, windows framed the night skyline of the city. Andy opened the door in almost a hallowed silence, like visiting a tomb of a loved-one. The only sound was the soothing gurgle of the aquarium.

"There," Andy said. The tank glowed in the darkened room.

Tyler grabbed her before she could enter. "Someone's here," Tyler whispered. A man in a white catering jacket crouched in the shadows, searching behind the aquarium.

"Who are you?" Andy asked racing in although Tyler restrained her.

The man jumped up, pocketed something and darted out a side doorway.

"I think he's got it," Andy said.

"Stay here," Tyler called over his shoulder as he followed him out the door.

Andy ran across the industrial carpet to the aquarium, the low hum of the oxygenator the only sound in the room.

"Please let it still be here," she whispered.

She slid her fingers between the wall and glass. Andy willed her fingers to clasp around the jump drive. She scraped both the window and the glass. Nothing.

Andy's heart plummeted. It was like hearing and feeling Brad die all over again. Frustration boiled in her heart, clinched her jaw, and inflated her lungs. Feeling powerless, she let her fist fly out and hit the wall. A framed picture of an ink blot, red as blood, rattled under her rage. She couldn't fail Brad. This was the last thing he'd asked of Andy.

Andy placed her hands on the cool glass. It hummed gently under her touch. Colored fish swam by, flashing a tail, darting in and out.

Some part of her wanted to shake the stand, knock over the fish, to let them flounder as their gills fill with oxygen, to be shaken up, spilled out and gasping. Like her.

She sank to the floor, burying her head in her hands. Then she spotted something.

A small corner of a piece of paper.

"What's this?"

Her finger pinched it to the carpet and pulled it free. A sticky note.

She read the sticky, memorizing it, and tucked it in her bodice.

Flashlights beamed around her. She ducked behind the tank.

"Who's there?" someone called behind her.

Security detail.

Without comms, Tyler warned her not to leave, but she couldn't stay either. As silently as she could in her ruffled dress, she hurried through the doorway after Tyler.

"There!" Another security agent called behind her.

Andy's heart lunged. Caught. She raced through another room filled with desks and computers to another doorway at the other end. She had no idea where Tyler had gone and no way to connect with him. There was no way she could take two armed security herself.

She ran into another room, but the locked door at the end stopped her. Frantically, she searched for another exit through another hallway, her hair slipping from the millions of bobby pins, blocking her sight. She tucked back some strands spying another doorway to her left. Footsteps sounded closer.

In a second, she darted through the doorway and realized it was the stairwell again. Once through the doorway, someone grabbed her from behind, hand over her mouth, pinning one hand behind her. He was strong, and he got the drop on her. She was only disoriented a split second until reflexes kicked in.

She chucked her elbow with all her anger and might into the assailant's gut. An "oof" escaped his mouth, but it didn't loosen the grip on her hand. She bit a finger over her mouth and stomped on his instep. Grabbing her attacker's hand, she twisted herself around and faced…Tyler.

"It's me, Andy," he said. "I have something to tell you."

"No time. We gotta run. Security."

Andy hit the stairs in a run, spiraling downstairs. Tyler followed her, their foot falls echoing on the walls. Their pursuers climbing after them. Andy just had to focus on her feet going downstairs, one misstep could be dangerous at the speeds they flew.

Her calves burned. Sweat pooled under her armpits, her hair lay completely limp and hanging on her bare shoulders from the humidity in the non-ventilated stuffy stairwell.

Chilled air greeted them at the bottom. She and Tyler both hit a door at the same time opening it to another blast of cool but foul-smelling air. A few florescent light bulbs cast shadows on old tables, tablecloths, broken chairs, chandeliers, and office equipment.

"The basement?" Tyler asked hitting a shelf. "Where are we supposed to go from here? We're trapped down here." He knocked on the cement wall. "On the other side of this passes the largest river in North America."

Andy scanned the room and breathed, calming her

breath, thinking of her options amid the shelves of storage. "Is there another exit?"

"Why couldn't you have gone up? Haven't you noticed in the movies, they always go up?"

"Up?" Andy breathed, wrinkling her brow, still breathing hard. "In a dress? I would've tripped over the skirt a thousand times."

"But if we were up, there would've been more avenues for escape."

"Do you have a B.A.S.E. wingsuit under your tux?"

"No."

"Repelling equipment disguised at a bow-tie?"

"We probably could've used your skirt as a parachute."

Before she replied with a terse har, har, footfalls echoed in the stairwell. Without a word Andy disappeared between the rows and rows of shelves. If they couldn't run, they could hide.

Gun shots rang out.

****

Tyler ducked behind a row of shelves.

More shots. Andy dove beside him, her skirt cushioning her fall.

Tyler whispered, "I've been able to follow your every movement just by listening to your flounces. As far as stealth goes, you get an F for the day."

Andy gave him a disgruntled glare.

"Are you going to take your skirt off?" he asked.

"Are you propositioning me?"

He resisted the chance to banter. Any other time, her question would have turned him on. Okay, if he was being honest with himself, it did turn him on, but he couldn't think about Andy undressing right now. Not with those goons hot on their heels. And he didn't want Andy to know how great her frilly pink dress would look, lying on the floor next to—he had to stop himself.

Focus.

"No, you're going to get us killed. It just sounds like the rustling of a tornado in here, plus," he added, smoothing the skirt away from him with annoyance as it foamed up around his suit lapel. He couldn't think about how it accentuated her feminine curves. Girls didn't usually distract him. Andy was the one girl who could get him killed. "It's getting in my way."

"I can't. I have too much stuff stashed in here." She grabbed the hem of her dress, lifting up to reveal quite a bit of leg, Tyler noticed, and rows upon rows of pockets sewn into her petticoat. With a flick of her wrist she fished out a flashlight on a lanyard, clicked the button and flashed the small LED beam, slipping it around her neck. There were other things he caught glimpses of, a pocket knife, duck tape, floss, rubber gloves, and throwing stars.

"Nice, what is this?" he asked. A red string dangled from somewhere in the back.

"Don't pull the cord. It's a flotation device. Self-inflatable."

"Really?"

"Hey, you've got to be prepared. I couldn't very well waltz in here with my huge bag. This was a clutch-only event."

"An ice pick? I thought I was being poked."

"Funny, I thought that was you."

Tyler smiled.

"Okay, let's find a way out of here," he said.

Andy paced the perimeter of the basement. Black and orange mold bloomed around the lower edges where the river licked the bottom of the building. It smelled like rotting forest, making her nostrils sore, her lungs ache. The damp mustiness made her claustrophobic. On the other side of the foot-thick concrete wall churned the Mississippi River dangerously fast.

Tyler tore off his jacket, thrusting it to the ground. "We're like trapped mice down here."

"I'm not giving up. There has to be a way out, a dumbwaiter or something."

Tyler kept his hands to the walls.

Andy turned up her nose. "This orange, slick, oozing mold reminds me of somebody's Sunday morning sick attack."

Tyler ignored her. "Often in these old buildings there is something useful." He ran his hand along the wall as he paced.

"What are you hoping to find?" she asked. But Tyler ignored her as he was stalked away from her.

He ignored everything but the banging at the door, causing his heartbeat to rise to his throat.

"Tyler," she hissed. "Where are you?" She drew closer, her flashlight beam finding him. "They've found us. We've got to hurry."

He returned into the light. "Okay, you go to the left, I'll go this way. We'll meet at the front."

"Tyler."

He raced along the wall in darkness, his hand along the concrete, feeling rather than seeing. The faster he ran, the faster they could get out of here. Then a shelf overturned making a terrific noise, and Andy screamed.

He tore toward the sound. He found Andy, unconscious, lying on the floor, in a puddle of dress, a gallon of paint can nearby. He lifted her gently, in case she had hurt something. Her face was so sweet when she was relaxed.

His gaze flit to her lips, defined with lipstick. They parted slightly when he tilted her head upright. There was something about her skin, smooth and a little glistening, her cheeks flushed red. All around her hairline were beads of sweat, the crown of her head matted with blood. He held her head in his lap, a bright stain spreading across his shirt. Her eyes blinked open.

"Hey, are you all right?" he asked. Andy just stared at the paint can, then at a shelf leaning toward the wall. Tyler checked her for a concussion.

"My skirt." She winced with pain. "It knocked a feeble shelf."

"I knew it would be the death of you."

She smiled.

Tyler breathed a sigh of relief. "Can you stand?"

"I think so."

Tyler lifted her to her feet, Andy winced more and grabbed his chest, falling into him. He held her close, even if it meant blood stains on his tux. A crash sounded nearby. They froze.

Footsteps flooded the aisle. Tyler's hope failed. There was no way he could escape with a wounded girl, or attack all these men and keep Andy safe. The two of them together, at their best, could possibly take them all, but Andy was like an abandoned baby zebra on the grasslands.

Tyler just had to think. He needed a plan, a strategy. Smelling her scent so close, he couldn't concentrate. Tyler inspected the walls. And there he spied it. A little door painted over with thousands of layers of paint, but it was what he wanted, at least he hoped it was.

"Andy, you're brilliant." He might have missed it circling the perimeter so fast. But Andy hurt her head right underneath it. "The coal chute."

He stood to examine it, but it was no use. They were upon them.

Tyler immediately jumped into action. His foot caught one man across his cheekbone, smacking his head against the shelf containing more paint. Another man lunged and leaped onto Tyler's back while a third man approached to throw a punch. Tyler swung the man on his back, walloping the other, knocking them both down to the ground. More men spilled down the corridor of shelves. Tyler glanced behind him. Men in suits. He surveyed in front of him. More men in suits. He breathed a huge sigh. This wasn't going to be easy. He shot a glance at Andy fading as pale as her bodice. They had to get out of here.

A man tackled Tyler against a shelf, spilling a flashlight, batteries, and cases of light bulbs in boxes. He wrestled the man to the ground by grabbing his shoulders and then kneed him in the chest. With the wind knocked out of him, he should be out of commission for a while. Tyler stood and blocked another uppercut from another guy. Holding on to his opponent's wrist he pulled it upward, then around until it snapped in a joint lock, then Tyler flung him on to another oncoming man.

He stood, pleased. His actions ebbed the tide of flowing men.

Andy's eyes fluttered. "Just leave me, Tyler. Run."

"I can't leave you," he said.

"Now's your chance."

"No."

"Tyler—"

Blood from his lip, mixed with saliva, sprayed as he faced her. "I won't leave you."

More footsteps.

Tyler had been in tougher situations, Djibouti, Jakarta, Senegal, a Somalian pirate brig, less maneuverability, more men, but tonight he was worried about time. Andy was bleeding out. He readied himself to attack again, but the group of men only gathered at the end of the corridor of shelves, the foremost man retrieved a gun from under his jacket.

"Enough," he said, leveling the gun right at Tyler's heaving chest.

Tyler was a duck in a gallery, and he knew it. The man had a straight shot at ten feet, bodies blocking a way for Tyler to even reach them. Breathing hard, blood dribbling from his lip, Tyler held up his hands to surrender.

"Take them," the man said. "The boss wants them alive."

Scattered men on the floor began to rise, shaken, with firm grudges fixed in their eyes against Tyler. Two of them apprehended Tyler, none so gently, one on each arm, holding him fast.

Two others yanked Andy to her feet. Pain shot across Andy's face, and he wanted to hit the guys again.

"Let's go," the man said. "And no funny business."

The small entourage marched around the lines of shelves to the basement stairs. Following them, the man with the gun stayed close.

At the elevators, the gunman and a man in a brown tux chatted. "Are they working, Bobby? Cuz I'm not hiking up no thirty flights of stairs."

"Yes, take them up," Bobby replied, clicking the button. "He's expecting them. I'll be up after I take care of a few things."

If Tyler ran, they would just shoot him and haul his corpse back. And Andy couldn't follow him out. No, if they broke out, they broke out together. Never leave a man. Or a woman.

A familiar face flashed in his mind. A friend. Bleeding, his receding hairline flapping open with a gash. Christiaan had offered his hand, but it wasn't enough.

BING!

Tyler's eyes flew open at the sound of the elevator, his heart pounding. The two men forced him inside the elevator car, Andy beside them.

The button for the PH lit up. Tyler's stomach lurched when the car began to ascend. Upward. To Tyrone.

Tyrone.

They would not be welcomed warmly.

Andy leaned against the wall as the elevators opened, eying the man who kept his gun firmly to Tyler's head. The men forced her out of the elevator and into the lush apartment.

With the abundance of antiques, Andy would've enjoyed seeing the apartment under any other circumstances. It was a pity she was there as a quasi-prisoner/medical patient.

She followed behind Tyler who strode confidently

across the marble floors, straight to a dining room table where Tyrone sat.

"So you're here," he said, concentrating on his food.

His face reflected in the polished inlaid wood, over which glowed two chandeliers. To his right was a professional kitchen, gray granite, white cabinets, and subtly hidden stainless-steel fridge.

Behind him a wall of glass revealed the speckled lights of the city.

Without glancing up, he gently patted his lips with a napkin and drank red wine from a goblet. "You know it's extremely rude to interrupt a man's meal." When his beady eyes met Andy's, his eyebrows raised as he grimaced. "This is a pleasant surprise," he said. Andy faced Tyler hoping for some clue. He had none to offer. Tyrone continued. "It's not every day the person you are searching for marches to your doorstep. Welcome. Andrew Baker, is it not?"

Andy's heart lunged. Her head throbbed as her heartbeat quickened.

Tyrone's eyes narrowed. "I owe you a little something, don't I?"

Andy didn't know what he was talking about.

Tyrone's eyes widened, his fingers placed on his fork and knife. "Did you know in historical times in ancient Korea, cooking for the king was a sacred privilege?"

Andy didn't understand what he was talking about. Either she wasn't all there or Tyrone wasn't.

"Food controls destiny. How many people do you think had their fate changed through the food they eat?" He leaned forward. "How many kings were poisoned to gain control?" His eyes narrowed. "I could kill you right now."

Tyler remained confident, cool, despite the gun at his back. "You can't kill us. We have powerful friends who know we're here. You kill us; they'll track it down to you."

"Yeah," Andy blurted out. "Don't mess with him, he's FBI. You don't want to tangle with the US government."

Tyler flinched.

"I have a great interest in the US government." Tyrone gave Tyler a more thorough inspection, regarded him as he would a suit he was interested in purchasing. His eyes pinched together scrutinizing him anew, white puss weeping from the corners. He returned to his meal. "No, this man has deceived you. He is not FBI."

Andy's heart stuttered.

Tyler remained confident. "He's just trying to introduce doubt, Andy. Don't listen to him."

"Don't listen to me?" he shrugged. "I know every FBI agent assigned to this area. I pay for them to be, shall we say, myopic, on certain occasions. This man is not local FBI."

Andy's head throbbed, her mind hurt. Her heart ached. She was confused, and she didn't like it.

"What do you want with us?" Tyler demanded.

"You come in here, threaten my security, set off the fire alarm during my daughter's engagement party, and my men find you sneaking around my building. I should ask you, what do you want?"

They didn't set off the alarm. Or Tyler lied.

Who was the man running out of the room?

Something didn't add up.

Tyrone rose, strode to his kitchen and extracted knives from their case with the sound of metal against metal. "I don't want to have to hurt you."

"Why not use a gun?" Tyler asked.

Tyrone laughed. "Guns? Guns are for the weak. It's much too easy. And mostly painless." Tyrone pitched forward. A knife flew through the air. Tyler blocked it, slicing his hand. Tyler, bent, attempted to grab the knife, but another one whizzed through the air, landing next to his foot.

"You get the idea. If you twitch, I hurt you. But don't worry, I won't kill you this way. Too messy to clean up. I prefer," he paused, "other methods. Now tell me, why are you here?"

Though his aim was accurate, his knives sharp, he had only a limited supply of them.

In a flash, Tyler removed both knives and ducked for cover behind a huge black pillar as Andy kicked her captives with a mule-kick followed by a quick side-kick, rolling to safety behind a second black pillar. No plan, just survival.

Tyrone, surprised, hesitated, unsure where to throw his knives—at his enemy in the big dress with blood overtaking her or the unstoppable man. His mark was on the man. He threw a knife at Tyler. Bright red soaked through Tyler's shirt, blood spilling on wool carpet.

They needed to get to the elevator. A knife glanced off the wood. Andy prayed he wasn't coming closer. When she ducked around the corner, she saw the elevator. The elevator dinged announcing its arrival. She dug into her skirt for her fireman's key.

Just as the doors open, a man in a brown tux exited.

"Bobby, get them!" Tyrone yelled.

Before she could react, Tyler kicked Bobby, grabbed his doubled body and smashed his face into his knee, shoving him out as he sidled in. Another knife whizzed, nearly hitting Andy as she ducked into the doors.

Bobby struggled to his knees, stopping the doors from closing, grabbing Andy's leg. Tyler, with a weight and strength advantage, lifted Bobby up as a body shield just as a knife sliced through the air. A sickening thud broke the air. Bobby's eyes bugged out and blood blossomed on his brown tuxedo. Bobby stumbled to the ground, a knife caught in his back just as the doors closed.

Tyrone's man stabbed by Tyrone himself.

****

"Uh-oh," Tyler said, once they started descending. He sat back contemplating what just happened.

Tyler caught his breath while holding his side, blood covering his hand. They were safe. For now.

"The fireman's key will allow us to go uninterrupted," Andy said weakly, a pallor creeping over her face.

"Where are we going?" He smiled through a wince. "I told you we should go up, not down."

"Up? Tyrone was there."

"But the roof. There are dozens of ways to get off a roof."

Andy crossed her arms, her lips pale, her body listing toward the wall.

"Okay, basement it is." He slumped to the floor, holding his side, then *sensed* the gun on him.

She held the gun firmly toward him. "Who are

you?"

"Not who you think."

"You work for them?" She tossed her head upward.

He glanced sideways at her. "Depends on which 'them' you're referring to."

"The bad guys?"

"No."

She held firm.

"I'm a good guy," he said.

"How can I trust you?"

"You can't." His voice softened. "Except you know me, Andy."

"I don't think I know you. I know lots of lies about you."

Even with a gun and him wounded, Andy, in her condition, was no match for him. In a flash, he held her immobilized on his lap. She still had her gun, though, pointed at him. He let her keep it. He had counted its shots. "You're out of ammo."

Andy let it drop. "Why did you lie to me? Why do you always lie to me?"

"I couldn't let you go. You had the entry code. And it's not every day a witness to a murder of a person of interest falls into your lap." He cocked his head to the side for emphasis, giving her a half-smile. "Literally."

Ding. The doors parted, and he leaned on them, holding them open. Andy elbowed him, but he held her firm. "You can let me go now."

Begrudgingly, he let her go. She stalked out the elevator but before she exited, he grabbed her and passed his hands up her skirt.

"What are you doing?" she asked.

"You've got something I want."

"What?"

"The Personal Flotation Device."

Sighing, Andy flipped up her skirt to reveal the PFD. Tugging on the cord, he propped open the elevator doors as the PFD expanded to fill the gap, preventing them from closing. "That should hold them," he said as he started down the hall.

"Who do you work for?" she asked.

"Classified information."

"What do you want?"

"Classified."

Andy let out an exasperated sigh. Her struggles weakened; she was waning.

"So, what's your real name?" she asked.

"Classified."

"Okay, where are you from?"

"Classified, too."

"Can't I know anything about you?"

He flashed her a wide grin. "You know I'm hot."

Andy frowned. "Listen this partnership isn't going anywhere if all you feed me are lies. Lies, lies. Men are good at telling lies."

"Sounds like you've been hurt." It was a tease, a jab, but he couldn't help but probe for information.

"That's classified," she said.

"Classified, eh?"

"Yup."

He snorted and stopped in the hall to face her. "So, it's okay for you to have classified secrets, but not me."

"But I don't lie about mine."

"Yes, you do."

"Not like how you lie," she said.

"What's wrong with lying?" he asked.

"People hurt others when they lie."

"Hmmm, not unlike Andy Baker."

"What's that supposed to mean?" Her eyes flashed as she faced him.

He gave her a sly, knowing glance.

To his amusement, Andy scrambled to justify herself. "But I have to use my aliases. If not, it is certain danger or death."

His tone changed, serious now. "Then maybe, maybe you understand," he said, all playfulness gone, "why I can't tell you anything."

"Yes, but it's different—"

He was dangerously close to her. For once he let his veil slip, the real him showing through. "You're right. It's different. They trained me for years, robbed me of my life, any hope of family, made me perceive the world differently. They transformed me into a killing machine."

Andy faltered as she spoke. "I understand."

"No, you don't." The words tore at him, but he needed to say them, shooting out of him like ammo from AK-47. "When I meet someone, I don't see a person, Andy. I see a target. There's a chance I might have to kill one of them. If I have to take some guy out, I can't wonder if he's got a family at home. He's a mark, Andy, like a tin can sitting on a log."

"I just want to know who you are."

"I can't just tell you whatever you want to hear, indulge your curiosity because you want an emotional bond with me. It just isn't going to happen. You get to know what I want you to know. What *they* want you to know."

"They? Who are they? Wait, I know. It's

classified." Andy didn't bother waiting for an answer from Tyler. "So, do 'they' know about me?"

He nodded, taking her hand, heading down toward the storage room.

"What did you tell them?"

He grinned, giving her a glance from the slit of his eye. "I told them you lie all the time."

"Not funny." She weakly hit him on his shoulder, stopping for a breath. Andy paled. "You think I enjoy lying with my body, being so emotionally dishonest? For once I want a guy to wrap his arms around me and love me and whisper in my ear, 'I love you, Andy.' Not Gertrude or Mary Lou or Tiffany. I hate living a lie. For once, when I'm with someone, I want there to be complete and utter honesty between us, no lies, no masks, and no aliases. Just pure simple truth."

He arched an eyebrow. "Not love?"

"Truth is a part of love."

He faced away from her. "Then I will never know love."

"You will never let anyone in?"

"How can I? Will you? Will you give up your charade, Andy? For love? Would you give up your life-long goal for it?"

"I would. If I could. Wouldn't you?"

"I guess my goals are too deeply engrained." He continued down the hall. The basement was a maze of whitewashed limestone walls. Every doorway was too similar to the next, and last time he was in too much of a hurry to remember specifics.

"Aren't you lonely?" Andy followed.

His shoulders gave a clipped shrug. "There are plenty of women in my business," he said, adopting the air of nonchalance.

Andy snorted. "I'm sure there are. But anybody you can trust?"

"I don't trust anybody."

"Not even me?"

He grinned and winked. "Especially not you."

"Have you been lying this whole time?"

"It's hard to tell, isn't it?"

"Arg, you are so aggravating!"

"Just keep thinking that."

"Do you even know when you're lying?"

He stopped. "Does it matter?"

Andy glowered.

"So my name isn't Tyler."

"Oh?"

"It's Axil."

Andy raised her eyebrows.

"Zane," he said.

Andy frowned.

"Proctor?" he proffered.

Andy rolled her eyes.

"Granite," he said with eyes bright, laughing at her frustration. But really, he was trying to keep her mind off the pain.

"Fine, if you won't tell me, I'll call you, Angus," she said, leaning against the wall again.

Lifting his arm, he flexed. "Because I'm so beefy?" He was pleased she smiled.

"It was the name of my dog," she said. "I bet Angus isn't from Brooklyn or Kansas, either?"

He carefully weighed his answer, tilting his head to respond. "No, but—"

"I knew it. Liars. Men. All of them." Her energy

ebbed. Her body weakened. The light faded from her eyes.

They needed to stop again. He halted, listening for footsteps. "Nothing I told you was a lie, Andy. I did grow up on a farm, just not in New York or Kansas, then ran away and lived in a rough neighborhood. Made friends with a mentor who taught me how to take the fight externally. Someday, I'll go after the very people who stole my parents away from me."

"I'm sorry," Andy whispered between blanched lips.

"I'm sorry I had to tell you."

"Your parents are dead?" Her eyes grew heavy.

He hesitated. "Yes."

Andy sighed. "So why can't you tell me everything?"

"To protect you. You said yourself it was okay."

Then he found the door to the storage room.

Chapter Ten

"We got out of there too easily," Angus-Tyler said as he jimmied the lock with the ice pick. "He let us go."

Andy shrugged, her body losing blood.

"But I was impressed you had a fireman's control key so you could override the elevator."

"Respect the pockets." She patted her skirt like a zombie.

"Do I even want to know how you secured one of those?" Angus asked.

"Lots of kisses."

"I'm sure."

They threaded their way back down through the rows and rows of shelves. Andy's energy withered with each step.

"You doing okay?" he asked.

Andy nodded, her breath labored. "Just let me rest here for a minute."

"We don't have a minute. Tyrone's men are following the elevators. I'm sure they have realized we are down here."

Her skirt weighed her down.

"It's time to nix the skirt," he said, his voice tense.

"That's not how I was hoping you'd persuade me out of this."

Angus smiled. With her arm over his shoulder, they continued on.

167

Andy continued. "Sorry, but there's too much we need in here. The dress stays."

They found the coal chute. Angus pried the door.

"I can't open it, too many layers of paint."

"See? Here's a knife," Andy slid her hand up her skirt, and handed pocket knife from a pocket.

"Thank you," Angus said, slicing the layers of paint holding the little door closed.

Angus's tux clung to him in the moisture. Sweat dampened his shirt and dripped from his brow as he scraped as quickly and as noiselessly as he could. Each stoke pained his wounds.

Trapped. With the knife, he slit the sleeves and up his chest, he ripped his shirt off, leaving a white undershirt, drenched in sweat and blood.

"The lock's been picked," a voice called to the other guards. Angus paused. They were closing in. Angus had almost finished the first side.

"I'll help." Andy crawled up beside him and commenced on a second side with a flathead screwdriver. Fear and pain flashed in her eyes as she clinched her jaw against it, scraping paint as fast as she could.

The second side finished. One last side.

Andy's screwdriver slipped in her weakness and caught Angus in the fleshy part behind his pinky, he barely noticed the sting.

"Sorry," Andy said, slumping to the ground.

"I've got this," he said.

Thankfully, they worked safely in the shadows, but Tyrone's men would get here eventually.

"Almost there," he said.

Angus slid his knife in the opening, prying. With a

pop, the door swung open.

Angus faced to Andy to celebrate, but she had passed out.

"If I have to carry you up, I'm taking off your skirt. Any objections?" He searched for the buttons.

"This is not how I imagined undressing you for the first time," he muttered. "And I prefer my women conscious." He breathed out. "I wish you'd slap me for my impertinence."

Andy woke while his hands were inopportunely around her thighs, sliding them from her dress, leaving her in a pair of little white shorts and her bodice top. Her lips white, her face wan. "Are you stripping me?"

"You can't make it up the shaft with your dress on."

Her pale lips parted. "That sounds really dirty."

He slid her from the battle array of barbarous cotton candy. He placed her through opened shaft door.

"Can you climb?" he asked.

Barefooted, she hoisted herself up the chute.

"There they are!" Men approached. Shots ricocheted around them.

Angus used the steel door as a shield as the sounds of gunshots rang in his ears. He thrust Andy upward and climbed up himself.

Up the shaft they climbed, Andy's head throbbed. She was grateful to still have her LED light hanging around her neck, illuminating the way as she held to the edges of the chute.

"I keep slipping on dust," she said.

"Don't worry I'm behind you," Angus said.

The door at the top had to be forced open. Andy enjoyed the rush of cold fresh air even if her dizziness increased.

The little doorway allowed them passage to a small landing, the river churning below. "Now what?" Andy asked.

Darkness surrounded them. Tyrone's men scouting the perimeter of the building limited their options. Men shook the metal as they scaled the chute below.

"Trapped," he said.

Suddenly, a flashlight beamed on them and a voice yelled, "There!"

Andy didn't have time to shield her eyes to confront their accuser.

"Jump?" Andy panted, fighting to stay conscious. "I wish I had my PFD."

Angus and Andy dove off the edge into the water below.

****

Disoriented in the dark, Andy swam, the water rushing fast around her. Her head throbbed as the icy, dark, and dirty water stung the wound.

Weightless. All she had to do was open her mouth and breathe in. Then suddenly, someone grabbed and hauled upward. Her head broke the water first, and she gasped for air.

"Can you swim?" Angus spit water, trying to keep her head afloat, treading water, while being swept around. His usually blondish hair plastered dark against his head.

The current rushed faster than her locked muscles could swim. They ached, and her head throbbed. Angus tugged her diagonally across the current toward the shore. Andy swam the best she could, but Angus was doing most of the maneuvering.

Finally, they attained the shoals.

"We made it," Angus said, dragging Andy to where she could reach the bottom and crawl through the water to the bank. He attempted to stand, but slipped, splashing into the water. Grasping some earth, he hauled himself up and out of the water onto the marshy bank. His frequent breaths made puffs of steam in the icy air. "You're lucky you're wearing an LED light. It was the only way I found you under there."

"You lost your pants," she said.

He wore only a pair of muddied brown-white boxers and t-shirt. His shirt clung to him, making his shoulders and chest even more defined.

"Kicked them off in the river."

Her brain wandered. Cold. Very cold.

Once safely on land, she glanced at the far away city lights, civilization, and laughed between chattering teeth.

Angus, still catching his breath, leaned close. "What?" he asked.

"What would people think if they met us, two people half-dressed." Her jaw clenched against the chattering. Her body ached, her head hurt. Her mind, drifting. "Out here in the middle of nowhere."

"They would think, they must've had a great time escaping from a very snooty party."

Andy's jaw shook uncontrollably. "Thankfully nobody's around. Where are we?" Andy scanned the banks. Dark barges piled with train car-sized containers of coal ran parallel to the river. A few trees, skimpy, waterlogged, cloistered nearby. Flat grasslands stretched behind them.

"Illinois."

Her muscles ached, her toes numb. Clenching her jaw against the cold made her head ache all the more. Everything sounded far away, distant. The wind snapped around her.

"I had matches in my dress," she managed to get out.

He laughed again, this time a full, hearty laugh filled with irony. It was cold. Cold enough to die. They were miles from St. Louis and not a road in sight. The cold river staunched the flow of blood, but it started to bleed again, making its own black river down her forehead.

With so much lost blood, the cold, fatigue, she passed out.

Angus didn't panic. Years of survival training kicked in. He wrapped her head in his undershirt, scooped her up under her neck and knees. He laughed at her name for him. Angus was no worse than any other alias he'd had. He indulged her in it.

He had her in his arms now, blood spilling down his chest where her head lay against his pec. He never wanted to let her go. But he couldn't love her. People in his line of work couldn't afford to have love interests, family, or anybody they cared about. They became a liability. A distraction, deterrent, a bargaining chip. He'd been able to avoid it for so long.

If only he could tell her what he really needed. But that would be stupid. He must never tell Andy the whole truth. Doing so would endanger them both. But he'd been stringing her along too far. She deserved some truth.

Of course, if she died now, there'd be no chance to tell her anyway. Angus ran. Without glancing at her, he knew Andy was fading. He kept moving, pumping legs, numb with cold, toward the lights growing brighter before him.

Soon, he distinguished cars parked by a building, then people. A man exited his car a phone to his ear.

"Hey!" Angus hollered, his voice strange to him. The man swiveled briefly, glancing away, then did a double-take. Tears flowed down Angus's cheeks. He hadn't realized he'd been crying. "Can you help us?"

The man grimaced at the strange sight of a man in his underclothes carrying a woman not much more dressed than he was. Steam escaped from Angus as he exhaled.

The man dropped his phone to his chest. "What do you need?"

He needed her warm, some place safe. He read the sign flashing above him.

River Bottom Topless Bar

"Can we use your car?" Just until the extraction team could come and get them. "And your phone?"

"My car?" The man shifted feet, hesitating.

"We're not carjackers." He breathed the icy air biting his lungs. "My girlfriend and I…" Why couldn't he think of anything convincing? "We wanted to go for a swim."

The man raised an eyebrow, but Angus didn't care.

"And my girlfriend hit her head. Please, sir, can we just warm up in your car?" He didn't want to take her inside. A strip club was not a place for Andy, especially when underdressed. He didn't want men, *those* men, staring at Andy.

The realization he wanted to protect her scared him, more than bullets, more than death.

"Can I use your phone, too?"

When the man handed him his phone, Angus thanked him before stepping away to make his call.

"We need extraction," Angus said into the man's cell.

"What phone are you calling from?"

"Don't worry, I'll scrub the number when I'm done. We need EMS. Now."

"We'll need your location."

Angus gave the information. He sighed. "And my cover's been compromised."

"Andy's not with you, is she?"

"She's inside, warming up," Angus stood off from the car, outside in the wind, the man's jacket around him. The man sat in the car with the blasting the heat on Andy in the front seat.

"What happened?"

He described the night, from beginning to end.

"How was I supposed to know Tyrone employed local FBI agents?" he asked. Of all the things Tyrone had to be honest about.

"How's Andy?"

"Not well. Still unconscious."

"No, I mean, does she still trust you?"

Angus glanced back to the car. He could only make out her outline through the fogged windows. "I don't think we can recover from this one with protocol."

A swear word passed through the phone.

"Listen, there's only one way to get her back. She feels emotionally close to me. But I will need to be on my own. Completely on my own. No back up, no ears, no tails. Just me and her."

No hesitancy on the phone. "No."

"It's the only way."

"It's against protocol. And a huge risk."

"She's not going to trust me if she doesn't feel completely safe. I have to earn her trust. She's still withholding information."

"How do you know?"

"I just know things." Angus could be persuasive. "I'll report when I have updates, but I control when I check in. This is the only way you're going to get your man. Andy has skills. She's not trained, but don't underestimate her. She'll take us right to him."

There was a long pause. "And if not?"

"Trust me."

A sigh. "What other choice do I have?"

****

Tyrone glanced at the bloody mess in his penthouse. Glass shards, men struggling. Then one body, facedown dark liquid saturating his brown suit around a knife wound, caught his attention.

Tyrone knelt beside him and slid out the knife, inspecting it with wonder. It wasn't his hand that threw the knife. It was not him who threw the knife.

Bobby twitched.

"He's alive," he said, his voice sounding strange to him.

A few men helped staunch Bobby's wound. Another man called the infirmary. Tyrone had his private doctor on retainer. He'd spare no expense for Bobby.

While waiting for the doctor, Tyrone held Bobby, using a napkin compress for the wound in his back. But the wound cut deep. Tyrone cursed Andrew Baker.

Covered in Bobby's blood, Tyrone gritted his teeth.

How was he going to tell Hazel?

The elevator pinged. "What happened up here? Where's Bobby? Am I to be abandoned at my own engagement party?" High heels sounded on the parquet floor. Then they stopped. Hazel gasped behind him.

"Bobby! My Bobby!" Hazel ruined her designer gown in an instant as she knelt in Bobby's blood, scooping up his pale face, covering it with kisses. His breathing was shallow, but there.

"What happened?" she asked. "Who did this?" So much like her mother. Tyrone couldn't bear it.

"Andrew Baker did this." Tyrone was too ashamed to tell the truth.

"Why?" Disbelief dissolved into tears as Hazel struggled to choke back emotion. She'd seen too much as Tyrone's daughter to be too emotional, but even this was too much for her.

Hazel bent over Bobby, her smooth, white shoulders shaking, sobs wrenching Tyrone's soul.

Tyrone barked orders. "I want their names. I want their addresses. I want to know where they attended high school, who their friends are, what people they've dated. Get our connections in the FBI, track their movements, their cards, their phones. Everything! I want an interview with the editor of the *Times*."

He needed to appease his conscience. He needed Andrew Baker to take the heat for Tyrone's mistakes. He needed his daughter to stop crying.

****

Darkness. A knock wakened her heavy and dull body. Even opening her eyes was a chore. Finally, the room swirled into view.

"Yes?" she said, taking in her surroundings. An IV

and cords ran from her arms to monitors beeping in concert with her heartbeat. The hospital gown and thin blanket offered little warmth. Her bandaged head didn't throb. Now her body rose, light and airy. Like she was floating. And so relaxed.

"How are you?" Angus asked when opened the door.

Andy cracked a smile when he approached. Was that his name?

Angus stood next to her bed. "After twenty-one stitches and fighting a nasty bacterial infection, you look great."

She glanced sideways. "I can never tell if you are telling the truth or lying." Where had they left things?

"Stop trying to guess, then." He shrugged. A few heartbeats passed. Angus slid a small black visitor's chair from the wall and sat, facing her. "So you withheld something from me."

"How did you know?" she asked.

"I found a sticky in your clothing."

She'd stuck it in her bra. She blushed.

"Did you find it at the T-Building? Why didn't you tell me?" His face fell.

Andy ignored his hurt expression, assured it was an act. "Why should I trust you?"

Hints of her memory slapped at her. Angus, that was what she'd decided to call him, sat almost immovable, only the slightest twitch of his eyelids.

"I can't work with someone when there's no trust," she said.

"I've never told you a complete lie."

"Ha!"

"You don't have to believe me."

177

"I don't believe anything you say anymore." Andy didn't mean to be so honest, but the drugs made her mind foggy.

Angus averted his gaze.

Plucking a cord stuck into her vein, Andy airy, mind dulled asked, "What's this? Truth serum?"

"Pain killers and heavy antibiotics. All legit. Unfortunately, our little dip in the Mississippi wasn't the cleanest thing we could have done with open wounds."

Andy's brow furrowed. "How long was I out?"

"Three days."

"Where have you been?"

"I was getting stitched up in the infirmary."

More details floated back to her. The attacks, the flight. The pain. "Your side?"

He tucked up his shirt to reveal a bandage taped to his torso. "Not as bad as your head. I worried you weren't going to make it. They gave you lots of blood."

A bit of pity softened her. "Thank you for saving my life."

His gaze fixed on something in his lap. Conversation stopped. Tiny muscles in his jaws flexed, the beeping monitor the only sound in the room.

"Since you're feeling better," he started, "are you going to tell me what was on this yellow sticky?" He held up the dry but watermarked square between his pointer and thumb and tapped it with his middle finger. It was blank.

More memories flooded her. Tyrone's penthouse. FBI. Not FBI. "Who are you?" she asked, her mind clearing. She had glanced at the sticky briefly in Brad's office. But she couldn't remember the name, even if she'd wanted to tell him. If she could just fight the cloud in her brain. There were other things she hadn't told him, too. About Dr. Armstrong. Glad she didn't even mention him. "Why should I talk?"

Angus didn't have a leg to stand on.

Andy narrowed her eyes to little slits. "Who are you?" she asked, sitting up straighter, still feeling weak, but strangely strong by having a piece of the puzzle he didn't have. A bargaining chip. She wasn't sure who these people were, whether FBI or CIA or MMA. She wanted answers.

"I've trusted you with my life," she said. "I need to know who you are."

"I can't tell you." He almost pleaded with her. His eyebrows peaked on his forehead. He shook his head and repeated it. "I can't tell you."

"Because I'm not talking until I get information. The truth, this time, only the truth and nothing but the truth."

His expression darkened. "You don't want the truth."

"Yes, I do. If you want to progress on this case, I need the truth."

But he didn't start talking. There were lines on his face, dark circles under his eyes. "Hasn't it ever occurred to you I can't tell you because of who you are? You're a journalist and they aren't exactly known for keeping secrets."

Andy's jaw dropped agape. "Fine. I'm leaving." Andy grabbed tubes, trying to dislodge them.

"I wouldn't if I were you."

"Why not?"

"Mr. Hershal, your editor, is dead."

Andy grew more light-headed, then a heaviness settled into her chest diving into the deepness of her stomach. Mr. Hershal was a dear friend of her father's. Even though he was tough on Andy, she owed him a lot. It was weird mourning a man she'd never met in person.

"What happened?" she asked.

"They say it was an accident. Fell off his horse while riding at the club yesterday. But I'm sure it was more complicated than what they want us to believe."

Her stomach ached. How many more people would die?

He continued. "Tyrone knows all about you now."

Andy scowled. She hated the name. But she wasn't too happy with Angus trying to manipulate her, either. "Don't worry. He couldn't have given him too much information."

"What do you mean?"

"I've never met him. He couldn't point me out in a crowd. I set up an LLC under a C-corp umbrella so I couldn't be traced."

"But what about your father? Mr. Hershal knew him, too, didn't he?"

Andy blanched. Sandra wasn't safe.

"You're safe here," he said. "We can protect you."

"Can you protect Sandra? You couldn't even protect Brad or Conner."

His lids flinched a bit.

"I'm not letting Tyrone kill Sandra."

Suddenly, he stalked over to her machine and unplugged it, a flatline sound followed. His entire manner changed from tired-worried to active-urgency.

"What are you doing?" Andy asked.

"Disabling the bug."

"What? Who is listening? Your team?"

He nodded. "Don't ask questions. Check the time," Angus said forcefully. "You'll need to know how long you have until a nurse comes in. She'll say the machine is broken, and will replace it. *They* are monitoring you through this machine, listening to everything you say and do. In a few minutes, they'll replace this machine. If you want to make a run for it, you'll need to know how much time you have before they realize you are gone. I don't blame you for leaving, but let me help you go and save Sandra. Unplug the next machine when you are ready to go. We can meet up after you escape."

"Why are you helping me?"

He shoved his hands into his pockets and stared at the floor. "Because you don't deserve this."

She couldn't tell if it was an act, or if they really were monitoring the room. But she needed him if she wanted to get out of here.

"I smuggled in your clothes and bag from your condo," he said as if this would convince her he was really helping her. Andy had to take a gamble.

"Where do you want to meet?" she asked.

He smiled. "Meet me at the Cafe Reginald and you can tell me everything there."

"And *you* can tell me everything there."

"Of course." He nodded curtly.

"With nobody else."

"Nobody else."

"Time?"

"Think you're feeling well enough to break out and meet by three p.m.?"

Andy nodded.

"Until three, then, Cafe Reginald." He raised his eyebrows in goodbye, but paused at the door. "Be safe. Stay away from Tyrone's men. Don't try to confront them alone. You're not well enough." He ducked out as the nurse entered.

Andy glanced at her clock when the nurse opened the door. Five after eleven. Only five minutes. More than enough time.

As soon as the nurse finished and closed the door, Andy leaped out of bed. The first few steps caused her to pause at the foot to catch her breath. Sitting in bed for three days on meds made her lightheaded, weak. But she didn't have time for weakness. Persisting on, she had to dress and get out of there, STAT.

Waiting until the last minute to pull her IV line, just in case they were monitoring her, she tore open her bag. True to his word, Angus had left her clothes and her phone, all her cards and money were in there.

And phones.

She called Sandra.

Voicemail. Andy would have to go to her house first. She wondered how much she would have to tell her to convince her to leave.

To escape the hospital, Andy couldn't resemble a patient. She painted her pale face with bronzer, to give it color. Then wrapped a scarf around her bandaged head.

"I don't know if turbans are in right now, but better to appear ridiculous than get caught," she said to her reflection.

All dressed, her hair tucked up, she cut the medical tape from her skin, then gently pulled the IV from her vein.

The countdown was on. As she had no intention of meeting with Angus, she had to make arrangements to warn Sandra and leave town before three.

****

Andy rapped at Sandra's door outside the city, a small brick house about sixty or seventy years old. The shutters needed a coat of paint and the flowerbeds needed weeding. Andy hadn't been there in months, but knew to dig in the plant boxes for the spare key. The door swung open to a small, mousy middle-aged woman.

"Mandy! You're here. Your head." Her eyes widened in concern, taking Andy's head, bandage and all, in both hands, kissing the side of her smarting head. "What happened?"

"Listen, Sandra." Andy's heart was up in her throat, and she couldn't speak. Andy didn't know how to tell her she continued on in her father's place doing dangerous things. Too much to explain, too many lies to confess. She'd have to opt for a quicker route. "I've gotten into trouble."

"Trouble? What sort?" Her expression changed from concern to worry.

Andy shook her head. Her throat dry, her head still hurt. Andy navigated the cluttered mess, years of memories, dust, and junk mail sat around in piles; picking up stuff would be important, Sandra's wallet, her keys. Brad was right. Sandra was a hoarder.

Andy continued. "I bought you a ticket to visit your sister in Ohio. Your flight leaves in three hours, so don't pack anything. Just go. I sent your boarding pass to your phone."

The horror on Sandra's face tortured Andy, her

biggest nightmare realized.

"Just like being married to your father," her stepmother said. "For how long?"

"I don't know." Andy needed time to think. She didn't know how long it would take to track down Dr. Armstrong. "Maybe change your name, color your hair."

With the Internet, relations could easily be tracked down. "Close out your Facebook account, and don't tell anyone where you or I are going."

"What is going on, Amanda?" Sandra stood resolute, her arms crossed her chest.

Andy didn't want to lie. She swallowed hard. "I should've told you years ago."

"Told me what?"

With a deep breath, Andy started. "Before he left, Dad passed the torch of Andrew Baker on to me."

Her mother drew a sharp breath. "He dragged you into his mess, too, eh? I should've known."

"Sorry, I didn't tell you. Dad didn't want you to worry."

"Worry? I have to mysteriously leave for some unknown reason."

"I shouldn't have lied to you."

Sandra nodded her head. "You think?" She paced, wiping her hands across her face. "I hated the lies your dad told to keep all his secrets. But it's more than that, Mandy. Now he's got you into the same habit."

Sandra paced. The lines on her face were deep. Her hair far too gray. A pit formed in Andy's stomach. How could she add to her pain? "Also, Brad was involved in something."

"Brad?" Sandra's face paled. "I haven't heard from

him in a week. Is he okay?"

Andy's stomach knotted. She bowed her head. "He's not coming back."

Sandra's expression fell. "They got him, too, didn't they?"

"You knew?"

"I had a feeling. The police told me he was missing. I didn't believe it. He's involved in this mess somehow, too?"

"Yes."

"He lied to me, too."

"I know."

"Just promise me one thing," Sandra said, halting Andy who was grabbing her purse and packing it with her passport and cash. "Promise me you won't lie to yourself."

Andy had fifteen minutes to gather her stuff from Sandra's house before she needed to catch her flight to Boston. The house was disorganized, sloppy. She bounded upstairs to the bathroom, digging through pink foam rollers, old hair brushes; grateful Sandra had kept everything. Finding everything she needed would be the problem. She needed cosmetics and hair holders and her old curling iron. A miracle it still worked. She wrapped the cord around the barrel. Clothes, fingernail files, fishing line, toenail clippers, floss, duct tape, and razor blades. She hadn't lost it all in her dress at Tyrone's, but she'd lost a lot.

Andy stuffed cotton balls into small zippered pouches, but it just wasn't all fitting. She tossed in a blush brush. The mascara fell out. Hands trembling, she picked it up. She had too much. She was about to fetch a backpack from downstairs when the doorbell rang.

Andy froze. She didn't want anyone knowing she was here, least of all any of Sandra's friends. Anyone she had contact with was a liability.

Andy ducked behind the half-wall leading to the downstairs, peeking through the plants for cover. Sandra's youthful stride negotiated the cluttered space, her keys jingling at her side, matching her pace. She opened the door.

Andy's blood froze when a familiar voice said, "Hello there, ma'am."

Tyrone himself.

Chapter Eleven

Tyrone barely acknowledged the small homely woman with unkept semi-curly hair as he peeked around the house of crazed disorder. He shivered. The disorder disoriented him, but he was here to deliver a message. He had to maintain control. "May I come in?" Two of his men remained at the door, another in the car.

Tyrone used his large frame to bulldoze past the woman without waiting for a response. He inspected the lack of taste in what little dusty decor hung from the walls and crowded surfaces. He sneered at the piles of magazines on the coffee table and the pyramid of shoes by the door. Mrs. Miller nervously buzzed round him. He grew bold under her fear.

He stopped at a picture of a girl hanging near the foyer. Her skirted leotard hung over skinny little legs, stretching up to her jazz hands. Though it was an older picture, he recognized her. "Is this your daughter?" he asked.

"Stepdaughter."

Tyrone studied the girl behind the glass for a few seconds, as if he were an old family friend. How could this one little girl cause all this trouble? Then with one hand clutching his hat, he suddenly strode into the living room, observed an overstuffed chair marked with stains and decided to stand.

"You know," Tyrone said, taking out a hanky and

wiped his eyes, gleaming with tears. "Last night, I ordered Maine lobster tails, clams, and shrimp from the grocer."

"What?" Mrs. Miller trembled. He smiled.

"Yes, I ordered the tails, boiled them, steamed the clams, peeled and deveined the shrimp, then brined, shredded, and combined them all into a seafood mixture."

"You're giving me a recipe?"

"Hush. Just listen."

He wandered to the kitchen, which was just in view of the little front room, sneering at the crusted dishes in the sink. "Then I mixed them with panko crumbs, you see. Now here's the secret, I used a watermelon baller to make the balls—the only way to form them to a perfect uniform size every time. I liked to cook. I attended École de Cuisine. Unfortunately, my father had other career plans for me. Thankfully, I can still cook.

"Sadly, three days ago, I fried my little balls in safflower oil, you might want to remember this, safflower oil is better for frying delicate meats like the seafood because it reaches a high temperature faster."

Mrs. Miller stared at him. Giving these little lessons disarmed his victims.

"It sounds wonderful," she said. "I'm sure you enjoyed them, now if you excuse me—"

"I'm not finished yet. You shouldn't be so rude. I need to tell you my story."

Sandra sat back down. He continued his culinary lesson.

"I like to fry mine at a temperature of three hundred and fifty or so, just to give the panko crumbs the right golden-brown texture on the outside." He pinched the air with his forefingers and smacked his lips. A hint of a smile played on the lips as if he were savoring the meal all over again this very moment. Then his face changed, hardened, darkened. "But I never got to enjoy my Three Seafood Fried Balls. Do you know why?"

Sandra shook her head.

"Because last night, I received some very sad news while I was frying my seafood. In fact, some of them burned, and I do not like that.

"The doctor said one of my men, one of my *sons*, my baby girl's only love, Bobby, may not make it out of the hospital."

"I'm very sorry—"

"Your stepdaughter is responsible."

Her hand flew to her face to hide her gasp. "Mandy would never—"

"I don't know if you know what your stepdaughter has been doing lately." Mrs. Miller didn't know. He could tell by her shock and horror on her face. He continued, "They were going to be married in the spring, my daughter and her fiancé. Now my little baby girl is mourning a husband she will never have. Do you know what it feels like?" He paused near the knife block. "It cuts like a knife."

From the block, he slid out an eight-inch chef's knife. Not bad quality. Not the best, either.

"This is a beautiful collection of knives, Mrs. Miller. I hope you don't ruin them by washing them in the dishwasher." He thumbed the edge of the blade, cutting himself slightly. A line of bright red slid down from his thumb. "Oh, and sharp, too."

Mrs. Miller shivered, staring wide-eyed at his hand. He headed to the door. She was on the point of breaking. Fragile. Just the way he liked them.

He opened the door, put on his hat, and gave her a smile he could have sold used cars. He disturbed the pile of shoes. A cricket hopped toward the open door. His smile disappeared. He grimaced and shuddered. Then stomped on the bug.

"You have a pest problem, Mrs. Miller. When I have a pest problem, I call the exterminator. I have a pest problem, too. I hate pests. Hate them with a passion."

Then quickly he flung the knife forward into the picture with the jazz hands, slicing it through, shattering the glass.

"Remember Mrs. Miller, a life for a life."

****

Andy persuaded a hysterical Sandra to drive to her sister's house in Ohio. She calmed to a smoldering silence and dropped Andy off at the metro. Andy paused at the door of the car, throwing her red weekender tote over her shoulder. Sandra had new wrinkles and dark circles under her eyes. Her shoulders slumped.

"I'm sorry I never told you I picked up my dad's investigative work," Andy said.

Sandra didn't reply, staring into the distance, toward the haze clouding the sun. Everything had changed so quickly. Things will never be the same. At least not until they put Tyrone away.

"I'm sorry about Brad."

Sandra nodded, tears welling in her eyes. She put the car in gear and Andy closed the door. She had to make this right.

****

Andy hated flying.

She hated all of it. Not just the packing, but security as well. And turbulence made her nervous. Ever since she watched a show where an alien ripped a plane apart, she never wanted to fly again. But since someone else paid for the flight, and time was of the essence, fly she must.

Using Mrs. Vehemia's voucher, she purchased a ticket to Boston. She could get out of town for a while, keep her promise to talk to Scott, find Dr. Armstrong the professor in Boston.

While in the winding security line, full of impatient travelers, she tried to remember the name on the sticky. The name meant something. It sounded familiar. Though until her head cleared of the fog from impact and painkillers, she'd just have to wait to remember what it was. In the meantime, she headed for Boston.

She checked her phone to make sure she was on time. Then she noticed a voicemail message. She clicked on the icon.

"Hi." The voice on the line had a thick accent. "This is Juan Martinez. A mutual friend said to call you." There was some unintelligible Spanish. Then ended.

Juan Martinez.

The name on the sticky.

She now had his number on her phone.

Some foreign number.

Her finger hovered over the redial button. Voices rose behind her.

"Where are you going?" a lady asked a man behind

her.

"Excuse me," he replied, his head down. "Sorry. Just catching up to my fiancée."

Andy swiveled. Angus, with a satchel over his shoulder, bent to kiss her. "Thanks for saving our place in line, honey. I got our bags all checked." He raised a scarred eyebrow, and his eyes twinkled, his chin thrust forward in his cocky manner. Andy's mouth fell agape. Andy's mind sputtered with questions.

"Next," the TSA man called.

Andy pivoted. She was next in line. Stepping up to the TSA podium, she showed her boarding pass and ID before entering the tunnel x-rays. The bored expression of the man in the blue and black uniform juxtaposed with her own anxiety. "Name?" he asked.

Andy couldn't find her voice.

"Name?"

"Amanda," she squeaked out, the corner of her eye following Angus as he stood at the second podium. How did he get there? Her heart nearly strangled her breath.

The agent, an elderly man perhaps in his fifties stared over the top of his glassed tucked underneath graying temples. "Full name?"

"Oh, Amanda Loraine Miller." Loraine was her aunt, her mother's sister. The bored TSA agent lazily shone a light on her ID. Andy glanced at Angus who casually passed an ID and boarding pass to a female TSA agent at the other podium.

Her TSA agent scribbled something on her pass and handed it back to her.

"Next," he said.

Andy stood in line and removed her shoes, placing

them in a bucket. Angus got behind her.

"Name on the boarding pass?"

"John Smith."

Andy snorted. "John Smith? Not very creative."

He didn't answer, but put his shoes in a gray bucket.

"How did you—?" Andy started.

"Get a ticket so fast? Or find out where you are going?"

Andy stood there, her eyes little slits. Annoyed for so many reasons. "Did you put a tracker in my bag?"

"You'll never know, will you?" Angus bent close, his eyes sparkling blue, full of amusement. "You didn't think I'd let you go to Boston by yourself, did you?"

"Tyrone's been to my house."

"Everybody okay?"

"Sandra is on her way to Ohio."

"Good."

Andy's face flashed with heat as she placed her bag in a bin and marched through the metal detector.

Beep! Beep!

A portly TSA man pointed to Andy. "Please step over here, miss."

Andy followed the gloved hands of another TSA officer as they waved the wand over her.

As a stout woman passed her hand over Andy and patted her down, she noticed the first officer secured her bag and rummaged through it.

"Miss?" he asked. "Is this your bag?"

Andy nodded. Angus didn't even try to hide his smile from her. Andy shot him a scowl.

The first TSA agent dug out throwing stars from her side bag pocket. She forgot she stashed them in there. You never know when you might need them.

"You know these are outlawed by the TSA," he said.

Andy burned with embarrassment. She'd meant to store those in her checked luggage but was so rattled after Tyrone's visit, she forgot.

"You cannot carry weapons on a plane. I could have you arrested and detained as a terrorist."

Andy's heart lunged. Andy had pretended to be many things, a terrorist was not one of them. Fear replaced indignation. "I'm a martial arts instructor, I always carry weapons in my bag."

"Weapons?" He continued through the bag. "There are fire crackers, a punch can opener, a four-inch Swiss Army knife, a wrench, and a lock pick kit." He laid the items out as he mentioned each one.

Another reason to hate flying. Andy's face burned with embarrassment as Angus inspected the contents with a trained eye. She didn't even care about the agents or the people behind her making comments. Only Angus's smug laughter bothered her. As if she were playing nurse and he was the surgeon. Her stomach soured like she'd eaten too much cheap Chinese take-out.

Angus stepped between her and the agent. "Sir, I'll be happy to take them back to our checked luggage."

"Who are you?" he asked gruffly, his whole body puffing up, objecting to Angus even speaking.

Angus didn't even blink an eye. "Her fiancé."

"You two traveling together?" Now it was the agent's turn to glance back and forth accusingly between Andy and Angus. His round face bubbled with little sweat drops on it, as if he were a rag being rung out. Andy was sure his nerves were also ratcheted up a bit. Dark circles seeped under his arms.

"No," Andy said just as Angus said, "Yes."

The agent frowned.

"I mean yes," Andy said, her head bowed.

The agent glanced back and forth between them. "You're together?"

"She's just a little nervous. We're on our pre-honeymoon." Angus slipped his arm around her waist, and bent to give her a kiss.

His lips grazed hers. She breathed him in. Her stomach fluttered again, but for a different reason. Confusion, anger—she didn't like being used as a cover—bubbled in her heart, even as she continued to kiss him. She couldn't help it, he was kissing her. The kiss deepened until the agent coughed uncomfortably.

Angus pulled back and opened his eyes, catching Andy's and gave her a smile.

The security man zipped up her bag. "Promise me you won't carry this kind of stuff through a security again. You gave us quite a scare, lady."

"She has that effect on men," Angus replied, winking to the officer, who pretended not to notice.

Andy, still dazed, barely aware and nodded.

She shouldn't have kissed him back, but she had to make their cover realistic. Why didn't he say they were brother and sister? Of course, they would have checked their IDs to validate matching last names. But Andy wished for any other story other than lovers.

Angus slid his hand down her arm and caught her hand and squeezed it. "I'll go check this in. I'll be back, honey," he said as if this parting were tearing him up inside. But Andy recognized a threat.

Angus shouldered her red bag and galloped back to the checked luggage while Andy waited at the gate. The passengers began boarding. Minutes passed, and he was back through security.

"Let's go honey, we don't want to miss our flight," he said as he threaded his arm through hers, showing him his seat number next to hers.

"How did you get here?" Andy asked, but he just stared at her, smug, superior, and calm. Andy's face fell. "You're not going to tell me are you."

"You're dealing with a professional here."

"I'm a professional."

"Tsk, tsk. You've got moxie, I'll grant you, but you're not a professional. You lack a certain edge, experience, and knowledge."

"You're so…" Andy compiled a list of insults, but Angus interrupted her.

"Careful," he simply said, breathing it out, his gaze intense on her.

****

While the other passengers boarded, she thought about her message from Martinez, and again when she and Angus settled in their seats. Martinez sounded scared, nervous. Desperate. Andy wished she'd been able to talk to him. Her mind whirred. Since she couldn't call him now, not with Angus there. She must think about something else. She faced her seat-mate.

"Did *they* tell you to follow me?" she asked.

"I will neither confirm nor deny." He flipped through the complimentary magazine, ignoring her completely.

"How did you know where I was going?"

Still silence.

"Are you going to report everything to them?"

"Why do you ask me questions when you know I'm just going to lie?"

"You can at least tell me your name. Or at least a name I can call you."

"Christiaan."

"For reals this time?"

"For reals."

"First or last name?"

"First."

"No last name?"

"Don't push it." He paused.

Frustrated, Andy studied her pamphlet on Boston University, with smiling co-eds lounging on green grass. She slapped it down and faced to her seat-mate. "Tell me something about yourself…not a lie."

"I don't sleep with a pillow."

"Odd."

"For years I slept on the streets. No pillows."

Andy's eyes narrowed. "Weren't you at your grandparents' place?"

"I was. I didn't lie. But I was getting into fights in school, I was bored, angry. I didn't want my grandparents to have to deal with my anger, so I left."

"You left? You ran away?"

"Yeah, I ran away to the nearby city."

"But it wasn't L.A.?"

He shook his head.

Andy nodded. "So how did you get to be doing this? I really want to trust you but I need answers, real answers, truth."

Angus or Christiaan put down his magazine, and stared into her eyes.

"From this point on, I will not lie to you. I may have to withhold information. Maybe someday after this whole thing is over, I will tell you all the truth." He bowed his head, his lashes concealing half his eyes. Then in a moment of bare naked truth, he whispered, "If I live long enough." His fingers played with the pocket in the seat in front of him.

"I can ask whatever I want and you will answer truthfully?"

"Or not at all."

"Where are you from?" she asked. "You're not from the States."

He arched an eyebrow. "How did you figure that out?"

"You kept using words Americans don't use like 'flat,' and 'expiry.' And you called the Bruce Lee movie *The Way of the Dragon*. It was released in the States as *Return of the Dragon*."

He sat back and grinned. "I'm impressed, Andy Baker."

"Tell me how you acquired such an authentic American accent?"

"Are you going to ask me questions for our entire flight?"

"No, I plan on falling asleep and drooling on your shoulder."

"Pleasant."

****

Andy, true to her word, did fall asleep on his shoulder and drooled on his collared shirt. Breaking out of the hospital, the pain throbbing in her head, she zonked, an hour into the flight.

"So, what's our first stop?" Christiaan asked when

they landed.

"Are you just going to follow me around until I reveal to you what was written on the sticky?"

"Something like that."

"So, like house arrest."

"Think of it as security detail."

Andy sighed. She'd have to find some way to get away from him to make her call. He was like a dangerous, spying puppy. "We have to visit a friend—a guy." Andy wrestled her bag down from the overhead compartment. Christiaan stopped her and lifted it down with one swift yank.

His eyes glimmered. "Oh? This is even more interesting. You must have guys stashed all over this nation."

"A *client*."

"Where?"

"Boston Psychiatric Hospital."

"About what I'd expect from one of your boyfriends."

Shaking her head, Andy disembarked the plane.

****

Andy gave the hospital her name. They okayed her from a list of approved visitors. They scanned her ID gave her a visitor's badge with her driver's license picture.

"And you are?" The nurse faced Christiaan. Andy had no idea what name he was going to tell her.

"Her boyfriend," he said without blinking an eye.

"Name?" The older lady stared at him over the top of bright red readers, unrelenting. Andy faced him, amused that this lady wanted something Andy hadn't been able to extract the whole time she'd known him.

Andy smiled. Because her visit here was so totally unexpected, Christiaan couldn't fake his way in.

"Christiaan"—he shot a glance at Andy's smug expression—"Johnson," he said, breathing out.

"I'm sorry, but you're not on the family's visitor list. You'll have to wait here in the lobby."

Andy laughed to herself. Johnson wasn't his last name, but he knew he wasn't on the list anyway. Triumphantly, Andy waved to him as they beeped through the security doors. "I'll be back shortly, honey."

Grumbling, he sat on the orange vinyl chairs.

Andy's smile soon faded as she found the smell of cleaners revolting. It was unnaturally clean. With her own doctor escort, she passed nurses in the hall, carrying clipboards, the florescent lighting emphasizing the wrinkles in their brows.

They stopped at room 405. Andy wasn't sure what to expect. She wasn't even sure what Mrs. Vehemia wanted her to find out.

The doctor opened the door to a sparsely furnished room. Only a bed, a small table, and a chair. A small square window high above them gave little light.

Scott sat in the corner. He was plainly not well. Since their last meeting, his face was paler, his hair grew longer. Dark stains circled his eyes. Still, he had a charming smile.

"Amanda," he slurred. Andy was glad he remembered her. "You're here. Carla said you would come."

"Of course, Scott. You and your family are dear friends."

He extended his hand to her. Andy almost gasped.

Three of his fingers were scarred bright pink nubs, shortened at the blunted knuckles. Only his thumb and forefinger remained whole. Andy could only stare.

When he saw Andy's horror, he retracted his hand, the smile leaving his face.

"How are you?" she asked, keeping her voice low.

"School is hell," he stared at the wall near him.

"What happened?"

He shook his head, his hair in greasy spikes flailing around.

"Carla told me you got into trouble. Can you tell me about it?"

"I miss my car."

Andy wasn't sure if he was cognizant, or if he heard her. She approached the bed and slid her hand over his. She allowed him to talk. His eyes rolled in his sunken sockets.

"It was a nice car. My father bought it for me." He spoke with a slur, like he had been sedated. "A McLaren F1. GT. My father bought it for me."

"Uh, huh."

"I used to go for long drives in my car. As a way to de-stress from school."

"Was school stressful then?"

He faced her, gazing from his sunken eyes. "I don't feel well." He leaned a shoulder against the wall. Andy's pity was stirred.

"What can I do for you?"

His eyes started drooping. Andy wasn't sure if she should wake him up. With his neck angled awkwardly over his shoulder, he started to snore. She'd sacrificed so much time to come and talk to him. Letting go of his hand, she dropped hers in her lap and sat back in the chair.

"Now what?" she said aloud. Shaking her head, she glanced around, about ready to leave when she noticed his bedside table filled with pictures. Andy leaned in closer. Carla and her family were there, of course. Carla never had a bad hair day in her life. But another picture caught her eye. Scott and another man, an older man. He looked familiar. Andy picked up the photo. Her eyes didn't deceive her. It was Dr. Armstrong. She recognized him from her Internet searches. The frame slipped from her hand, knocking two cups of meds over. Four little white pills scattered on the floor.

The noise woke Scott who frowned at Andy. The glass only cracked slightly, but the frame was dented. She scooped it up along with the meds. Not knowing which ones went in which cup, she just dumped them together.

"I think I broke it," she said holding up the dented frame.

With eyes wild, he glanced from her to the frame. He tried to grab it from her, but he couldn't wrap his fingers around it. "Go."

Andy wasn't sure what he said, for it was said in such a whisper. Surely, he didn't want her to go, she just got there.

She stepped closer. "Go!" he yelled, almost rabid, sinking farther into his bed. His timbre and forcefulness shook Andy, her heart lunging. Trembling, she placed the broken picture on the nightstand. Scott sobbed repeatedly before the doctor let her out.

"Perhaps it's best," the doctor said. "It's time for his medication, anyway."

Andy, still shaking from her experience, forgot to

ditch Christiaan to call Juan Martinez. In the lobby, she broke down in tears, causing him to wrap his arms around her and take her to the nearest cafe to calm down.

"What did Mrs. Vehemia tell you?" Christiaan had just handed her a cup of hot chocolate. "Careful it's hot."

"Thank you." Andy let him slide next to her in the booth, taking a drink of the dark, creamy liquid chocolate. It made her insides warm. "I don't know if I'm supposed to tell you. Carla said it was a great secret."

"Let's pretend like I can keep secrets."

Andy snorted. "Yeah, I guess if anybody asks, you've got a string of fantastic lies you could tell them." Andy held the chocolate in her hands and breathed in the steam the cocoa produced, her mind still harrowed from the memory of Scott's shouts, his empty hand. "Okay, but you can't tell anyone, not even the people you work for. This has nothing to do with whatever you're investigating." When he nodded consent, she started. "Scott, Carla's brother, is finishing up his undergrad. He had begun a few of his graduate-level courses for his MBA since his junior year."

Christiaan sipped his cocoa, his gaze rooted on her. "Go on."

"Well, here's where it gets kind of crazy." Andy paused, uncomfortable even with the memory of the conversation. "He was accused of doing some very bizarre things."

"Elaborate."

"Well, during his late-night studies, of which he had many, I'm sure since I know Scott, he's totally studious…"

Christiaan's eyebrows arched in a tease. "Oh? You know Scott well."

Andy ignored the jibe, her mind still fresh of visions of Scott's sunken eyes. "He's studious and brilliant. He wants to do well so he can take over his dad's business when he's done with school."

"Not your typical frat boy."

"Not at all. He was his parents' Golden Boy. I think that's why Carla rebels a bit. He was always doing the right thing and Carla wanted to be different."

"Makes sense. So, while he's studying…"

"Yeah, while he's studying, it was like he tossed his cookies."

"Eh?"

"He went crazy."

"Define crazy."

"Attacking people in the dorms."

"Not crazy. Violent," he clarified. "I know lots of violent people. I work with them every day."

"No but, he…" Andy set down her hot chocolate for it no longer had taste to her. "He ate them."

Andy was glad he flinched a little bit. Only a flicker at the corner of his eyes. She was beginning to wonder if he had any sort of feeling. "Ate them?"

"He bit off chunks of flesh from their bones. While they were conscious."

"Did he kill them?"

"No. He just ate off bits of flesh."

"Interesting." Christian sat back. "What did the police say?"

"Well, they think Scott was doing some sort of drugs, like bath salts."

"Of course, erratic behavior, violence."

"Forensics ran a urine test but they didn't find anything in his system."

"They wouldn't. Bath salt recipes change all the time. There isn't anything traceable to find."

Andy loved having these conversations with someone who understood, who solved and thought. Maybe working in a two-some wasn't so bad.

"What's the verdict?" he asked.

"He's awaiting trial."

"What's the defense?"

"His lawyers are saying he was crazy, asking the court for him to be evaluated by an independent psychologist. They are thinking maybe he flipped over the stress."

"How did the family react?"

"Carla says when the lawyers advised him to plead insanity, her father totally blew up. He's groomed Scott to take his place in his business. Until now, they've managed to keep it quiet, but money can only hush things up for so long. If you're wondering why the media hasn't had a heyday with this, it's because Carla's dad donates a lot of money to the campus, his *alma mater*, and they don't want to him to retract his money. He donates millions of dollars to their chemistry department."

A grim silence passed between them. "There's one more thing I need to do in Boston," Andy said, fingering the brim of her mug. "Something I need to do alone." Andy had found an address for Dr. Armstrong. She wanted to talk to his wife, a relative, someone.

Christiaan eyed her suspiciously.

Maybe it was the firmness in her voice, the

resolution in her eyes, but Christiaan met them, nodded. "I'll take you as far as you want."

****

Christiaan drove a rental to the outskirts of Boston, searching for an address. He parked at the curb of a tall building, an apartment.

"You know which number?"

"Three-forty." Andy tucked something into her bag and stepped out. She probably thought Christiaan didn't catch it, but he did. A note.

Andy searched along the buzzers on the plate fixed into the cement just outside the glass front doors. Her silken hair flew in her face with the breeze. She swooped it out of the wind to read the nameplates. Bending for a closer look, she threw her bag across her shoulder, then buzzed one of the buttons.

He sat back in driver's seat, focusing through the windshield. Probably another one of Andy's boyfriends.

What did he care? After this assignment, they'd never be together again. He needed to get his head in the game. He'd only just managed to convince the boss to let him come to find out what was on the yellow sticky. Maybe it was nothing. Maybe Andy was playing them all to be fools. No. She couldn't be that tricky.

Christiaan peeked at her, tapping her feet against the stone stairs and suddenly wished his life was his own, to be free to love who he wanted, to live where he wanted, to anticipate to the future. Christiaan scanned the street for the zillionth time, soaking in every detail of the brownstones, probing the windows, his gaze sweeping the rooftops. Would he ever be able to just relax and enjoy the moment?

Movement caught his attention. His gaze flickered

to the rearview mirror. A car was coming down the street awfully fast. A window rolled down. Christiaan caught a glimpse of a gun barrel.

Christiaan's instincts kicked in. He rolled down the window.

"Andy." She glanced his way before he slid himself down into the foot well, his hands on the keys.

Christiaan held his breath his muscles tense.

Nothing happened.

The car passed.

Andy approached the open window. "What were you doing?"

Christiaan straightened up and gazed after the car. It was only an umbrella poking out of the passenger side window. Someone was pointing with it.

"I thought…" Maybe he'd been doing this too long. Everyone was an enemy. "Never mind."

Andy opened the door and slid across the seat.

Christiaan was a bit relieved. "Where to?"

"I don't know, I'm emotionally drained. Dead ends at every turn."

"I know just what you need."

He slid his hand over her back as if to emphasize his point, tenderly working a few muscles between her shoulder blades. He hoped Andy would melt under his strong persuasion. She was withholding information. And it was his job to get it.

****

Andy collapsed on her bed, ready for a hot shower. Christiaan stood back aloof.

Physically, emotionally the last few days had been killer. "I'm going to take a nice hot bath. I think I need some Epsom salts." Andy raised up on her elbows.

"Thanks for coming. I'm actually really glad you were here with me tonight."

Finally, Christiaan gazed up at her. "Take off your clothes."

"What?" she sat up.

"I mean, go take your bath. Wrap yourself in the bathrobe, backward. Leave your back exposed."

When Andy, in the hotel bathrobe, exited the steam-filled bathroom, Christiaan was kneeling on the bed, shirtless, a bottle of wine and several glasses on a tray near his knee. Only the cotton balls and lighter didn't make sense. Andy eyed his toned shoulders and arms.

"Lie down on your front," he said.

"Are you going to tell me what you are doing?" The backward robe was awkward. Andy pinned it closed behind her with a hand. Eying the wine, she hesitated before she hiked up the bathrobe to climb on the bed. "I don't drink on the job."

The last thing she wanted was to be too loose and friendly with Christiaan while only wearing a bathrobe.

"I think you misunderstand. We're not going to drink the alcohol."

"Oh?"

"I'm going to help you relax."

"How?"

"*Zhēnjiǔ hé báguàn, chāoguò yībàn zhìyù de bìbìng.*"

"Say what?"

He picked up each cup, rubbing the rims with lotion. "An old Chinese proverb, 'Acupuncture and cupping, more than half of the ills cured.' "

Andy was glad he didn't ask for her sewing

needles, although she did have some in her bag. Acupuncture wasn't something she wanted to try in a hotel room. "Lie."

"I don't lie, how 'bout you?"

He smirked. "On your front."

Gingerly, she lay on her front on the bedspread, the robe opening slightly, tickling the sides of her breasts. His warm hands opened the robe, exposing all of her back.

He warmed lotion in his hands then spread it on her back in long forceful strokes. Andy's skin prickled with goosebumps. She couldn't remember when she'd been touched by a man in such a healing way.

With her head tilted to the side, she watched him expertly wipe the glass with wine and light cotton balls on fire inside before setting them on her back.

"Woah, fire," she said, raising her head. He was probably violating some fire code.

"Shh. Relax." He soothed her head back down. "Traditionally this is done with horn or bamboo."

A warm sensation filled her back, painful in a weird sort of way, but wonderfully calming as well. Soon serene warmth replaced the ache in her back.

"Where did you learn this?" she asked.

"China."

"Right, I don't know why I bother to ask you anything."

"Andy, when are you going to trust me?" He sounded so hurt, so saddened, Andy's heart ached, almost as much as her back. She yearned to trust him, despising the suspicion, the lies between them.

He replaced the burning cups on her back. As each cup cooled, the muscle bubbled into a deep tissue massage, a mixed sensation of pleasure and pain. He continued until he had covered all of her back, releasing stress and tension.

When he finished cupping, he massaged her back in strong strokes. "The massage will help with the blood flow so the bruising will heal faster."

"Bruising?"

"The cupping leaves bruises, like hickeys."

"Won't be the first time I've had a hickey on my back," she muttered under her breath.

His fingers glided strong across her back, skin against skin. He leaned to whisper in her ear. "You are really tense."

Goosebumps attacked her skin, her senses alerted. Andy controlled her breathing, her body trembling. Each stroke aroused her senses. His fingers worked through the tension in her shoulders, easing down the sides of her back, dangerously near her breasts.

"The stress has been too much."

Christiaan worked in silence, allowing her to talk.

"Brad. And Conner, then Jack. Mr. Hershal. And Scott. I'm not sure which is the most haunting."

Christiaan murmured something.

"I thought I was strong, that I could handle it all, but I am falling apart, Christiaan."

Christiaan leaned over her. His lips brushed the nape of her neck, his warm breath tickling her skin. She closed her eyes against the sensation, quivering.

"Let me take this burden from you," he murmured close enough for his lips to touch her lobe.

Andy tingled, her breath quickening. His hands continued to smooth her back, another kiss, farther down her neck, then her shoulders. Andy swallowed, struggling to maintain her control.

His hand slid near her breast as he easily flipped her over, the robe falling loosely across her chest. He held her under her neck on top of his knees. She basked in his gaze as he stared down at her. His eyes glowed.

As he brought her close to him, she slid an arm around his neck, crushing herself against him. His lips brush hers; he closed his eyes taking the smallest kiss on her upper lip. Then kissed her again, sending chills to her every extremity.

Some part of her wanted to give Christiaan everything. Let him examine all of her. His hands continued to stoke her back. His breath intensified with each kiss.

"What was on the yellow sticky?" he asked. He held her lips against his.

Lips pulsing, hungering for more, Andy knelt, her robe slid, exposing her shoulders, their legs intertwined. His hands caressed her neck, her exposed shoulders. Andy half hoped the robe would fall.

"A name," she said, sliding her fingers through his hair before kissing him again. "He called me."

"Number?" One hand held her against him, while the other leaned back.

Andy leaned back with him, her mouth never leaving his. "On my phone."

He broke from kissing long enough to say, "Good." Then letting her rest on top of him, massaged her back again, holding her into him. "Name?"

"Juan Martinez."

His fingers continued up her back, still kissing, then stroked her neck, firmly at first.

Then his fingers held her neck. Then nothing.

Chapter Twelve

Smoke rose from the tables clouding the room in a veritable haze. The music was loud, but the man entering the lounge liked it loud.

His white linen suit pants and large floral shirt almost allowed him to blend in with the other cruisers. It fit his rather large physique. His arms were tanned from the last week in the sweltering open water. This was the first time he ventured into the theatre to make a connection with his mark.

A seating host approached him. "Do you need a table, sir?"

"For one, please."

"This way." The man pointed to rows of seats with small tables.

Christiaan sat at a table in the audience.

His mind flicked back to Andy. Regret was not an emotion he was often familiar with, but for some reason, he had a soft spot for her. The sleeping grip wasn't his first choice, just the most convenient.

Christiaan imagined her waking after a ten hour rest the grip induces, disoriented, alone. She'd understand. He had to do it. He probably saved her life. This was no place for an amateur. She served her purpose back in the States. He left her money, her bag. Hopefully, she was smart enough to just take herself out of the game, go somewhere and start again, free from

Tyrone and his gang. Free from him.

They were getting close. Too close. He didn't want to admit to himself just how close he'd come to her. The memory of her kisses played on his lips, his biggest regret.

He picked up a fork and tapped the handle on the table thoughtfully. There were a few minutes before the show began, he could unwind.

Maybe if they weren't working on a case, if they'd just met as strangers somewhere at an ice rink. He'd ask for her number. They would've flirted a bit.

Of course, if she was just a normal person, he probably wouldn't have found her so attractive. They understood one another, and that scared him. And for some reason, a reason he could not fathom, she trusted him. He craved her trust.

Wanting her was dangerous. She was dangerous to him, and she jeopardized his career. Their closeness jeopardized everything he'd worked for the last few years. He couldn't throw it all away.

He clenched his jaw, staring at the fork, which he was pounding mercilessly into the table, leaving divots in the wood. It could never be. No matter how much he wanted her. Work came first. It always came first. Whenever he got close to someone, bad things happened.

What was Andy doing now, he wondered. She was mad at him, of course. Oh well, she'd never find out who he really was anyway. And he'd go his way, and they'd never to meet again. An unfamiliar feeling crept in his heart. He didn't take time to label it, shoving it away.

The music grew louder, the lights illuminated the

stage. This was what he needed. A new task.

In Boston, he'd stolen Andy's phone. Still, a week later, Juan hadn't answered any of his phone calls. He finally asked for a call tracer from his connections. Though they couldn't find a name directly, they found it belonged to Mexico City. Too many people lived in Mexico City. He had to try a different angle: social media. At last he found a girl who might know him. A girl Christiaan planned to get acquainted with after this show. Totally routine job, get in, get information, get out.

Curtains parted. Semi-clothed ladies danced in sequined outfits, feathers in their head pieces fluttering with each step, accentuating the movement. Christiaan searched among the dancers hoping to catch the eye of a young dark-haired girl—his mark.

The girls marched downstage, parting in the middle and forming a line across the stage, moving in time with the music.

Christiaan scanned the dancers, searching for her. He did a double take. He caught his breath.

Then his jaw dropped. A blonde smiled down on him, shimming her shoulders to the salsa tune. His surprise only lasted a split second. Then he smiled back at her, warmth rushing all through him.

Andy Baker.

****

Andy ran off stage, hot and sweaty, yet gleeful in her heart. Triumph! Christiaan's surprised expression was worth every price she paid to be here first.

After a small breather, she rushed back on stage, adrenaline coursing through her. She refused to make eye contact with him during the second number, only scanning the crowded room over his head, teasing him. He wasn't there for her, anyway. He wanted the dark headed girl who danced to her left.

Without meeting his gaze, she knew he watched her. His disbelieving stare gave her even more energy. Into every little hip wiggle, every dip, every cha-cha, she gave something a little special.

Music crescendoed. The finale, big finish. Pose. Wait for the lights to dim, curtain fall. Rush backstage.

The cramped dressing rooms smelled of alcohol, stale smoke, pungent stench of body odor, and cheap perfume. Fresh air was a luxury one didn't enjoy down here. After living below decks like chattel, Andy decided her dream of going on a romantic cruise someday was ruined.

Andy removed her sequenced costume, listening to the conversation.

"Did you notice the man out there smiling at me?" bubbled an attractive petite Latina, tugging on her fishnet stockings, then moving her palms over her calves to straighten the lines. "The tall one, in front. He couldn't keep his eyes off me. Which one of you has his table tonight?"

When dancers weren't rehearsing or producing a show, they waited tables in the lounge area.

"You mean Gorgeous at table eight? I got it, Carmen," a taller girl with a sultry voice and a thick accent added.

"Trade me?" She put on a pouty face, her red lip protruding, her dark eyes pleading. "I want to meet him." Carmen patted her breasts, adding plastic bags to her bra, enlarging her cleavage.

"What's it worth to you?" the taller girl asked.

"Half my tips."

The taller woman nodded, and Carmen nearly squealed with delight.

Andy overheard the conversation while she affixed her pin-striped apron on the front of her mini-skirt. A flouncy thing with a perky petticoat underneath. Before exiting the dressing room, Andy adjusted the strap on her shoe, her face down. "Be wary of his back rubs."

Carmen paused at the door. "What?"

Andy straightened, smiling. "Nothing."

Carmen smiled quizzically and exited.

While the next show dazzled and amazed the audience, the hour grew later. More and more people drank more and more. Andy had the fortune to have the row of tables right behind table eight where Christiaan had chosen to sit to admire and make eyes at Carmen.

Carmen reciprocated his attention. After every order, she paused at his table, to linger and smile. Pouty lipped, voluptuous curves. She was cute.

Andy brushed behind him after Carmen left for a soda and scotch. A napkin fluttered behind Christiaan's chair, Andy bent to pick it up, whispering in his ear.

"Not quite as sophisticated as I imagined for you, but she might be your type. Half of her boobs are fake, by the way."

Christiaan leaned back in his chair, subtly tilting his head back. "How did you get here?"

"Ah-ah! A professional doesn't give away her secrets." And Andy fluttered off for a gin and tonic.

When she returned, Carmen was draped over his table, her white teeth contrasted against the dark stain of her lipstick, her legs on display. It must be so easy for him. Just smile at a girl, and she was a goner.

Maneuvering between the stadium seating tables was tricky. There was barely enough room for a person to pass through the aisle, much less room for a woman, a drink charger, and an extremely fluffy miniskirt. Andy used this to her full advantage. She bent over to give the man at table sixteen his drink, letting the ruffles of her skirt brush against Christiaan's neck. He leaned forward in his seat toward the petite brunette. Then Carmen was called away by another customer.

Andy glanced over her shoulder to Christiaan who swiveled, giving her a raised eyebrow, his face perched on his hands.

She didn't bother reacting. The costume accentuated her body, and she worked it to full advantage. She floated off with her charger in request of another patron. When she swept back, a piece of napkin fluttered to her. Andy caught the paper. It was almost too dark in the hall to read it, but she barely made out the words.

Back door five mins.

Andy crumpled it and stuffed it on her tray with other napkins and straw wrappers, and dumped it in the bar garbage.

"I'm going to take a breather," she told the bartender. She left the charger at the table and headed toward the back door. Before she could get there, someone grabbed her out of the darkness.

Christiaan held her close. He smelled of fresh air. His strength surrounded her. "Meet me on the back deck." Then his arms released her, and he was out the door.

Hitched up in five inch heels, Andy's feet were killing her. She exited and climbed the swaying metal stairs to the main deck. She wasn't sure if she was allowed up there and wished she'd had a change of clothing so her costume wouldn't give her away.

It was the first time she'd breathed fresh air the whole week she'd been on the boat. And she drank it in. Compared to the noise of the lounge, the deck was quiet. The dome sky was full of stars.

Her heels made a clacking on the wooden decking as she headed stern-ward. Christiaan faced her and smiled. If she had just met him or if they had just been friends, her heart might have made a little leap when they met. But she wasn't sure what was going on. She wanted to trust him. In her heart, deep in her heart, she hoped she could trust him, but he kept estranging her with lies. She flushed from anger.

When she got close, he unhitched his arm from the railing. He glanced at her name tag. "Amelia, eh?"

"How dare you show up here and talk to me."

His smile broadened. "And I was going to comment on your costume."

"I don't trust anything you say." Andy tried to strike him, but he deflected it easily, catching her wrist. She broke his hold and landed a smack across his face. "You used me and left me there."

"I deserved that." Suddenly, he grew serious. "One day, I promise, I'll tell you the whole truth. I just can't right now."

"Why did you get rid of me?"

"Do you want another lie?"

"You knocked me out and stole my phone. I am furious."

"I know." Christiaan leaned close. "I'm sorry. I didn't want to. I had to. My boss would've called me off the case. I had to give them something. You're a tough nut to crack."

"Is that supposed to be a compliment?"

"So, how did you find her?"

Andy lifted her chin. "I've impressed you, haven't I?"

Christiaan avoided her gaze.

"I have!"

"Okay, maybe a little."

"Well, some secrets I must keep to myself."

He faced her. "Andy, I'm tired of playing games. Let's call a truce."

"A truce? You mean, you stop lying and manipulating me?"

"No, I mean, we work together so we don't lose the bigger fish. You flouncing all around me while I'm trying to work my mark is distracting."

"Distracting?" Andy reeled. So something was going on. She puffed out her chest in defiance.

"Distracting." Christiaan never said more than what he wanted to say.

"Okay, what do you suggest?"

"Why don't you tell me what you know, and I'll tell you what I know."

Andy couldn't help but be a little suspicious. "Hmm, okay fine."

"Promise?" He had some quirky expression on his face. Andy couldn't figure out what it was.

"Promise," she said, eyes squinting, not sure he was telling the truth.

"Pinky-swear?" Christiaan proffered a pinky. His eyes shone with secret delight.

Reservations sliding, Andy held out her hand. "Do

you say this to all your other secret agent partners?"

He leaned close, inches from her, and locked pinkies, staring into her eyes. "Oh no, this is much more intimate."

Hands locked, gazes locked. She was on a ship in the middle of the Pacific Ocean on a starry diamond night.

"Okay, you go first," Andy said, not completely trusting his promise.

"All right." He breathed deeply. "We don't know anything."

"What?"

"Now what do you know?"

"Wait a minute! You're sneaky. You don't know anything? I'm not telling you anything."

"You pinky-swore."

"Pinky-swore?" Andy stepped back. "You lied again."

"No, I told you I'd tell you what we know, which is nothing."

Andy spun on her heel, whirling on the wooden deck, her heels clacking in the varnish. "I know what happened, you hit a dead end and want to know what I got from Carmen. Am I right? Worried your charm will fail you? Your sparkling eyes won't cut it?"

"It's not fast enough. We are running out of time. My boss wants us to work together as a team now."

"A team?" Andy was pacing now. "A team trusts each member. And I don't trust you."

"Listen, we dock tomorrow morning. I need information from you or from Carmen."

"Carmen has been my friend for the last week, and she's told me a lot about her ex-boyfriend." Andy liked having the upper-hand. It made Christiaan powerless. Grasping. Desperate. "And you are just going to use her just like how you used me."

He grew in size as he puffed himself up next to her. "Do you think I was using you? Every day since I left you I have thought about you, replayed the last night in our hotel."

"I'd have to be a fool to believe you."

His voice lowered, softened. "I've wanted to make you care. Trust me, Andy, if there was a way I could love you how you needed to be loved, I would've done it already. There is just so much going on I can't tell you about."

"You only kiss me when you want information."

"I can get information from the girl in there. What I want from you is this." He kissed her on her head, lowering his voice to a whisper. "You have to know in your heart this is real, Andy. Let me in."

He wrapped his arms around her, drawing her close, hungrily pressing his lips into hers, nibbling at her cheeks, her chin, down her neck.

"Excuse me?" said a voice across the dimness.

Andy and Christiaan whirled. Carmen stood on the deck, her eyebrows drawn in confusion. Then glancing back and forth between them, her eyebrows gathered on her face. She spun on her heel and retreated.

"Great," Christiaan muttered under his breath as he chased after Carmen, catching her arm before descended down the stairs.

Andy couldn't understand what they were saying in Spanish. She should watch more Telemundo.

Whatever the conversation was, Carmen slapped him and left in a huff. He didn't even try to block it.

When Christiaan returned to her, he was visibly annoyed, rubbing his cheek. "We lost an asset."

"What did she say?"

His shoulders sagged, deflated. "She says your number's on."

Andy's heart lunged. Well, she was fired.

"That's not all," Christiaan continued.

Andy arched an eyebrow, questioning.

"She called you a hussy."

"Not true."

"Okay, you're right. She called you something worse than a hussy. But to make you feel better, she called me a few choice words about me being a player."

Andy nodded in agreement. "That is true."

He glanced sideways at her, then slid down the wall, sitting on the floor. "And she said we're through." Andy gloated a bit. He glanced up at her through his hands covering his face. "Don't be too pleased."

But Andy still kept her smug expression.

"You're still pleased with yourself."

She joined him on the floor. "But you said yourself, we don't need Carmen anymore. I already got the information we needed."

"You said 'we.' "

"Oh, I guess I did."

"So are we a team?"

"You better kiss me some more."

Moving to kneeling, he tenderly kissed her upper lip, then kissed her shoulders. His hands graced her thighs, as he leaned her back onto the chaise. Her hands found his neck, drawing him closer. His hands crossed the bare shoulders of her costume, caressing the skin above her collar bone.

Finally, all barriers down, alone in the Pacific Ocean, Andy could let her heart be free. With all the intensity of her pent-up passion, she hungered for his breath, the poofiness of the skirt a barrier.

"Hey, get a room," a man yelled across the deck.

Breaking from the embrace, Andy's whole body pulsed. "Do you have a room?"

Christiaan's eyes lit up.

****

Christiaan guided her to his room. "It was better we stopped," he whispered as he nuzzled into her neck. Andy nodded, her body radiating pleasure.

He opened the door to a spacious room colored in pastels and grays. A balcony faced her. On the wall to the right a large screen TV, a softly patterned couch, a bouquet of flowers overflowing on a bureau, and romantic lighting.

"You can freshen up in there," he said pointing to the small bathroom. Andy barely had enough time to return to her room and grab her bag and clothes where Carmen had dumped them outside their room before coming here.

In the bathroom, she changed into her pajamas—micro shorts and a tank top. When she entered the room, only the half-light of the moon shone through the thin balcony sheers.

Christiaan, standing at the edge of the couch, had stripped down to his white undershirt, the definition of his triceps and biceps bulging from the sleeves. Andy swallowed hard.

"Tomorrow we can plan about where to go to find Juan Martinez," he said, staring at her, as she crawled on the king-sized bed. Desire crackled in the air.

"Yup."

Andy shivered under his intense stare, every sense awakened. She knelt there on the bed. He dropped his shirt.

"I made some phone calls. I think I know where Martinez lives." He sauntered to the foot of the bed.

"That'll make it easier." Andy's heartbeat strangled her breath. Her exaggerated breathing loud in the stillness. She slowed it down by closing her eyes and focusing on her breath, like in meditation. With a rustle, she opened her eyes. He stood near her, and stroked a strand of hair out of her face. Her breath blew out low and slow. He bent and kissed her collar bone, her neck, the jaw line. Andy's body flushed.

"I wasn't lying when I said I couldn't go all the way," he said, sliding a strap off her shoulder, kissing the whiteness. Christiaan was sending intensely mixed messages. Andy held him close, her lips parted, he rubbed his cheek against hers.

"Why not?" she asked through quickened breath.

"Excellent question."

A shrill sound pierced the air.

Andy leapt up as Christiaan threw himself into action. He flew to the door, opening it a crack to peek into the hall. Passengers pooled there.

Andy threw on her pants and a shirt. "What's going on?"

"Fire alarm." He shut the door. "How have you been paying for things?"

Andy panicked. "Credit card."

His face contorted. "Amateur. If Tyrone does have the FBI on his payroll, we're screwed. You need a ghost account." He grabbed her hand and hauled her to the window, but not before she plucked up her bag and slung it over her shoulder. Christiaan glared at the bag.

"What?" she asked, breaking from his hand. "It's got my passport. And my stuff. Trust me, you'll be glad I have it."

He smirked, pulling back the curtains to the balcony window. "Were you planning on using your passport once we dock?"

Frowning, Andy bit her lip. "It's the only one I have."

"We'll have to change that, too."

Andy halted before the window to the balcony. "Are you saying someone is after me?"

"Me or you. But I don't make mistakes." He unleashed the sashes.

"A fire alarm goes off and you assume the world is out to get you? How do you sleep at night?"

"Sleeping—another amateur mistake." Christiaan slipped out to the balcony and climbed onto the rail to his escape route. "I booked this room because it has at least two exits."

"Why would they set fire to the whole boat?" Andy asked.

"Your innocence is endearing. I honestly can't remember being so green." He peered up the side of the boat. "The first night, I tied a rope with a rolling hitch to the railing in the upper deck." He yanked on the rope to test its security. "Diversion, distraction, and chaos are a hired gun's friend." He mounted the rope, hand-over-hand, leaving Andy staring up at him. "Start climbing!" he shouted over the wind.

Andy climbed up the rope after Christiaan, grateful her martial arts training helped her maintain upper-body strength.

"Why not just pick the lock and kill us?" Andy asked, the spray made her hands slip, making it difficult to retain a grip. Her hands ached. She grasped with her legs, but still slipped.

Christiaan called down. "It's sloppy. Too much media attention. You need chaos. Accidents are poetry."

"The rope?" she asked hand over painful hand, gaining on him. The wind tugged at her clothes.

"Tied it myself. As a secondary escape route."

"What if someone cut it?"

Christiaan climbed to the top. "We'd be going with the tertiary."

"What was the third one?" Andy asked as she followed him to the top.

"Down."

Hair blowing, Andy glanced down to the dark and cold spray churning around the boat nearly a hundred feet below.

"Open water?" Andy asked in disbelief. "We were going to take our chances on swimming in open water?"

"I didn't know you were going to be here. I was hoping I didn't get too desperate."

"Do you always do this?"

He was already taking in his surrounds. Lifeboats lashed to the sides, people flooding the passageways. Charging forward, he ran up the next flight of stairs. "Only if I think I might be followed."

Andy followed. "So, someone on the ship is hunting us?"

"For *you.* Most likely."

"We can't go back to our cabin?"

He motioned forward, and they rushed forward to the main deck. "Only if you want to wake up dead. Come on, we need to find a place to hide."

When Christiaan opened the door to the main deck, he stopped short. Passengers in pajamas, panicked, yelling, wearing life jackets packed the main deck. Smoke billowed from the bow of the boat.

A scene flashed in his eyes. Different time. Different place. People screaming, blood, smoke. He could taste vomit in his mouth, and fear. Everyone speaking Russian.

Christiaan shook the image from his head. Focus.

"I don't like crowds," he muttered, elbowing through shoulders of swaying passengers. He'd been in tighter situations before. Tumaco, Tripoli, Dakar. "Let's go."

They maneuvered through a crush of people. "Why don't you like crowds? It's easier to blend in," Andy said.

Christiaan's gaze flitted to each face.

"Easier for our hitmen, too." He shook fear from him, pressing through the crowd toward the stern, grasping the door to a covered gangway. Through the hallway, passengers shouldered Christiaan and Andy in their haste to reach the bow. Not the lady in her bathrobe. Not the balding man with a gut. Not the twenty-something with a hangover. His mind did a quick filter.

A familiar man in a suit. No fear in his eyes.

Alarmed, Christiaan's head followed him * as* he passed.

The man opened his coat pocket. And *on the* alert, anticipated the threat, swiveled grab* *him by* the neck. The hitman reacted fast by lashing out a front kick. Christiaan stepped back in surprise.

Andy spun, crashing the man against the Plexiglas windows, a nickel-plated Kimber with a suppressor clattered to the ground. Christiaan kicked it, a scraping sound echoing in the metallic gangway. The man rose attacking Christiaan by grabbing his back.

Christiaan, using the small confines of the gangway, thrust him against the steel walls, kicking him in the chest.

Picking him up by the collar, Christiaan questioned him. "Who sent you?"

The man stared through swollen eyes. "Why, hello, Wayne."

"Wayne?" Christiaan whispered the name he hadn't heard in a long time. Fear constricting his throat. They'd found him.

Christiaan slammed his knee into his head. The man fell backward, incapacitated from the blows.

"Let's go." Christiaan yanked Andy's arm.

"Who was he?"

"I can't say."

"Who is Wayne?"

Christiaan didn't answer.

"Was he one of Tyrone's men?"

As they approached the door, another man opened it. With adrenaline rushing, Christiaan instinctively grabbed his collar and pulled him between the door and frame, slamming the door on him, sending him reeling.

"What the—" the man said from the ground where he f̶ "Why'd you hit me?"

̶istiaan stepped over the man. "Sorry, thought you w̶ someone else."

Outside, fresh and cool air greeted them. They raced along the outdoor gangway.

"Are we safe now?" Andy asked.

"Can't be sure. There's always the law of redundancy."

"Huh?"

"Always send at least two people to get the job done. We're not safe until we're off the boat."

"Let's hide."

"Where?"

Andy motioned to the life boats. "In here."

"Too cliché. People hide there in the movies."

"A reason why he won't search here. He'll think we're smarter than scriptwriters."

Christiaan couldn't argue with her logic. He unbuttoned the tarpaulin and heaved her inside, careful not to attract attention.

A voice sounded over the speaker. "The emergency has been resolved. Thank you for your patience. You may all return to your cabins. The bar will be open..."

When he was sure no one was around, he jumped in, flipped the tarp over and buttoned it back on the locks as best he could from the inside.

The speaker continued. "...Anyone who needs to speak to a licensed professional about tonight's events, meet in the Emerald lounge."

A couple outside was talking.

"There was no fire. Just smoke bombs," the man said.

A woman replied, "They said the kitchen caught fire."

"But why all the smoke out here?"

Christiaan, still tense from the fight, waited until it

was quiet again. The thickness of the tarp made it hard to discern anything more than Andy's dark outline. It was hot. And stuffy. And cramped. He longed for fresh air. Christiaan didn't like being closed in. Reminded him of a tent in Sri Lanka.

In the quiet, his stomach growled. Andy dug around in her bag and retrieved something crinkly and placed it in his hand. A granola bar.

"Thanks," he uttered. He tore at the package and bit into the bar.

"When we get back, I'm going to order room service."

"It's not safe to go back. Until we dock, we'll have to spend the rest of the night here."

"What's left of it." Andy was seated at the bottom of the boat and laid her head back against the bench seat, her knees against her chest. Several minutes passed. She tried different positions.

"Here." Christiaan stretched his legs across the boat parallel to the benches. He motioned to his chest. "Come lay down here."

Andy pivoted her head to be next to his. "Place the bag behind you," she said. "I promise it's more comfortable than a bench to lean against."

"Thanks." He slid the bag behind him. "Okay, so the bag has its pluses. Now if only there was something in your bag to help us get off without being seen, that would be something."

"How did Tyrone find us?"

"He wasn't one of Tyrone's men."

"He wasn't? Then who was it?"

"My past catching up to me."

Chapter Thirteen

Christiaan woke up to a hot and bright tarp. And Andy was gone. Even her bag. Then, the tarp flipped back, and he was in the full sun. Christiaan jumped, blinking against the sudden light change.

"You must've been pretty tired," Andy said already dressed and refreshed.

"Where have you been?"

"I had to go pee. And I brought breakfast." Andy tossed him warm breakfast burritos.

Christiaan rubbed his eyes, opening a foil wrapped burrito, taking a bite.

"They're disembarking."

After finishing, Christiaan jumped up from the boat, following Andy down to the main deck. Passengers streamed off the gangplank, holding cameras, maps, sun hats. Despite the ocean breeze, it was hot. Andy had wrapped her bag in a shopping plastic bag, hiding its tell-tale color.

Andy and Christiaan followed the crowd. Christiaan continued to scan for any irregularities. A man in a floral shirt and hat caught his eye. "Notice the man in a short-sleeved shirt, open at the neck?"

Andy nodded.

Something was different about him. Christiaan continued to stare as he held the railing, descending the gangplank. His instincts told him something was off.

"He has a white neck," Andy said. "He's not a tourist."

Christiaan and Andy halted on the gangplank, allowing the elderly couple to go ahead of them. "Time for plan C."

"What's plan C?"

"Jump!"

He stood up on the railing.

Without hesitation, Andy followed him into the water. Bag and all. Gasps and shouts of the crowd sounded before the sea swallowed every other sound. Christiaan swam underwater until his lungs almost burst. When he broke the water, Andy was close behind.

Swimming to shore without being spotted left both out of breath. Andy hauled herself up the cement wall, water cascading around her, clothes hugging tight around her shapely body.

"What's next?" Christiaan asked her.

"Find Juan." Her bag had now been immersed in sea water, leaving its contents intact but soggy, only mildly protected by the bag. But she didn't have time for self-pity, police searched the cement bank. "Follow me."

****

Christiaan knocked on the door of the flat. From an open door above the stairwell a hot breeze blew in, and with it, a rancid smell. Chipped paint flakes dusted the floor like the dandruff on the shoulders of the kids playing in the streets. Their dark shirts, smudged, ill fitting. Yet they smiled. Reminded him of home.

Christiaan knocked again, a sharp, impatient rap. The breeze wafted in and out again, blowing in or taking away some smell he couldn't put his finger on, while Andy blocked the stench with her hand.

"What do we do?" she asked.

"Ask one of the neighbors, I guess."

"Let me try one more time," Andy said and pounded slightly harder. Timidity was never her strength. The door popped open a crack as it slid out of the lock.

"Real secure here, huh?" Christiaan said, opening the door. Timidity wasn't one of his strengths, either.

Andy entered the scarcely furnished room. A lamp with exposed wires clung to the unpainted brick. A soiled pillow sat in a corner under an open window. "I guess when you haven't got much, you don't have to protect it."

But when she closed the door, she found the inside covered with a smattering of locks, some of them brand new. "Or not."

Small noises rustled inside the room, movement or music maybe. Hope rose in her heart. Perhaps someone was home. The wind shifted, and Andy's nose caught a whiff of stench, like rotting meat.

In the kitchen, the linoleum floor was covered with a tar-like substance, pooling in the low spots, sludge oozing from the small dorm-sized refrigerator which hung slightly ajar. Christiaan called out Juan's name. Andy couldn't imagine anyone living in this apartment. Christiaan slid open the door to a bedroom. A rat, almost the size of a cat, ran from the room across her toes. She muffled her scream with her hands.

After a glance in the room, Christiaan recoiled, backing away from the door, his face contorted in disgust.

"What is it?" Andy asked, heart still beating from

the surprise rat. She attempted to squeeze past him, wondering what could repulse this man. But he stopped her with his hand.

"Don't go in there," Christiaan said.

Andy almost vomited from the fetid stench, the heat of the apartment making it unbearable.

Christiaan sighed. "I think it's Juan."

"No." Andy's throat roiled with acid. "The smell."

"The rats got to him."

Acid forced its way up. She ran to the window and hurled onto the muddied streets two stories below. Feeling better, she sat back. But Christiaan entered the room, and she caught sight of a foot, the heel gnawed to hamburger, bone exposed. She swiveled and dry heaved, holding on to the splintery wooden sash to keep her body from lurching out the window. Andy trembled.

She'd seen death before, but not like this. The indignity of human life haunted her. "Tyrone's men have been here," Christiaan called, his voice sounding tinny and far away in her ears.

Clammy, thirsty, a bitter taste of bile, she wiped her mouth on her sleeve. "How do you know?" She breathed the moist, but fresh air from outside, her heart still pounding, her body shaking, trying to erase the single image from her mind, quieting her body's reflexes.

"Drug cartels bust in, shoot the place up. These shots are close, accurate. In fact, they questioned him for information."

"How can you tell?"

"Shots in the back of the head, execution style."

"Did they get what they wanted?"

"That remains a mystery."

Stomach reeling, she clutched her head. She leaned against the stained wall, unable to stand. Chasing two-bit hoods, scamming con artists taking advantage of little old ladies was one thing, but this—

It comforted her to have Christiaan there, someone who spoke the language, understood guns, who wasn't afraid to inspect a rat-infested body. She couldn't think of it.

Christiaan washed his hands in the filthy bathroom, wiping them on his pant leg. They hurried out of the apartment and closed the door on the horror.

"We should call someone and have them bury the body," she said, once she was out in the hall. He wiped his face with his hand. She guessed what he was thinking.

"Dead end."

"Literally."

Just then, an older man exited his apartment, but when he spied the two *gringos*, his eyes widened with fright. He quickly retreated and closed the door.

Andy and Christiaan faced to each other. "He knows something," she said.

Christiaan pounded on the door. No answer. He continued to pound, likely to bust the door in. He shouted something in Spanish.

"What did you just say?" Andy asked when he stopped pounding.

"I just said, we know you're in there. We want to ask a few questions."

Andy snorted. "Yeah, that's a friendly way to get someone to open the door."

She noticed two shadows of feet under the door. She got an idea.

"Got paper?" she asked, eying him. Then realized how stupid her question was. "What am I thinking? Asking *you* for paper." She rummaged around in her bag, finding paper and a pen, uncapped it with her teeth and held the paper up against the door.

"What are you doing?"

Andy passed two years of high school Spanish. "How do you write, 'We are friends of Juan'? '*Amigos des Juan*,' right?"

Christiaan snatched the paper from her. "Give it to me. What do you want me to say?"

" 'Juan called us and wanted to talk with us. We think he is dead.' " The image of the heel flashed in her mind; she didn't want to write he was dead so she said, "No. 'In danger.' "

Christiaan eyed her. "What? Maybe he witnessed Tyrone's men come out. You remember the expression on his face? He knows something. He was afraid. Not afraid of the unknown, afraid because he knows something."

"I know people, okay. I understand them. If he saw something, he doesn't know who to tell. Don't tell him Juan is already dead. Local law enforcement is powerless in a case like this."

Christiaan arched an eyebrow. "All right, anything else?"

" 'We'd love to talk with you at the Cafe Rubio at one o'clock.' Maybe meeting someplace public will get him to come."

Christiaan continued to write. Andy envied his skills. To be fluent in Spanish. She should really branch out.

"Okay, done," he said.

"Fold it and tuck it under the door."

Christiaan stared at her intently, folding the paper, then crouched, sliding it under the door. The two shadows promptly left.

"Did he take the note?" Andy asked, hoping her scheme worked.

Christiaan knelt on the floor. "It's no longer on the floor." Andy was elated. Christiaan hopped up and dusted himself off. "But it doesn't mean he's going to come."

"We'll find out at one."

****

Christiaan tapped his finger on the table at Cafe Rubio.

"What time is it again?" Andy asked, leaning across the cafe table, moving into the shadow of the rundown building. Condensation fell from his glass onto the wrought iron table. The heat and humidity suffocated them. There was no air conditioning in the place, only fans, so they opted for the shade outside where at least the breeze could cool them.

Christiaan tapped his finger after glancing at the time. "One-fifteen. He's not going to come."

"He could be late."

No one spoke, the heat strangling the conversation.

"I like Mexico," Andy said at last, glancing at her surroundings. "A weird mix of old and new. Though it's scary there are bars on every window. And the roads need some upkeep. But it's pretty."

"I hate Mexico."

"Have you been before?"

"A few times."

Christiaan drank long from his cup. He'd had a

rough afternoon explaining to the local authorities why they should investigate Juan's body, how they stumbled upon it. He had a bad headache. He often did when he didn't know what was next. They were on their own. If he returned empty handed, he would have a lot of explaining to do. He hoped something would happen.

Despite the heat and the headache, he smiled at his companion. He sat across from her at the table, admiring her youthful ponytail, the humidity making the fine hair at the base of her neck and around her hairline curl into ringlets, framing her face. An impatient expression, almost like a child, crossed her face as she scanned the road. There was something about her. He wanted to protect her, keep her from knowing how terrible the real world was, hold her in her arms and keep her safe. He wanted her, everything deep within him wanted her, yet he had to refrain. If he could just tell her…

"*Hola.*" A man clutching a paper envelope cast a shadow across the table. Despite the heat, his shoulders were squeezed into a brown cardigan.

Andy's face lit up. Christiaan recognized him as the man from the apartment and asked him to sit down. Fear and suspicion still held the man's face. He didn't sit.

"You speak English, no?" They said yes. "Americans?"

"Yes," they both replied. Only Andy spoke the truth.

"How did you know Juan?" the man asked, his accent thick.

"He called my cell phone. I think he might have known a friend of mine, Conner Flannery."

The man nodded. "Andy Miller?"

Andy's eyebrows raised. "Yes."

"I've been expecting you." A grin of missing teeth finally played out on his face. "I have something for you, something I think will help you. Come, let us go somewhere more private so we can talk."

Christiaan leaned forward in disbelief, examining the small man with a brown cardigan even in the heat.

"As an old man, I have no muscle. I get chills. Even to the smalls of my toes."

Andy and Christiaan followed him to a field nearby. Christiaan told him about how they found Juan. The man nodded soberly.

"Do you know what happened to Juan?" Christiaan asked.

The man brushed the dry grass, his gaze and head low, speaking in English.

"I met Juan when he returned from his studies in the States. He fell ill, and always acted suspicious."

"Acted suspiciously? How?" Andy asked.

"He was suspicious of everything. Like a mouse."

Andy recoiled at the rodent allusion, her stomach roiling at the memory.

The man continued. "Like somebody was out to get him and wouldn't talk to anyone for several months. No visitors, no friends. But after a while, we confided in each other as we chatted on the balcony together. He was not well, dark circles under his eyes. I wanted him to confide in me, tell me what was bothering him. Everyone has a story, everyone has some deep burden, and what are we here for except to share those burdens?

"He worked in a physics lab in Boston. He told me something terrible happened to his professor, murdered, he thought, when he went home for holiday. When Juan returned to work, all the professor's documents, notes, and computer files were taken or destroyed. Juan had fled with this, which he'd taken with him to study on his vacation." The man, raised his head, with a tear in his eye, uncovered something he hid in his cardigan. "He gave it to me. I don't know what this is all about. But I know at least two men have died because of it. I have not opened this. He told me a man called him, an American named Conner Flannery, who had a girlfriend who would help."

He pressed the envelope into Andy's hand, her name and number were scrawled at the top. The man held his soft wrinkled hands in hers, pressing them against her chest, his eyes fervid with emotion. "Juan was my friend. He had a lot of potential. Don't let his death be in vain."

The little old man in long pants and a sweater, bowed and shuffled through the field, leaving a trail of bent grass.

Christiaan was the first to speak. "All right, let's open the envelope."

Andy unclasped the brass tabs and slid out the papers Conner died for.

Andy with Christiaan over her shoulder, standing in the blaze of the sun in central Mexico couldn't believe her eyes.

"A scientific paper?" Andy asked Christian.

Christiaan leaned close. "It's in German."

"Don't you speak German?"

"Fluently, but I can't understand all of what's written here. They are technical words."

Christiaan flipped through the charts.

"Why was this worth killing for?" Andy asked.

"I'll have to read it in depth."

Andy folded the papers, placing them carefully in the envelope, tucked them under her arm as they returned to the hotel.

Christiaan and Andy mounted the stairs to their hotel room, the wood creaking under their weight. Christiaan stopped at the top step. A slight breeze blew from their door left ajar at the end of the hall.

"Someone's been in our room," he said, turning toward Andy, ushering her down the stairs.

"You're not going to check?"

"Nope." He forced her out to the lobby and into the heat of the street, fear rising in his chest. Only someone trained could have found them. Christiaan used every caution in the book. They needed a safe house.

Christiaan scanned the road for anyone suspicious, seeing only a throng of people at the bar, bicycle rickshaw, two old men playing checkers in a store window front, a big beefy man with a mustache leaning against the crusted wall. Nothing out of the ordinary. "We have what we came for. We need to get home. I don't trust many people here."

"I think I know someone who can help," Andy said.

****

Andy and Christiaan pulled up and inspected the hangout.

"I don't like places where the bouncers are bigger than I am." From the driver's seat, Christiaan eyed the two men standing at the door, a velvet rope between them. Broad shoulders, deep chests, and large biceps. Big didn't mean skilled. Andy and Christian could still take the guards if they had to. Music poured from the black hole of the front door. Above the door in neon lights said, *PULSE*.

"Relax," Andy said. "José works security here. He can help us get home."

"How do you know this guy?"

Heat rose from her shirt. "We dated briefly. He's one of Scott's old bodyguards."

Christiaan eyed her with mistrust.

A valet waited to park their car, and Andy stood outside, letting the music seep into her soul. Tonight, she was a club-goer, the younger, hipper version of herself. Christiaan reluctantly agreed to come in costume as well. She faced him as he relinquished the keys to the car to the valet.

He exuded charisma in a tight shirt stretched over his pecs and a suit jacket. Dark-haired beauties in sleek miniskirts and jeweled tops smiled at him behind their boyfriends' backs as they strode up to the entrance. He was eating this up. Andy smoothed her own skirt against the stare of the first bouncer.

After announcing who they were, and who was expecting them, Andy dipped into a curtsey when the bouncer unhooked the velvet rope. She entered the renovated warehouse, feeling the music pulse against her heart.

Christiaan's lips brushed against her ear.

"I think those guys are checking you out." A group of men with drinks in their hands, lounging against the bar did little to hide their interest. "I'd better protect you." He slid his arm around Andy's waist and kept her there, tight, throwing the boys a possessive glance to stem the gawking. Andy smiled inwardly.

Andy searched the throng for José. She hadn't seen him in about eight months. The hulking Mexican leaned against the bar.

She easily recognized his huge build and friendly smile. He lit up when Andy approached. Andy loved his soft brown eyes.

"Andy." The muscular Mexican gave her a bear hug, enveloping her in smells of chile and salsa verde. And expensive cologne. "More beautiful than ever."

Andy flushed at the compliment while Christiaan soured.

"We shouldn't be here," Christiaan whispered in her ear, scanning the crowd.

Andy ignored him, addressing José. "You, too. I mean, you look great, too."

José smiled. "Who's your friend?"

"Sorry, this is Christiaan, my friend I told you about."

José gave him a scrutinizing glance. Christiaan gave him a curt nod.

"Pleasure to meet you," Christiaan said.

"The pleasure is all mine, I assure you." He glanced around, biting his lip. Then continued. "I have a work thing, really quick to do, then we can talk. If you'll excuse me." José nodded and left.

They listened to the music for a few songs until Christiaan leaned toward her. "What is his job here?"

"Head of security."

Christiaan fidgeted.

"Why are you so nervous?" He just gave her a doomed stare as José returned.

"Sorry about leaving. No more work, only play. Tell me, what brings you to Mexico?" he asked in heavily accented English which Andy found attractive. His arm slid around her waist as he drew her closer to the bar.

"Just touristing." She shrugged.

His gaze caught the lie. "Not much going on in this part of the city, *amiga*."

Andy held out her arms. "Well, this is fun! Thanks for inviting us." José nodded his head, smiling again. He ordered them drinks.

"So what's new?" Andy asked, glancing at Christiaan, who glared at José giving her such rapt attention.

"Just working my job. It's great to meet up with you, though." He sipped his drink, staring at her, his eyes bright and interested. "What's going on in St. Louis?"

Before she could respond, movement next to her caught her eye. A woman, clad with fewer than forty-two square inches of fabric, asked Christiaan to dance. He followed her out to the dance floor. Andy scowled, turning back to José, but always keeping an eye on Christiaan. "I'm sure you heard Scott's in trouble."

"I had heard, *amiga*," José said shaking his head, grabbing his drink with both hands, staring into it. "I never figured Scott could be so violent. He was always so friendly, nice. He'd never hurt no one."

Once Christiaan was out on the dance floor, the woman with luscious hips and long, thick hair wrapped her arms around Christiaan's neck. He caught her hand, then followed her arms down until his hands encircled her waist, holding her, with only a breath between them.

"I agree." Andy couldn't take her gaze off the

dancing couple.

José kicked back his drink. "But he had his faults, man, like anyone else. Stressed too much. Maybe he was drinking too much." Andy was only half listening. José noticed, following her gaze out to the dance floor. "It seems your friend has found Yolanda. Or Yolanda has found your friend."

Christiaan's nose was on Yolanda's, their foreheads touching. She wrapped a leg around him, her pelvis pitched against him. Starting with her knee, he stroked her leg up to her hip. She smiled as he whispered something in her ear. Andy had a weird sensation burn in her chest.

José continued, talking faster, the drink loosening him up. "I wasn't just his bodyguard, I was his driver and friend. I had some pretty heavy influence on him."

Andy wasn't even listening. Her heart pounded in her ears as the woman hooked her finger on Christiaan's waistband, drawing him closer.

"He always had the nicest cars. He had me put one of those converters on." He was a little proud. "Do you have one of those yet?"

The question upended her. "I don't have a car. What are the converters?"

The woman kissed Christiaan's neck. Then continued down his torso. Andy couldn't breathe. Like she'd been kicked in the stomach. What was worse, Christiaan enjoyed it.

"The CO2 converters? Everyone has one these days. Gets rid of emissions like magic, something an imbecile like me wouldn't know nothing about. Scott knew. He's smart like that."

Andy attempted to focus but the woman ran her

hands up Christiaan's thighs. José continued, a wide smile across his face. "Although, I'm smart too. I installed it for him when he couldn't. At first, they didn't have no installers in Boston, but I figured it out."

When the woman rolled up his shirt and ran his hands across his chest, Christiaan drew her in closer.

"Oh," Andy absently said, taking a drink. "Where did he get it?" she asked automatically.

"I don't know where he got the first one." José protruded his bottom lip in a frown. "Now they're everywhere, man, but here in Mexico, we put them on ourselves since the government picks who gets to put them on, you know. Too expensive." Then suddenly he asked, "You wanna dance?"

Christiaan scanned the room over Yolanda's head, his gaze absorbing every detail. His heart beating in time with the bass subwoofers. When the music slowed, they danced over to a single guy in a suit. Christiaan thanked his partner who reluctantly switched to the next man. Something wasn't right.

After ditching Yolanda, he found Andy dancing with José, and scowled. José lifted his fingers from where he held her firmly on her back and stroked her cheek, then delicately combed them through her hair. When Andy rested her head on his shoulder, Christiaan faced away, a weird feeling pinching his chest, and continued to scan the room.

He didn't like crowds. Hated them. He tugged at his jacket. It was hot. The heat in there weighed on him, smothering him. He shouldn't have let Andy convince him to come here. Too much time had passed.

Something was amiss.

A group of ladies passed, each giving Christiaan a

broad smile. Christiaan had his eye on something else. Two men stood in the corner by themselves. Nothing odd about them, he guessed. But Christiaan didn't like their scowls. They weren't there to dance. He recognized them. Manuel and Ricardo. Christiaan gulped. The Habanero Cartel.

Christiaan found Andy in raptures wrapped in José's arms and was only too pleased to interrupt. "We've gotta go."

Andy's smiling face fell to a pleading glance. "We just got here."

José whipped her around to face Christiaan. "I'd like to finish my dance with Andy," he said.

Christiaan gave José a hard stare, then headed for the door. Christiaan glanced over his shoulder. Andy gave José a hug goodbye. He searched the room for the men.

They were gone.

"Why were you so rude? And why are we leaving?" Andy asked when she caught up to him. "I didn't get a chance to ask him for help."

"He's not going to help us."

Now was not the time for self-doubt. Christiaan threaded through the haze of the fog-filled room. Once outside, Andy stopped him by tugging at his shoulder making him face her. "What is going on?"

"Always trust your gut," he said, glancing over her head. "And my gut told me to get out of there." The valet wasn't at the stand. Christiaan found the box and lifted his key.

"No, I mean what is going on with Yolanda."

"Our dance bothered you?"

"You were getting pretty friendly."

"Like you and José."

"We've known each other for years."

"Then I was just doing, what is it you do? I was just collecting a little DNA."

"More like donating some."

He couldn't focus on her right now. Instinct ruled as he searched for their car. The streets were lined with cars bumper to bumper along the narrow roads. Inconsistent lamplights cast changing shadows. He did three-sixty sweeps with his head.

Every shadow, someone was hiding, every alley way an attacker. He hoped he wasn't going crazy. His intuition was on alert. He glanced behind him. One of the men followed them.

He swiveled to alert Andy. Instead, she spoke first. "I see him," she said. "I spotted them at the club, too."

He smiled inwardly. So, she wasn't as into José as she pretended to be. "How do we shake him?" Andy asked.

But Christiaan, so concerned with the man behind them, didn't anticipate the man who jumped from the alley.

Chapter Fourteen

The man in the leather jacket stepped out of the alley and faced Christiaan.

"Johansson," the man said, his accent deep, stepping out of the shadows.

"Ricardo," Christiaan replied, stepping forward.

"You should've known better than to come back to Mexico, my friend." Ricardo opened his jacket, revealed a well-used Taurus, and pointed it at him. "*Abuelo* told you if you returned, you'd join your friend. *Adiós*," he said, aiming it at Christiaan's head. Manuel closed in from behind, gun at the ready.

Andy struck first, her reflexes released a front-kick to his gun-arm, sending his shot up to a building. Ricardo released the gun. Andy back-kicked Manuel's leg then disarmed him by catching his gun-hand swinging it behind him knocking him off balance.

Christiaan followed up with a joint-lock to Ricardo's arm and a kick to his leg, knocking his body on the ground. His shoulder joint cracked. Christiaan crushed him with another kick to the ribs. Manuel, temporarily shocked at Andy's offensive strike, paused two seconds before kicking her in the back, searching his jacket for another gun.

"I always keep a spare," he said.

Andy, reeled from the hit, but returned with a front kick to his face. Christiaan push-kicked his chest, sending him and the gun flying in opposite directions.

"I'll grab his gun," Andy said.

"No using guns, except my biceps."

Andy smirked. "I'll at least keep him from using it."

Christiaan nodded. Andy dropped the ammo from the Taurus, tossing the metal into the alleyway. Then they ran like hell.

****

With her back throbbing where Manuel kicked her, Andy halted down the street when they were both out of breath. She slipped off her heels and tossed them. Running in heels and a mini skirt wasn't very comfortable. Men had it so easy.

"I think your friend José ratted us out," Christiaan said as they jogged to a new hotel.

"No."

Christiaan shrugged. "Did he keep going on and on about nothing? Stalling tactics. Because no one else knew we were here."

"Who were those guys?" Andy asked.

Christiaan hesitated. "Habanero drug cartel."

"Why were they after you?"

Christiaan was silent for a few breaths. Andy didn't let up, still expecting an answer. A truthful answer.

"I might have busted up a few of their runs, sent a few of their guys to prison. Ricardo's father is in prison because of me."

Andy had more questions, but saved them until they checked in to their hotel. The hotel clerk, a looming man in black with a gold tag with "*Pablo*" written on it. He sneered under his thick mustache as he showed them to their room. They followed Pablo, behind his massive back and his long pony-tail, as he led them down the dimly lit corridor.

The Spanish-style room had leather high-backed chairs, wide windows with bars, and *one* bed.

"I hope you like sleeping on Saltillo tiles," she said, throwing herself onto the bed, staring up into the wooden beams above her. What a day.

She sat up, facing Christiaan. "Okay, so why were you busting up drug cartels?" she asked.

Christiaan checked the windows, secured the doors, and she was sure, planned a few escapes. "It's a job."

"A job? Filing paperwork and sending emails is a job. Busting up cartels is like military task force stuff."

Christiaan pointed his finger to his nose. "I'm going to shower."

Andy shook her head and fell back onto the bed. To keep from thinking about him undressing in the other room, Andy switched on the TV for company. Weather channel. Everything was in Celsius, but the prediction was going to be unusually hot. She flipped the channel.

Telemundo.

She couldn't understand what they were saying. But followed the plot for a while. A rouge, charismatic young man from the drug cartel saves a girl from the ugly guy taking her land. Bored, she flipped the channel. Soap opera, soap opera, more soap opera. Oh, American news. In English, even.

Only slightly less depressing.

Andy left the remote on the TV stand. Fetching her bag, she dug through coffee filters and bandages to grab the paper. While flipping through and studying the charts and schematics, she listened to the news with only half a brain until her ears caught a familiar name.

"Senator Granger has been instrumental in leading the Committee of Energy Efficiency in the approval of the law," a well-groomed lady told the camera. Then Senator Granger himself was in front of a bouquet of microphones. "The new emission conversion negates greenhouse gasses with no negative side effects, only fresh, pure air."

Next, it showed pictures of the new converter. Voice over: "These converters fit right onto your exhaust pipes turning emissions into earth-friendly vapors."

A representative of Vehemia Manufacturing spoke next on the screen. "It's amazing the technology our scientists are able to produce."

Andy stepped closer absorbed in a digital demonstration how the converters chemically changed the carbon monoxide into friendly gasses.

Andy held the paper up to the screen. The schematics in the paper and the ones on the news were an exact match. Andy dropped the paper and yelped, her gaze glued to the news.

A lady standing out front of the Jefferson Monument in DC. "The Elimination of Greenhouse Gasses law, nicknamed EGG, will federally mandate every car to install one."

The shot jumped to a friendly male anchor in a suit. "Remember, during the voluntary phase-in period IRS rewards citizens with tax credits until the complete adoption is complete in five years. Be sure to get your tax exemption now."

Andy flipped off the TV as the shower ended. Andy's heart pounded. They needed to get the paper back to the States and analyze it. If she only spoke German.

Christiaan appeared in the doorway, clutching a towel around his waist. Lights glistened off his rippling muscles in his chest and arms. The sight immediately forced everything else out of Andy's brain. She caught her breath and closed her eyes. But the image of his toned chest was still there.

"Forgot my bag." He leaned over to pick it up.

Andy peeked. "We've got to get back home," she said. "Now."

He cocked an eyebrow. "You don't feel safe here?"

Andy shook her head not daring to tell him what she learned. She still wasn't one-hundred percent sure she could trust him. "We need to go."

Christiaan nodded, returned to the bathroom, and in a few minutes appeared in the doorway fully dressed. "Let's go."

Andy packed her bag and then paced until Christiaan was ready.

They opened their door to the room.

Pablo, the hulking front clerk, filled the frame.

"I guess they found us," Christiaan said, seeing the menace on Pablo's face.

The Beretta strapped to the inside of Pablo's jacket was nearly invisible. But Christiaan anticipated him and with a swift calculated chop, knocked away Pablo's gun.

Christiaan landed a push-kick square in Pablo's large chest. Pablo didn't budge. He didn't even flinch. Christiaan raised his eyebrows in surprise, strategizing a new attack.

Andy, seeing Christiaan's failed attempt to knock

Pablo over, hit his knee sideways, knocking his kneecap, the sheer volume of his size sending him off balance. Christiaan hit Pablo on the back of the head as he doubled over to respond to his hurt knee, sending him to the floor.

"Follow me!" Christiaan shouted, stepping over Pablo's fallen body, bracing himself for the next attack as they ran down the ornately decorated hall. In the half-light of the wall sconces, two men wearing black ran toward them. Christiaan didn't falter. Running straight on, he clothes-lined one, then kicked the other with a side kick in the ribs.

Christiaan and Andy rounded the corner. Christiaan grabbed Andy's hand and led her over the bodies.

"Grab a gun," she said, but he ignored her, preferring to flee instead. "How are we going to get out of here?" Andy asked.

"Out a window," Christiaan said, running in a specific direction. But the window at the end of the hall was guarded by iron grates.

Using his might, Christian forced them open, ready to jump. Andy screamed as they jumped through the window. They fell like tumbleweed through rocks, cactus, and palm trees, until they rolled to the bottom of the hill. As evening fell, the temperature cooled.

"We need transportation," Andy said.

Christiaan glanced one last time back at the hotel now swarming with men in black leather jackets. "Everyone will be searching for us. The vengeance of the Habanero Cartel is thick."

In town, Andy checked the cars lining the road.

"For a country in poverty, they drive nice cars."

"What are you searching for?" Christiaan asked.

"Something older."

Then she spied the perfect car. An old, early eighties Mustang with a broken driver's side window. Andy slipped her hand in, popping open the car door, then knelt down under the steering column near the ripped leather seating on the pebble-ridden floor.

Christiaan blinked back surprise. "What? You know how to hot-wire a car?"

Andy waved her hand. "I'll have to bust the latching pins. They are sufficiently sun-rotted anyway." She searched through her bag, taking out a hammer and a flat-head screwdriver and banged.

"Can you hurry?" Christiaan asked, once she got the fragile plastic casing off, trying not to be impressed.

"I have to examine the wires. One false step and it could strip the shifting." Andy fumbled with colored wires, separating wires, then picking two.

"I think these are they."

"You think?"

"I don't have an owner's manual. You wanna search for this model?"

"No phone. What happens if you're wrong?"

Andy used her knife to splice off the plastic from the yellow wire. From her bag she fished electrical tape, cutting off a length. "Then you'll have a corpse *and* people after you,"

"Great," he said, not wanting that option.

"Here goes the test." Andy hit the two wires together, the dashboard lit up and the radio blasting the Beatles made Andy jump. "I'm not dead, at least."

"Isn't there a safer way to do this?"

"Yes, but I didn't pack my cordless drill."

A black Hummer rounded the corner just as the

ignition roared to life.

"Uh, are you done? They found us."

"Yes, just touch down on the gas when I touch these together or I'll have to start again." Andy wrapped the tape around the two, creating a solid connection while Christiaan, half-seated, slid his foot on the gas.

"Slide over, I'm driving."

"I got this," Andy said just as bullets sounded from the Hummer. Andy jumped to the passenger side, her legs over the console. Christiaan couldn't turn the steering wheel.

"Wrench it," she said. "You have to break the lock on the steering." Christiaan flexed his muscles until he popped the lock. He cranked the car onto the road, the Hummer close behind. Stepping on the gas made dirt and debris fly around with the open window.

"We're going to die," Andy shouted as shots rang out.

"Think positively," Christiaan yelled back, maneuvering through the dingy streets.

"Watch out!" Andy yelled as they turned a tight corner, narrowly missing a leaning stop sign and a stray dog. At the fifth tight turn, the Hummer wasn't in his rearview mirror. He relaxed a bit, still glancing behind him every once in a while.

"Where are we headed?" Andy called out.

"North," he yelled back. "Do you have anything for this window?" Christiaan didn't like the dust blowing in his eyes.

Andy rolled her eyes and dug into her bag producing plastic.

"What's that?"

"Emergency rain poncho."

After crawling into the back seat, she taped it to the window, blocking out the wind, the dust and the sound. Then crawled back.

"You know, one thought keeps passing through my mind," Andy said.

"Do share." Christiaan continued to concentrate on his driving.

"It is a small world."

Christiaan didn't respond.

"Or you know a lot of people," Andy shouted.

"Or bad people find me."

"Could be it as well."

They drove north until the lights of the city faded behind them and the darkness enveloped the city and overcame them. The scenery changed to scrubby trees and small bushes but mostly dirt, and Christiaan kept glancing behind them.

Several kilometers before the city of Chihuahua, they ran out of gas. Pushing the car into town, they found a hotel on top of a small bar, trading the stolen vehicle for a night's stay and a meal.

"You are going to recompense the owner, right?" Andy asked.

"Andy this is the real world."

"But you have all this money and resources, you should be able to find him, right?"

Christiaan, too tired and hungry to care, rolled his eyes.

****

Andy entered the hotel with some trepidation. The hotel could've been held together with twine, as if it would blow over with the next hoodoo. Bars laced the windows, and wires and pipes sprouted like vines on the exterior of stucco and wood. It was as hot inside as it was outside and possibly stuffier. But the ramshackle hotel was at least a place to sleep.

"What stinks?" Andy asked, covering her nose as she followed him up a flight of narrow wooden stairs. The wall's patina of time, grime, and filth chest high on the whitewashed walls gave Andy the creeps. Her shoes stuck to the floor.

"Tequila," Christiaan replied. "And smoke, urine, and probably some vomit."

Christiaan opened the door to a dingy room, with a sagging twin in one corner and a questionable plaid love-seat in the other. A lamp teetered on a small nightstand near the bed. A sink and a toilet occupied a small water closet.

"Cheery," he said, as he peeked through the broken shade at the window. "But it's a place to sleep. We have no money to get out of here. No using your credit cards."

Andy frowned. "There has got to be another way. You can't connect with your 'friends?' Can't they get us out?"

"I told you, we're off the grid." Christiaan shook his head.

Andy hadn't seen him so defeated. "We'll come up with something."

He tossed her a smile. "You will, I'm sure." With some rearrangement of the pillows, he plopped down, slipping his hands behind his head. "I'm not feeling very confident at the moment."

Andy slid under her sheets, sniffing to determine if they were fresh. They didn't smell too vulgar. Christiaan settled on the loveseat to read the paper Juan died to protect.

****

Christiaan didn't know how long he was asleep. Maybe a minute. Maybe hours. Or maybe he hadn't slept at all. His dreams were too much like his realities—disorienting, confusing, and tense. He preferred to be awake anyway.

Christiaan worried. It didn't happen often, and it was a strange sensation. He usually had contingency plans for his contingency plans. Maybe because he was with an amateur, or with a girl, things were out of control. They were out of money, out of supplies, unless you counted Andy's bag, which was more helpful than he first gave her credit for. But his boss had no idea where they were so he had no extraction plan.

He had taken a risk. He hoped it paid off. They had the schematics. Not what they wanted, but surely one of the team members would be able to figure out what it was and how it connected to everything.

His gaze followed a spider crawling along the corner of the wall and the ceiling. Evil men were crawling the city for them. They stood out as foreigners. They'd have to be really careful if they wanted to get out alive. He wished he hadn't put Andy in so much danger.

His mind whirled, planning, strategizing. If the Habanero Cartel searched for a couple, maybe they should split up. If only he had the funds, he could send her alone, on an airplane. It was his duty to make sure Andy was safe. Especially her.

It must have been late, yet the bar underneath them was still going strong. Music pounded upward through the wooden floorboards. Cheers rang up. Tucking his pillow under his head, he flipped to his back. He wouldn't be getting any sleep any time soon. How could Andy sleep through all of this? He peeked at her bed.

She was gone.

Alarmed, he dressed and crept to the door. Opening it, music flooded in, like a wave of the night breeze sweeping through an open window. With only his undershirt and a pair of jeans, Christiaan wished he had more than his belt to take out any attackers. He smirked to himself, remembering the time he bested five former KGB turncoats on a train outside of Moscow with only his belt and his fists.

At the end of the darkened hallway, light glowed from the stairwell below. He descended toward the light and the music, entering the bar.

The smoke-filled room crowded with men smoking, cheering and clapping and laughing at…

Christiaan shouldered his way through the group of men, holding bills in their fists and shouting encouragement in Spanish.

In the center of the man-made ring was Andy, in her sports bra and shorts fighting a man in a sweaty brown shirt. She'd just tackled him down, winning the bout.

"Ho, hello there." Andy faced him, smiling a crooked smile as men threw cash at her feet. She waved a coy, little wave, then bent to pick up the cash.

"Who's next?" she asked. Her eyes were glassy, and she blinked a few times.

"What are you doing?" he asked.

She cupped her hand around her ear. "Can't hear. Music."

"Let's get you out of here," he shouted.

"I'm fighting." She scooped up more bills and stuffed them in her bra. A challenger wearing a Stetson stepped into the ring.

"I can see that." But he was powerless to stop it. The man in the Stetson believed he could take Andy down. Poor guy.

After blocking a few hits, she dropped the man with a side kick to the knee and a knee to the face. The men cheered again. But Christiaan was not amused these men were ogling Andy. And egging her on.

"Don't you want to know why?" she shouted over the music.

"Why?"

"For travel money."

"Not this way. How many have you already knocked out?"

"Twelve." Andy bent to retrieve her winnings, her balance a little wobbly. "I'm getting to be a sure bet."

"Martial arts aren't for prize fighting. This is disrespectful. Come on."

He grabbed her forearm, but even drunk, she easily broke his hold, staring at him with defiance. He should've known better. Everyone learns how to break a hold the first year of martial arts training. Staring her down, he plotted the next attack.

But she made a mistake. She faced away from him.

In a swift jump, he executed a rear choke hold. Not tight enough to make her pass out, just enough to gain control.

To his surprise, she stepped to the side. Sliding her leg behind him, she rolled back on the ground, breaking the hold.

This time he jumped up, seized her about the waist and lifted her off the floor.

"Ow, let go of me," she said as he hauled her through the men, kicking and jabbing. But Christiaan kept his grip firm. The men groaned as he carried her away. Christiaan wished he had a blanket to cover her up. They headed for the stairwell for a bit more privacy, a little less music. But before they could make it, a man with a large mustache caught him by the arm.

"*¿De dónde crees que vas?*"

"*La joven viene conmigo,*" Christiaan replied. He was taking Andy, and that was that.

The mustache cocked back his arm to strike Christiaan, but Christiaan dropped Andy and easily caught his opponent's arm, twisting it back to its owner. The man cried out in pain. When the others realized Christiaan and their prized fighter were leaving, they headed toward Christiaan in a drunken-zombie amble, eyes bloodshot, angry, arms ready to rip, punch and pull Christiaan apart.

"That's not how it's supposed to be played," Andy said, forgetting she didn't speak Spanish. "It's supposed to be a one-on-one game."

Suddenly tired, Andy leaned against the wall, droopy and dopey-eyed and lazily, sleepily as at least seventeen men clamored for more action as Christiaan cocked back his arm, knocking one down after another. How he had so much energy at four a.m., she'd never know. They were no match for him, of course. Most of them were drunk, unable to walk a straight line, much less hit anything. He was a highly trained killing machine. Not a fair match, really. Andy wished she could've taken bets but there were no idlers on the sidelines. They were all in the fray. He was clearing the room anyway.

She was as disconnected from the room as an old Western bar scene from a movie. At last, the scuffle ended, with Christiaan breathing hard, his hair flailing, his undershirt untucked and sweat soaked. A trickle of blood seeped from his lips where someone got a sucker punch in while he had two guys, one under each arm, in a strangle hold.

He faced her and said rather angrily, "Let's go."

"Are you going to chew me out because I'm an amateur? I don't want to hear it tonight."

"Why did you do it, Andy?" He pointed back to the pile of men on the floor groaning, clutching their heads, their stomachs, and their legs. "Someone could've seen you and reported you to the cartels."

"Because you said we needed money to get out of here. You said I couldn't use my card to get money from an ATM or use it to buy plane tickets. I was just helping out." The logic was so sound after a few drinks. It seemed so stupid now.

"It's okay, at least I have on my wig." Andy patted her head. Then shook it. "I guess it's gone. I wonder where it went."

Despite his own fatigue, he helped Andy up the stairs, the smell of tequila heavy on her. She missed a stair and landed on him, collapsing both of them to the wall. Christiaan held her up, bracing her with her arm around him, holding her close. "I was only trying to help."

"Yes, but not this way."

"I like my way." Now she was crying. "It's the only way I can help."

Christiaan's heart did a weird flip. It couldn't have been compassion. He had believed it was all drilled out of him.

"We'll think of something else." He kicked open the door to their room, shuffling her inside and laying her sideways on her bed. He tucked the covers around her.

"But I got quite a bit of money." She dug into her bra to show him wads of cash and jangled a purse of coins.

When he didn't take the proffered coins, she set them on the bed next to her. Instead, he chided her. "You should've been more careful. What if they ratted you out to the cartel? Then you'd be dead."

"What does it matter?" Her words slurred. She faced away from him, the mattress squeaking under her, coins spilling on the red Saltillo floor.

She shook her head. "I couldn't save Brad."

Christiaan cocked an eyebrow, trying to figure out what she was talking about. Then he realized.

"You're still upset. Over his death?" Her head slumped to her chest.

"I didn't save him. I could've stopped them if I hadn't been so scared. And Conner. If I hadn't been an investigative journalist, but something better, I would've been able to save Conner."

She was bawling now, her shoulders shaking under the covers. He wanted to pound Conner. If he wasn't dead, he'd would have killed him. Conner was a pansy for leaving an amazing, beautiful, yet feisty girl.

She sobbed until her shoulders shook. Christiaan drew nearer. This was what propelled her forward. Guilt.

"I told you this before. You did the right thing. If you'd tried to save Brad, you would have died. And for what? Nothing. Because of you, we have hope for justice. Sometimes the bravest action is none at all." His voice sounded more tender than he expected.

Andy paused in her crying, peering up at him. Even with her stringy hair streaming across her face, her nose and eyes red, she was still beautiful. And she had pure intent like a child.

"Will you tell me a story? From your childhood. Something true. No lies."

Christiaan's mind traveled far from their rented room to a land far away, very different from where they were sitting. His memories flooded his mind, the smell of the sewers running in the streets, the sounds of mangy dogs barking and people shouting obscenities from ramshackle houses, broken windows. He remembered the laundry lines blocking the sun, hanging from building to building like unofficial telephone wires in the government projects. He didn't want her in to the dark corners of his life. He didn't want to relive it.

He searched his feelings for something to endear him to her. A turmoil of emotions roiled inside, thoughts he'd never let himself think, feelings he'd ignored for so long. He closed his eyes, thinking back.

He is in a broken-down mansion. A long hallway of doors is in front of him. Each locked room hides a memory he's wanted to keep tucked away, to forget about. Andy is knocking on the door. She wants to come in. Christiaan feels so ashamed. He doesn't want to let her in. He opens the front door. She wants to explore everything. She wants to clean the room. The house is filthy, he realizes, seeing it as if for the first time. Cobwebs in corners, paint peeling, dirt on the wall. Dust bunnies in the corner. He panics. What if she sees the dark and evil part of him he doesn't want her to discover? Andy starts to open rooms. He flies across the room in a speed exceptional even for him. He closes the door. She tries another. He closes it. Andy asks, "Isn't there anything I can see?" He opens some rooms, but doesn't turn on the light. He feels clever he is sharing, but she can't really recognize anything, can't fix anything. Then there is a large room at the end of the hall. The door is very dark. Finally, he knows.

"Hey, wake up."

Christiaan opened his eyes, disoriented in the dimness of the room, the bed seedy, decrepit window, the shade dirty and torn. "I guess I fell asleep." He wiped his eyes.

"I thought you were going to tell me a story. But if you're too tired, it's fine."

"No," he said, wrapping his arm around her, completely weirded out at their closeness. "I just have to think of something not depressing. I was a scrappy kid, right? Orphan on the streets. Well, I had a friend named Blaine. He was a few years older than I was. He sheltered me under his wing. He told me I didn't have to be alone anymore." Christiaan didn't want to say how harrowing it was to be alone, but how horrific it was with the older boys forcing them to do despicable things. He didn't want to relive those dark days.

"Blaine and I eventually ran away. A master found us, trained us skills and introduced us to a different path."

So many years ago. And Blaine so different in

those first tender years of friendship.

He glanced over at her, she'd fallen asleep. He then gave way to his sleepiness, allowing himself one indulgence.

****

The next morning, Christiaan counted up the cash. Luckily, Andy made quite a bundle in her drunken fights the night before. Not enough for two flights home, but there might be other options.

Cash in hand, he paused before going out, assuring himself Andy was safely asleep. He tiptoed out in the early morning light in search of supplies.

When he returned, Andy was up, clutching her head. "Drink this," he said, tossing her a bottle of colorful liquid.

Andy read the label. "A sports drink?"

"You're dehydrated."

Andy opened the bottle, then sat up on her elbow to drink.

He paced, floorboards squeaking under his feet. "We need to figure out how to get home."

"You can't call your people and ask them to send us two passports with fake names on them?"

"No. They," he paused, exhaling, "don't know where I am."

"You're *really* off the grid?"

"*We're* off the grid," he corrected.

"You can't call them?"

"I don't have a secure line. We don't know who has ties to the Mexican cartels. Using anyone's phone here would prove dangerous for them and for us."

"So, what's next? How much money do we have?"

"Enough for one plane ticket. I am sending you

home. You can claim your passport was stolen, then go somewhere in the States, anywhere but St. Louis."

"I don't think so. I'm not leaving you here. And we're going back to St. Louis together until justice is served."

Christiaan was touched by her loyalty, her courage. "Okay. The other option is bus fare."

Christiaan set down a map he purchased earlier that morning for his own route home. She unfolded it and spread it over the table.

"How much is a bus ticket? How far can we get?"

"With what you made, we could get as far as Oijinga." He pointed to the map to a town not far from the border. "Then we can cross on foot if we pack enough supplies." He slid more sports drinks and bottled water into a satchel.

Andy sat all the way up, quite pleased with herself. "Admit it," she said. "My idea worked."

Christiaan packed while Andy gloated.

"Haha." She threw off the covers, tossing her legs out of bed and landing on her feet. "I got us out of here."

Christiaan frowned and followed her out of the room.

****

At the bus depot, swarms of people searched for them. A man distributed papers with copies of their pictures.

"Your friend José sold us out," Christiaan said, picking up one of the fliers. "A picture of us from his phone. Now what?"

Andy didn't skip a beat. "I need a haircut and dye job. And so do you. But you need something more.

Give me ten minutes and a couple of pesos."

Andy sifted through items in the small shops bordering the bus depot. Leather goods, hats, bolo ties, some maracas. Andy bought a silver necklace as part of her costume since she'd always wanted one, stifling her worries about getting thrown into a Mexican jail if they failed to cross safely. She'd gotten them this far, she could get them home.

Andy fingered the textiles, cotton shirts with floral patterns stitched into them, raw hide belts and bags, sequins-speckled sombreros, and blankets dyed bright colored, roughly woven. Andy got an idea. She purchased a few items, shoe polish, a purse, and some clothing. Andy paid a women, wrinkled from sun and a hard life, more than enough pesos. Andy smiled at her.

Outside, away from the sun and searching men, Andy's scissors cut away. First on the purse, then on her hair.

"Here." Andy found Christiaan waiting for her on a shady side of grocery store. She held out a fuzzy black strip. "A mustache."

He did a double-take. "Woah, your hair."

Andy stroked her coal-colored bob. "Do you like it?"

He held up the mustache. He pinched the patch, feeling the fibers with his fingers. "Is this real hair?"

"It *is* real hair," she said eying him from the side, feeling especially clever. "Just not human hair. I borrowed it from a cow."

"A real live cow?" He wasn't sure what grossed him out more, human hair or cow.

"She's dead now. She was a purse." Andy held up the snipped cowhide bag. "I just borrowed a corner.

Glue it on with this." Andy proffered super glue and squirted it on the back.

"This is going to hurt when it comes off," he said, plying the bit of cowhide to his upper lip, pressing his thumb and forefinger over the top to smooth it.

"Do we look different?" Andy asked, turning him toward the foggy not quite reflection of the glass windows. His hair darkened, closely shaved, dyed with shoe blacking, his skin darker from her bronzer, his clothes local, a white shirt with only small white flowers embroidered. She couldn't afford boots; hopefully no one would be scrutinizing his shoes, which were a dead give-away.

"Your eyes are still blue," Andy said. "Keep them down."

He smiled.

"Good enough," she said, biting her lip.

Andy's eyes, heavy with liner, stood out, her skin smoothed with makeup, darker, too. Her clothes were more vibrant, and she hoped she would blend in, not stick out.

They boarded the bus with no problem. Andy's heart raced as men searched different busses, questioning people. Christiaan did all the speaking as he settled his bag filled with water, food, and supplies under his seat. Andy made a mental note to study languages once she got home and things calmed down. Being fluent in another tongue would be so handy for disguises. She wondered why she didn't think of it before.

The bus lurched forward, grinding like a tractor, the gears scraping as the driver drove out of the bus depot, leaving a trail of dust and exhaust behind them.

Andy couldn't keep her heart from beating wildly.

Darkness fell. She welcomed the relief from the oppressive heat, as a cooler breeze drifted in from the open windows. Of course, they had to sit with the only stuck window. But at least the radiant heat no longer burned them through the panes. Everyone else passively traveled, the mother with her toddler on her lap, the old woman. Everyone had a serious contemplative expression.

Andy's body jostled at every pot hole, every change of gear. She wondered what would happen if she had to go pee in the next four hours.

The road ahead was dimly lit by the faint headlights. Too tired to think about how dangerous this was, Andy was almost asleep when she awoke to sirens and flashing lights shattering the darkness.

Chapter Fifteen

As the police boarded the bus, Christiaan listened attentively.

"*Buscamos dos americanos*," the *policía* told the bus driver.

With a dry throat, Christiaan waited, his gaze downcast like the other passengers on the bus. They were searching for them.

Christiaan weighed his options. If they could get away, and that was a pretty *strong* if, they were still miles from the border. Darkness could provide them some cover, but there was little vegetation and even fewer hills and places to hide. Just flat land of century plants and sage brush. He glanced out the window. The moon shined too bright. They wouldn't get far.

They would stay.

For now.

Without the wind blowing from the windows, the stationary bus grew hot. Christiaan smelled the sweat of his fellow passengers. He understood what it was like to live in a place where the government was corrupt, where people lived in fear. Bits and pieces of their conversation hung in the air.

The uniformed *policía* made their way along the seats. Andy stiffened beside him. He placed a hand on hers. Sweat streaked her makeup. But in the dim light, he prayed it would go unnoticed.

The *policía* brandished a flashlight, waving it on the passengers, between seats a few rows ahead of them. Andy held her bag on her lap. Imitation designer totes were pretty common in Mexico, but it was still ostentatious.

The *policía* neared them and stopped to examine them. Christiaan kept his head down.

"*¿A donde vas, señor?*"

Christiaan's heart beat, but he kept his gaze downward.

"Chihuahua," he said. His accent wasn't perfect.

The officer bent down, examining Christiaan. Christiaan closed his eyes and stilled his breath, but he breathed out in nervous tremors. In a violent motion, the *policía* tore off Christiaan's mustache.

Christiaan tensed. "Yeah, that hurt," he groaned under his breath, knocking the *policía*'s flashlight out of his hand with a chop. Holding it like a bludgeon, Christiaan smacked him in the face with it, knocking him back into a row of passengers.

"Now we have to go," Christiaan said to Andy. An officer thrust forward with a Kimber.

Andy stood on the seat. Using the luggage rack above their heads for an anchor, she kicked the gun from his hand, then slammed her foot into his face.

"Get the gun," she shouted.

Grabbing his wrist, Christiaan twisted the *policía* around, forcing his face into a vacant seat, stomping on his shoulder. Christiaan picked up the gun, tossing it out the window before bolting for the entrance.

Andy ran with him. "Why don't you ever keep guns?" she yelled as she knocked out two more officers, disarming them before running toward the hills.

Perhaps it was time to tell her why.

Andy and Christiaan kicked up sand as they ran from the bus, hoping the cover of darkness would shield them from gunshot. Shots cracked in the night, a sound more terrifying than fireworks.

Andy ran, her red bag heavy on her shoulder, worried the burn of a well-aimed gunshot would pierce her. Men shouted in Spanish. Lungs burning, she dodged to the right hiding amid some spiky yuccas to catch her breath.

The men rushed forward, closing in the gap between them.

"Let's go," Christiaan shouted, sprinting away. Andy followed.

The landscape tilted upward, then down again. Sand filled her shoes, making them heavy and gritty. Rocks under her soles bruised her feet and stubbed her toes. Her heartbeat sounded in her ears. Blackness swallowed her vision, no sound but their feet beating dry sand and cactus.

Andy's lungs squeezed as she ran up another small rise in the ground, turning to the view below.

"They're leaving," she said, a bit of triumph in her voice.

"They're searching for us."

Jeeps left the road, driving in wide circles. Gun showered random shadows with bullets. The bus, with its twin dim lights, like a tired, hunched old man, waiting for something to either happen or for it to collapse. Finally, it kicked into gear and started up the road again. Leaving Christiaan and Andy.

Christiaan grabbed her hand, heading away from the road, but south, not north, pausing behind a cliff to catch their breath.

"We can rest here," Christiaan said as the sounds of gunfire cracked farther and farther away.

"Where's your backpack?"

Christiaan swore, his eyes hard. "We have no supplies. We're dead."

Andy frowned. "We need a plan."

"We're dead, Andy. Without my bag of water and supplies…" He swore again. "Why didn't I pick it up?"

"We need a plan."

"If only we'd gotten closer, or had water." Christiaan rubbed his hand over his stubbled chin.

Andy wanted to slap him. "Okay, our previous plan is scratched. So now what?"

Christiaan volunteered for first watch, on alert for the *policía*. He spent most of the night mentally kicking himself for forgetting the water. Failed to save Andy. Failed the mission. Failed.

Again.

Sleep must have overcome him sometime because the next thing he knew, the sun pierced his lids.

"What are you doing?" Christiaan blinked sand out of his eyes and peeled back a metallic space blanket Andy must have placed on him. "What's the story of this emergency rain poncho?"

Squatting, Andy had stretched plastic across a hole in the ground and held in place by a few rocks, a rock sagged toward the middle, like a giant plastic flower. "My father gave it to me years ago saying, as serious as ever, 'Keep this on you. It could save your life someday.' I just always thought I'd use it for rain. Not for harvesting dew.

"I plopped it in my bag, rolling my eyes. I used to

tease him about being so paranoid." Andy paused, her hands hovered over her knees, tears stinging her eyes. "I'd do anything to have him here."

"Is that how you know so much about survival?"

Andy nodded. "He made me learn. Why do you think I carry this bag everywhere?" Andy leaned back, patting the dusty, water-damaged red bag sitting in the sand. "He was the real Andrew Baker. No one knew, not even my mother. It was a secret only he and a few of his trusted friends shared."

"Where did he go?"

"He disappeared. He was working on something. Not in St. Louis."

"You were close."

"Yes. He had a passion for justice."

"A passion you inherited."

"I don't know." Andy stared into the white sand around her. "What am I going to do once I get back to the States? You're right. If Tyrone knows who I am, I won't be safe. What can I do?"

"What would you like to do?"

Andy shook her head, shrugging off the question. "First, we need to get to civilization. We can follow the road to the border."

"No," he said. "The police will be patrolling the road. But we can use it as sort of a guide."

"And we travel by night. It's too hot to travel during the day without adequate water."

****

Andy propped up an umbrella as the sun rose, the shade diminishing as it rose to its zenith. She curled under the shade of the umbrella. Christiaan's expression was tense.

"You still upset about the water?" she asked.

Christiaan grunted.

Andy patted the sandy ground next to her, inviting him to join her. She smiled holding firm to the umbrella staff against the hair-dryer wind. "And I thought I'd use this for rain, too."

Relaxing, Christiaan cozied up next to her under the umbrella, their feet still in the sun. "In Asia, they use them for rain *and* for sun."

"Have you been to Asia?" There was so much she really didn't know about Christiaan.

"I've been all over."

A silence prevailed. A brooding expression clouded his face, his mind elsewhere.

"Okay," Andy said, squatting. "Just to pass the time until sunset, how about we play a game? I ask you yes or no questions and you answer them. Fair?"

"Interesting. Do I get to ask you questions in return?"

"Sure, but I don't have anything to hide." She arched an eyebrow glancing sideways. "Okay," she said. "We'll take turns. First question: Have you ever killed anyone?"

"Out of all the questions, you ask that one?" He played with twigs in the sand.

"So, have you?" she prodded.

Christiaan quietly answered. "Yes."

"Lots of people?"

"Yes." He sat still for a while only breathing, his eyes solemn as if reverencing the memory.

"How many?"

"Not a yes or no question."

"Fine."

"My turn. Why did you choose that question as the first question?"

"Not a yes or no question but I'll answer it: I've never been friends with a murderer before."

"I didn't say I murdered them. Killing is different than murdering."

"You killed in self-defense only." A yes or no question formed as a statement. She hoped for the affirmative.

"No."

Andy's face fell. She chewed her lip. The silence growing more awkward.

"Yes," he said suddenly. Andy's head cocked. "Yes, what?"

"They were bad people," he offered. "I was sure you were going to ask."

"Whose definition of bad?" she prodded, her eyes little slits.

Another long pause. Christiaan stared off to the desert. "Not a yes or no question."

"We'll move on."

"No, I think you deserve an answer."

Andy stopped fiddling, her expression serious and attentive.

Christiaan couldn't make eye contact with her as he was about to unfold his history, something few people knew. Information enemies could use to harm him. Her goodness made her trustworthy.

Still, he hesitated. He couldn't even form the words. How could he go back to his past?

"You don't have to," Andy said, massaging his back, her touch full of tenderness.

"It's just hard getting started." He inhaled deeply.

"Remember how I told you about my friend Blaine?"

Andy nodded, but he could tell she didn't really remember.

"Blaine and I, and a few others ran away from a boys' home. Blaine wasn't afraid of anything."

"Was? He's dead?"

Christiaan hesitated. "Yes. I think so. He went mad." Then he continued. "Anyway, we got into trouble, in and out of prisons for stealing stuff, starting fights. Until one day, I was around fifteen. One of the guys suggested we sign up as mercs."

"Mercs?"

"Mercenaries. Hired guns."

"Oh." Andy's eyes lost a hint of light. She dropped her hand from his neck.

A sense of guilt burned in him. "There weren't many opportunities for a kid who only knew how to fight." Except the offer to start over from the professor he'd only met once, now a dead man who needed Christiaan to bring his murderer to justice. But he couldn't tell her everything.

"You're a mercenary?"

"No. *Was* a mercenary." Those were dark days. So much bloodshed. He could smell gangrene and quinine sweating out from his body. There were some horrors he never wanted to relive. He swallowed, but his mouth was dry. "We worked paid jobs for a few years until we got abandoned in Asia on an op. Bleeding, nearly dead." His fellow mercs left him for dead. Only Blaine remained. It was a wake-up call.

"Blaine carried me out on his shoulders even with a broken arm, saved my life in the foothills of Doi Nang Non." He paused seeing her confused expression.

"Thailand." Andy nodded. He continued. "We met a man. A simple Chinese man in a village in the foothills. He said his name was Master Tso. He returned us to the land of the living. After nursing us back to health, he asked if we wanted to use our talents for a higher purpose." Christiaan remembered the graying Chinese man who had a fondness for saying with a twinkle in his eye, "Common name, not common Master."

"And what did you say?"

"Yes, of course. Tso Zhu promised us a better way." Christiaan hadn't told many people about this part of his life. It was so different than what he was living now. "He led us to one of Seven Sanctuaries of the Destroying Angels."

Andy let out a low whistle. "What do you mean?"

"Their mission was to defend the weak and honor the good. In this way, I could make up for my bloody mercenary past."

"By killing the bad people?"

"More or less. God's swift retribution on those who disobeyed him."

"Wait, you were acting on God's orders?"

"When you think of God, you think of Jesus or some kind of loving God. This was in the East. Their definition of God is different. It was more like gods or Goodness or Rightness. It's hard to translate. Think of Yin and Yang. An opposite of everything. There is evil. We counter the evil. But you have to be above reproach to join. You make certain oaths."

"Would one of those be a vow of chastity?"

Christiaan smiled, his lips burning, but he couldn't help it. "Very astute."

Andy exhaled. Although he didn't tell her what his

vow of chastity entailed. She didn't need to know all the details.

"We also don't use guns."

Andy wrinkled up her nose.

"It has to do with ancient orders. They didn't have guns back then. Anyway, each neophyte was trained in the Arts, and once they'd taken their Oaths, they were branded with the tattoo as Brotherhood of the Order of Destroying Angels."

Christiaan was transported elsewhere, speaking in a rare moment of authenticity.

"In the Brotherhood, we wear masks to keep our identities a secret from our enemies. It keeps us safe. Anonymity is protection. It just doesn't protect you from traitors. Your own best friend, your own Brother."

"You were betrayed by your brother?"

"Not brother brother. A *Brother*." Christiaan sat still, barely breathing. His gaze not seeing the desert around them, instead reliving a different scene, climate, fear. Remembering. His mind replayed the images and scenes so foreign to their current surroundings. "Rather, Blaine."

"Blaine? The guy who saved your life?"

"Blaine decided the Order of Destroying Angels was outdated. He wanted to change things. Forgo the Oaths. He ended up destroying the Order itself. And himself."

"What did you do? How did he betray you?"

Christian silenced her with a withering stare. "Not a yes or no question."

"I guess I'm confused. What does the Brotherhood do? Who were your enemies?"

"Our targets were the same you'd pick, Andy.

People involved in human trafficking, drugs, murders, and secret organizations who try to destroy civilizations and capture others."

Andy's mouth fell agape.

"Let's change topics," Christiaan said. He'd perhaps revealed too much.

"Wow! You are part of a secret brotherhood seeking out justice. So, that's why you are going after Tyrone?"

"Yes and no."

Christiaan's thoughts tore him away from the desert floor to a completely different climate, cool and damp, the smell of mildew lingering in the air. Blood, so much blood. Maybe he should tell her all. Christiaan shook his head, sighing. He'd already told her too much. But her sweet face, so full of innocence, no, *nescience* of the world urged him on. "No. The Order was destroyed. But yes, I still keep my Oaths. I have to. They are eternal. I am still bound to seek out evil. Not knowing what to do with myself, I found my current employer." They were willing to make special arrangements to help him keep his oaths. And by traveling the world, it would help him someday find out who killed his parents.

"Wow, I can't believe you killed for money."

Christiaan wrinkled his nose, annoyed. After all he told her, she focused on this. "What about your journalism gig?"

"I've never killed anyone. And I don't do it for the money."

"Or the fame?"

Andy hung there in silence. The tension told him all he needed to know. "You're just as bad as I am," he said.

"I do it for justice," Andy said at last. "I want good to triumph over evil."

"I don't know if it's possible," Christiaan said. Only Andy gave him hope.

The heat bubbled up around them draining them of energy. He didn't feel like talking. His throat was dry. Several minutes passed before he spoke again.

"My turn," he finally said. "Do you like Mexican food?"

"Yes. Have you ever been in love?"

"Yes." He didn't even hesitate.

"Are you still?"

"Isn't it my turn?"

"Yes. That was your yes or no question. Now it's mine. Are you still?"

He sat contemplatively and answered slowly. "Yes." A deep hollow of sadness gripped his chest. He'd told her too much. The gnawing in his stomach weakened his mental guard.

Andy dropped her gaze. "Your turn," she murmured, squeaking out the words.

Christiaan narrowed his eyes, probing deeply. "Okay, since personal life is open season, have you seriously dated anyone since Conner?"

Andy's face flushed red with embarrassment. "Let's play a different game."

Kicking up sand, he sat up with mock delight. "Oh, no! You've already extracted secrets from me." Seeing a weakness in her armor, he urged further, adopting an air of mockery. "Is it because no one can compare to Conner? His lily-white hands and his wimpy chest must make all the women roar." Cocking back his head, he made a roaring sound just to prove his point.

"What have you against Conner, anyway? You've never liked him."

"I think he's an idiot."

"An idiot?" Andy's eyebrows raised defensively. "He got a job right out of college. Did you even finish college?"

"Nope."

"High school?"

He shrugged. "It's not the same where I come from."

"And where do you come from?"

"Not a yes or no question."

Andy groaned. "He graduated top of his class in accounting, one of the most math intensive majors. You think you're so hot and girls fall all over themselves for you." Andy shook. "Well, let me tell you, Conner loved me."

She readied to stand, but Christiaan stopped her, speaking more fiercely than he intended. "He's an idiot because he left you."

Andy's eyebrows shot to her hairline, choking on his words.

Christiaan continued holding her gaze. "No intelligent guy, who had your love, would ever leave you."

He stood, tossing his twigs away, dusting his hands.

Andy processed his statement.

"Are you so blind you can't see the truth?" he said turning away. "He told you he was afraid. Yes, he was afraid. He was afraid you'd mingle with Tyrone and find out he was a bad guy. Then Conner would've had to choose between his loyalty to Imperium or to you. He just made his choice early. He was going to propose to you. But he didn't choose you. For that, I say he was a damned fool."

****

The afternoon sweltered on. Even under the shade, Andy was too hot. Christiaan checked the condensation from the plastic.

Picking up Andy's previously unused urine sample cup she had in her bag, he offered Andy a drink. "Here," he said.

"You first," she said. He knocked it against his lips, then handed her the cup to drink. She wasn't sure they were going to make it or get rescued. Either way, she had a gnawing feeling in her gut and it wasn't from lack of food.

She broke out some breath mints she had in her purse and handed him one. "Only one calorie per piece," she said with mock cheerfulness. For once she wished she carried more food in her bag.

"I hate just sitting here wasting time," Christiaan said.

"If you go out there in this heat," she checked a small thermometer. "You'll die. Ninety degrees and it's not even two yet." Andy then noticed the Celsius line opposite the Fahrenheit. "Are you Canadian?"

"Nope."

"German?"

"Nope."

"British."

"No."

"Where are you from?"

"Not a yes or no question," he sighed, "but I will

answer it. Because we're going to die out here."

He said it with such a thick accent, Andy didn't catch it at first.

"Where?"

This time he exaggerated the vowels in American. "South Africa."

It was too unreal to be a lie. "Did you really live on a farm?"

He nodded. "Sugar cane farm, north of Durban. And yes, I did leave."

"Were your parents really killed?"

His head lowered but his irritation did not. "Yes."

"Why?"

"Wrong side of politics."

"And your grandparents?"

"I had to leave, Andy. You should've seen their expressions when I came home day after day, bloody lips, black eyes, and bruised shins from fighting. My grandma held me and cried, kissed my head, but I ignored her. I was angry and hurt. I couldn't keep disappointing them."

"So you left?"

"The first few nights on the streets in Durban I regretted leaving. Competing with the rats for food, sleeping among needles and the sounds of gunshots. I really thought I was going to die."

"Why didn't you go back?"

"The image of my grandma's face, her disappointment every afternoon before I left. It haunts me. I didn't want to tell you the truth, so I told you what was closest to the truth. Durban is like LA. Kansas was like our farm. If you had known from the start I was from South Africa it would have made you too suspicious to trust me. I shared the essence of the truth. I'm sorry, I did the best I could."

The conversation slowed. The heat becoming unbearable, sweltering, silencing all talk.

When the sun started on the other side of the sky, Christiaan grew restless. "Why don't we walk with the umbrella for shade? We'll die here of thirst."

Andy pointed north. "We'll die out there," she said, her tongue like a brick in her mouth. Heat waves blurred the horizon. Playing games or answering questions no longer distracted them.

"We're going to die here!"

"But at least here we can collect some water."

Andy trembled. There wasn't enough water to live. They had to get to civilization.

****

At dusk, Andy packed their collection with weakened arms, every resource burned away. They continued despite thirst, a lack of food, and throbbing headaches.

They hiked all night near the road, until a pink glow illuminated the eastern sky, then they traveled farther from the road.

At ten, they set up camp. Christiaan dug a hole for the plastic, his shirt around his head like an Arab, his back bare, glistening, tanned. Andy couldn't swallow, like she'd licked the desert floor. Her tongue stuck to the roof of her mouth. They huddled under the umbrella, the sun hurting her skin, her eyes aching from the constant brightness. By the afternoon, Andy checked the plastic, shared the trapped moisture, ripped it in half to make two. Andy no longer sweated.

Christiaan sat beside her, back bare, his shirt

around his head. His cheeks were red, his lips cracked. The seraph nestled on his lower back expanded slowly with his breathing.

"Did you tell me all your secrets because we're going to die anyway?" Andy asked, her ears ringing.

He faced her, a smile cracking his chap. "I have way more secrets than what I've told you. Don't you have any secrets you want to share?"

She would've swallowed if she had any moisture left in her mouth. "If we're going to die," she said slowly. "I guess I should tell you my secrets. If you want to hear them."

"I would love to know what a journalist has hidden."

"Not really secrets. Dreams more like."

"All right. Spill."

Andy hesitated before beginning. "Ever since I was a little girl I wanted to join the CIA. I wanted to make a difference in the world. I guess doing the investigative journalist thing was the closest I could get."

"Have you applied?"

"I go to their site a few times a week. Click on a few buttons, but I never hit Apply."

"Why not?"

"They want a bachelor's degree for one. I dropped out of university three years ago to start helping my dad with his investigative work and never graduated."

"Experience is more important. You have that in spades."

Andy cast him a doubtful glance. "They want SWAT team guys. Ex-Military."

"I think outsmarting me, getting information from Carmen, escaping drug cartels and greedy mobsters certainly qualifies you."

Andy smiled. Then she shrugged. "Besides, I have to keep doing this until my dad gets back."

"You think he's still alive?"

Andy paused, searching the hazy horizon. Her gut ached. "I don't know. I hope so." Then she dropped her head in a rare moment of humility. "You're right. I'm just as bad as you. I lie, too. I don't deserve to be in the CIA."

Maybe he chuckled, maybe he snorted, Andy couldn't tell but he leaned back, wrapping his arm under her, drawing her close.

"I think you're pretty amazing, Andy Baker."

"You, too." Her chapped lips stung as she parted them in a smile. "You're not ugly either," she said, encouraged by his strong touch across her back.

He snorted. But he held her close.

"I mean. If we're going to die, I should tell you." Her face nestled into his chest, she was glad. She didn't want to have to confess it to his face. "I really like you."

He didn't speak, but drew her closer, kissing her on her head. The gesture warmed her, comforted her to be cradled in his arms as death sneaked closer. They were dying and yet, she had peace. She leaned into him. Her eyeballs were too dry to cry. Why did she wait until now to confess her feelings? Her whole heart belonged to him. Everything was clear.

"If this was how I'm going to die," she said. "I'm glad it's with you."

Her skin stretched tight, like beef jerky, her thoughts incoherent. She slept sometimes and dreamed, weird nightmares of saying goodbye to Sandra, sometimes her father. "Thank you," she said out loud, to Christiaan or Sandra or somebody in her dreams. Her voice was strangely far away.

"I love you, Andy." Did she dream it? She wasn't sure her lips could even part to ask. She dreamed more. Zippers. Flush toilets. Noisy buses.

A plane.

An engine roared in the sky.

She opened her eyes against the blowing dust, and threw back the umbrella startling Christiaan. "What the…?" he said, squinting at her.

Dizzy, she searched the sky, wondering if she was crazy or delusional. Her ears rang, but the sound was true. There in the midst of gathering blue was a little spec of gray.

Andy searched through her bag with her diminished strength.

"What are you doing?" Christiaan asked.

Andy rummaged until she found an old relic left over from dating Conner. A mix CD he made for her. She kept forgetting to take it out of her purse. She used crystalline case.

Andy signaled with the reflective surface until the plane circled closer and landed, blowing up clouds of dust.

With great effort, Christiaan stood next to her. "What if it's the drug cartel? What if it's the *policía*?"

"At this point either of those would be more welcome than death." She squinted as the door slid open of the single prop, and out jumped a man in a suit.

"Oh no," she said as a dark skinned, dark headed man in a suit jumped out. "We've signaled the cartel."

As he approached he smiled too white teeth and

said, "We've been searching the desert. Luckily, we found you."

And with his words, Andy passed out.

****

Bobby didn't struggle for breath. Not anymore. The plastic chest tube still protruded from his chest, but the heartbeat was gone. For almost two excruciating weeks, Hazel sat by Bobby's side. Even after the surgeon had removed a damaged lobe, Bobby gasped and rasped for air, the blood filling his lungs. It had to be drained. As she sat through it all, silent, steady, courageous, optimistic even, hating the man who killed Bobby even more.

Hazel peered at Bobby, almost unrecognizable now, his face ashen, eyes wide and free of pain. The doctors shook their heads, murmuring apologies to her.

Pneumonia.

Not at all a glorious way to die. Not for Bobby. An ache choked her breath.

Hazel bowed her head when the doctors covered Bobby's body with a sheet. Her hopes, her dreams, her future, dashed. No promenade down the aisle in her designer Vera. No kiss from the father of the bride. No first dance. No celebration. No wedding toast.

All of Hazel's planning, all the money spent on decorations, flowers, wasted.

Flowers. Yes, there would be flowers. Wreaths of lilies, not a bursting bouquet of gardenias.

But Hazel didn't cry. She planned. A man had used Bobby as a body shield, a man she planned to find and make suffer. Hazel planned and executed on a large scale.

Chapter Sixteen

Once on the single prop plane, Christiaan attended to Andy's medical attention first. Ears ringing, muscles aching from carrying her into the shaded and air-conditioned cockpit, he dropped Andy's IV line, the man in the suit handing him a clear bag of fluid.

"Thanks, Antonio," he said, taking the lines, trying to focus, his mind a fuzzy blur.

"Let me do it. You help yourself," Antonio said with his lilting accent, wrapping Andy's IV with tape. "Boss doesn't want you to die."

Christiaan's head spun, especially since he usually only pretended to drink his share of the water in the desert. Christiaan swabbed his vein and stuck in an IV. A few heartbeats later, his heart rate slowed, his skin loosened, his muscles relaxed.

"How did you find us?" he asked as he leaned back against the seat, buckling in. Antonio jumped in, signaling to Christiaan to put on his headset.

"I'll let Boss tell you."

"You were following us? I thought we had an agreement."

"Boss couldn't let you go completely off the grid, you know how it goes. But we lost you when you left the bus."

Christiaan glanced nervously at Andy, still passed out on the seat next to him as they prepared for takeoff among the sagebrush and cactus. Christiaan frowned behind Antonio's back, fitting the headset over his ears and adjusting the mic over his lips.

"Are we called in, then?" Christiaan asked through the headset.

"For now. Until we decide where we are at." Empty space echoed in his ears. "Did you get it?"

Through the window, Christiaan stared at the small spots of green dotting the desert sod growing smaller and smaller as they rose into the air. Relieved, he patted Andy's bag. "Something," he said, grateful Andy insisted on carrying them in her red bag. He checked her color, glad she was reviving. "But it's not what we thought it was."

"We'll let the Boss examine it and make a decision."

Christiaan sat back, his body relaxing the first time since he'd left Boston, his mind drifting to the schematics, wishing he knew more scientific German. The lulling sound of the propeller relaxed him. Leaning back, he'd hoped they'd seen the last of the Habanero Cartel.

He woke when the pilot asked for silence in his headset. He listened to the control tower for clearance.

****

Andy woke glancing over the small airport, questioning with her gaze. Christiaan only smiled tightly. Once they landed, border control cleared them with some papers the man in the suit showed them. Andy figured they were faked.

"What's the plan?" she asked Christiaan.

"We're meeting up with my people."

"Truthfully this time?"

Christiaan smiled. "It's time to get some answers to your questions."

A man Christiaan called Antonio led them to another flight to St. Louis on which Andy mostly slept after downing airport junk food as if it were a lobster dinner, and slobbering all over Christiaan in her sleep.

Starting their approach to land, Andy's heart fluttered as she studied the river and the web of streets still far below. Tyrone had a bone to pick with her. He was out there, on the alert. But Andy couldn't give up now and hide. She had to persevere. Meeting up with Christiaan's team would give her more information, at least a change of wardrobe. From what she'd seen so far, they all were extremely well-dressed.

From the airport, they drove Antonio's car to a warehouse out by the river. With low-lying cloud cover, the day pressed on them, cooler and humid. The gray dampened Andy's mood, too.

Antonio left the two of them alone outside.

Christiaan stuffed his hands into his pockets, his flight jacket accentuating his broad shoulders. He paused before opening the door for Andy. They entered in the nondescript building with florescent lights and gray doors.

"Okay, my boss is in there." He pointed to a room at the end of the hall with double doors.

Now she would finally be in the loop, trusted. She hated being in the dark, wondering, always wondering. The florescent lights made his scars white, contrasting sharply with his tanned skin. A four days' growth of stubble still dotted his chin. His lips no longer chapped.

They shared something in the desert. It had to be more than ramblings of heat stroke. Maybe now was the time to get answers for more than just one question. Or to tell him what lived in her heart.

"Christiaan, before we go in there—"

"Andy, I wanted to ask you," he paused.

Andy's heart leaped. He was going to confess, too. Maybe they could run away and leave the converters and Conner and Scott and all the other mess behind.

He continued. "They want to know if you know anyone on the local police force you trust."

Andy frowned, biting back disappointment. Oh, yes, the mission must go on. "There is only one person I know who doesn't care about money or being bribed."

"Who?"

"Fred."

"Okay, we may need to connect with him. Also…" he hesitated, glancing over her shoulder. "You may have to go into the Witness Protection Program."

"Why?"

"If you testify, they'll come after you."

"They'll be in jail. They can't get me."

"You think so? I know many men in jail with influential arms extending far beyond the borders of their confinement. Do you think a prison will stop them from taking their revenge on you?"

Andy's heart lunged, tightening. The thought haunted her. "I can be careful. I can use disguises."

Christiaan grew passionate. "For the rest of your life? You'll need a new Social, a new name, not just for you, but for your family. They will come after you, kill you. Or your loved ones. They will take them away, kill them or make them suffer. It's the price you pay. They will make you suffer until everything you hold most dear is either destroyed or theirs."

"I don't understand."

"Don't you understand? Brad and Conner didn't want to be the ones to rat out Imperium. They left it to you. Death was the easy way out. Connor is a piece of crap. You were going to take all the fall. No, you aren't evil. You cannot understand evil."

"And you understand evil?" Andy asked in a small voice.

He didn't respond for a few heartbeats. "Just promise me you'll be safe."

"I will," she said.

"Promise. In a sentence."

"I will be safe."

Christiaan sighed with relief. "Before we go in there…" He paused. He sounded tired, fed up or annoyed.

Andy anticipated he was going to say something about the time they spent in the desert. Andy wanted to make the first break. "Before we go in there," Andy halted, "I should explain what I said out in the desert—" He hadn't yet said anything about her confession of love. Andy didn't even know if the words had been audible. Now, Andy wished she hadn't said anything.

But Christian stepped forward, searching her gaze with his. Andy held her breath as he spoke. "Actually, there's something I need to explain—"

But he was interrupted. Antonio slid out of a set of double doors on the other end of the hallway. "We're ready for you." He held the door open for them, waiting.

Christiaan nodded vaguely toward Antonio, the urgency in his manner dropped. The moment was lost.

He faced Andy, his eyes full of feeling. "You don't need to say anything more. I think we both feel the same way."

In some part, his words relieved her. But another part of Andy roiled in anguish.

Then in a flash, Christiaan smiled, all the hidden meanings wiped away. He clapped his hands. "Shall we go in?"

And he led her to the waiting doors.

Inside, a woman sat at a long table. She stood when they entered. She fit the role of secretary for the boss with gorgeous, matte finished olive skin, silken shoulder length hair, lacquered nails and lips. Stunning. Antonio joined them and sat at the far end of the table.

"There you are," the woman said, with a slight accent, greeting them in a wide smile. The dark-haired vixen flipped her hair over her shoulder with the grace of a shampoo commercial. Her examination of Andy was scrutinizing. Andy extended her hand for Christiaan's when he stepped toward the woman.

"Andy Baker of *Baker's Dozen,* Sabrina Guterelli…"

Andy thrust out her hand to Sabrina as Christiaan continued to speak. "My boss."

Andy almost recoiled. *She* was his boss? He couldn't be taking orders from a girl. A woman could be a boss, but she was so *Vogue.* He was so alpha.

"Project lead," she corrected him.

Christiaan slipped his arm around Sabrina's waist to continue.

"And his girlfriend," Sabrina said, kissing Christiaan on his cheek. He tilted his jaw upward, observing Andy intensely.

Andy's heart lunged in her chest, her temperature rose, her stomach roiled. Despite her physical reaction, she had to say something.

Though Andy had told many untruths, white lies and downright whoppers in her time, but no lie was as big, as incontestably false as what slipped from her mouth next:

"It's nice to meet you." She smiled broadly, struggling to suppress all tells of emotion, her heartbeat constricting her throat. "I've heard so much about you."

Sabrina assessed Andy, then flattened her lids to flirty little slits as she glanced sideways at him. "You weren't bragging about me again, were you?" Her gaze lingered on him and then refocused on Andy. "Did he tell you how I disarmed him with only my high heels and a lace thong?" Her gaze flitted to Christiaan, slapping him slightly on his huge shoulder. "He's always telling that story."

Christiaan dipped his face into her neck, giving her a quick kiss there. Andy's stomach soured. Heat drifted up through her shirt. Her insides burning.

"We called her the Italian Battalion," he said.

Sabrina tossed her head back in a laugh. "I shouldn't have given up the field. But to be project lead…"

"She was incredible, Andy." He gave Andy a quick glance.

"*Is*…Is, darling," Sabrina said, running a fingernail against his cheek. "Not past tense. Never think of me in the past tense."

The room tilted. Andy closed her eyes against the scene. She had to get out of there. Her lungs hurt, her heart seized.

Andy faced away from them and marched through the double doors into the hallway.

"Andy," Christian called.

If she could just reach outside. Andy struggled for breath. Footsteps followed her.

Christiaan touched her shoulder, stopping her. "Wait."

Reflexively, Andy's hands flew into action, knocking his hands away with a forceful block. His face twisted with concern. Her hands flew to her own face, shutting him out.

"You okay?" he asked.

There are times so painful, only a lie will do.

"I'm fine." Her voice wheezed from her constricted throat. Andy stifled a sob by suffocation.

"Lie," he stated, his face inches from hers, his gaze searching hers. "What's really wrong?"

"Girlfriend?" She couldn't even look him in the eye. She breathed deeply into her hands. Nothing would be okay after this.

Grabbing her shoulders, he leaned in. "I was going to tell you. There just wasn't time."

She dropped her hands, staring at him with all the disgust she could manage. "Why should you tell your *mark* you're in a committed relationship?"

He stepped back, his brows furrowing. "Is that what you think is going on?"

Andy crossed her arms. "I *know* that's what's going on."

He threw up his arms.

"I do it every day," she said. "I should know."

Christiaan leaned in, his whisper, rugged and intense in her ear. "There are so many secrets I can't even tell you about. It's complicated. Dangerous even. I wish I had power to make it right. To make this right."

Retreating from him, Andy stood firm. "Let's get one thing straight: I am here for Brad. I want Imperium taken down for him."

Andy's face hurt from trying to keep the tears in. Her nose burned. She dared glance at his eyes. They were big and wonderful and full of pain.

"At least come in so we can explain what is really going on."

Just then, her phone rang.

Christian had his secrets. It was part of who he was. Sitting around opening up to people didn't come easily to him. Emotional "kum ba ya" wasn't his strength. But it hurt him to hurt Andy.

"Andy," he said, as she slipped her hand into her bag for her phone. "Don't close yourself off to me." All this time, he'd used her, lied to her, and still managed to regain her trust. But this might have been too much.

Pent up emotions hovered too close to the surface. Admitting his feelings now would destroy everything he'd worked for. Andy faced way from him. "I wanted to tell you earlier, but, there's just too much." Christiaan added as a last-ditch effort, "I need Sabrina."

Without a word, her eyes still cold and steely, Andy slid out the doorway.

****

Ricardo and Manuel couldn't let Christiaan off the hook. He was back in North America, and Ricardo would not rest until Christiaan suffered. His father must be avenged.

His men had found a man, Miguel, a worker at the Sierra Vista Municipal Airport who cleared the single prop. The *policía* tracked one leaving Mexican airspace and figured it was Christiaan's extraction team.

Miguel in his green uniform, his hat in his lap, sat in front of Ricardo at his safe house in the town of Sierra Vista, Arizona just inside the US border. Ricardo stared him down. Everyone could be bribed. Everyone had something they needed. This man was deeply in debt.

"I am searching for this man," Ricardo said holding up a picture of Christiaan. "He crossed these borders into US, no?"

"*Si,*" the man said, plucking at his mustache. "With a woman and another man."

"Where were they headed?"

Miguel recognized this man from the drug cartel. His armpits moistened with sweat. If this man was chasing someone it would mean their death. But if he didn't tell him, it could mean his own death.

"I don't know."

Ricardo leaned closer. Spittle flew in Miguel's face as he talked. "I will only ask you one time again. Where did they go?"

The offer of money had just been a feint to get him here, but Miguel half hoped he would still be able to leave alive. He had three children who just started school after being sick. What did he owe to the stranger? He loved his family. "They took the next flight to St. Louis, Missouri."

"*Gracias.*" Ricardo thanked him with a shot to his head.

"St. Louis," he said to Manuel. "Time to call our friends in St. Louis. We will only have one chance at this. Christiaan cannot leave this continent alive."

****

Once out the door and into the crisp air, Andy berated herself for not being impervious to his charm. Finding out about Sabrina pained her. Like her insides would fold inward. She was a fool.

Flipping over her phone she noticed the missed call.

Carla.

Andy didn't want to talk to her. She didn't have any answers. Not about Scott. Not about Imperium. The whole world weighed on her chest, making it difficult to breathe. Andy had failed.

Andy glanced around not wanting to go back inside, but not wanting to linger outside. She wasn't sure she could face Christiaan. Their relationship was all an act. Andy hung her head. Surprisingly, this realization stung her more than knowing Brad was in Imperium. Movement in the corner of her eye caused her to do a double take. The ground moved. Andy studied closer. A nest of cockroaches! Ugh!

Repulsed, Andy slid her hand into the handle of the door. She had told Brad she would dismantle Imperium. Do it she must. No matter the personal pain. She returned inside.

Although the outside appeared to be an ordinary abandoned warehouse, the inside, after passing through the secured entrance, transported Andy into another place. Refurbished with new wood paneled walls and polished tables gleamed in the light, the temporary base was sleek and modern. Andy opened double doors. Sabrina, Antonio, and Christiaan chatted around the table. Andy joined them by choosing the furthest seat from Christiaan, avoiding eye contact.

Sabrina stood at the front of the room. "It's time, as you say, to lay our cards on the table."

Andy just shrugged, shaking her head. To them it was business. To her, personal.

"From the beginning, please," Christiaan said.

Sabrina stood like a model at the head of the table. "A year ago, a visiting professor at an American university was murdered in his home in Germany. Since it didn't happen on American soil, your government didn't do anything about it. However, the Germans were exceedingly upset their respected physicist and professor was murdered. Suspecting it had to do with some of his research for a certain US company, suspicions turned to its share holders. The Germans are convinced the members of the company were facilitators of his death. The German government called us for investigation and arbitration."

"Who is 'us?' " Andy asked.

"We are a UN-Sanctioned world police unit. We were organized to solve disputes between states, quickly, silently, efficiently. We are OverSight."

"Kind of like Interpol?" Andy asked.

Sabrina nodded, flashing her too-white teeth between red lips. "But better equipped, more sanctions, and immunity."

"And cooler tech," Christiaan said and grinned. Andy ignored him. She hadn't so much as made eye contact with him across the polished table.

"Except the US government doesn't like us, understandably," Antonio said in a lilting accent, his hands clasped in front of him on the table, smiling charmingly at Andy. This didn't go unnoticed by Christiaan who tried to ignore Andy's reciprocity. "We don't want to breach diplomatic trust."

Sabrina cleared her throat and continued. "The Americans have the biggest egos, preferring to be the biggest guns, the world police. But America is becoming corrupt."

Antonio flashed her another million-dollar smile. Andy returned it. His teeth were blindingly white. "We are sent to make peace by ensuring justice for the Germans without upsetting your government."

"Do you mean you have higher security protocol and protections than the CIA or FBI?" Andy asked in awe, wondering how they accomplished a higher level of diplomatic immunity.

Sabrina gave her a sly sideways glance. "They wouldn't admit it if you asked them."

"How can I believe you? You've lied to me this whole time."

Christiaan winced.

Sabrina smiled her eyes dancing with delight. "We have proof."

"What could you possibly give me to convince me?"

"Here," Sabrina said. After unfolding a small wallet-sized bi-fold, she handed Andy an official document for her to study. An embossed hologram seal of the United Nations gleamed across the top. "Or if you'd like, we can call your president."

"This is enough." Andy handed back the bi-fold.

Christiaan continued the narrative. "Back to Germany. We followed the money trail from the professor to T Enterprises, owned by none other than Michael J. Tyrone."

Sabrina continued. "We had been following him

since we figured he must have constructed Herr Doktor Professor Mertz's death. Tyrone invested millions of dollars developing Herr Doktor Professor Mertz's technology. Something went wrong, and Tyrone silenced the Doktor Professor. Though we have our suspicions, we needed evidence for conviction. Tyrone has so many minions to do his dirty work for him."

Christiaan finished. "Last year, I concocted a deep cover, to get close to Tyrone only to discover he was in the upper echelons of a secret society called Imperium. So instead, I made connections with those lower in rank within the organization to dig up evidence of foul play."

Andy opened up with the understanding. "Conner."

Sabrina nodded. "Conner was one of our CIs."

"CI's?"

"Criminal Informant."

Andy bristled thinking of Conner as a criminal. "You blackmailed him."

Christiaan shrugged. "Sometimes we have to in order to get the information we need."

Sabrina leaned forward, placing her hands on the table. "You witnessed Brad's blood out, he told you of his suspicion of Conner's blood out. Mertz, Martinez, and your editor are all dead. These murders will not bode well for Imperium."

Andy leaned toward the table. "What do you need from me?"

"We need the authentication code for Conner's jump drive," Sabrina said.

Andy squinted. "You have the jump drive? How did you get it?"

A few heartbeats of awkward silence followed. No one spoke. Andy glanced from face to face, confused.

Finally, Sabrina broke the silence. "The other team recovered it."

"What other team?" Andy asked her heartbeat quickening.

"The other guys we fought in the hall who made off with the jump drive." Christiaan answered this time. "I tried to tell you."

Andy flushed, turning to Sabrina. "You sent in a second team? You didn't think we could do it?"

Sabrina wasn't even abashed. "Actually, you were the distraction. They were able to get out clear because Tyrone only knew about you two."

Andy's heart pumped blood to her face, her lungs constricting. "Did you know about this?" She faced Christiaan for the first time since their conversation in the hall.

He nodded. "I told you about redundancies."

Used. Andy didn't bother concealing her anger, glowering at him

Sabrina continued. "Our team tried cracking the code, but it's too secure. We figured Brad gave you the encryption code."

Andy pointed with her thumb at Christiaan. "So you sent him to follow me." Everyone nodded in unison. "You told me you were off the grid."

"I lied," he said. He lowered his head and avoided eye contact.

"But it paid off," Antonio said in a soothing accent. "We were able to find you in the desert. We saved your life."

"Thank you," she said, forcing her chair back. She was through.

Sabrina stopped her by speaking. "We have the

schematics you recovered. We just need the encryption code."

"What's on the jump drive?" she asked.

Sabrina continued. "We hope it's the exchange of emails between Tyrone and Herr Doktor Professor Mertz's proving Tyrone had knowledge of the professor's findings. And a clue as to where the prototype went. We were hoping Martinez had it. But it doesn't matter because now we have the plans."

Christiaan spoke. "In the paper, Herr Doktor Professor Mertz recorded strange side effects of irrational behavior in test subjects. He guessed they reacted to a byproduct of the intermediary gasses and recommended they not go forward with manufacturing because they couldn't isolate the variable. They found a correlated link, not a causal one."

"Which was?" Andy asked.

"He was not exactly sure." Sabrina's expression remained passive. "He was after all a physicist, not a medical doctor. The gasses altered the brain chemicals."

"He recorded all this in his paper? But no answers." Andy asked again, trying to make sense of this.

"He didn't know why. And it troubled the professor."

Andy swiveled, intrigued. "Sounds like he didn't want to continue, but Tyrone did."

"Tyrone had too much money invested in the technology, having sponsored the studies. Tyrone bumped off the professor to keep him quiet."

Finally, Christiaan commented. "To be fair, the side effect was random. Only about one in a thousand were affected, but it wasn't consistent. Mertz recommended more testing, or to can it all together. It was already in late stages of manufacturing, and Tyrone decided to cover it up."

Sabrina leaned closer. "We need the encryption code to find evidence to convict Tyrone. Then we can extradite him to Germany where he can stand trial."

Antonio tapped his fingers together. "One more thing. In his paper, Herr Doktor Professor Mertz mentioned a collaborator, but as the paper wasn't finished yet. It might be mentioned in the emails. It's another professor, but he gave no name."

"I know." Andy glanced up. "Dr. Armstrong. Brad gave me his name before he died."

Christiaan stared at her in disbelief. "Have you gotten ahold of him?"

Andy shook her head. "He's been missing for months."

"Imperium?"

"I don't think so. I don't know."

After breaking for lunch, Andy stood outside, preferring even the roaches to the company inside, to eat her sandwich. She also needed to confirm something. Andy had subscriptions to many white pages listening. After much digging around the Internet, she finally found a home number for Dr. Armstrong.

"Hello?" a small voice answered the phone with much hesitancy.

"Hi, Mrs. Armstrong?"

Again, hesitancy. "Yes."

Andy hoped the wind didn't affect the audio. She stepped out of the wind. "I'm Georgia Haines, I was one of your husband's students. I left a note for you at your house."

"Yes." Still no change in her small and timid voice.

"I was just wondering if he happened to know anything about an emissions converter prototype."

"Who did you say this was again?"

"Georgia Haines, a former student."

"He did have one, yes."

"Do you know where he got it?"

"My husband is a very curious man. As usual, he was intrigued by the new technology of one of his co-workers, a pompous German professor, was working at a lab here in Boston."

"Do you know what happened to it?"

"I gave it to one of his students who was interested in the technology and wanted to buy it from the German professor."

"Scott Vehemia possibly?"

"I really don't remember. Too much stress has happened in my life since then. If you'll excuse me…"

Andy continued. "I was sorry about your husband's disappearance. Just out of curiosity, was he acting strangely before he left?"

Silence on the line.

Andy continued. "This is really important. I'm trying to help my friend who might have had the same problem. Did your husband act out in violence or do things he wouldn't normally do?" Mrs. Armstrong sniffled into the phone. "Mrs. Armstrong?"

"He did terrible things, to our dog, to me. I'd never seen him act so brutal before. He's usually so gentle. Just a chemistry professor. Eccentric? Neurotic? Yes, but never brutal. Always so curious about things. But then he"—she stifled a sob—"he threw our dog against the outside of the house and bashed in his head."

"I'm sorry. Did he say why?"

"He was barking too loud." Mrs. Armstrong sobbed again. "Two days later, he went missing. It's been six months of pure torture. I've hired private detectives to find him, called the police. No one can find him."

"I am so sorry, Mrs. Armstrong. I will do everything I can to help you find peace."

"He's out there, all alone. I don't know if he's suffering. Or even still alive. No one is watching out for him. He's not taking his meds."

Andy paused. "Meds?" Andy needed a connection, anything linking him to Scott.

"He takes a statin drug for a heart condition. I wish I knew where he was."

Scott wasn't taking statin drugs. He was young and athletic. Andy drew a blank.

Then as almost an afterthought, Mrs. Armstrong added, through tears. "And his depression meds."

Andy's heart beat faster. "Do you know what depression meds he was on?"

"*Cymitol.*" The woman cried inconsolable sobs. "For anxiety. I must go."

When Andy hung up the phone, she glanced around the windblown trash scattered about the abandoned lot.

"I just need two data points," she murmured. Andy didn't have all the links but she was closer. She had to call Carla.

"Did you get to visit Scott?" Carla asked when she got on the phone. "How is the case coming?"

"It's coming along," Andy said. "I have a question. Did Scott take anti-anxiety meds?"

"Ugh. My mom would kill me if I tell you."

"Which one?"

"Uh, I don't know. *Alinor*? They all sound the same to me. I don't know their names."

"But he took them. For anxiety?"

"Yes. But really you can't tell anyone."

"I think I might have found the missing link."

****

Andy returned in a quickened pace, opening the doors and busting into the room, still holding her phone.

"I think I figured out the cause of the problem with the converters," she said.

Sabrina glanced down her nose at her. "Oh, do tell."

"I think the converter gasses are reacting to anti-depressants, or anxiety medications." She explained Dr. Armstrong's strange disappearance. "Both Dr. Armstrong and Scott were taking them. And both name brands contain a chemical called, flaxoprime. If the studies found random patterns they couldn't duplicate, it could be they couldn't find the hidden variable, and it would appear random."

Christiaan stood. "We have to stop it."

"The law is going into effect. Other people may be having problems, and we just don't know it yet."

"But if we have the authentication codes, we can convict Tyrone."

And she still held her trump card. And now it was time to play it.

"Okay, but I want *all* of Imperium arrested."

Christiaan and Sabrina glanced at each other. Christiaan spoke. "We'll talk about it."

Sabrina, Antonio, and Christiaan conferred. Antonio was chosen as voice.

311

"We'll trade the codes for a guarantee Imperium will be taken down. With one condition."

"What's your guarantee?"

"We will share the evidence on the jump drive with the US government. Although not our original goal, this must happen. I assure you, we will have the cooperation of the US government."

Andy nodded.

Christiaan spoke up. "But, we'll need a plan to persuade Tyrone to come to Germany."

"You mean kidnap," Andy said.

"I don't think he'll come willingly." Sabrina smiled at her, wrapping her arm around Christiaan. "And Germany's extradition treaty with US didn't go so well. They said we can only prosecute Tyrone in Germany. Well, to Germany we must go."

"What's your condition?"

Christiaan folded forward in his chair facing Andy. "Kidnapping for extradition is kinda tricky business. If you help us capture Tyrone, we'll make sure Imperium goes down."

Andy had to continue to the end. She wanted justice for Brad. A man she loved like a brother. His gaunt face haunted her. "You want my help and the codes."

Antonio gave her a persuasive smile. "You've been in there. Christiaan says you have an almost photographic memory. You know his apartment, the details. We need details, Andy. And you are an American. You know things about your culture we could never know. You have a distinct advantage."

"Okay," she said, acquiescing. "I will help you, but I have my own condition."

Christiaan arched an eyebrow and rocked back in his chair.

"I take no part in it."

"But—" Christiaan said, leaning forward, protesting.

Andy held up her hand. "I don't want to be around for it. I will give you one plan and a method for getting into his place in exchange for a new identity. I trust you. But just in case, I don't want to be the one left holding the bag. If this was a frame-up for me to take the fall, if this goes south. I don't want any part of it."

Christiaan's expression fell. "You'd think we'd set you up."

"After all we've been through, I don't think I could believe otherwise. Meet me back here in a couple of hours," Andy said, picking up her bag.

Christiaan tried to stop her as she headed for the doors. "It's not safe for you to wander around the streets by yourself in St. Louis. Tyrone is still free, his men are hunting you. I'll come with you."

"No."

Christiaan persisted. "I'd feel better if I—"

"I'll be back in two hours. I'm just going to say my goodbye to a great city I love. I'll have a plan when I get back."

Andy meandered by the open-faced windows of the downtown boutiques in a haze. Evening replaced afternoon, the shopping changed from an afternoon drizzle into a flood. She was occupied with how they were going to get into Tyrone's place again. Security would be on high especially after their break-in at the engagement party.

What haven't they tried? Perhaps a fat suit. Nah!

Although how lovely Sabrina would be in one. Maybe someone could fake a heart attack and they could dress up like EMTs, but someone had to be inside already to fake the heart attack.

Ideally, Tyrone's people should do the calling to give them an excuse to go in.

She stared absentmindedly into the windows not seeing her reflection until she glanced to something on display, something she'd seen before. At Tyrone's apartment. A lightbulb of inspiration caused her to smile. For the first time, Andy stepped into a cooking store to make a purchase.

Then on the way back to the warehouse, she picked up a few friends.

****

Christiaan worried about Andy until she returned to the temporary base less than two hours later with two paper bags tucked under her arm. Antonio, Sabrina, and Christiaan waited for her in the meeting room, Christiaan sat on the table.

"I've got it," Andy said, a gleam in her eye. "We'll knock him out with this."

Andy retrieved matching silver cylinders from the first paper bag.

"Huh?" Christiaan asked.

Antonio was more kind. "Andy, I don't think salt and pepper shakers will knock him out."

Andy was not deterred. "Not unless we put something else in it first. Like oxycontin. When he eats this in combination with alcohol the interaction will have some really nasty side effects."

"Brilliant." Antonio grinned from ear to ear.

"But how are you going to get the poison in there?"

Christiaan asked.

"Hold on, I'm getting there. He needs to call us."

Christiaan rolled his eyes. "I don't think he'll just call us up and invite us in."

"Yes, he will."

"But he'll recognize us." Tyrone had already seen Christiaan. And he was pretty sure Tyrone will kill him if he goes into his building.

"No, you wear disguises."

"The disguises are in your bag?"

Andy smiled, shaking her head. So cute with her eyes aglow. He didn't want to squash her with his pessimistic realism.

"It's like we're playing the yes/no game again. No." She patted the bag. "This is *why* he's going to call us." Opening the bag, she showed Christiaan the crawling creatures. She smiled wide. "Infestation."

"Cockroaches?" he asked in confusion.

"Remember your robotic cockroaches? These little guys will follow your bugs to his Penthouse suite." Andy crossed her arms in self satisfaction. "He'll call the Pest Control but you'll answer the call before they do. By the time the real Pest Control comes, you'll be long gone."

"We can monitor his phone call with the bug as well." He grabbed her shoulders. "Andy you're a genius." And he kissed her. On the cheek.

Chapter Seventeen

Tyrone sat down to lunch. *Poulet basquaise facile.* His pinkies outstretched, his fork and knife properly aligned at seven and four respectively. Where was Andy Baker?

His men had been combing the city, searching his contacts. Perhaps she fled the town, maybe the country. All the better. If she was gone then he could go back to business as usual. But, someone else would take her place. No, she must be stopped, made an example. People needed to know who was in charge of this city.

He sliced delicately into his filet when movement caught his eye from the corner of his penthouse suite. He blinked, mouth open, staring at the crawling carpet. Then he swallowed, his gut sickened. Closing his eyes to fight the nausea. He wiped his eyes with his napkin. Then yelled.

****

"I'm here for a bug problem," a man said with a slight twang. He consulted his clipboard. "An emergency. Penthouse suite."

"Hush," the concierge said, shifting his gaze left to right with his crow-like eyes. "Come with me." He swiftly escorted the bug man up in the elevator.

****

"Clean every surface!" Tyrone was yelling at the new maid who hastily collected spices and jars, condiments. "Yes, sir," and cowering murmurings of, "Right away," were followed by doors clanking and people scurrying about.

Tyrone wiped his eyes with his napkin, then his brow. He didn't dare touch anything.

****

The concierge followed the pest man as he sprayed the penthouse suite. After a time, he grew bored. "I'll come and get you when you are done." The bug man nodded, his hat hiding his face, and continued spraying the corners and baseboards.

"The sheets, the curtains! Everything, everything has to be washed!" Cleaners washed the windows. Fresh linens applied.

In the evening, the maids rehung the curtains, men vacuumed the floors. The concierge returned upstairs. "Is the pest man still here? He was supposed to page me when he was done."

A woman, attractive, exotic, probably too exotic to be a maid was replacing salt and pepper containers. "He left when he was finished."

The concierge's old crow-eyes scanned the room checking the men and women cleaning furiously and figured the room was safe enough. Satisfied the bug man had left, the concierge descended in the elevator.

Tyrone breathed in the toxic fumes. It was better than to share air with one of those... He couldn't bear to recall what he'd witnessed. A cockroach. He shuddered. Where there was one, there were one hundred. He forced the thought from his mind before it soured his stomach. He finished preparing his meal. A light salad, though it was late when he could finally sit down to dinner. Chateau Mouton-Rothschild 1945 at his side. He needed an old friend after a day like today. He downed a glass. Then a second.

A little salt, a little pepper. Oil and vinegar. After finishing his salad, he told his man he was going to lie down. His head throbbed. Maybe it was the nausea from the intruders earlier today. His head spun.

He nestled in his bed, still feeling groggy, he couldn't get the bugs out of his mind. Soon he was seeing his dinner all over the freshly shampooed carpet.

Shaking, his eyes watering, bile still on his lip, he clicked his button for help. His eyes clouded with darkness, sickened by pain. He recognized the pest man.

Then he realized. He'd been poisoned.

****

Christiaan didn't have time to change when he hid in the broom closet. As Tyrone ate, Christiaan knocked out his guard. After Tyrone lost his dinner, Christiaan was ready to carry him to the elevator shaft. This was no easy task. Christiaan was strong, but Tyrone's mass tested him. His face resembled a pasty bagel. Pinched, glossy, his eyes watering, drool coming from his mouth. He smelled awful.

Christiaan hit the elevator button to Roof. When he entered the elevator, the guard monitoring the feed downstairs would spot them both and call backup. He had just minutes before his men would arrive. It would be too late. Sabrina would be there with the helicopter.

His footsteps echoed down the hall until he opened the outer door. The cool blasted him as he kicked it open, an alarm sounding. He searched the skies.

Two red lights splashed shadows on the roof. People shouted inside the hallway. He jammed the door shut. Almost there.

The helicopter landed with wind blowing all over. Christiaan heaved Tyrone up into the door. He wasn't going easily. Dead weight weighed more than active. Shots ricocheted behind him. He ducked behind the tycoon, shoving him in at the last minute. Then they lifted off.

Hours later, Christiaan sat across from Tyrone, the latter had his hands bound in cords to a chair at the refurbished warehouse base.

"It's going to be a little tricky getting me through customs," Tyrone said, still a little blue around the gills, like a blueberry bagel or more accurate, a green bagel.

Christiaan smiled, relishing his victory, wishing he could thank Andy one last time for her perfect plan. But there wasn't time. He had to deliver Tyrone to the German government as soon as possible. "You're not going through customs."

"I don't have my passport on me."

"I've got all the paperwork I need." Christiaan poured over a file folder in the dimly lit room. Sabrina observed behind the one-way mirror. "You killed Herr Doktor Professor Mertz."

"I know my rights. I don't have to say anything without my lawyer."

"I'm afraid you've mistaken me for an American law officer. I am not bound by American law." Christiaan scowled as Tyrone paled. "Now let's try this again."

"I didn't kill anyone."

"Oh, yes, probably not with your own hands, but ordered the hit just the same. I've got emails here to prove it."

"You don't have anything."

"I have repeated emails from you to Herr Doktor Professor Mertz about some concerns he had about his emissions converter. Then he sent you some interesting emails, saying your prototype was defective. You knew they caused problems. They made people go crazy."

Tyrone shrugged. "Rumors. I don't believe anything not written in a peer reviewed journal."

"Oh, okay. Glad you're skeptical. It will make this experiment more interesting."

Tyrone's eyes watered, but with his hands tied behind his back, he couldn't wipe them. He kept the air of nonchalance just the same. "Okay, I bite, what experiment?"

"Oh." Christiaan gazed at the ceiling casually. "We decided to link a couple of the converter's intermediary gasses to this interrogation room. We'll leave you in here for a few days, and observe your behavior."

Christiaan pushed back his chair as if to leave. Tyrone visibly shuddered, casting his gaze upward in fear.

"You didn't."

"There have been repeated cases of insanity. We'll test if it really is output gasses. Or maybe you'll be one of the lucky ones who isn't affected." Christiaan smiled.

Tyrone's puss-filled eyes grew wide. Christian liked him scared. He had the emails from Mertz, but he needed a confession from this weak man to take down all of Imperium for Andy. What a pathetic mess he was, sweating, eyes watering. It would be his pleasure to put him behind bars.

"What do you want?" Tyrone asked.

"Just a confession. Some closure for the poor family of Herr Doktor Professor Mertz." Christiaan only met the tall, dark-headed professor once as a child. Christiaan's mother had made the professor *dampfnudeln,* a pale poached bread from his hometown of Kandel. How Herr Doktor got his email and connected with Christiaan during a troubled time, he'd never know. "Why did you do it?"

"I'm an American. I have my rights."

Christiaan placed his face within inches of Tyrone's face. "You threw out those rights when you crossed an ocean to kill."

Tyrone struggled some more.

"Perhaps I should come back later."

"No," Tyrone yelped.

Christiaan leaned over the table. "Why did you do it? Did you want to scrap it because it was a terrible failure and couldn't afford the losses? Were you worried about lawsuits? Worried you couldn't sell your technology you'd dumped millions into?"

Tyrone's eyes hardened, squinting into small pits, his voice sounding rough like pebbles at the bottom of a lake. "You have no idea, do you?"

Christiaan stepped back, involuntarily. Even in a room protected by cameras, guns, and his own hands, Tyrone's words had influence and power.

He smiled causally. "I'll come back in one hour."

Christiaan left letting the door's automatic locks shut behind him. Heaving a sigh, he let his head rest against the wall. Sabrina exited her viewing room. They strolled down the hall together.

Christiaan grew tired of his games. "Give him some awful food. Maybe some tap water and canned meat on stale crackers. He's got to crack sometime."

Sabrina cast a sideways glance at him. "Telling him about the gasses was clever. Too bad it's a lie."

He glanced over his shoulder to Tyrone's holding cell. "I wish he would go crazy." Christiaan wanted Tyrone dead. For Andy's sake. But OverSight didn't want him dead. They wanted a confession.

Sabrina's glittering green eyes probed him. "You like the American girl, don't you?"

Christiaan shrugged and cleared his throat uncomfortably.

"Your feelings are all over your face, Christiaan. I am not stupid. You have been depressed since she said goodbye."

He glanced up, feeling all his strength ebbing. Finally, he nodded.

"Then you should tell her the truth."

"I'll never see her again."

"More's the pity." Sabrina stared at him for a few heartbeats, then swiveled and left him in the hall.

Andy. He thought about texting her, but decided against it. He closed his eyes. He remembered her eyes, full of anger. She'd never forgive him now. How he treasured the tender words spoken in those last few hours of being in the desert together. Surely she didn't mean them, did she? He'd hurt her too much. Or was it all an act? His lips twitched in a smile. She lied as much as he did.

Four hours later, he interrogated Tyrone again. His food laid untouched, even though his bands had been loosened enough to eat.

"What's the matter? Food does not appeal to you?"

"This is inhumane treatment. Where's the UN?

This is torture as defined under the Geneva Convention."

Christiaan just raised his eyebrows. He was cracking. And they didn't even need crazy gas.

"No one could eat this mess." He toppled the plate with his knee. "If I starve, powerful people will avenge my death."

Christian only sighed. "Powerful people who would murder Herr Doktor Professor Mertz?"

He glanced around, searching for gas. "You don't know who you are dealing with," he sputtered again.

Tyrone's puss-filled eyes made even battled-hardened Christiaan, who had seen visceral parts litter the ground, nearly lose his lunch. "Why don't you tell me then?"

Tyrone focused his bloodshot eyes, directly on Christiaan's. "You think this is all about money. Ha! Money, if used correctly, can buy you power." Tyrone's puffy bagel face flamed with rage. "But money can be taken away. True power is giving the people what they want."

Even while pretending not to, Christiaan listened hard. He didn't take one word coming from his lips, puffy and pink though they be, for granted. This man blustered like a raving lunatic.

"There are people far more powerful than me. Men who have far more to lose than I do."

Christiaan raised his head. No, he wasn't confessing. He was tattling. Andy was in danger.

****

Hazel Tyrone wore grief like a mink fur. Her pallor gave her blazing gaze power. Pain gave rise to a fire of revenge. In a sleek, black pantsuit, she stood at the head of her father's table, surrounded by men her father used for advantageous purposes. She had never ordered a hit on anyone. Bobby always did it. But she knew how.

She would never be Mrs. Sharp. And Bobby would never inherit her father's empire. In fact, she hadn't seen her father in days. And in his business, missing bosses only meant one thing. He would want her to continue on. She trembled as she stood there, searching the challenging faces of her father's most loyal men.

"Who put you in charge?" Her eyes shot to the man who spoke. It was Rodgers. One of Tyrone's more higher-ups.

Hazel gave him a confident stare-down. "Father being kidnapped can only mean one thing. With his lawyers, I perused the paperwork and have discovered my father left the family business to me." It was a lie, of course. It was meant to go to Bobby, but she had the lawyers on her side. They didn't want Rodgers to take the reins. He was full of bloodlust.

Rodgers scoffed.

"I am in charge, and you will listen to me." Her knees knocked against one another, and she was glad the great table covered it up. "I'm searching for this man," she said, her blood red lips trembling. Her hair was soft and blond. This was personal. "Bobby Sharp's killer." On the screen was the security feed from her father's personal penthouse where Christiaan had used Bobby as a body shield. Christiaan and Andy's faces were the size of throw pillows. "Shoot to kill."

"And the girl?" Rogers asked.

"She's of no consequence to me. Kill her as well."

"They are both trained."

"Are you afraid?" she asked, staring at him without

flinching.

Rodgers leaned back. "You are asking us to risk something for you. You, who are merely a girl."

Hazel mustered her courage and stood straighter. Her voice loud and commanding. "I am Hazel Tyrone, and I am in charge."

Her declaration silenced the men, and they glanced around at each other.

"We'll need men." Rodgers had been in the penthouse the night of her engagement party. "I've seen these two in action. I know what they can do."

"Then gather up as many men as you need. I want his heart so I can bleed it out myself."

Chapter Eighteen

Andy called Carla in the morning from the hotel phone. OverSight had paid her a chunk of cash for her help. She'd be getting a new social and a new name. But the money sickened her. Money purchased with her heart and tears. The envelope on the nightstand disgusted her. Like blood money, only worse. She was just as bad as Christiaan. She could be bought.

Carla picked up.

"I need to talk to your dad," Andy said. Andy figured if she told Mr. Vehemia about his son, he would stop production on the converters.

"Daddy is in Boston, but he'll be home in time for tonight's soirée."

"Soirée?"

"Senator Granger is hosting a fundraising event this weekend."

"Where?" Andy asked.

"At the theatre, of course."

"How do I get in?"

"The invite list is super exclusive. I'm not even invited."

Andy's hopes dropped.

Carla continued. "And security will be tight because Senator Granger is running for president. You should just text my dad."

"I need to talk to him in person." Andy couldn't

predict his reaction. Perhaps he'd be angry. Or grateful. Or Mr. Vehemia might resist her recommendation to halt production. She might have to go straight to Senator Granger to change the law.

"If I know you, Andy, you're already thinking of a way to get in."

Andy smiled. Carla knew her so well. Parties were hard to control. People crashed all the time, friends of bartenders, musicians, or lighting crew. It was just a matter of finding out who was supposed to be there.

"Who is catering?" Andy asked. She needed a name, clothes, and a new body.

****

Lights flooded the lobby of the Granger Theatre, shining through its expansive glass doors. Ribbons of red, white, and blue decorated the columns as the formally dressed visitors swept up the stairways and into the warmth of culinary spices. In the corner, a string quartet played patriotic songs.

Too nervous to pay attention to the music or smell the food, Andy jumped at the sound of champagne corks popping at the populated open bar. Latex prosthetics covered her face, giving her a double chin and thicker cheeks, and she worried she might startle herself right out of it.

Andy spent hours enhancing herself. She grew several sizes since noon. After she found out which caterer would be serving the event, she executed her plan. Applying for a job just in time to help for the biggest night of the caterer's life.

She trembled as she placed appetizers on a gilt plate with an inflated hand. Mini cheesecakes and chocolate covered strawberries with nonpareils sprinkled on top. Though the fat suit restricted her movements, she spent the last six hours in the kitchen preparing for the shindig, and her feet were killing her. The suit weighed a ton.

And she decided she hated food.

At least she vowed to never become a caterer. It was no longer like food; it was consumable art. What was even more disgusting, no one noticed the details, the equidistant bites on white plates, the crystal, the silver. They just sipped and nibbled at the little tidbits.

Andy's stomach growled. Weakened by the burden of carrying her extra bulky body, Andy found everything tempting. Even the beluga caviar, scooped on thin, crisp toast with mother of pearl spoons smelled tasty.

Andy glanced up from her duties at the table, refreshing the buffet, scanning the room for Mr. Vehemia just as the guests left the lobby, leaving cocktails on napkins, food uneaten, to migrate toward the theatre where the program commenced.

Once everyone settled, the speeches began. With so much alcohol consumed, everything said was brilliant and worth clapping for. Andy waited and listened to the Senator's speech from the corner of the room.

"A toast to a cleaner, greener future," he said at last holding up a champagne flute.

"Here, here!" Hundreds of cries sounded, the flutes raised, and drinks guzzled. Andy bit her lip. This bill was extremely popular. Her empty stomach growled. Mr. Vehemia might resist. He would lose a lot of money if they stopped manufacturing the converter.

Finally, before the program ended and the flood of people returned to the lobby, she hefted herself up to a table. She couldn't think on an empty stomach.

One little bite won't hurt.

As she munched on chocolate covered fruit and dry toast in a corner, she scanned the flow of people. Perhaps the Senator was the best person to talk to.

She liked the Senator. Perhaps he read her column and praised Andrew Baker as a hero. Her gaze tracked him. Several men and women congratulated him, patting him on the back.

With eyes glued to the crowd, Andy munched on a lettuce wrap with something akin to tuna salad in it, but way more expensive. No one would miss one. She moseyed back to the theatre.

Alicia Reshad, in a stunning white gown, sang for the remaining audience. For some reason, perhaps the slow sultry tune, made Andy think about Christiaan. Maybe he didn't go to Europe. Maybe he stayed to say goodbye, sneak up on her and scare her.

Andy's heart beat a little faster, scanning the crowd now with greater curiosity. Face after face flit by her gaze. No Christiaan. Nobody with his broad shoulders, marked grace, sandy blond hair.

Andy's heart fell. All day, as she shopped for supplies for tonight, she'd seen him everywhere. A man wearing a flight jacket on the metro, but was too short to be Christiaan. At the mall, cargo pants reminded her of him. Somebody tonight wore his cologne. After their last conversation, she needed to get him out of her mind. And her heart.

Andy waited until the ceremonies and congratulations finished, the food cleaned up and stored, tables collapsed. The remaining crowd encircled the Senator, hands grasping his, clasping his back.

Since she finished her catering duties, she ditched the black apron, and struggled up the flight of stairs leading to the back of the theatre. The fat suit considerably limited her range of motion.

Crossing the green room, the smells jogged her memories. After years of performing there, memories tugged at her. She'd met Conner here.

She paused by the unlit dressing room, wondering if she should take off the fat suit now or wait.

Andy kept the suit on, better to keep it as long as possible. On stage, she peeked out of the curtains. A tight group holding Senator Granger's attention huddled on stage as the light and sound crew packed up cords, stored mikes, and dropped the lights to darkness.

She still hadn't seen Carla's dad. Maybe his flight was delayed. If she couldn't talk to Mr. Vehemia, she would have to talk with the Senator. A crowd still surrounded him on stage.

Andy waited behind a black curtain, breathing quietly. They continued talking. Andy couldn't make out what they discussed. So she waited. Just as Andy's heart rate had settled to a resting pace, and she was about to give up, someone spoke.

"I'd been wanting to talk to you all night." The male voice sounded familiar. "I don't think we should force this through."

Carla's dad.

They crossed the stage in a cadence of footsteps. Andy was about to come out of her hiding place when the next man spoke.

"You worry too much." Senator Granger. She was pretty sure.

Mr. Vehemia again. "I've seen firsthand what the

converters can do." Andy's mind whirled, her heart wanted to jump out of her chest and make a run for it. "It must be an installation problem."

"Problem solved when we helped Tyrone. We made a law requiring only certain, properly trained businesses to install them. Tyrone gets his business, people are safe. Problem solved," the Senator said, his voice low and soft.

"But helping him doesn't solve *my* problem," Mr. Vehemia said. "My son is going to trial for something he's not responsible for."

"Not my problem."

"If we just—"

The Senator interrupted him. "What? Tell the world the catalyst causes violent behavior? Let the fear destroy all we've worked for? Would you sacrifice the group for the solution of the one?"

"I don't care. I want my son to be absolved." Mr. Vehemia's voice trembled. "He can't go to prison. It was not his fault."

" 'At the altar of progress one makes many sacrifices.' " Granger remained calm. "This has gone too far, too much is at stake to create a PR nightmare now. The reaction never bothered you before your son became ill. Such a turncoat."

"You can't take everything from me," Mr. Vehemia shouted. "You won't get away with it."

"Don't threaten me."

"I'll halt production," Mr. Vehemia said. Then he slowed his words. "I'll go to the press."

A blunt blow sounded, then a groan, and a body collapsed.

"Take him away. Naturally, this was an accident,"

said Senator Granger, hissing snakelike.

Footfalls pattered on the wood floor. She caught sight of a pair of men in suits dragging a body out the door. The sound of the door slamming startled Andy.

But what chilled her the most was what the Senator said next.

"I'm sorry you witnessed this whole display of unprofessionalism. But you can come out now."

Andy almost didn't leave her secure spot.

"I know someone is there. Your feet are peeking under the curtain."

Senator Granger stepped closer.

Andy couldn't run. Her suit was heavy on her. Being restrained left her few options.

Shaking, Andy stepped from behind her curtain, waddling in her fat suit.

Two suited men latched onto Andy from behind. She struggled to get free.

Granger examined her closer, then pulled the latex. Andy's face burned as he ripped the chin and cheeks free.

"Amanda Miller. Why I am surprised you're here." A flash of fear splashed in his eyes. "You're not Mr. Vehemia's bodyguard, are you?" He chuckled, sweat glistening on his forehead. Unfolding a handkerchief, he dabbed forehead. "I'm really getting too old for this."

Andy's gaze never left him, her throat dry, arms burning by the men's grip.

The Senator addressed Andy, pocketing his hanky. "Too bad we have not met under different circumstances. You're quite attractive when you're a little less of a woman." He stroked her neckline, flashing his too-white smile. Andy stomach dropped.

"We already know about you," she said, glaring at him. "It's all going to come out. You might as well give him what he wants. You don't have to kill him."

The Senator shrugged. "He's no longer a team player. He thinks more about his son than about the goal of the whole. I can't have insubordination."

"People will get hurt."

"It's not really bad, Amanda. I think you are seeing this all wrong. We are the good guys. We are saving the world."

"But the converter sends out poisonous gases."

"Only to individuals in certain rare cases. No one needs to know."

"But they do." Andy couldn't grasp why he couldn't understand. "Now Scott is going to jail."

"Do you know how frustrating it is to find something so perfect only to have a few snags? Tyrone invested millions developing the technology. Vehemia spent millions manufacturing it. We can't stop just because a few people get sick."

"But people should know it is at least a risk."

He waved his hand in the air. "What they don't know won't hurt them, will it?"

"Yes, it does."

"Listen, we can't figure out what causes it. It's completely random. It may not be the converter after all. We couldn't duplicate it."

"We figured it out."

"Oh, you've figured out what Mertz never could, did you?"

"The intermediary gasses interact with certain psychiatric drugs."

"We'll have to ban those drugs. No big deal."

"This is a big deal. You'd be a fool not to comprehend what's at stake."

Granger only mildly smoothed his mouth with his forefingers. "One does not get to be President by being a fool."

"You could put off the distribution, wait until they find out which drugs."

"Amanda, timing is everything."

"For your Presidential bid? It's just a cover up, plain and simple."

"Yes. Now are you going to be a friend and help me keep our secret? It's not such a very bad one, is it? One in a thousand, maybe, are affected."

Andy remained quiet, pondering his speech. The converter was a brilliant idea for eliminating emissions and protecting the environment. But they manipulated and killed to cover-up the truth.

The Senator continued. "Besides, there might be some reward for you, too. How much money do you need?"

Andy stepped back, repulsed.

He stepped closer. "I'll tell you what. I'll make sure several thousands of dollars, say a hundred or two, show up in your bank account. And we both pretend nothing happened."

Andy licked her lips. "You think I want money? This is about justice."

If she didn't expose their corruption, Scott would never be exonerated. And Brad and Conner would've died in vain. And Martinez. Mr. Hershal, as well. Andy gulped, gathering her courage. If he was willing to pay big, he must be desperate.

"The people should know the risks," Andy replied, head high, standing firm.

Granger balked, as if no one had ever said no to him before. His usual amiable demeanor changed. His teeth flashed, spittle flying from his mouth.

"You want your fifteen minutes of fame, do you? Yes, I know who you are, Andrew Baker. You want your Tweets. Your likes. Your shares. You'll have your fame and then, when people realize it's not that big of a deal, they'll forget about you. They'll call you an alarmist, a fear-monger, an anti-progressive." His tone changed becoming more pleading. "I can give you a new future, a life where you never had to worry about money."

Andy always wondered why she did her vigilanting. Not for the money. Did she really love justice or was it about her ego?

In this case, if she wrote the story, something beneficial would be stunted—the Elimination of Greenhouse Gas law, which would help the environment. But if she didn't tell the story, the whole story, these men would get away with murder, manipulation, and cover-ups.

Andy wanted justice. She wanted it for Brad, for Conner, for Martinez, for Scott. For Mr. Hershal.

Straightening up, staring him straight in the eyes, Andy faced him. "I won't take your filthy money."

A hint of fear brushed the edges of his eyes. "What will happen if you tell? I might suffer momentary embarrassment. Will it hurt my long-term goals? Not a bit. People have short memories. Will it delay the law? Yes. Will we get it back on track once we prove yet again it is safe and effective? Yes. But you'll be halting progress. Wasting time. You"—he pointed to her—"are killing the earth."

Andy realized she had the upper hand. She had the truth, the truth about Imperium, and every bit of it mattered. Her eyes blazed as she stared him down.

"But you spilt blood to cover it all up." Andy stood strong in her fat suit. "You can tell Tyrone I will tell all."

"Tyrone?" He let loose an odd snort of a laugh. "Tyrone is nothing."

Andy reevaluated her previous assumptions. She hesitated. "I thought Tyrone was the leader."

"Tyrone?" Granger scoffed. "He can't tie his shoes without permission. He's like a bludgeon. I'm like a rapier." He made a quick motion with his wrist, as if he'd studied fencing. Then laughed, his fake-white teeth gleaming in the dim light. His fear disappeared, replaced with confidence. "Anyway, darling, if you are not going to accept my offer, I can't allow you to expose this little hiccup, so I'm afraid this is where I make my exit."

The two men grabbed her arms and pinned them behind her back. Andy immediately flew into action. With latex flying, she tripped the man to her left, kneeing him in the face as he stumbled. The second man reacted too slowly. Andy elbowed him with her blubbery arm in the sternum, shouldering him until he fell over backward on her outstretched leg. Even with the restrictions of the fat suit, she acted with greater agility and ease than Granger's men.

Swiveling, Andy kicked the first in the head, sending him backward to the wood floor of the stage. The latex didn't hit as hard as bone, and the men recovered quickly. With a swift spin, Andy wrapped the second guy in a black leg curtain, then pummeling him until he fell to the floor. The first man attacked, choking her from behind.

Andy, using her bulk, lifted up onto her back, spun him around, then rolled on top of him. But the latex wasn't real weight, and he landed a hit to Andy's face. Rubber flying off her face and chin, Andy knocked his head repeatedly into the floor until his was out. Feeling quite proud, she glanced up to Granger who had another six men facing her with suppressed Glocks. Andy swore.

"Most entertaining," Granger said as the men surrounded Andy, and she struggled to her feet. Two of the men stripped Andy of her fat suit. The cold air chilled her sweaty clothes.

"You going to kill me here?" she asked as he opened his suit jacket.

"I can't have your blood in my theatre," he said pulling out a gun pointing it at Andy.

****

It wasn't a gun, Andy decided when she woke up with a bad headache later. It was a Taser. Her bones hurt, her head hurt from falling. Cold seeped through her bones as she lay inside some hard, concrete manger-like tomb.

Andy glanced up. Above her loomed the underside of a bridge, water lapping nearby, the city lights far away, creating a halo of light on the dark clouds. A bridge under construction, a yellow rusted excavator nearby, more cement mangers, some wire mesh littering the ground. The rumblings of a truck alerted her, and Andy, though tied hand and foot, propped herself up on

337

her elbows. A cement truck pulled up under the bridge.

"There, you are up," the Senator said behind her, still in his silver suit, smoking a cigarette. "This one I had to see myself. Tyrone oversees all his victims himself. I'm too squeamish, I don't like blood, you understand. Don't have the heart for it. But you, you are so clever, Andy Baker. I had to make sure you didn't escape."

Andy's voice was hard to find, her throat was dry, and she had a bad headache. He must not have caught her when she fell. The heathen.

"There are always consequences," she said, like a schoolmarm.

Granger flicked his cigarette butt on her chest, the flame burning a little hole in her shirt before the wind blew it out. He leaned close into her. "Yes, I will be President."

His eyes glinted in the dim lights. His wind-tossed hair danced around his head like a mad man. With all the strength left in her, Andy lifted up and head-butted him in the face, hearing the crack of his nose.

"Why you little—" Granger swore, backhanding her head into the concrete, covering his swelling nose with his other hand rolled into a protective fist. Blood issued forth, spilling on her shirt and the trough.

"Enjoy a broken nose on the campaign trail," she said, smiling through the aching pain. Seeing his blood dribbling down his shirt and the ground—his beautiful face, marred, made the pain easier to take.

"For that," he said, his eyes little slits, "I'll give the order myself. With pleasure."

The cement truck backed up, the red lights cast an eerie glow under the bridge. Andy's headache worsened with the beeping, but she knew a little head trauma was the least of her worries. At first, she didn't understand why there was a cement truck when she was already tied up inside a trough. But as a man pushed the chute toward it, Andy's heart sickened with realization. The chute landed with a thud against the concrete trough.

"You got this?" the Senator asked the man exiting the cab, hovering over Andy with a Kimber. The other man nodded. The Senator gave Andy a sinister sneer, giving her one last bloodied stare as the sound of cement slogged down the chute. He then stalked away still clasping his nose with his handkerchief.

If she could just get out, distract them both. If she had her bag, something to throw, anything. But her hands were tied, she was at the bottom of the trough.

She glanced to the spinning drum of the truck, to an excavator crane barely visible against the skyline, to the cement wall behind her, to the river rushing nearby. Her final destination.

The cement fell, weighing her down.

Her ankles were covered in gray heavy, thick, cold sludge. She struggled to get up, using her elbows as leverage, but the man held her down. The other held her feet until the cement covered her legs.

The cement weighed on her chest. She stared hard at the men holding her down, but they didn't make eye contact.

Cement pooled around her head, filling the box and matting her hair. A tear slipped down her cheek, an angry tear. Helpless, powerless, stupid tear. She struggled again.

She glanced once more to the sky. Cement filled her ears, and the world muted.

This was it. The cement covered her hair and cheeks.

She glanced up. A dark streak flew across the sky. Andy followed it with her eye. Then one of the men fell on top of her, struck from something forcefully behind him.

Andy glanced around again.

Another streak of black through the night. Another man crouched over her, his eyes wide, wary, holding her down. Emboldened by the chaos, she struggled against the crushing cement. Using all her strength, she kicked through the muck and knocked the guy backward.

Someone was helping her. Andy struggled through the heavy cement, but it weighed her down, stifling her breath, pressing her under.

Through the last remaining bit of eyesight, Andy caught a glimpse of a pulley and sheave with a lifting hook.

A hook?

She managed to drag her face out of the gritty cement.

The pulley and sheave was the size of her face, and it swung around one more time, knocking out the last of the men. The contraption lowered gently toward her.

Breaking through the heavy mire, she fastened her hands on the safety latch. Immediately, it raised her up, tearing at her wrists with incredible pain, extracting her from the mire.

She glanced around for the source of the hook. Men ran toward the crane which was all lit up, and inside sat a familiar face. His hands were too busy with the controls to wave, and time too precious to waste on such a formality.

Christiaan set her down gently, her head, hands, and body aching. A man approached her. She head-butted him then jabbed with an elbow.

He dropped.

She was too slow for another man behind her. He grabbed her, but she managed to slip free, kicking him with both legs bound together, both of them falling to the ground.

Andy flipped to her feet and readied to attack another man, when the hook swung around nearly clashing with her face. She dodged it with a quick side-step.

"What are you doing?" she yelled to Christiaan in the cab. "Are you trying to kill me?"

But he was busy. Three other men cornered Christiaan, but he was holding his own by kicking them one by one down off the chassis as they comically ran one at a time to the door.

When the first one raced to the excavator, Christiaan slammed open the door into his face. Blood flowed from his broken nose as he staggered back. The second caught the door, tearing at Christiaan as he climbed onto the crawler tracks. Christiaan smashed his foot into his face sending him backward to the ground.

The third grabbed a steel rod, thrusting the jagged end toward Christiaan in the cab. Christiaan batted it away with a kick, then jumping, he exited the cab, just as the man jabbed forward. Christiaan easily side-stepped him, blocking the plunge with his left hand, then with his right, backhanded him twice in the face before stepping inside the man's spread legs, grappling him behind his neck and flipped him over, landing him in the mud. Christiaan crashed down on his chest with a stomp.

Free of the men, Christiaan ran down to meet Andy.

"We better get you into the water," he said, picked her up under her legs and neck, sticky with hardening cement. The extra weight made him groan.

"Still trying to kill me, then?" She tried to smile but the heaviness of the cement clinging in clumps and smears to her face made it difficult. "I always wanted to model a cement kimono."

He stepped into the river, up to his waist then lowered Andy down into the water, in a sort of baptism, the current washing away much of the thinner parts of the cement. Christiaan, hand still under her neck, wiped her body free of cement, legs first then ending with her hair.

At first, Christiaan frantically thrust cement from her legs and clothing, but then he slowed with the washing of her face and hair, letting his hands wash over her forehead, down her hair, making sure all the grit washed free, his gaze deep in hers.

Time stood still. He lifted her out of the water, his hand under her head, supporting her, his thumb brushing the side of her cheek. His face was near hers. Andy held her breath in anticipation. Closing his eyes, he bent over and grazed his lips on hers. As if a graze was all he would allow himself, he drew back.

From his jacket pocket he drew a knife, slicing through the ropes, first on her ankles so she could stand. The current rushed all around her, tugging her downstream as her feet found the bottom of the river. When her toes landed in the silty mud, she found her balance and stood. "I have your bag, too," he said.

Relief flooded her as she threw her arms around his neck in a spray of water.

"Thank you," she said, when he finished blinking off the water dripping from his face.

Gun shots sounded.

Chapter Nineteen

Christiaan snatched her bag from the cab of the excavator and grabbed Andy's hand as they ran northwest for the city lights.

"Hurry. More of Granger's men are coming."

Shadows stretched across the horizon from the north.

"Who are they over there?" Andy asked as he draped his flight jacket over her shoulders.

Several thugs in turtle necks and masks approached from the west. "Tyrone's men."

"What?"

"They've been following us since we captured Tyrone."

"And those?" She pointed to more men in suits coming from south.

"Granger's."

A few shots rang out ahead of them. "Then who are those guys?"

Still running, he squinted back over his left shoulder at the black leather jackets, sawed off shot guns coming southwest. "Mexican cartel?"

"Are you kidding me?" Andy shivered both from the cold and the realization all these men were all trying to kill them. They paused, crouching in the tall weeds to catch their breath.

"They've been tracking me since we left Mexico."

"Is this just everyday life for you?"

Christiaan tossed his head back and forth trying to determine if what she said was an accurate statement. "Maybe seven out of ten days. Yeah."

"Okay we need a plan to get rid of these guys."

Christiaan nodded forward, then crouch-ran halfway up a slight hill, the weeds offering some cover in the darkness, his breath blowing from his mouth in a steady stream. "What do you suggest?"

Andy crouched beside him, glancing over at the hordes of people chasing after them. "Get some guns, mow them down."

"No guns. I told you. I don't use guns."

"Right the only guns you have are your biceps."

Gunfire crackled around them as someone spotted movement. Both crouched farther into the grass.

"Okay, well let's survey the situation," she said.

Andy glanced around where they stood on a small rise covered in prairie grass. "There's roughly five to seven guys from the cartel coming from the southwest with automatics and what sounds like sawed off shotguns trying to kill us. And from the city we have oh, ten to twelve of Tyrone's men after us with semi-automatics. And last, but not least, from the prairie we have, my guess would be, about ten henchmen of Granger's also with handguns, trying to get us. I think we need guns."

Christiaan still crouched in the hill, the grass blowing over his head, offering little protection. As the thugs crept closer, zero protection.

Andy was not going to die this way. Trapped, no way out.

Andy studied Christiaan's face in the dim light the

reflection of the city lights in the cloud cover. He concentrated on the problem, his jaw clinching. Twenty yards down a road, an abandoned warehouse broke the horizon. "We don't need guns because they brought guns. They will be their own undoing."

As the men approached, fear nearly crippled her thoughts. "What if we are caught in their crossfire?"

"We'll probably die."

Then an idea struck her. "What if we caused a crossfire?"

"What?"

She dug around in her bag. She pulled out a wig, her umbrella, and floss. She opened the umbrella, putting the crown upside-down on the ground, then tied the floss to the handle.

"What are you doing?" Christiaan asked, unable to make sense of her actions. She maneuvered a few stones around to help make the umbrella stand upright.

"If we convince them we are still crouched here..."

Christiaan broke into a wide smile. "A dummy."

She stashed her bag as a counterweight on the other side of the umbrella's cup. Once the umbrella was secured and stationary, she put the wig on the handle. She slipped off the jacket.

Christiaan grabbed the leather. "Not the jacket."

"I'm sacrificing the bag. The jacket or your life."

"Are you sure this will work?"

The wind howled around them echoing with gunfire. They were getting closer. Andy met Christiaan's gaze, his face inches from hers. For the first time, fear shone in his eyes.

"No. I'm never sure anything will work." Her heart raced so hard, it was difficult to speak. But her hope urged her onward, and she clung to it for she had nothing else. "But I hope it will."

Christiaan leaned forward and pecked her on the cheek as he removed his jacket from her. "If we live through this, you owe me another jacket."

"If we live through this," she said, throwing the jacket around the umbrella and wig concoction, a bent scarecrow. "I'll buy you a hundred jackets."

She unraveled the floss behind her as they crouch-ran down the hill toward the empty building, with the cover of darkness and tall prairie grass hiding their escape. Andy unwound the floss until nearly the end, then lobbed it up into a broken window before finding the entrance.

Andy arrived at the doorway first and stepped inside, smelling rotted wood and mold. Low hanging wooden rafters grew splinters and cobwebs. Light from a streetlamp seeped through the broken windows. Still outside the brick building, Christiaan scooped up a rock and knocked out the flickering streetlight. The building plunged into darkness.

Only Christiaan's broad shoulders were visible as he led her up some creaking stairs. They bumped their way to the window, and Andy found her floss. Below them, the scene unfolded.

The Mexicans from the prairie fired first from the southwest, their MAC-10s and sawed-off shotguns sprayed bullets, the sound echoing off the building. They were anxious to fire at the anything moving. Andy tugged on the floss, and the bag acted as a counterweight. The wig and jackets swayed like people crouched in prairie grass.

Granger's men, across from them, reacted with the

precise aims of their nickel-plated 1911s with suppressors to systematically and silently deliver death with each shot, the sleek whisper of metal the only sound from their hands.

Tyrone's men, defending themselves from the north, held their automatic pistols close to their chests, letting loose a rapid-fire spread of bullets from their MAC-10s crackling in the night, but the kick of the guns prevented accuracy. Some aimed at the leather jacket and wig, undulating with the waves of grass and hits. Others just retaliated blow for blow.

At first, the Mexicans appeared to be winning by the long range of their guns, open chokes of their shotguns, wiping out or wounding men, silencing their opponents. But as they burned through their ammo, the more precise gunners of Granger's men crept closer for more accurate shots. Men dropped, blood splattered, and shots echoed in the night.

Andy's plan played out beautifully. She was both horrified at the bloodbath as bodies fell, each killing the other without thought, yet relieved it was neither her nor Christiaan. If the sounds hadn't assaulted her ears, the smell of powder so sharp, it would've been like a movie. Surreal.

Soon, the sprays of bullets became fewer and fewer until silence reigned. Only three suited men remained, one hulking man with a bald head and dark eyebrows, a scowl across his face as he stalked among the fallen. A shorter man accompanied him. Then a tall agile man with angular features crept from his cover, a patch of red blooming from his arm. Granger's men. Their marksmanship and cover allowed them to survive. The biggest and the strongest, yes, but also the smartest.

They threaded through the fallen, collecting inherited guns. Standing at the jacket and the poor umbrella and wig, now crumpled to the ground, riddled with holes, the bald one kicked it. He followed the floss with menacing eyes to the building.

Christiaan drew breath. "They're coming here," he said.

The men cut across the hill leaving trails of broken grass.

"We can take them," Andy said, her heart leaping in her throat. "There's only three; we have the cover of darkness."

Andy squared her shoulders. Granger's men had guns, but they had the darkness and surprise.

Andy leaned to tell Christiaan a plan, but he was nowhere in sight. Her heart lunged, her eyes widened at the sound of approaching footfalls.

Christiaan hoisted himself up onto a wooden rafter beam while Andy's back was turned, waiting for the first suit to come up the stairs. He hoped Andy had taken sufficient cover. Even self-defense martial arts were no match for automatic weapons. He couldn't see her, but hoped she was smart enough to hide.

The men spread out, searching the building. Perfect. Easier to pick them off one-by-one. A small but stacked man marched up the stairs. Christiaan only had once chance. The man roamed slowly, carefully, overly attentive, searching the shadows for movement, anticipating trouble. He just didn't anticipate it to come raining down on him.

As soon as the man stood directly under Christiaan, he leaped onto him, landing on his shoulders, kicking the gun from his hands before they both tumbled to the ground. The gun sounded a few shots before it flew from the man's hands, scuttling across the floor. They both stood, Christiaan grappling the man's collar behind his neck with his right hand, bending him forward, his left hand controlling the man's left arm.

Using a Russian Sambo take-down, Christiaan kicked both legs around the torso of the smaller man, letting his weight collapse the man on top of him, then rolling him through until he was on his back, Christiaan's legs pinning him across his chest, still in control of his arm. Christiaan forced his leg down on top of his ribs, knocking the air out of them. Then hopped to his feet to kick him again in the head. He wouldn't be getting up for a while. Christiaan disarmed him further.

The tall lanky man ran at Christiaan. A shot fired. Christiaan kicked the gun out of his hand. Then grabbing his right hand in a joint lock, he used the man's thigh as a step, mounted him, legs straddling his neck, still holding his arm. Christiaan leaned. The man lost his balance and crashed to the floor to his right. Both rolled then stood upright, searching for an in. The lanky man attacked first, Christiaan blocked him, joint-locking his arm, rolled him backward to the floor, then stepped on his crotch, twisting his leg away from his body. Once he was immobilized, he collected the guns and tossed them out the window.

He halted when a shot rang out below, and a body fell. He rushed down the flight of stairs.

****

Andy freaked a little when she found she was alone. But she had no problem using a gun and wanted the first one she could get. Andy hastened down the stairs to the entrance, hiding behind a leaning board, waiting to take out the last guy. She let the first two pass and spread out. The third, Baldie, was huge. Andy gulped before deciding to take him out. He passed by her. He had a gun. Andy wanted it.

Sneaking behind him, she made a noise. He faced her. She attacked the right arm.

The gun wasn't there. He was a lefty. Why didn't she catch it before?

Andy kicked the left hand as he swung to point his Kimber at her. The gun clattered away. Andy headed for it, but the man caught her by the leg, hitting her down with his fist on the back of her thigh. Andy collapsed a few feet from the nickel-plated gun. Baldie, by her leg, grabbed her calf, pulling her toward him.

With her free leg, she whacked his face, then using the heel of her foot, stomped him in the chest. His eyes glowed with anger.

Taking courage, again, she kicked him in the head, he yanked her foot out from under her, causing her to fall on her rear and elbow. He stepped down on her leg, crushing Andy's ankle. Andy sat up, using her arms as supports and threw her leg back into him, causing him to stumble off balance. He fell back, jumping up quickly. He found a two-by-four with a jagged end.

Andy stepped into his swing, blocking his arm, joint-locking it behind his back in one swift motion, smashing his hand across her knee. The board fell to the ground with a clatter. Andy shoved him forward, until he fell to his face. With his free hand, he found the gun, twisting it backward, pointing at her. Still in control of his arm, she lifted it up shielding her as his shot pierced right through his own body, blood spurting on Andy.

Pausing to make sure she wasn't shot herself, Andy let his lifeless body drop, her ears nearly deaf from the proximity of the shot.

Christiaan rushed down the stairs where Andy stood over the man, the gun in his hand, blood across her, but the man dead.

"Well done, Andy Baker," he said surveying the mess, shaking his head.

Andy kicked the lifeless body, retrieving the gun. From upstairs, a shot rang out, just missing Christiaan. The glow of a red laser pointer focused on his chest. Andy estimated the distance from the gun and shot in the dark. The sound of a body collapsing, reassured her she hit her mark.

"You never use guns, eh?" she asked. "I think you should rethink your policy."

Christiaan grunted a thank you, far too manly for too much gratitude. "Did you say you had a friend in the police?"

"Fred?"

"Let's get this mess cleaned up."

Andy called Fred who sent out a couple of cars and an ambulance. The police taped off the scene and listened to testimony; forensic guys scoured the place gathering evidence, guns, blood samples, and empty brass for hours.

Andy had to tell Fred she wasn't Bethany, but Andrew Baker so he'd believe her story. He listened, eyes bugged out. Andy wasn't sure if it was from the story or from her confession Bethany was fake.

Fred shook his head. "Senator Granger will just deny he was here. His word against yours."

"Oh, Fred," she said. "If you check the trough over

there. It will be covered with Granger's blood.

Fred smiled and sent some forensic guys over to investigate.

"DNA all the way, eh?" Christiaan asked.

"He didn't want my blood left at the scene, so I made sure he left some of his."

Christiaan smiled his approval on her. Warmth bloomed inside Andy. "You are a clever girl, Andy Baker."

****

Early in the next morning when all the bodies were safely tucked into brown body bags and hauled to the morgue, Andy finally retrieved her red bag, which was no longer functional except as a sieve. There wasn't much left of the flight jacket, either. When Christiaan picked it up, a sleeve fell off. He tossed the rest of it back into the pile of debris.

"I owe you a jacket," Andy said.

"I think you said a hundred jackets."

"I will deliver."

Andy crossed to him, just as the sun broke over the horizon. "I thought you were taking Tyrone back to Germany."

"When Tyrone spilled Granger was the head of Imperium, I knew you were in danger. So, we turned around. I broke into your hotel room, only to find a bunch of latex. You really should clean up after yourself."

Andy rolled her eyes. "Whatever."

"I called Carla to find you, and she told me about the party. I dodged you in the fat suit all throughout the party until the end when I lost you. Then followed Granger out here."

"Thank you."

"For what?"

"For letting me finish off Baldie."

"He was a nasty one, huh?" He paused, his hands in his cargo pants. "Are you going to print the story?"

"The people have a right to know. It's the only way Imperium is really going down. It's hard to believe in government anymore."

Now the case was solved, they would be parting ways. No more competing with him, no more outsmarting him. A weird sort of hot pain shot through her chest when she imagined next week, and he wouldn't be there to tease her. She ached at the thought.

Nor did she want to dwell on the way his shirt tugged at his chest and arms. She couldn't figure him out. Sometimes he was intense, feeling. Other times it was like he didn't care. Which was the lie?

"What are you planning on doing now this is over?" Andy asked.

"You know, I thought it was time for a change, but I think—"

An officer called him away.

"Well, I guess this is goodbye," he said.

He flicked his head in a nod and left.

****

Andy typed her story from her hotel room still in St. Louis, under an assumed name until she could decide if she wanted to be relocated in a Witness Protection Program. As she typed, sometimes the words flew from her fingers. Others had to be squeezed from a stone. Hours ticked by on her digital clock.

When she glanced up from the screen, she was surprised at the darkness and the lateness of the hour.

Her laptop was the only light in the room.

A sound in the hall startled her. Outside her door. Andy's heart beat fast as her ears prickled at every sound.

She almost laughed at herself. In a hotel, she wasn't the only person on her floor. Her neighbors had every right to go thumping and bumping around. There was no reason to be afraid of small sounds.

No reason, except she was a few minutes away from exposing the most corrupt political scandal of the decade. The hair on her neck prickled.

Andy's laptop screen darkened. The total darkness made her blink her eyes. It was just her screen saver, of course. A pair of feet stayed outside her door. Slowly, slowly, she shut the laptop lid.

She swallowed hard. Her ears straining for more sound. Andy slid the laptop from her lap, her muscles tense.

A knock shattered the silence. Andy tried to calm down, but adrenaline coursed through her body enough to make her shiver in cold sweat as she kicked her pile of papers under the couch. She made her way to the door.

If it was Christiaan playing a joke on her…

She peeked through the peep hole, half squinting her eyes as if squinting would protect her.

Carla.

Andy nearly laughed with relief.

She swung the door open.

Carla's beautiful features were drawn up in pain, her eyes red and puffy and yet, she was still unflawed.

"Why did you let them kill my dad?"

"Carla, I couldn't save him. Granger killed him

because your dad cared more about Scott than he did about Imperium."

"You could've saved him."

Andy's heart shuddered. Those were the very words she thought about so many people in this case. Brad. Conner. Juan. Even Mr. Hershal. She hadn't saved any of them. And she couldn't have saved Mr. Vehemia. "It all happened so fast."

Biting her lip to keep them from quivering, Carla shook her head.

"I can't stem the tide of corruption, Carla. I do my best, but I can't stop everything." But it did make her wonder. Could she have done more? Andy had to toss out such self-doubt. She did what she could.

Carla's eyes filled with tears. She wanted someone to blame. Andy slipped her arm around her as Carla cried into her shoulder. Andy held Carla's shaking body.

"I am so sorry," Andy said.

"You'll always be here for me, won't you?"

"I can't promise you."

****

The next day, the news showed pictures of the bottom-feeding reporters clinging to the gated estate of the Vehemia family, hoping to catch any morsel of the story Andy broke. Social media shamed the venture. People demanded the converters to be recalled, the business to be examined, and Granger's affairs investigated. Imperium was going down. Andy danced in front of the TV with delight.

But when police found Mr. Vehemia's body, Andy didn't dance. She called Carla, but to no response.

Two days later, Carla attended her father's funeral. Andy, tucked into an alley unseen, stood across the church decorated with lilies and gardenias. A throng of reporters lined the steps of the stone church, catching every moment. Men dotted with red flowers loaded a casket into the back of the hearse. Closed casket, Andy remembered. She wondered what Granger's men did to him.

A black limousine led a row of cars. Scott, in a dark suit had fewer circles under his eyes, and his color healthier than their last encounter. The story acquitted him. He held the door for two women in black.

Andy caught a glimpse of Carla, her hair a sheet of black satin, blown by the wind. She glanced up before stepping into the limousine. Her gaze met Andy's, staring at her across the street. Andy had never seen such grief in her expression. Carla returned to the limo as she ducked inside.

Andy roamed the street, the wind hollowing out the canyons of the cityscape. No matter if she chose the Witness Protection Program or to hide on her own, she could never meet with Carla again. She stuffed her hands in her pocket, mourning the loss of her friend.

Epilogue

There are awkward times in any parting relationship after two people have suffered so much together. Neither were sure if this relationship would continue or how it would continue, unsure if the other even wanted it to continue. And certainly, they didn't want it to continue under the same amount of stress and difficulty as before. Andy hoped it would continue.

Andy and Christiaan stood on an empty road, in an undisclosed location, far from St. Louis, dawn creeping from the east. Early morning frost linked arms across the window panes of Andy's waiting taxi.

They hadn't seen each other in the past few weeks. Andy revamped her wardrobe, colored her hair, and relocated. Two days ago, she received a mysterious text to meet Christiaan. She took a taxi to his exact GPS coordinates. Andy's heart thundered in her chest. She was not disappointed. He leaned against his car, more well-rested and relaxed than when she last saw him. No jacket despite the chilly morning. Same Porsche.

His eyes lit up. "Hey," he said, his hair fluttering in the sunrise. His smile alone was worth the taxi fare.

"Long time, no see," Andy said, trying to keep it impersonal, though her heart pounded just at the sight of him, her gaze lapping him up.

"Been busy. Had to fill out numerous forms for Tyrone's extradition." When he spoke, his accent was now pronounced.

"He's safely away then?"

"Trial is upcoming. I'm optimistic for a conviction."

"Granger is facing trial, as well."

"Your story broke all the records."

Andy bowed her head modestly. Her hits were at the top of the charts. "The converter will go back to testing. It's such a great idea. Too bad so many people were killed to cover up its defects instead of getting it properly vetted. Granger needed it as a matter of political expediency. Timing was everything for his Presidential bid. Tyrone just had too much at stake."

They stood there facing each other for a few heartbeats. All the questions were answered. Well, almost. "What did you want to talk to me about?"

Christiaan slipped his hand from his pocket, grabbing hers and placing a heavy, metal object into her palm. "I, uh, realized I borrowed your pocket knife. I still had it."

"Thanks. That reminds me," she mumbled, throwing her straps off her shoulder, then digging through a brand new brown weekender tote, producing something of her own. "I said I owed you a jacket. Here." She handed him a brand-new leather flight jacket. "It's not exactly the same." This one had darker leather, almost black.

"You really didn't have to." He threaded his arm into the jacket. "It fits perfectly. Thank you."

"Oh, and here's your cufflink from the party. I used it to prop a door open while escaping from the hospital." She handed him a little metal clasp.

"*Lekker.*"

Andy gave him a questioning stare.

"It means awesome. Oh, and this," he said, reaching into his shirt pocket. "I had this earring, too."

Her hand instinctively found her ear, though it was from the pair she wore to the engagement party. "Thanks, I didn't realize I was even missing it." She dug some more into her bag. "And here's a mouthwash cup I snatched from your apartment. I was going to return it after I did some DNA sampling on it to discover who you really were."

"Shame." Opening his jacket, he pulled out her handgun. "Here's your Sig Sauer you, uh, *left* at my house." He held the object in his hand then suddenly, threw back his head and laughed. "Ag, we're quite the pair, aren't we?"

His laugh almost made the tears behind her eyes disappear. She hefted the Sig, glad to slide it into her bag.

"What are you going to do now?" he asked.

"Guess finally hit the Apply button at the CIA. My story broke big, but I can't stay in St. Louis anymore. I think I'm ready for the next level."

Cocking his head sideways, he smiled. "Sure you won't join us? We could use you."

"I may be interested. But I need a break."

"You know where to reach me when you're ready."

"I do?"

"Just send me a text. And I promise I'll respond, even if I'm over China."

Andy stepped closer, remembering how he'd said he was over China the week before the engagement party. "Were you really over China?"

All pretenses, all covers down. Christiaan trusted

her, and she trusted him. "Yes."

So, this wasn't the end. He wanted their relationship to continue. He just told her this might go on. Her eyes leaked water onto her cheek. His forefinger caught the tear. He drew her close. Andy shuddered, searching the depth of his eyes. His hand pressed against the small of her back, drawing her into him, grazing her lips with his. Andy inhaled his intoxicating breath, releasing her desire.

Trembling from her own heartbeat, she parted her lips as he pressed his own warm and tender on hers. Andy succumbed to his gentle touches, breathing him in, feeling his warmth, her own flush. Andy craved him, her desire growing fierce. She slid her arms around his neck, reciprocating his touch. His pressing intensified. Her heart rate increased as he pinned her to the front panel of the cab, expanding all her pleasure sensors. Her thoughts wandered unrestrained, full of yearning.

"I ain't gettin' paid to watch you tongue your girl," the cab driver called out his window.

Without breaking the undulating rhythm of his caresses, Christiaan slipped his hand into his pocket, produced a Benjamin and handed it to the cab driver, who, after taking it, slid his hat over his eyes to nap.

When they finally broke, still holding each other, Andy could hardly find words.

"And what if I don't want to send a text?" she asked, trembling in spite of herself, fearing he detected her attraction, how she wanted so much more.

He winked. "You'll have to, if you ever want another kiss from me."

"What about Sabrina? Your *girlfriend*?"

"Always a little hypocrite, even to the end."

Andy crinkled her brow, questioning him.

He leaned in close, so close his breath tickled her cheek. "How many fake boyfriends have you had?"

And with one last kiss, he released her, leaving Andy confused and lightheaded. "Text me soon," he said. "We've got work to do."

He turned and climbed into his Porsche, the engine roaring away, sounding long in Andy's ears as a smile crept to her lips.

A word about the author...

Amey Zeigler received her B.A. in Communication from University of Arizona. While attending university, she put her studies on hold to live in France and Switzerland for a year and a half.

When she was nine years old, she started writing romantic mysteries and has been obsessed with the genre ever since.

She lives with her husband and three children near Austin, Texas.

http://ameyzeigler.com

Thank you for purchasing
this publication of The Wild Rose Press, Inc.

If you enjoyed the story, we would appreciate your
letting others know by leaving a review.

For other wonderful stories,
please visit our on-line bookstore at
www.thewildrosepress.com.

For questions or more information
contact us at
info@thewildrosepress.com.

The Wild Rose Press, Inc.
www.thewildrosepress.com

Stay current with The Wild Rose Press, Inc.

Like us on Facebook

https://www.facebook.com/TheWildRosePress

And Follow us on Twitter
https://twitter.com/WildRosePress